DARKEST DANIEL

CHARLIE DEMPSTER

Without these people my work would never have been published

Heather Jane

My brilliant wife and best friend

Mary Young

A truly amazing lady and editor

Jane Haggarty

Danny's first Fan

Lyn Failes

&

The Wee Book Club

who blew away the cobwebs on this work

When you are uneducated and grew up in the 60s in Glasgow it is difficult to believe that you could ever write a book. I did exactly that, but I needed help and encouragement which I received from the people mentioned above.

A girl working in a well-known bookstore once told me never to change my work to please others, so I haven't. Darkest Daniel remains earthy and definitely falls within the 'hard-boiled' category of detective writing.

This story is completely true – except for the parts I have made up. Most names have been changed, but places are real.

Promoted by Belter Books, Glasgow

https://www.facebook.com/damngoodreads

CHAPTERS

1.	Daniel	6
2.	The Past	27
3.	Carolyn	40
4.	Jenny Gunn	53
5.	Kelly	58
6.	Philip	63
7.	Kinlochard	67
8.	Sylvia	76
9.	Lunch	84
10.	The Private Detectives	87
11.	Los Angeles	94
12.	The Teenager	99
13.	The Girls	109
14.	Aston Martin Day	114
15.	The Boyfriend	118
16.	Jenny, Janet and Lesley	126
17.	Surveillance Day 3	142
18.	Doubles	149
19.	Tell Me	155
20.	Second Thoughts	173
21.	All Fucked Up	177
22.	The Morning After	186
23.	Kelly's Night Out	192
24.	Blow Off	196
25.	Katie	203
26.	Softly, Softly, Catchee Monkey	210
27.	Jenny Does Danny	215
28.	Rejection	223
29.	If You Go Down to the Woods Today	228
30.	Hell	233
31.	God Help Me	240

32. Knock Knock	242
33. Stage Fright	247
34. DCI John McLeod	253
35. Claire	270
36. Gone	282
37. MV Titan	285
38. Bring Up My Dead	291
39. Body Snatcher	309
40. The Dark Past	316
41. Gone but not Forgotten	324
42. Conal Fury	333
43. Here They Come	348
44. Dog Gone Day	361
45. Happy Days	372
46. A Bad Day at Pitt Street	384
47. Suspect	400
48. Plan B	408
49. Park Circus	412
50. Red	423
51. Heather	429

Chapter 1

Daniel

It was a beautiful sunny Monday morning in early Spring. The view from the top of the park where the lodge was perched was stunning. There was no wind, and the loch below reflected the beauty around its shores. Blue skies, mountain tops and Caledonian pine trees were perfectly mirrored on the flat calm water. Oystercatchers flew overhead, their unmistakable call piercing the still morning air. Danny stood on the wooden deck that surrounded his lodge, a cup of coffee in his hand. He was 6’4” with ice blue eyes and thick dark hair, a small scar below his right eye – the result of a knife fight when he was younger – marking his otherwise perfect skin. Danny was athletic and kept his toned body in good shape with daily visits to the gym and long hikes in the mountains. He had a mesmerising smile and a fantastic strong Scottish accent, said by many girls to be sexier than Sean Connery’s voice. Girls loved him, and he loved himself.

Today was shaping up to be a good one and Danny was looking forward to the coming summer. He was now forty years old, hungry for money and with a lust for the opposite sex. The Mountain View holiday park in Argyll was his hunting ground and the season had just started. He walked back inside, smiling, and headed for the shower. His previous jobs had been located on parks south of the border, in England. Working so far away from home meant he had to live there for nine months of the year. This park, however, was in Scotland, home to his beloved mountains and his beautiful home. His house was now within easy travelling distance, allowing him to go home on his days off, which he often did.

This was Danny's second month of the new season and year two of being on this particular park. It was a large park with over a thousand static caravans and lodges spread over two hundred acres of beautiful, landscaped gardens and woods. Many of the lodges were upmarket and situated at the water's edge. Owners kept boats and jet skis moored at their private jetties dotted along the shoreline. Danny was off to a good start this month having sold three caravans that weekend.

He was in a great mood, as the following evening he would be heading home for his two days off. He got dressed in a royal blue suit and light blue shirt and dark blue tie. Admiring himself in the mirror, he tied a perfect Windsor knot. He looked fantastic, like a male model, even at the ripe old age of forty. It was 8.50 am and time to go to work. He grabbed his keys and jacket, jumped into the Audi A5, and drove towards the sales office at the front of the park. Someone waved and he stopped the car; it was the groundskeeper Willie who was tending a flower bed at the side of the road – he was as mad as a box of frogs.

Danny lowered his window, to be met with Willie's shout of 'Show us your big hairy baws,' as he cackled away to himself. 'Good morning,' Danny replied. Willie said the same words every day and always laughed, which made Danny laugh too. That and the fact that Willie wore yellow yacht wellies all year round even though he did not own a yacht. Danny got out of the car to have a quick chat.

'How are you this morning, Willie?'

'Great, Mr Bond,' was Willie's reply; he thought Danny resembled a James Bond type of character and had named him so. 'How was your weekend? Did you sell any vans, Danny?'

'Of course, Willie. I sold number 10, and also 29 and 31. Could you make sure the gardens outside look pretty for the new owners next weekend?'

'Of course, Danny; I will go round them in the week and make sure they look pretty.'

Danny shoved a twenty-pound note in the old man's dungarees pocket as the old boy wrote the numbers down in his wee notebook.

'Thanks Danny, you're a gentleman.'

Danny left Willie tending the flower beds and sucking air between his two remaining teeth, white saliva visible around his mouth. The old man worked away vigorously, probably thinking of that bottle of vodka he would be buying later with the money Danny had given him. Willie's wheelbarrow, which held his garden tools, spade, rake and a hessian sack, stood by his side. The sack hid the half bottle he had already started drinking that morning. Danny left Willie daydreaming about more booze and drove the rest of the way to the sales office. He parked the Audi in the sales parking slot and raced up the stairs and into reception.

Standing and awaiting his arrival were the three amigos – Big Bob Two Bellies, aptly named because he was indeed a fat bastard who really looked like he had two bellies under his sweat-stained t shirt. He was a fat stinking slob who had not seen his cock since he was a kid and whose BO would make you gag if you got too close, especially in the summer.

Bob, believe it or not, actually had a wife whose name was Sheena. She was fatter and uglier than he was and should have been named four bellies. Her bellies were stacked up on each other like the tyre guy you used to see in the Michelin tyre commercials. Even their ugly kids were fat. Sheena also stunk of BO and had an arse the size of a hippo. She sometimes wore leggings – not so much camel toe, more like T rex toe, disgusting!

Standing next to Bob was Smudger, who was lacking in the height department, but he was a good laugh, a right cheeky bastard and the best of the three.

Finally, there was Dave, known simply as Dave who was the leader of the three amigos. He was not much of a conversationalist and drier than the Nairobi desert.

'Morning, boys.'

'Morning, boss, what have you got for us this morning?' Dave asked.

'Fuck me, boys, let me get my jacket off,' Danny said as he

walked to his office, quickly followed by the three muppets. The men crowded into his office where they all discussed the caravans he had sold that weekend and which plots they had to be sited on. He handed the list to Dave who studied it: Smudger reversed his baseball cap and saluted before all three about turned and left. He could hear them shout sexual comments to the girls in reception.

Danny walked into the reception and watched the three minimum wage monkeys board the tractor and the pick-up truck parked outside. They were happy as shit in their little caravan park world, where the Rangers football team, Tennents lager and their work were all these poor bastards had to live for. Danny watched them leave for a day's toil shifting caravans, happy in the thought that he was not joining them.

In reception today was Janet who was blushing. She was not the prettiest woman in the world, a bit of a plain Jane. Not as bad as the cleaner at the leisure centre who looked like Plug out of the Beano. However, Janet was good at her job and had a fine figure hidden under her drab looking clothes. She fancied Danny even though she was married.

'Morning, Hunk,' she said.

'Morning, honey,' was his reply, 'how are you?'

'I am as well as to be expected on a Monday morning, kind sir,' she replied, and curtseyed. He left Janet to answer the ringing telephone and walked into the kitchen where he made two cups of tea with just milk, before heading into the sales office. Gordon, the general manager, was his usual Tourette's self, shouting and swearing down the phone at the gas engineer. 'I don't give a fuck,' he yelled, his neck swelling and his face turning purple. 'We have four vans to be sited today so you had better get yourself a fucking Lemsip, shove it up your fat nose and get your fat fucking arse up here! You fat useless shit!' Danny handed him his cup of tea which he duly spilled as he slammed down the phone in anger.

'Morning boss, having a good morning I see.'

'Fuck off,' Gordon replied. 'That prick was trying to throw a Monday morning sickie, the fat fuck said he had a cold.' The fat fuck he was referring to was Graham, the resident gas engineer, who connected and disconnected the gas supply to the caravans and carried out general maintenance and gas safety checks when required. He was all doom and gloom. A right boring wimpy bastard that spent most of his spare time sitting in his little sailboat. The boat was tied to its mooring, which it never seemed to set sail from. Graham also did not look after his pretty church-going wife in the bedroom. Danny did but that's another story. Gathering in Capt. Tourette's office for the scheduled 9.30am meeting were Gordon aka the Capt., Lorna from admin, Janet from reception, Linda from the gym, Morag from housekeeping and Gavin from Entertainment. Gavin was also known as Flash Harry because of his pencil thin moustache and resemblance to the guy from the St Trinian's movies. He was a creep and Danny did not like him one bit.

Last, but not least were Duncan and Ruth, the owners and directors of the park. They were a husband and wife from England and thick as two planks of wood. This pair of stupid twats could not run a burger van between them. They had been left the park by Ruth's father who had bought it 28 years before and built it into a good business. He had died two years previously. This pair could not fail. The site fees paid by the caravan owners every March totalled nearly two million. Add that to the holiday rentals, say another one million. And the money brought in by the various bars and restaurants on the park and you had a pair of very stupid millionaires grossing about five million a year. They were spoiled rich kids and not very popular.

The purpose of this meeting was to discuss the start of the new season. The new seasonal staff intake consisted of usually low paid immigrants, and various other shit that went to work on caravan parks. On the agenda were new caravan and lodge models, departmental budgets, staff, targets and so on. Future general and sales meetings would be held weekly thereafter and usually on a Friday morning. Capt. Tourette's started off the meeting by talking about the fantastic season the year before, with sales surpassing expectations despite a recession going on everywhere else. Danny was impressed with Gordon's control over his Tourette's when in the company of his directors. Danny was also convinced Duncan was shagging Linda. He had once seen both their cars parked outside a hotel in Gourock. You could also tell by the way they looked at each other when they thought no one was looking.

Linda was from Glasgow and married to an IT computer geek called Trevor; she would shag anyone to death if they were rich or famous. Danny never had the opportunity to explore that sweet tight-fitting pussy because he was neither. Sex with Linda would be like a workout in the gym and leave you physically exhausted and walking like John Wayne for weeks. I mean this bitch had a six pack! Fuck that. Danny preferred to be in control.

The meeting was incredibly boring and lasted three bloody hours. It was now 12.30 pm and lunchtime, this meeting was over, and Danny needed sex! He also knew exactly where to get it. Danny would have to wait until Gordon was out of the way, which he would be shortly. Capt. Tourette's always went home at lunchtime, which would leave Danny to do his own thing. The manager lived in a swanky lodge on the park with his wife Laura who had just had a baby girl named Abby who kept Gordon and Laura very busy indeed. Gordon always went home at lunchtime to give his wife a break and to see his baby daughter.

'Catch you later Danny,' said Gordon as he walked out to the car park, "one is going for one's fucking lunch.'

'Me too.'

'Be back here for two,' Gordon shouted as he started up his Toyota pick-up. 'We need to go over your monthly target.' He laughed as he drove away.

‘Whoopee fucking doo,’ Danny replied as he jumped into the Audi A5, aptly named the Black Pearl and started driving up and down the endless rows of lodges and caravans. He needed to find his prey quickly. Her name was Natcha, she was 23 years old, from Thailand and was stunning with beautiful black hair, olive skin, lovely brown eyes and a body to die for. She was very petite and looked about seventeen which turned Danny on big time. Eastern woman loved to please their men and even though she was still very young, she was an expert at all sexual activity. Natcha had no boundaries in the bedroom, none at all. Danny now understood why so many fat-bellied, over the hill old men went to Thailand. Young Thai girls would do anything to please their perverted ways.

Thai girls were desperate, keen to escape their lives of poverty in Thailand, and up for anything, poor things. They could be easily dominated and there was no back chat from these young girls who were also very beautiful and feminine. It would be very unlikely that old perverts would get the same response from a seventeen-year-old British teenager. Natcha came from Thailand via a Thai bride website when she was discovered online by Malcolm, a 67-year-old petrol station owner. Malcolm owned a 30-seat coach which he used to bus the blue rinse brigade round the three lochs. Natcha was young, sexy, and beautiful and totally wasted on Malcolm. She was simply his plaything to be used when he felt like it. He could not fuck her even if he wanted to! This was due to his age and limp dick. Everyone knew about it in the local village. This was thanks to his ex-wife's vicious tongue. Unfortunately for Natcha, Malcolm used her as his skivvy around the house and his business. He was also a tight bastard with money. The poor girl worked her cute little buns off. She also worked on the park cleaning the caravans and lodges. Malcolm beat her and took most of her earnings. What she had left or had managed to hide was sent back home to her Mum, leaving her very little for herself, although she did manage to put what little that was left in the bank. It was her insurance, something she might need later.

Danny knew she was around somewhere and kept looking. He glanced at his watch. Looking up, he saw her minivan at the end of Lochside number 12. YABBA DABBA DOO! She was cleaning one of the holiday lodges. Perfect! He could feel his cock already growing in his trousers. He parked his car behind her little white minivan and climbed the wooden stairs, opened the gate and walked on to the decking. Natcha heard him coming, turned and instantly smiled that beautiful smile. Her teeth were brilliant white and perfect. She was wearing a pair of brown Ugg boots, blue jeans and a white top which showed off her beautiful olive skin.

'Hi, babes,' he said and smiled as he closed the door.

'Danny!' Natcha screamed. She threw off her top to reveal she was not wearing a bra, her small breasts and tiny nipples bouncing slightly as she ran to the bedroom. Danny followed her. She was now practically naked and, stepping into the en suite shower, Danny watched her soap herself while he undressed, to reveal a very impressive hard-on. He played with himself as he lay back on the bed watching her soap her body. Danny got up, cock in hand, and joined her in the shower. She immediately squatted and took his hard cock in her mouth. The pleasure was intense. Natcha could suck his large cock for hours and was always very willing and able to please him. Danny aimed to please her in return and lifted her up. She immediately wrapped her legs around him tightly and he lowered her onto his throbbing cock. He thrust it into her pussy, holding her cute ass in both hands. He pumped her up and down on his rock-solid cock. Both were wrapped up in the ecstasy of the moment, Natcha screaming and moaning. He had his finger in her ass, as he fucked her even harder, holding her against the wet shower wall. Her skin made squeaking noises as it rubbed up and down against the wet glass. She loved it and shouted, 'Fuck me! fuck me! fuck me!' as she bit and sucked his lip hard! Her cute tiny ass was so small he could practically hold both cheeks in one hand! She was now going wild and moaned and screamed in pleasure. Danny lifted her legs onto his shoulders. She balanced her arms on the top of the glass walls of the shower, looking down, watching, as Danny sucked, bit, and licked her clit. He gave her sweet pussy some oral as he gently moved his finger in and out of her ass. Natcha had a massive orgasm, a lot of which Danny could taste in his mouth. She had come five times before they had moved out of the shower.

Danny threw her face-down on the bed, pulled her upwards and backwards, fucking her from behind. She reached behind and gently massaged his balls. He fucked her hard, alternating his cock between her ass and pussy; sex with her was out of this world. Eventually he could not hold back any longer – stopping, he lay down on the bed and pushed her head down on his cock. She sucked and licked it as she massaged his balls and then licked his ass. Danny loved to watch her; she was really happy pleasing him. Finally, he couldn't take any more and lay watching as she finished him off by taking his pulsing throbbing cock out of her mouth and wanking his cum all over her pretty little face. His cum looked brilliant white against her skin and she put his cock back into her mouth in time to taste the last of his spurting juice. She liked to watch him, looking on with those beautiful brown eyes. His cum covered a large amount of her small pretty face and went over her beautiful black shiny hair. Exhausted, they both lay down on the bed. He could not think of a better way to have lunch!

Danny later carried Natcha back to the shower. She washed him down, paying special attention to his cock and his ass. She then dried him off with a soft Egyptian cotton towel. 'I love my Mr Danny,' she said in her cute native twang.

'And Mr Danny loves you, babes,' Danny said in his best Sean Connery voice. Both were hugely satisfied. He could gladly have spent the rest of the afternoon with her. That, however, was not possible due to their impending work. They both got dressed and chatted for a while before she started cleaning up the lodge and Danny headed back to work. He felt great as he headed into the sales office.

He started the afternoon by heading back into the Capt.'s office for the second time that day. Gordon went over the stock list and prices and his monthly target with him, a target that Danny could reach with ease. Gordon annoyingly kept a parrot in his office, an African Grey called Moby who was even more foul-mouthed than his owner. The stupid bird swore that much that it had to be put in the stationery cupboard when there were customers about and during meetings. It told Danny to 'Fuck Off, Wanker' and screeched 'Danny's a dick!' about a dozen times. It was getting on Danny's tits, and he made a mental note to kill the fucking bird at the first opportunity. Gordon laughed every time Moby did it and thought it was hilarious. After the meeting Danny spent most of the afternoon talking to Janet who obviously thought he was hot. Periodically, he glanced out of the window, looking for any potential customers that could appear in the showground where they kept the display caravans.

Danny had not given Janet a second thought last year, mainly because she really was not that pretty; she had a better chance of winning the bingo than riding his large cock. But then you never know – sometimes it's sexy to fuck really plain chicks, and Danny had started to notice that she was wearing more revealing clothes than previously. Her summer frock was showing off more of that fine slim body beneath. Fucking her would give him that control of a girl who lacked good looks and was married. They were usually easy to abuse and kept silent. Abusing girls was a pastime that Danny absolutely loved and thrived on. Was that not what God invented him for? Maybe he would fuck the bitch; why not? she might let him go further than most.

At 5 pm Danny had three choices on leaving the office; **one,** go back to his lodge and make his dinner; tonight, he was having M & S Scottish salmon with mashed potatoes and string beans, after which he could watch some Kodi TV with a couple of JDs. **Two,** stand at the bar in the Leisure Dome like the Lone Ranger and watch a smaller TV which would be further away, just in the hope of picking up some new female flesh. Or **three,** go for a couple of lengths in the pool; again, hoping there might be some female flesh on show there. Danny decided to check out the centre just in case there was pussy about. He entered the bar/leisure centre hoping there would indeed be some fresh pussy and preferably young. He popped his head through the open door of the bar. It was empty apart from the barman. Danny had never seen him before and thought he was probably a Pole or a Romanian or some other foreign dickhead – Danny hated the immigrants. The conversation with him would be shite and probably about football, badly spoken in broken English. Anyway, he hated male company and avoided it at all costs. The bar was, however, worth checking out in case there was a barmaid or other females in there worth fucking. There was not a single bit of talent around. It was still too early in the season and the park was still very quiet. Fuck it! Danny decided to head back to the lodge as he was getting hungry anyway. He was a good cook and dinner was mucho tasty. After cleaning up he sat down, flicked on the TV and was in the middle of scanning the channels when his iPhone vibrated on the table.

It was a text from Barbara, a married 55-year-old MILF with the most amazing tits. She had a caravan down at the front on Sea Breeze. Barbara was married and totally bored shitless with her husband. She just adored Danny and loved to fuck him. He always kept her on standby when there was a shortage of new females around the park. Or he was just horny, which he often was, or simply just bored. Fuck it, he thought why not; Barbara would not show up until it was late and dark outside anyway. This was because she was worried about anyone seeing her. She was also scared of someone telling her husband who was unaware that his wife was a sex mad slut, fucking a guy 14 years her junior and 20 years younger than him. Anyway, by the time she sneaked up here in the dark Danny would be well up for another healthy sex session. Barbara was a school administrator who came to her caravan during school holidays, her husband, Eric, who worked offshore, joining her when he was onshore. Danny had met her on his very first day on the park. He was driving round the park in the golf cart. Barbara was there on her own, leaning over her balcony displaying those wonderful breasts which were bursting out of her halter top. Danny stopped the buggy to introduce himself. Twenty minutes later he was fucking the screaming slut in every hole. Barbara was now one of his sex slaves and madly in love with him. She did everything he told her including when she could come and play and when she had to leave. She was older, but great fun in bed, absolutely up for anything. Danny spent the next couple of hours watching Lock, Stock and Two Smoking Barrels which was one of his favourite films. He drank JDs while rubbing his cock and looking forward to the horny slut's arrival.

She arrived at 11 pm clutching a bottle of JD and kissed him. 'Hi babes,' she said as she groped his hard cock through the fabric of his trousers. She pursed her lips; 'I want you so much,' she moaned. Danny thanked her for the booze and poured them both a drink from the bottle that was already opened. Barbara closed all the blinds, nervously looking around. She really had what he could only call awesome tits – they were simply huge. Not just saggy useless lumps of flesh, these beauties held their own. Ladies with tits of this magnitude usually had the huge ass to go with them, but Barbara didn't; she had narrow female shoulders and a medium-sized ass. Danny never did like fucking fat birds although he had done on occasion. He preferred feminine and petite girls or skinny women in their late fifties and sixties that he could throw about the bed. Barbara was great company and really wild in the sack. This was partly the fault of her husband. He had not fucked her in years and because of this she was a desperate horny bitch. This apparently happens a lot to women when they are married, and their husbands do not want to play anymore. Danny had heard every excuse under the sun as to why the married women he was fucking were up for anything – anal sex, rimming or oral and swallowing, twosomes, threesome, orgies and so on. Most of the girls used the excuse that they were doing it to please him because they loved him. Or they had simply too much to drink. When in fact a lot of them just got lost in the ecstasy and could not help themselves. To be honest, a lot of them were just neglected wives hungry to be fucked by a hot handsome man with a big cock. All women had heard of multiple orgasms but very few ever experienced them.

Danny believed that if a man is not fucking his wife, then someone else will. Probably him! He laughed at his own joke; this brought problems, as a lot of his one-night stands would fall in love with him. They would be great at the start and then become a nuisance by phoning, texting or even following him. Because of this, Danny preferred to keep only the married ones to play with on a regular basis. Married women kept quiet and normally did as they were told. They were also an opportunity to blackmail. They never complained even if the sex got a little rough. Another reason these randy females kept quiet was because they did not want to get caught by their husbands or found out by their friends and family, especially the posh ones.

Like Victoria, his ex-wife's best friend. She was a high society lady who played tennis and golf, often rubbing shoulders with politicians, royalty, and stars. In bed she was a dirty slut and up for everything. That dirty bitch was fucking Danny when her surgeon husband was working, saving lives. Lovers did not want to risk losing everything that they had worked their entire lives for. They preferred to keep their affair a secret, especially if they had children. This suited Danny just fine. He kept two mobile phones in his possession. One was a pay-as-you-go burner phone kept for calls with the ladies and the pests. The other one was legit and for business. The burner phone could be switched off or dumped at any time, especially when leaving a park for pastures new.

Yes, married women were definitely easier to control and much less hassle. Danny did have a soft spot for Barbara, Natcha and the late Sylvia. All were allowed a tiny part in his little world. They were his and owned by him. They were his toys, his playthings, standing by eagerly in reserve – simply and only for his pleasure. The rest of the sluts he met were mere whores to be used simply for his pleasure. These women were slags, sluts, whores, and bitches who gave their bodies free of charge and deserved to be treated with contempt.

Danny put on a Black Keys CD and walked back to the couch where Barbara was sitting. She placed her drink on the table and pulled him closer. 'Come here honey, I want to taste you. I want your hard cock in my mouth, all of it.' She unzipped his fly and took out his cock. She wanked it a few times before putting it in her mouth and sucking it hard. Barbara could get the entire length of his cock in her mouth and looked as if she had a big gobstopper in there – you could see it pressing against her cheek from inside; getting it all in was not easy, but deep throat was a fabulous speciality of hers that Danny loved. He put down his drink, reached down and undid the top of her dress and bra. He played with her beautiful tits, now free, in both hands as if he were trying to guess the weight of a couple of melons. Barbara stood up, wiping her face of pre- cum juices, and Danny moved his hand under her summer dress, to be greeted by a very clean-shaven pussy and a very wet one. He fingered her as she stood facing him, but she stopped him. She picked up both drinks and headed for the bedroom and Danny followed her, his hard cock poking out in front of him like a water diviner.

They lay on the bed where he made Barbara lick his shaved balls as she played with herself using her pink rampant rabbit vibrator. He forced her head down hard between his legs making her lick his asshole while pumping his cock. Danny returned all three pleasures before some hard fisting and fucking in every position. Tiny beads of sweat were visible on both their brows. Danny pulled her up onto her knees as he buried her face into the pillow. He then slid his hard 12 inches into her moist honey pot, a muted moan escaping from the pillow as his full length reached its goal. He fucked hard, his hard cock slowly going in and out of her soaking wet pussy. He would stop every now and again, to grab and pull at her tits, his cock held pressed inside her, because he liked to watch her tits as they moved back and forward just above the sheets to the rhythm of his thrusting. Danny fucked her long and hard until eventually they both collapsed in a heap. Barbara finished him off by sucking his cock until he came all over her teeth, lips, and face. Barbara had another great sex trick of wanking his cock over her teeth and mouth while keeping her teeth clenched shut until he had come. She would then lick her lips to get all his cum into her mouth. It was pretty amazing and a trick he would have to teach Natcha.

Barbara lay back on the pillow, her heart beating wildly in her chest. She was in heaven as she lay exhausted on the bed beside him. 'JESUS, DANNY!' she said. What a guy, she thought. He always delivered and delivered well; he was a sex god. Barbara knew he fucked other girls, but she did not care. She could not remember the last time Eric fucked her and even then, he could not make her come. Tonight, she had a total of eight orgasms, some of them massive. She loved sex with Danny it was truly amazing. The best bit this time was when Danny did his reverse thrusting fuck. She would be on her back with his ankles near her head, and he would be on his front face down on the bed and facing away from her. He would bend his fabulous big, long, thick cock downwards and backwards and slide it inside her. He would then thrust back and forth, his hard wet cock sliding inside her as she played with his shiny balls and fingered his ass. She watched it rise and fall, her finger sliding in and out of his asshole in perfect rhythm as it rose up and down. Number two was when he was licking and sucking her clit with his tongue while ramming three of his strong fingers hard inside her soaking wet vagina – she thought that one was going to kill her. She now lay on the bed, her entire body shaking; the orgasms made her weak and legless and all her energy was drained from her body. Barbara also liked it when Danny took her from behind, fucking her ass and pussy while she was tied, blindfolded, to the bed as he spanked her and called her a dirty girl. He could get carried away sometimes and had physically hurt her on more than one occasion. It was difficult to hide a load of finger slap marks that had been left on her bum and had later turned into bruises. He was, however, a fantastic lover and worth the pain. Barbara had never had a single orgasm in her life until she met Danny. She was now making up for lost time and loving it!

Chapter 2

The Past

Danny had grown up in Faifley, Clydebank, a tough housing estate in Glasgow. His early years were marred by hatred, drugs and violence, gang warfare and knife crime – all part of his daily life. When he was a kid, he was bullied by adults and older children. His own parents' abuse included being referred to as little Hitler. Shouts of Heil Hitler and Sieg Heil were common most days. This was due to his thick jet-black hair and brilliant ice blue eyes. He hated the name and the people who used it.

The name little Hitler derived from his likeness to a boy who played a part in the film *The Boys from Brazil*. The 1978 film starred Gregory Peck, Laurence Oliver, and James Mason and was about Josef Mengele, the infamous Auschwitz death camp doctor who was played brilliantly by Gregory Peck. In this film Mengele had secluded surrogate mothers in a Brazilian clinic and fertilised them with ova containing Hitler's DNA. The result was ninety-four perfect clones of Hitler. Once born, these children were placed with foster parents around the world who could not have children of their own and were happy to accept a child from the doctor without asking too many questions. They were not concerned with the child's real mother or the child's origin. These boys when old enough would carry on with Hitler's dream. To do what? Danny had no idea. It was a good film and he had watched it himself; however, he hated the name and the resemblance, nonetheless.

His early years were like living in a cesspit full of sharks. The dismal concrete jungle that was his home turf was full of junkies, thugs and neds and Danny disliked every last fucking one of them.

Most had turned to drugs and crime to make money. Danny however did not. He was not interested in drugs, burglary or robbery, although he had dabbled in it during his teens. He would rather escape to the mountains or enjoy the sanctuary of an older woman's breasts.

He was no angel and had enjoyed some of their crimes like snow- dropping, going out with the boys at night to steal clothes from washing lines and stuff from garages and sheds. Snow dropping got its name from the snowdrops that started flowering in the spring and were scattered on the ground in the woods that they used as their path between the housing scheme and the posh houses. The gang of youths also broke into some commercial premises – all were very beneficial pastimes.

It wasn't all doom and gloom, and the gang did have a few laughs. Like the time Melly stole the John Morrow luxury coach from outside the driver's house. The driver lived in a top floor flat and had run an extension cable from his house down to the bus so he could vacuum the seats and carpet. His wife had then shouted on him to come up for his dinner, which the daft bastard did, leaving the keys in the ignition.

Melly saw this and jumped in and sped off, pulling the plug out of the wall as he did so. Danny was inside the bus stop outside the Co-op store, snogging a girl, when suddenly the coach pulled up, with half the Faifley Mad Squad hanging out of the windows. It had already been around Faifley picking up neds and was nearly full. Melly opened the door and screamed 'all aboard!'

With cops hot on their tail who were trying to avoid the flying objects that were thrown from the rear window, including the Hoover and a few seats, the bus went via Carbeth, Drymen and then Balmaha before Melly stalled it on a steep hill. The cops managed to catch a few of the boys and nine were charged with theft, even though only one person stole the coach.

Danny was more interested in escaping from this world of shit than living in it and did not intend to remain in a Clydebank housing scheme for the rest of his life. Fuck that! Instead, he used his charm and handsome good looks to his advantage. He learned that older women would pay to sleep with him; if they did not, he would just steal from them anyway. He started to pick up and fuck these women and, in return, they gave him gifts and money. He enjoyed the attention and sometimes even the sex, depending on how old they were – the rewards were usually worth it.

By the time he was twenty years old, he had saved up enough money to escape his life in the Faifley back streets. He would not be going back there ever. Nor did he want anything to do with anyone from his past; they would only drag him down. Danny packed up and left. He was now 23 years old and bought a flat with his hard-earned cash. It was in the West End of Glasgow in the Byres Road area. He then got a job working in a bar which was on Byres Road itself. The area was awash with students from Glasgow University which was located in the same area. The job was really just a front, as his main source of income was from fucking older females out of as much as he could get. His cock and his bank balance were his gods, the latter of which was now growing by the day. He targeted middle-aged women with low self-esteem and average looks, usually divorced or dumped by their men for a younger woman. They would usually have a few quid in the bank after their divorce. Most were very willing to spend it on their new handsome boyfriend. They would parade him in front of their friends like a prize peacock. Once used and abused, the majority of these women were left with empty hearts and matching bank accounts. Lessons in love they would not forget. Danny took no prisoners – women were stupid when it came to love, sex and marriage. Did they really believe that someone as hot as he would marry an over the hill, fat, middle-aged woman who was past her sell by date? Come on! Did these women really think they could buy him? Fuck them! It was their own stupid fault. A few of the women he conned were good-looking and intelligent; he fucked them senseless and even took them out, but took their money, nevertheless.

Danny cared very little for anyone but himself. He also dated a long list of females for his own sexual gratification, girls a lot younger than any of his cons, though he was never tempted to break the underage rule. He sometimes dated up to a dozen girls at the same time. He was a god, a sex giant in a land filled with man dwarfs with tiny dicks. His parents had given him only two things, a large cock, and good looks; who needed anything else?

During this trail of fuck destruction Danny hit the jackpot when he met Gillian, a tall blonde sex goddess. She was stunningly beautiful and intelligent. He met her in a bar in the West End where he was working. She was ten years older than him and crazy about him. Who fucking wouldn't be! Danny saw her as the potential for an easy life. Gillian was well off financially and could support him without any difficulty, plus she wanted to! The thought of not having to work again or live in his shag pad in the West End was very appealing. Yes, fucking older ladies was sometimes fun and the money good. He would rather live in luxury with a stunning woman than continue eating pussy for cash. He did enjoy it though. Another reason for opting out was he had been rough with a few of the ladies and had been close to borderline to being arrested more than once. He had fleeced and hurt many ladies over the years and jail was always a risk. A woman once parted from her cash and dumped by Danny often became that woman from hell. Not only were they fucking dumped, but they were robbed as well! Cleaned out – bank:

empty: so sad: too bad: bye bye! A few ladies had threatened to go to the police. This really worried him as the prospect of prison was one of his worst fears; he could not stand being confined. He would rather die than be imprisoned. He loved his freedom as much as money and sex and did not want to lose it.

With that thought in mind he decided to work hard on his relationship with Gillian and started romancing her for the next two years. He was a perfect boyfriend and Gillian was showered with expensive gifts, flowers, romantic dinners, sexy weekends away and exotic holidays. He had a few quid in the bank from his cons and spent a lot of money on his new bride-to-be. During their relationship Gillian still worked in London which suited him as it gave him plenty of freedom to continue having affairs. He stopped fleecing older women and was very careful who he fucked, mostly only dating girls outside his local area. He avoided going to places with Gillian where he might be recognised by a lover, and he got away with it. He was the perfect partner in her eyes. He later tied the knot with Gillian in a small romantic church in the village of Luss on Loch Lomond two years to the day they had met. The wedding was huge with many professional and high society guests. Danny even managed to fuck a nineteen-year-old waitress at the wedding reception in the Cameron House hotel. The girl was giving him the come on all day, as were half the female wedding guests. Danny got his chance out in the corridor and took her upstairs and fucked the young slut in a laundry cupboard. He could hear Gillian talking and people passing outside – a quickie but exciting. The sweet little thing managed to swallow his cum without getting a drop of it on his £3000 Armani suit. After the wedding Danny and Gillian enjoyed a honeymoon in India Shores in the Florida Keys. He loved it there; they rented a condo on the beach and watched dolphins and sunsets from their balcony. Apart from his new wife, Danny did not fuck anyone while on honeymoon. To be honest, he did not get a chance as she was always by his side.

On their return, the new Mr and Mrs Fleming moved into their new home in Newton Mearns, the £750k mansion complete with pool that was inherited from her parents. The wonderful Mrs Fleming was fast becoming a very successful solicitor and was earning a respectable two hundred and fifty grand a year. She was a fine catch. She had also inherited her parents' estate, bringing her total worth to about £1.8million; this was what Danny was looking for, to live in luxury, never wanting for anything, to be kept by an older woman. At Gillian's request Danny stopped working and was now officially a house husband. He lived the next few years by sponging from his wife's high earnings, the money from her inheritance and the cash he had conned. He also sold the flat and was doing very well. Gillian was besotted by him and gave him everything and he, in turn, worked hard on improving his knowledge and his social standing, not forgetting to keep his new wife happy in every way possible. That stopped temporarily two years later when Gillian gave birth to a son whom they named Jason. Danny was unhappy about the child's arrival. He was left at home and made a weak attempt at being a father. It was quickly established that this was not working, and Gillian insisted they hire a live-in nanny, which would allow her to continue with her career and give Danny the freedom to continue to improve by restarting his classes.

The new nanny, a French girl named Genevieve, was nineteen years old, slim and pretty. Danny was fucking her within the week. She was a raving nympho and could not get enough of him. Gillian's work in London was now keeping her away from home the entire week, only arriving home late afternoon Friday and leaving again early Monday morning. This allowed him endless opportunities to have sex with Genevieve. He screwed her constantly in every way and she loved it, most of the time on his marital bed which turned them both on, not to mention the bathroom, baby's room, kitchen and just about everywhere, including Gillian's car. They both lived in the house just like a married couple and went out often. Danny also fucked countless other females he picked up at classes, in bars, shops, clubs, even the dentist. Over the next year of his short three-year marriage Danny slept with just about everything that moved. Young or old, it did not matter; his sex drive was a monster and whatever morals he had were lost a long time ago and now floated in a cesspit somewhere in his past. Life was great for a while and Danny continued to better himself with an education, something he never had the opportunity to do when he was younger.

He had been expelled from school at fifteen for assaulting a teacher and now many years later regretted it. Education was the way to go if you wanted to survive in this world. To improve his knowledge and social standing Danny spent days reading books, lots of books, and attended day and night courses on subjects such as elocution, etiquette, history, politics, and travel. He also gained his Private Pilot's Licence and flew a light aircraft. He dressed impeccably and wore the finest designer clothes, with an £18k Rolex on his wrist, a birthday present from Gillian. He was fast becoming an intelligent man, mixing with professional and intelligent people, many of them Gillian's friends from university, work associates and colleagues. Gillian loved to show off her handsome young husband. He was well and truly away from his shit past. Danny was now a man with style and class who had left those humble beginnings behind. He had a passion for climbing and had climbed all the Munros in Scotland and a few mountains in Switzerland.

Switzerland was a place he liked to visit whenever possible. He rented a chalet there, The Chalet Schwalbennest (swallows' nest) located in Zermatt – an expensive private chalet with stunning views of the Matterhorn Mountain. Danny loved to travel and had travelled extensively with Gillian over the last few years, visiting France, Germany, Switzerland, Norway, Austria, and Hong Kong. He had also spent long holidays with his new family in the United States. Past holidays had been spent in Florida, Texas, San Francisco, Los Angeles, Boston, New York,

Hawaii, and Las Vegas. Las Vegas was one of his favourite destinations and a place he planned to visit again soon without his wife. Danny was living the fucking dream; life was just a breeze for the ex-street kid. His friends from the past were still petty criminals and drug users stranded in their fucked-up life of hell. Danny, however, lived a life of luxury and did everything and anything he wanted. He was still living on the edge every day which suited his adrenaline-fuelled body and mind; he was buzzing and on fire. Constant affairs were fun and risky, and he just loved sex with multiple partners, Danny thought he was untouchable, immortal, a king amongst slaves and peasants. Sadly, for him he was nothing of the kind.

His easy life came to an abrupt end when Gillian caught him screwing her best friend Victoria, and Genevieve, by the indoor pool. Danny and Victoria were fucking by the side of the indoor pool, and he had persuaded them both to indulge him with a threesome. As Victoria was married, he frequently fucked her at the house when Gillian was away. Genevieve living in had ended that arrangement, so he now fucked them both at the same time.

Genevieve was kneeling at the poolside sucking Victoria's clit as she lay on a sun lounger. It turned out Victoria had acquired a taste for young pussy during her boarding school days. Danny was behind the young nanny fucking her tight little pussy. Victoria's face was turned towards the patio doors as she bit down on the green and white striped cushion of the sun lounger, her arms above her head, her huge diamond wedding rings blinking in the sunlight. Gillian suddenly appeared in the back garden. She always parked her car in the garage and entered the house by the pool doors. She stood frozen, staring through the glass at her husband, best friend, and nanny fucking by her pool like something from a porn movie.

Danny pulled his wet hard cock from Genevieve's ass, and it now stood out in front of him like a baby's arm holding an orange. Victoria nearly knocked the young nanny's head off as she scissor-kicked her legs closed, launching herself from the lounger as if it had suddenly caught fire. She screamed, grabbed a towel and ran away, Genevieve hurriedly following behind. The look on Gillian's face said it all. He found out later that Gillian had decided to return a day early from London to surprise him for their wedding anniversary the following day. She stood stunned, a bunch of red roses in her hand. She looked mad as hell and did not say a word. Instead, she simply about turned and left.

Danny pulled on his trousers and ran outside, only to be met by the Porsche screaming out of the drive, its broad tyres smoking and leaving black tracks on the paving stones. The roses were lying on the ground. Shit, he thought, this was not good. Danny never saw her again.

The end came swiftly, with him being quickly tossed out of the house by men he had never seen before who were accompanied by the police. His joint bank and credit cards were stopped, and the locks changed on the doors. She even took back his car. He was stunned at the speed of it all. Gillian would not even talk to him, ignoring his calls before blocking them altogether. He was now well and truly fucked by his now very livid wife. She later won her divorce case by a mile; this of course was of no surprise to him. He ended up with fuck all except for his watch and clothes. He was forced to spend the next few months floating between various lovers' domains. He had his cash stash now sitting at £127,678 which he had been topping up from their joint bank account but wanted more. He went back to his old ways of fucking for money and working in bars, but he was getting tired of it. He lasted twelve months doing it before he applied for and got a job selling caravans on a park in the Lake District. He needed to escape from his gigolo lifestyle. A few of the ladies he had fleeced were turning up at the bar – it was time to go.

The job was good, and he lived and worked the rest of the summer there. It was better than working in bars and the money was good and it was an excellent place to pick up girls. Danny of course was now fucking lots of them on a regular basis. His ex-wife was apparently dating a local GP and Danny had not seen either her or his son since his departure. Good fucking riddance he thought. He was charming, funny and, most importantly, handsome; he did not need anyone; he was independent, a survivor. He was a professional con man, full of charm and wit – a proper ladies' man. He really did not give a fuck about anyone but himself. One minute he could be one of the lads, a bit rough and tough, who could, and would, kick ten colours of shite out of you and the next minute he was a sophisticated and adorable educated gentleman lover. Woman loved to love him, and men loved to hate him. Danny was first and foremost a prolific con man, a compulsive sex manic, a wild lover. However, he also had a much darker side. An evil side seen only by a very few unfortunate people.

Chapter 3

Carolyn

The fasten seat belt sign was on as they continued their descent into Glasgow International. The 787 flew over Milngavie reservoir as they descended on the glide slope for runway two three. Her jump seat was on the wrong side of the aircraft. If she were sitting on the opposite side, she would be able to see her house and the children's school. Thank God, she thought; her feet were killing her, she had just come on a period mid-flight and her stomach ached. Carolyn, a 40-year-old air stewardess from Milngavie near Glasgow, was on a return trip from Los Angeles. She was married to Philip, an optician who had his own optician practices in Milngavie and Bearsden and they had a 15-year-old daughter Emma and a 13-year-old son Jonathan. She lived with her family in the Castle Mains Estate, a posh part of Milngavie. Emma and Jonathan went to Douglas Academy just a five-minute walk from home which meant they could walk to school every day by themselves.

Carolyn worked with Virgin Airlines on the long-haul flight out of Glasgow International, on the 787. Life in general used to be pretty good for her but not anymore. Now there was something wrong, something very wrong with her marriage. Her love life with her husband had practically stopped. Her husband of twenty years had not made love to her in six months. They never seemed to do much together anymore. Either he was too busy with his business, or he was playing golf. She had the kids and her job. Carolyn was not sure what exactly was wrong, just that something was not right. Philip had not even touched her in ages and blamed the stress of work. What stress? the business was doing very well. She could understand if she had let herself go, but that was not the case. She was an attractive 5'7 blonde with an ample bosom and a knock-out pair of legs. She was slightly curvy after having the kids but still looked good. Carolyn had received plenty of offers from young first officers and pilots on her route, although, to be fair, pilots did love themselves and think every female wanted to screw them. She had many opportunities to dabble in many an affair on stop overs. However, she had always declined and had always remained faithful. She had never been tempted on any occasion and had only ever been with Philip, a true virgin to the man she loved.

She was looking forward to seeing the kids and having a hot bath. Carolyn thought a lot about her marriage to Philip while she was away. Like the way he was now secretive with his mobile and how he worked late when she was home and finished early when she was away.

Philip also went out a lot more than he did in the past. He told her that he was going to the golf club with his friend Kenny. She had checked once, and he was not there. When she confronted him, he said he and Kenny got bored of golf talk and went to the pub instead. Previously on stop overs when Carolyn phoned home Philip would normally chat to her for a few minutes and would say things like 'love you darling, miss you'. Now he would simply ask how the flight went and how was the weather, before quickly handing the phone to the kids. He was pretending to be happy to hear from her but was clearly not interested in chatting with her for very long.

The Dreamliner touched gently down on two three, the main wheel making a thump, thump noise as it ran over the centre line runway lights. Carolyn cleared customs in double quick time and drove out of the airport, heading west towards the Erskine Bridge. There was not a single traffic light between the airport and home which made it possible to make it there in about 20 minutes. Happy days, she thought as she would have been in no mood for traffic delays today; traffic, though, was light as it was now only 1 pm. She arrived home at 1.25 pm – the kids would not be out of school until 4 pm and Philip would be at work till about 7 pm. Carolyn headed straight for a bottle of wine and a glass and headed upstairs to run a long-awaited bath. On the passing she found herself drawn to the laundry basket in the closet upstairs and started flicking through the dirty clothes which was a mixture of Emma's sexy panties and bras and some school clothes and Jonathan's rugby gear, plus Philip's shirts. She started to smell his shirts, not really knowing what to expect; they still smelled clean, but she was sure one smelled of perfume, or was it aftershave? Carolyn's mind was in overdrive as she lowered herself into the bath, selecting a bath bomb from her Lush collection and popping it into the water. She was so glad to be home, albeit in a troubled state of mind. She placed her iPad on the tiled alcove windowsill and listened to Adele as she soaked in her slipper bath, a luxury she enjoyed. After her bath Carolyn started preparing dinner. The shopping she had ordered online from the local Tesco had arrived ten minutes previously. The kids were home and as always were delighted to see her, but after a short chat they both headed to their rooms for homework and teenager stuff which they would spend the rest of the evening doing.

Carolyn felt sad and scared about both her and the children's futures in this house. They had a beautiful home – surely, they would not have to leave. Emma and Jonathan went to a great school, had great friends and were both achieving great results and reports; they would be devastated. Was Philip going to throw all this away? Was it maybe her fault; was she going through the change of life? Maybe it was all in her imagination. She would confide in her sister tomorrow.

She stood in the kitchen, busy preparing dinner. Her thoughts were interrupted by the sound of Philip's car as it arrived in the drive. He walked into the kitchen and gave her a peck on the cheek. He asked what was for dinner and if she had a good trip, that was it! He then headed straight for the lounge and the TV and started watching the news. There were no cuddles, no sexy groping of her breasts or her butt. No 'I missed you darling'. Her mind started racing again and she felt sick with worry. Carolyn insisted that family dinners were always held in the dining room as it was the only chance they all got to communicate as a family. The last few days were the topic of discussion. Both Emma and Jonathan then retired to their rooms to continue their little teenage lives.

Carolyn disliked the atmosphere between herself and Philip at dinner. It was awful. It was more like they were flatmates than husband and wife. Both then spent the remainder of the night watching TV before going to bed about 11 pm. Yet again no contact, just idle chit chat during which Philip announced he was buying an Aston Martin DB9. A fucking what! Who does he think he is, Daniel Craig? Was it possible that Philip was having a midlife crisis and it wasn't her? Perhaps this was a penis extension to make up for the lack of sex in their marriage. She could not sleep the rest of the night and was now raging! What was he thinking, she thought, did he simply not care about his family? An Aston Martin! She was definitely going to see her sister in the morning, in fact her Dad too! This whole thing was making her ill. Philip had finally convinced her that there was indeed something wrong. He was becoming selfish, a complete wanker! It really looked like he didn't care. Carolyn closed her eyes she tried to sleep. She was jet-lagged, her mind racing. It looked like being a long night. And it was. She eventually drifted off to sleep as it was getting light, and the birds had started singing. She woke later that morning to find Philip was gone. He went to the gym every second morning before work. She wondered if he was simply keeping fit or was there another reason perhaps?

Carolyn had breakfast with the kids before waving them off to school. Douglas Academy was a great school with a fantastic reputation and the kids loved being there. She closed the door and went upstairs for a shower. Catching a glimpse of herself in the mirror, she looked rough and tired. The sleepless night and her period were not helping. The thought of Philip having an affair and what it would do to her and the children's world was not helping either. She got dressed and then telephoned her sister. She agreed to meet her at the Boatyard Inn at Balmaha for lunch. She then called her Dad at home. There was no answer even though it was only 10 am. He had a mobile which she tried but it was not answered either. That did not surprise her as it was usually always switched off and used only in emergencies. She decided to drive out to where he would be.

Fifteen minutes later she turned her VW Beetle into the Queens View car park. There was a small grass landing strip there for radio-controlled model aircraft. Dad had taken up the hobby after her Mum had died of cancer three years previously. Carolyn wished her mother was still alive; she missed her very much. More so in times like this, especially in times like this. Mum had been the rock of the family and great to confide in. She was also her best friend, a beautiful woman and dearly missed by everyone. Carolyn drove into the car park overlooking the moor. Ben Lomond in the distance still had a small patch of snow on its summit as it towered above the loch's glistening waters, casting a shadow over its eastern shore.

A tall figure of a man stood alone on the small neatly cut grass of the miniature runway. He was there right enough. Dad was looking up at the sky; no doubt his little plane was in the air. There was another on the ground nearby. Carolyn parked her car next to his and watched him for a while. She texted Sarah her sister and told her that she had found Dad and would meet her as discussed earlier. Carolyn waited until her father landed his little plane before she got out of the car. It was not a good idea to interrupt him when he was pilot in command of his aircraft. Dad's hobby could be expensive if he crashed one of his little planes, something he found out to his cost after a previous lapse of concentration. Carolyn shouted and waved at her Dad. He immediately looked confused and puzzled at seeing his daughter out at the strip. He waved back and placed his remote control on the ground. Dad walked towards her and gave her a huge hug. It felt nice. Is everything okay?' he asked. 'Yes, Dad, everything is fine, how are you?' 'I am fine, my dear.' Dad was a tall strong man with impeccable ethics, a retired Fire Chief, with sound judgement and high moral fibre. He was also a good listener just like her Mum had been.

'Sarah and I are going to the Boatyard for lunch; we were wondering if you wanted to join us. I am buying,' she smiled. Her Dad agreed but he knew that a chat about something important was coming up as lunch was not arranged via the usual channels, and Carolyn never bought lunch either. Carolyn helped her father load up his estate car with his equipment, being careful not to touch his delicate little planes – she knew much better than that! She gave him a huge hug. 'I will pick you up at 12.30 pm sharp, Sarah is making her own way there as she is working later.' She left her father packing up his gear and headed home where she spent the next hour getting ready before heading to the filling station at Baljaffray for fuel. She then picked up her Dad as arranged and headed out towards Balmaha and The Boatyard Inn. It was a lovely country pub, famous around the world for its charm and beautiful setting. It was adjacent to the Balmaha Boatyard which still delivered the Royal Mail to the twelve islands out on the loch. The restaurant was just a stone's throw from the loch itself.

They drove quietly at first, barely speaking. Dad asked the usual how were the children and how was work, then there was a long silence until he asked. 'Is this about Philip?' God how did he know that? Carolyn had not mentioned it to a soul. 'Yes,' she blurted out, 'I think he is having an affair or a mid-life crisis or something.' She told him what had been happening, like the mobile phone, the gym, the new car, the late nights at work. Her father was quiet for a time and then said, 'If Philip is having an affair, then you need to decide what route you intend to go down.' This was very serious indeed. More importantly it would massively affect the children as well. 'I will support you a hundred percent but can only advise you on what you should do. I can also tell you what your mother would say.' Carolyn burst into tears and eventually had to pull over as she could not see where she was driving through the tears in her eyes. Dad squeezed her hand and held her. He told her not to worry, everything would be fine. After a few minutes they eventually got underway and drove the rest of the way in silence. They shortly arrived at The Inn, to find Sarah sitting in the corner admiring the view across the loch. She saw them both walk in and could tell that Carolyn had been crying; Dad also looked the same sombre way he had looked on the day of Mum's funeral. Something was obviously wrong, and she had a good idea what.

During lunch the chat was the usual small talk about work and stuff. Sarah worked at the Waitrose supermarket in Milngavie as a floor manager and was married to Bob who was a joiner for a local company. She did not have all the lovely trappings that Carolyn had but was pretty much content with life in general. Sarah had a son Billy aged 17 who was now at college studying business management, and life was pretty happy and normal. Sarah had never been envious of Carolyn's life, she just wanted her to be happy. Sarah decided to start the serious conversation. 'What's up, honey, is it Philip?' God, thought Carolyn, had she missed the obvious; was everyone else seeing something that she had not, or did everyone know except her? 'Yes,' she said, 'I think he is having an affair.'

'Who with? What makes you think that?' Carolyn went on to describe why. Both Sarah and her father advised her to stay calm and stop stressing. They all agreed she should employ the services of a good private investigator to find out for sure if there was something to worry about. Carolyn felt a little better with her family around her and they all agreed not to mention it again that afternoon. It was tiring and distressing, and Carolyn had had enough. The trio managed to enjoy their lunch before Sarah headed off to work. Carolyn drove her Dad home as he was planning to spend the rest of the day in the garden. She went home and prepared and had dinner with Philip and the children. That night was a repeat of the previous night, both sitting in front of the telly and not saying very much. He was acting a little more on edge than he did last night. Carolyn slept better, and the next morning, after Philip and the kids had left, she went into the office next to the dining room and Googled private investigators, Glasgow.

There were a few listed, such as PI-1, Joe Stern Private Investigations Ltd and so on. They offered services such as matrimonial relationships, vetting, fraud, tracing, and the like. She chose a company called Frank McKnight Investigations and nervously dialled the telephone number. A female answered who sounded happy and cheerful and put Carolyn at ease right away. Carolyn arranged an appointment at their office in Glasgow at 1 pm. It was now Tuesday and she left for Los Angeles on Thursday morning. She had to know; she could not go through another trip like the last one. She texted Sarah to inform her about what she was doing, Sarah called her back to say she was taking a couple of hours out of work and coming with her. The sisters met at Milngavie train station and boarded the 12 noon for Glasgow which, in hindsight, was probably a mistake as they could not really chat about things due to the other passengers being in the carriage.

Thirty minutes later they departed the train at Glasgow Central and walked the short walk to Renfield Street. Carolyn was nervous about seeing the private investigators; they entered the lift and ascended to the fourth floor. The girls both walked into the reception area, to be greeted by a pretty blonde girl about 20 years old sitting at the reception desk. She immediately put Carolyn at ease again and asked their names before lifting the phone. 'Your one o'clock is here,' she said to whoever was on the other end of the phone and hung up. 'Mr McKnight is expecting you, this way please,' she said as she walked round from her desk.

Carolyn and Sarah were both shown into a plush office with dark rosewood furniture and fittings. Sarah squeezed Carolyn's hand as they sat down at Mr McKnight's desk. Mr McKnight was a fit looking guy about 6ft tall, very much a military kind of man. Frank, as he preferred to be called, was very blunt and straight to the point; he asked Carolyn to start from the very beginning and not to miss anything out. She told him of her suspicions about Philip from the beginning and when she had finished Frank explained to them both that even though this was very personal to her, it was in fact a job that simply just needed to be done and needed to be done quickly. If Carolyn wanted an outcome and an answer quickly, she must listen and comply with Frank's instructions, no matter what she thought.

He first explained that following a person or tracking a person to gain pictures of adultery can become very expensive. Carolyn should allow his team three days at the outset to gather video and photographic evidence of any possible adultery. The cost for two manned vehicles would be £2k per day plus expenses. Carolyn was quite shocked about this, but she had to know, and she had already spoken to her Dad about the cost and if she could not manage, he had agreed to cover it. Carolyn instructed Frank to proceed and asked when they would start their surveillance, telling him that she thought it best to start when she left for her flight to Los Angeles in two days' time as Philip seemed to be more active when she was away. Frank informed her that a private detective would meet her later that day in Milngavie to collect the spare key for Philip's car. This was to allow them the opportunity to place a tracking device in his car, Frank explaining that having a tracking device in the car would save time and money.

Carolyn was lost. 'Let me explain,' said Frank. If, for instance, they were spotted by Philip and had to back off, or they simply just lost him in traffic, they would be able to find him quickly again with the aid of a tracker. Not having one fitted could result in them having to start over, possibly even starting again the following day. Carolyn thought she knew what he meant, read and agreed to Frank's terms and conditions, signed the paperwork and shook his hand. He seemed like a no-nonsense type of guy, and she felt better already. Carolyn and Sarah left the office and went for lunch in the Italian restaurant in Buchanan Galleries when they discussed the next few days in great detail, especially what Carolyn would do if Philip was indeed having an affair. Carolyn had already decided that if it were true, Philip would have to leave the house immediately. Sarah had agreed to help out with the children when Carolyn was away; Carolyn would look at coming off long-haul and sticking to domestic routes instead; the children were old enough to be left on their own during the day, just not overnight and it was also not fair to leave Sarah to look after them.

Chapter 4

Jenny Gunn

Jenny was a 60-year-old widow, lonely but financially secure, her late husband Robert having left her a portfolio of 23 properties mostly located in the west end of Glasgow and enough cash to leave her very secure after his passing. She was also a horse breeder and owned a farm and equestrian property near Balfron in Stirlingshire where she bred heavy horses and ran a nice little coffee house. Jenny deemed herself as a tough cookie; she was pretty and feminine but managed her businesses with an iron fist.

It was Monday morning and Jenny was sitting in her car on the 10 am Gourock to Dunoon Ferry. She had done this trip many times when Robert was alive, but never on a Monday morning. It was a calm sailing, which pleased her as she admired the nostalgic paddle steamer the Waverley as it passed behind the ferry on its trip (Doon the Watter), a regular trip from its base on the river Clyde to the Isle of Rothesay. It brought back fond memories of her childhood holiday to Rothesay with her family.

Jenny was making the crossing to deliberate whether it was time to sell her caravan at the Mountain View Caravan Park. She was deep in thought, thinking about all the good times she and Robert had at the caravan park; they had had a static caravan pitch on the park for over 20 years, had spent many weekends there, and had made some very good friends. Now that Robert had passed on, she thought of selling the caravan, because coming here was just not the same without Robert anymore. She was looking for a reason as to why she should keep it or not. She intended to discuss it with Lucy, the sales lady, before she decided. She drove the short distance from the ferry to the Mountain View Park, admiring the beautiful scenery in the late March sun. On arrival at the park Jenny made a quick visit to the sales office with a view to making an appointment with Lucy.

Lucy had sold the couple their various caravans over the years. Jenny and Robert had always dealt with Lucy who had been at the park for as long as she could remember, in fact they bought their very first caravan from her all those years ago. She entered the sales office and asked Janet if she could speak to Lucy, but Janet informed her that Lucy no longer worked there as she had retired and that she would fetch Danny, the new salesman, to have a word with her. While she waited, Gordon approached her from the back office. He was the foul-mouthed general manager on the park who could always be heard shouting obscenities from his office; how his wife puts up with him is a miracle, Jenny thought.

Gordon chatted to her, rubbing his hands with joy at the idea of what he thought was the prospect of her buying a new caravan. Janet's return interrupted their conversation, as she approached them. Janet then said the words that Jenny would never forget. 'Jenny, this is Danny.'

Walking towards her was the most gorgeous man she had ever seen; he was six foot plus tall with jet black hair and the most beautiful ice blue eyes; a very athletic body, muscular but not too much as to make him a beefcake. His shirt, trousers, belt and shoes were all designer and fitted him like a glove. Jenny was stunned – he was not only extremely handsome, he smelled gorgeous, He also had a killer smile which lit up his entire face. Extending his hand, Danny thought to himself 'fantastic, what a fine-looking lady.' Jenny obviously kept herself fit and trim and still had all the right bits in the right places. She had brown hair and dark eyes and judging by the Bentley in the car park, she was worth more than just a sale, maybe much more.

'Good afternoon, Jenny, I am Danny; would you please follow me into the office,' he said. As Jenny followed him to the office, she felt excited, and very aroused between her legs, a feeling she had not had in a long time; in fact, she and Robert had not had sex since at least ten years before he died. Danny seated Jenny and offered her a coffee, making sure she got a whiff of his Mont Blonc aftershave as he lingered near her. Jenny accepted his offer and Danny dialled reception and asked Janet to bring two coffees.

'How can I help you?' he said as he hung up, looking straight into her eyes. Women just loved his blue eyes and this bitch, by the look of her, was totally hooked. A sale was on the cards, Danny thought.

Jenny started by informing Dan that she was recently widowed and had decided to sell her static caravan as, since her husband had died, the park did not have the same appeal. She explained that she now only visited the caravan on very few occasions, sometimes with her friend Lesley, and was unsure if it was worth keeping. Danny was now even more interested in Jenny; widows generally were left money by their deceased husbands, and she looked like she had plenty of it, going by her jewellery and the car outside.

'I am sorry to hear that, Jenny. You are on a very desirable pitch with a great view right on the loch; it would be a shame to give it up,' he said, 'however if it brings back painful memories or it's a financial decision, then I understand why you wish to sell. However, it would be a pity to see you go; you have been here such a long time.' What a nice guy, Jenny thought; maybe she was being too hasty in selling up. Danny could be the reason to stay on the park at least for this season. Jenny was unsure if he really was flirting with her or was it just charming sales talk, but then she was not buying anything, was she? She could not tell and was reluctant to make that decision right at this moment, although she might have fun finding out later; she could not wait to tell Lesley. Jenny explained that it was not a financial decision but more a personal one and she would think about it during the week and get back to him before the coming weekend. As she stood up to leave, she felt weak at the knees, hypnotised by this wonderful specimen of a man.

Danny came out from his desk and walked her to the door; he gave her his card stating it had his mobile number and that she could call him any time. Her heart was thumping in her chest as she said goodbye, shook his strong warm hand and sat outside in her Bentley feeling weak and thinking naughty thoughts; she had not felt like this in years. Jenny still looked good for her age and was never short of admirers; most, however, just wanted her for her wealth and she did not think Danny would be any different but if she was careful, she could have some fun. Jenny would have to think seriously before allowing this hunk into her bed. She had not been with anyone since she married Robert. Danny would not be short of a few dates, that is for sure, but he was definitely coming on to her. Danny appeared from the office and was now standing outside in the sunshine talking to another customer; Jenny took a picture of him on her mobile – just to show Lesley, of course.

Chapter 5

Kelly

Kelly lived in a penthouse flat in Partick overlooking the River Clyde; she owned a hair and beauty salon on Glasgow Road, also in Partick. She drove a nice white Range Rover and life was bobbing along quite nicely for a 24-year-old Wag. She had a fantastic body, green eyes and blonde hair which flowed right down to her fabby tight ass, and the tan was real, as were her nails. She was at that very moment in time seeing Paul, a 30-year-old fireman and part time actor/extra and model. She met Paul when he was a bouncer at the Arches night club in Glasgow and had been dating him for about a year. Paul had his own flat which he said he needed as he worked shifts although she knew he really kept his own pad to sleep with other girls there, but she couldn't give a toss; it suited her anyway. It was nice to have your own space and do some girly stuff and she also needed a place to play with Philip. Paul was fun to be with, was good to look at and was a whizz in bed. He tried hard at his model and acting work and had changed agencies on many occasions with a view to getting better work; however, she could never see him hit the big screen and become famous. He had had walk-on parts in various soaps over the years and a few commercials, but blink seriously and you would miss him. Let's face it, as hot as Paul was, he was never going to be able to give her the finer things in life that she craved for and was determined to have, whatever the cost. That is where her very own sugar daddy came in – Philip.

She had met Philip at the gym. He was averagely handsome and successfully ran his own business and he also paid for the Range Rover's lease. The salon was performing well but not just well enough to pay for all the expensive things she must have, wanted, and loved. The penthouse she owned looked great and had all the gadgets a penthouse should have, but most were paid for by Philip. Paul thought Kelly's business was doing really well and Kelly had paid for all her new shiny toys herself. Kelly was a single child from a modest house in an average private estate in Bishopbriggs where her Mum worked at the NHS as a nurse and her Dad was a train driver with Virgin trains. After leaving school she went to a hairdressing college in Anniesland before working in a few different salons until finally Dad provided the funds and helped her open her own salon. Kelly was heading there now to check all was well and collect the weekend takings for the bank; Kelly simply owned the salon but did not do any actual manual work herself. However, she did manage it; one had to look after one's business. Zara, her manager, pretty much ran the salon with Kelly stepping in on Zara's days off and on holidays.

Kelly sat and had her nails done while Zara went through the usual stuff – bookings, takings and so on. It was eleven o'clock and after makeover and doing the banking, Kelly was heading down to the Marina on Loch Lomond to meet her best friend Zoe who was shagging a footballer from Spain. He had a massive boat moored down at the Marina and was having a party later that afternoon. Both she and Zoe had had their fair share of footballers over the years, having frequented and been part of the night club scene in Glasgow since they were old enough to go. Most of the professional footballers were fit with good bodies; however, they were only interested in themselves and would never commit to a relationship. Footballers were also tight- fisted with their money, unless they were spending it on themselves, or they were in a night club trying to get your panties off; they really were not easy to get money from. Zoe still did the Wag thing with the champagne, the footballers, and the cocaine. Because it was what she loved. Kelly, however, soon got tired of being a flash tart for these athletic overpaid dickheads and had really given it up, well sort of. Kelly arrived at the marina to be met by Zoe who was sitting with three guys at the bar on the back of a huge boat which was definitely the biggest one there. They hugged and kissed, and Zoe introduced her to Stevie, Dominic, and Sebastian. Seb was her current boyfriend and the one she was sleeping with; they were all footballers, of course, and all giving Kelly the once over, undressing and riding her in their heads. After a ten-minute chat and a glass of Dom Perignon, they decided to sail out on to the loch towards Luss, and the big powerful cruiser headed up the loch. It was a fabulous sunny day and it looked like being a fun one. It was not warm enough to don a bikini, so Kelly kept her street clothes on and sat out on deck as the boat powered towards Luss pier.

Seb stopped the boat at the pier simply to pose in front of the common people and drink more champagne. They remained at the pier for about thirty minutes, enjoying the envy of the holidaymakers and day-trippers who watched them. When he was bored with that, Seb decided to head for the island of Inchmoan, aptly named as Cheryl found out later, to have a barbeque on its fabulous sandy beach. The island had a wonderful beach indeed, and Kelly went ashore with Dom and Stevie to set up the barbeque. The day was heating up, however, and Kelly decided to go back to the boat to put on her tiny bikini. She had a fabulous body and did not mind showing it off. She left Stevie and Dom cooking burgers on the beach and headed for the luxury boat moored at the small wooden jetty; the boat looked massive tied to the small wooden structure. Kelly hopped on board, only to disturb Zoe and Seb who were going at it big time on the sofa in the lounge. She walked past and went downstairs, had a pee, got changed, and was about to head back upstairs when Zoe shouted her back. Seb was snorting coke from her belly, and Zoe asked Kelly to join them. Fuck it, why not she thought; she had not had a good blowout in a while, mostly because she was now seeing Paul and Philip. Stevie and Dom came back on board, Kelly removed her bikini, walked over and started snogging Dom while she groped Seb's groin. Let the party begin! The rest of the time on the boat was a blur of Coke, Pussy, Cock, and Champagne. She could not remember anything else until the next morning when she woke up in her penthouse with Dom lying in bed beside her; she felt like shit and quickly kicked him out in case anyone turned up. The penthouse flat had a controlled entry system with CCTV which was great for stopping anyone reaching your front door, especially as there wasn't a back door to let anyone out unseen. Kelly was meant to be seeing Paul that night and then a free night before seeing Philip on Thursday night after his wife had left to do her trolley dolly stuff. Paul would have to be postponed as she was in no fit state to see him; her jaw, fanny, and ass all hurt, and she had the worst headache ever. She texted Paul said she was not feeling too great and would make it up to him on Friday; then she headed straight back to bed with a bottle of water.

Chapter 6

Philip

Philip got up at 6 am, leaving Carolyn in bed, got dressed in his running gear and headed outside. Every morning he went for a jog around Castle Mains Estate which normally took him about thirty minutes to complete. He was thinking about Carolyn's outburst the night before; she was being stupid about the Aston Martin and was obviously on a period, hence the mood. Carolyn used to be fun and was once hot to look at; however, after a couple of kids and a few extra pounds, she was not so hot now. He thought about Kelly, and how they met; now she was hot! And half his age, she gave him everything he desired in the bedroom, and was fun to be with. Kelly was wild and did things that Carolyn would not.

He first saw Kelly at the gym when it was obvious by the looks she was getting that every guy in the gym wanted to be with her physically, and she was just out of this world. They met when Philip had gone to the sauna after his workout; he was lying on the top bench soaking up the heat when the door opened and she came in, whispered an apology, smiled, apologised about letting the heat out and placed her towel on the bench opposite and one lower than Philip's. She was wearing a bright peach coloured bikini which left nothing to the imagination. The girl had a fabulous body, with long legs, a tight butt, and flat stomach. Nice firm breasts which were not too big for her frame, and which were also perfectly shaped. She had long blonde hair and a beautiful face and smile. She lay on the bench with her eyes closed and he could not take his eyes off her. He stared, following the line of her body from her lovely face down over the ample curves of her breasts which were now glistening with beads of sweat, further down over her flat stomach to the top of her fluorescent bikini bottoms; she had a pelvic bump which he loved in a woman and looking at the imprint on the cloth she looked like she was completely shaved; her entire look was amazing.

They both managed to stay in the sauna for another 20 minutes before she sat up and went outside to the shower. Philip could see her showering through the sauna door window and watched her every move; he was hoping she would return to the sauna, but she did not, instead heading for the sun loungers at the side of the pool; she lay down on her stomach and started to read a book. Philip left the sauna, had a shower himself and went for a few laps in the pool; he could not get her out of his head and was trying to build up the courage to chat to her without making it too obvious. Philip could not take his eyes off her perfect ass as she lay face down on the lounger not more than 20 feet away. He continued swimming only to be disappointed to find that after a few lengths of the pool, the lounger where she had lain was now empty. He felt a sinking feeling in his heart and was thinking that he would probably never see her again; disappointed, he headed for the changing rooms.

He had a shower, washed and dried his hair, and got dressed. He was wearing a two-piece grey suit with a light blue shirt and no tie. He headed into the café to pick up a coffee before heading into work, something he always did after his workout. As he stood at the counter a voice behind him said, 'I hope you are not stalking me.' Philip could not believe it; the girl was standing right behind him, looking even hotter with her makeup and her hair brushed and dried. Philip was stunned and blurted out 'No, of course not; anyway, you are behind me so it must be you that's stalking me.' They both laughed and Philip stuck his hand out. 'Philip's my name.' 'Kelly,' she answered, as she shook his hand. He offered to buy her a coffee, she accepted. and they both sat down at the same table together. Philip learned that, like himself, Kelly ran her own business – a beauty and hairdressing salon and she also had her own penthouse flat at the Quayside and that she was single! Philip explained that he owned two opticians, one in Milngavie and one in Bearsden.

The couple chatted for another hour or so before agreeing to work out together at the gym. There was no harm in that, Kelly said. Philip arranged to meet her on Thursday at the gym with the possibility of having lunch afterwards. It was the perfect opportunity as Carolyn would be in LA and would be none the wiser. Philip felt fantastic and did not feel any remorse whatsoever; he would be the envy of every guy in the club. Why should he not have some fun; he worked hard for his family and was a great provider. Carolyn jetted all over the world, stayed in fabulous hotels, went out for meals and got to visit all the sights in lots of different locations. Philip meanwhile stayed at home with the kids, with only work and the occasional round of golf to keep him amused. This was his chance to have fun; it was every middle-aged man's dream, and he was going to take it; Carolyn would never know anyway.

Chapter 7

Kinlochard

Danny left the park at 5 pm on Monday evening and headed for the Dunoon ferry; he was looking forward to going home. Home was The Bothy located between Aberfoyle and Inversnaid, a gem of a place, beautiful and remote and only accessible by a 4 x 4 even in the summer. This was due to the rough forest track you had to drive along to reach it. To overcome the issue Danny had purchased a twenty-year-old Toyota Land-cruiser Amazon 4.2 turbo diesel which sat in an old barn at the start of the forest track about three miles from the Bothy. The two-mile drive from the nearest road to the barn was tarmac. The Audi A5 Quattro could not be used beyond the barn even though it was a four-wheel drive because it just did not have the clearance to drive over the rough ground. The Audi was good for his image and saved him from having to drive around in a 4 x 4 fuel-guzzling battered old jeep all year round. Danny's hideaway had not been disclosed to anyone; he had given out that since his divorce and departure from the marital home, he was now residing on the caravan parks where he worked.

Danny had bought the property and 120 acres eighteen months ago. The house was surrounded by hundreds of acres of Forestry Commission land. It had no mortgage and was his alone. He had spent a fortune modernising and renovating the property to his own taste and two new extensions had now doubled its size. He had decided to keep the Bothy's name even though it suggested a smaller property. Once the building work was completed Danny would have loved to brick up the workers in the walls like the Pharaohs did when they built the pyramids, thus keeping the house a secret forever; this was the extent of his paranoia. He even went to the trouble of hiring contractors from outside the area. As far as he was concerned the fewer people knew it was there, the better; locals were gossips and well avoided. If anyone knew he actually lived at the Bothy, his mail would have been held at the local post office in Kinlochard, where he would have to collect it. The Wee Blether Tea Room doubled up as the local post office. Danny, however, had his mail delivered to whichever caravan park he worked on. The lodge address was his official residence.

Danny and the Bothy did not exist on paper or otherwise, except with the deeds he held in the safe. He sat in his car on the quayside, watching the little red and white ferry docking with its full load of Dunoon visitors and residents. People started their engines, as did Danny, and the waiting lines of vehicles drove onto the ferry. A member of the crew marshalled him into a spot on the deck where he parked his car and showed him his pass. Danny could not imagine a more boring job. It must be so boring being a member of the crew doing the same thing over and over again, just like Bill Murray in *Groundhog Day*. The trip was unexciting, and he disembarked twenty-three minutes later; it was good to be on the other side of the Clyde and closer to home.

Danny turned left and settled down and tuned into Radio Clyde for the drive home. It was a good hour's drive along the west side of the Clyde over the Erskine bridge and then down the opposite side of the River Clyde towards Dumbarton until eventually turning east towards Stirling. As the crow flies, from his work to his house was only 18 miles; however, by car it was 32 miles. He stopped off in Greenock at the Tesco superstore to pick up some groceries, he was looking forward to being home. The lodge was luxurious, but it was certainly not home, and he had spent many a sleepless night being kept awake by the rain drumming on the roof.

The grocery shop was pretty humdrum, but there were some nice bits of skirt about. Danny decided not to chat anyone up as he was just in the mood to spend some time on his own at home. His phone vibrated in his pocket; it was a text from Barbara to see if he was on the park. He replied no, he was not and was heading home; pity, if he was on the park he would have seen her; it would have been nice to play with Babs for a few hours; the last session was really satisfying, Danny felt his cock grow in his trousers but dismissed the idea. The drive home was the usual with holiday caravans and fucking cyclists whom he hated; he would gladly run over every last one of them. The traffic was at a crawl as these ignorant stupid morons cycled ahead. Why would anyone want to cycle on country roads in heavy traffic; they had to be raving bonkers, it was so dangerous. Every other mode of transport has moved on, we don't still fly about in biplanes and go to the likes of Australia by boat or travel around in cars with no air bags or power steering, that are only capable of 40 miles an hour. Imagine if we still travelled around in steam engines! Cycling tossers made him mad; they were rude, arrogant, ignorant and selfish. All cyclists should be put off the road.

Danny's trip ended up being a half hour longer than normal due to the slow-moving traffic because of these cyclists. He eventually arrived at the barn and transferred his groceries to the old Toyota Amazon which he had grown to like as it had never let him down and always started first time no matter how long he left it. The 4 x 4 could also cope with anything the weather or terrain threw at it; Danny started it up and headed for the farm, driving slowly along the forest tracks. His property was located in the Queen Elizabeth Forest just west of Aberfoyle; there were stone viaducts coming out of the wooded hillside on the right, which crossed the valley and disappeared back into the hillside opposite, the viaducts carrying water to Glasgow from Loch Katrine. The River Ard on his left starts at Loch Ard further up the track and is visible from his property; it runs all the way to Grangemouth. The river is deep and slow and is void of fish due to the high falls at Callander, and also because of its acidic water polluted by the soil from the commercial forests.

Scotland's most southerly Munro, Ben Lomond, stands tall in the distance, towering over the Bothy located at the edge of the woods just below its east side. This location is spectacular; the house is surrounded by tall Caledonian pine trees, open moorland

and the river running at the bottom of the garden where red deer can be seen most nights, but especially in the winter. The approach to the Bothy itself is spectacular, more so after you round the last bend in the forest track and the Bothy comes into view. It sits about a mile away across the stone bridge over the river Ard.

Danny had spent thousands turning the property into a luxurious home and it was stunning. The stone oak and slate entrance cost £30k just on its own. The landscaped gardens with the bronze stag were £25k to create and blended into the existing landscape. The house was of stone construction with a slate roof and had originally been a sheep farm. The Bothy had now been heavily converted with lots of space created and was now open and bright, in fact it had tripled in size with larger windows and a new second floor, which had floor to ceiling glass at each gable end, allowing uninterrupted views of the surrounding hills. A high apex roof with huge exposed oak beams gave the property a modern look, and a large extension on the back with a 25ft conservatory on the east side added to its grandeur. Internally the house now consisted of a 30ft lounge; large, fitted Hacker German kitchen with Bosch appliances; four bedrooms, all of which were en suite; a master bathroom with a huge four-person all glass shower and a freestanding jacuzzi bath. The ground floor rooms all had interior stone walls with oak flooring and tartan rugs and oak beams; the lounge had a wood burning stove on a slate hearth with a floating oak mantel and a 16-point red stag shot in the very vicinity.

There was a Bang & Olufsen 65-inch state of the art TV and sound system, which played music via speakers in every room including the bathrooms. All the furniture was of top quality and the house was a fabulous haven, created to Danny's taste. This was Danny's sanctuary, his personal and private place, created by him for him; this was his very own Scottish Castle, something he could only have dreamed of. Outside consisted of a large patio with an eight-place glass table and chairs, a chimenea, and a barbeque and a free-standing hammock and sun loungers. The views were stunning; the garden consisted of beautiful mature plants, stunning neat lawns which ran down to the river, separated by the gravel driveway and dotted with patches of Mountain Fern (Oreopteris Limbosperma); the stunning brass stag on the lawn, bought from The House of Bruar at a cost of twelve grand, added that final touch.

Danny was really enjoying being home; he made himself a beef stir fry while he sucked on a Peroni beer and listened to some music, he went for a shower after dinner, changed into some cotton trousers and a t shirt and headed outside to the garden, the piped music purring quietly from the speakers integrated into the eaves of the house. Danny sat and admired the view. He loved it here, felt safe and was more than happy on his own. As the night wore on and it got dark, he lit the chimenea and watched the night sky with its billions of stars; there was no light pollution from the city and that made it a great place to watch this wonderful sight, a truly awesome experience with shooting stars and satellites whizzing across the sky. Danny was now on the JDs and thinking about the future. He had the house which was probably worth £700k plus and he had a total of £80k in the bank, very little of it earned: this was, however, not enough to retire on and Danny intended to retire before he reached 50 years old.

He needed to find a new, older, rich woman to feed off, probably Jenny; he would start the wine and dine, play hard to get routine when he got back to the park. He needed to get his cash up to £500k which would allow him the means to head down to the South of France or Switzerland, rent somewhere posh and work the rich ladies. The pickings were much better in these areas and Danny intended to retire a millionaire, one way or another. He went to bed about 1 am and masturbated before quickly falling asleep.

His first day off was another beautiful morning and Danny was out of bed and in the shower by 6 am; he liked to enjoy his time off and never was one for lying in bed when the sun was shining; he also had chores galore to do today. Breakfast was orange juice, coffee, and some toast before he got kitted out in his old working togs. The lawn needed its first cut of the season, and the grass was long. The Toshiba ride-on mower had not seen daylight since the previous September and would make short work of the grass. If he got time, he would get the chainsaw out and cut some logs for the chimenea and the wood burner: living rural and secluded like this brought additional work which had to be kept on top of or your property would simply be swallowed up by nature. Last year Danny had gathered a load of timber from the woods and now had a pile of it which needed to be cut down to size, a task that was harder than you think. He fired up the Toshiba ride-on which started first time; you could not beat the Japanese for reliability, he thought.

He spent the morning quite happily mowing his lawn, enjoying it, finding it relaxing and therapeutic. Job done, he stopped for lunch about 12.30 pm which he had on the patio before getting dressed in his protective chainsaw suit for a workout cutting timber; he looked more like a bomb disposal expert than a chainsaw guy. He oiled and fuelled his 24-inch chainsaw and headed for the log pile; a chainsaw is a very dangerous tool and if not handled correctly could leave you without one of your limbs, or worse, your dick! Being so far out in the country meant bleeding to death was also a good possibility if he had an accident – no phones here to call an ambulance.

Danny had previously had a few close shaves with the saw and decided to buy the suit for more protection. He cut logs for the next three hours before deciding that would do for now; cutting logs was like a workout in its own right. He took the cut timber and put it on the log pile inside the barn, which took another hour of his day. Admiring his handywork in the garden as he came out of the barn, he decided to head for the shower: the place looked great, and it was time to chill and enjoy the fruits of his labour. After his shower and with music and beer in hand, Danny sat in the garden drying his hair with a towel. It was a nice day, about 20 degrees, and he was feeling good about himself; he really loved his home and wished he could be here more often. His thoughts turned to the future; he disliked working and it had to change and soon. Working for a living was for fools. You only got one life and he intended not to spend it at work. His thoughts went back to Sylvia and how he ended up living here in the first place.

Chapter 8

Sylvia

Danny was able to buy the Bothy not just because of stealing or conning women, but also because of Sylvia. It was two summers ago in mid-July; he had just started working at Mountain View and was on his days off. He had bought a Cessna 172 four-seat aircraft which he kept at a Skydiving Center at Strathallan Airfield near Auchterarder. He bought the aircraft with money he had stolen from a woman in France a year previously. The airfield only operated at the weekends except for when they had their boogie week in the summer. Because of this, the airfield was deserted when he arrived, apart from Jean the old lady who ran the café at weekends; she was in re-stocking her kitchen after the weekend.

Danny entered the hangar through the side door. There was his C172 and two Cessna 206s which were bigger than his but only had one seat for the pilot and no side door; the skydivers sat on the floor of the aircraft. Both belonged to the Skydiving Centre and were parked at the rear of the hangar, a large Scottish flag hanging from the girders above them. These aircraft were powerful with 300hp engines and could climb to the 13,000ft height with five meat bombs (skydivers) and the pilot on board in about twenty minutes. Danny unchained the big hangar doors and rolled them back with ease. He pulled his blue and white Cessna aircraft out of the hangar into the sunlight where he carried out his pre-flight walk around. Once completed he continued with his pre-flight checks inside the cockpit. Ten minutes later he was rolling down the runway. He made a blind call to Strathallan Traffic even though there was none, before changing frequency to Scottish telling them of his call sign which was G-SCOT and his height, intended route and destination. Scottish gave him a squawk code which he entered into the transponder. The big Cessna turned onto a heading of 278 degrees and climbed to 4,000ft which was the minimum safe altitude to clear the mountain tops ahead. The 73 nautical mile flight would take Danny over loch Voil, Crianlarich, Tyndrum, The Cruichan Dam and North Connel before heading out to sea, passing the southern tip of Lismore Island. He started his descent over the sound of Mull for a landing on the grass runway 25. Danny had called the tower at Oban and acquired permission to land at Glenforsa, giving them an ETA of 35 minutes. They in turn would call Dave in his little shed on the airfield and tell him he was coming. Danny landed his Cessna 172 at Glenforsa airstrip bang on time. As he exited his aircraft, a female who was sketching on the shoreline next to the grass airstrip waved to him. Danny was never one to miss an opportunity where a female was concerned. He walked towards her only to discover when he got closer that she was pretty, but far too old to have any fun with; she might, however, be a rich old lady worth befriending and was worth further investigation.

Danny commented on a sketch she was drawing of Ben More and offered to buy it from her; it would look good in the Bothy. She declined the offer but was happy to let him have the sketch anyway. Danny, in return, offered to take her on a short flight over Mull. Sylvia was more than happy with the deal and accepted without hesitation. He excused himself and walked up towards the hotel where he paid his landing fee to Dave. He also told them of his impending short flight round the island. Sylvia climbed aboard, excitement written all over her face; she told him she had never been in a light aircraft. They flew over the brightly coloured houses of Tobermory and the harbour with its array of yachts and fishing boats. She really seemed to enjoy the flight around the island especially when flying over Iona with its white sands and wonderful view of Iona Abbey. Danny enjoyed her company so much that he decided to fly a little longer. He flew north further out over the Atlantic and over the Island of Staffa, flying low over the water They had great views of Fingal's Cave and then over the Dutchman's Cap and Puffin Island before turning east and back to Glenforsa Airfield. Sylvia loved the flight so much that she insisted on buying Danny lunch at Cafe Fish a restaurant located on top of the old CalMac Ferry Company's offices on the pier overlooking Tobermory Harbour.

They sat outside on the terrace enjoying the most delicious seafood. They had a great view of the harbour and chatted as they watched and admired the fishing boats and yachts in the harbour. Sylvia even had a glass of wine, something she would not normally, she said. He learned from her chat that his first instincts were correct – she was indeed very rich; she told him her late husband had owned a massive chicken farm in England, now run by three of her sons. She also had a fourth son who was a barrister. Danny knew he would never extract any money from her but was not that bothered anyway. Sylvia was intelligent, gifted, and good company. Like many other English interlopers in Scotland, Sylvia owned a home on the island and preferred to be here in his beautiful country than in England. She was very charming and invited Danny round for coffee to see her house. The property was large but old fashioned, a white colonial style house with stunning views out over the Atlantic. Paintings of boats, the island, and the surrounding mountains were on every wall in every room, and all painted by Sylvia; she was very talented indeed. Before he left the island Sylvia gave Danny a key to the house and invited him to fly over any time; she liked and trusted him and he was always welcome to stay, whether she was there or not.

Over the summer they became good friends and Danny visited her a few times, staying overnight with her on the odd occasion. He also visited the house when Sylvia was back home in England and was currently working his way through the local female population as well as fucking half the female holiday visitors. There was a huge old four poster bed in one of the master bedrooms which Danny used as his love chamber. On his days off and if the weather was good, he would fly to Mull and spend time with her if she was there. Later that year he got a call from Dave who knew Sylvia well as she often went for dinner at the hotel; one of her paintings hung on a wall in reception, a painting of the airfield with a couple of aircraft parked at the western end.

The news was bad as Dave informed Danny that two days earlier and while on the island Sylvia had died of a heart attack. Her wish was to be buried there; her funeral was on Friday in Tobermory. Danny wasn't that sad about Sylvia's passing as he struggled to mourn people dying. He was more annoyed that his handy holiday house-cum-shag pad would no longer be available. He would, of course, attend the funeral as it was the decent thing to do. Danny asked for the Friday off work and headed home on the Thursday night and checked the weather as he intended to fly to Mull. The Met Office forecast was not good, predicting rain with a cloud base of only 1500ft making it impossible for him to fly into Glenforsa the following day. Danny had an Instrument Rating which allowed him to fly IFR (Instrument Flight Rules) into airports that were instrument equipped with landing aids, like Glasgow or Edinburgh. Glenforsa had no landing aids to assist an approach in bad weather which meant that instead of a short 40-minute flight he now had a two-hour drive to Oban and a 40-minute ferry trip from Oban to Mull and back again.

He made the necessary bookings that night and left early the next morning. He was now leaving The Wee Café where he had a coffee and was walking the short distance along to the

Evangelical Church on Main Street. He sat at the rear of the Church, preferring to remain in the shadows. The Church was packed, and Danny recognised a lot of the people there, including the minister conducting the service; he was also a pilot and flew a light aircraft from Glenforsa, call sign G-ESUS; it was a compliment to the minister's sense of humour as he was one crazy dude.

After the funeral and while at the reception Danny learned from Sylvia's best friend and neighbour Patty Beggs that Sylvia had left him something in her Will. Danny felt excited as it could be the house; she knew how much he liked it and it was worth at least £600k. He doubted it and it was more likely to be a painting or some other small token. Patty gave him a card with the solicitor's contact details and said that Danny should contact him, which he did the following day and learned that the reading of the Will was the following week but that he would not be attending. The solicitor, a Mr Bainbridge, agreed to call him after the Will was read. About a week later Danny received that call from the solicitor who told him he had not been left the house in Mull but had in fact been left a whopping £300k.This was a massive amount of money, much more than Danny was earning from his cons or his job. No one had ever given him anything. For the first time in his life Danny was gobsmacked, and he didn't even have to sleep with the old bird. The money was a great bonus.

He did not go back to the park he was working that year and instead headed to Zermatt and some winter chill time. He rented the Swallows Nest and would spend Christmas there. He was getting fed up with the nomad lifestyle and wanted somewhere in Scotland he could call his own. He surfed the net most nights and came across the Bothy which was being sold by Rettie Country Homes. Danny decided that he wanted a property of his own just like this one. He returned to Scotland and was told by the agent that the property had received very little interest from other buyers due to its remoteness; there was no electricity either, and power came from either solar panels or a generator in the barn. There was also no mains water as it was provided by a spring, and no landline telephone also put people off, something that did not bother Danny.

He bought it immediately. The Bothy would be a huge part of his escape from his other life; in general, it would become his sanctuary, his bolthole, his castle. He was unashamed that everything he owned was either stolen, given, or received in an immoral way; let's face it, no-one was ever going to give him anything in this world, apart from Sylvia. Women had used Danny for years just as much as he used them, so fuck them all.

****

He headed back into the house and made himself a steak dinner with a baked potato and some salad, washed down with a nice Peroni. He went back and sat outside on the patio enjoying the views; this place was paradise. This year was looking great both sexually and financially and he was only into the first months. Danny had decided this week was the time to start his move on Jenny, He would first check she was not protected or related to any heavy-duty criminals or members of the law. Criminals could seriously harm him or even kill him, and cops could take away his freedom, none of which he cared to have happen. The internet was a great way of checking people out and there were plenty of other females to con without running unnecessary risks. Danny was always particular about who he targeted (The Mark) and thoroughly checked to see if they were indeed rich enough to warrant his attention and if the effort was worthwhile – if the cash balance was too small it was not worth the risk.

Chapter 9

Lunch

Jenny left the caravan park and returned home to Balfron, rising early to help Maggie the groom with mucking out and exercising the horses. Mucking out was not much fun but it helped her stay fit and in good shape. She had arranged to meet Lesley in Massimo's for lunch and a chat; she was keen to tell her all about Danny, who she could not help thinking about. Jenny had gone to the sales office to see him before she left the park, only to discover that he had left for his days off; she was tempted to call him for lunch, but decided it was too intruding and too soon.

She met Lesley inside the restaurant at 1 pm; she had been friends with Lesley for thirty years and they had shared in each other's joys and pains over that time. Lesley had divorced her heavy drinking abusive husband three years previously and rightly so. She had introduced to Jenny a few boyfriends over that time; however, they were more a sexual need rather than the want of a new husband. After being married for 28 years it was nice to be in your own space for a while anyway, she always said. They both ordered wine and food and chatted about various bits and pieces that had happened over the last weekend. Lesley informed her that she had missed all the excitement that had happened over the last few days; thieves had stolen the overhead power cables in the village leaving everyone without power. Lesley had explained that apparently they were stealing the copper cables for their scrap value. Lesley was also excited that one of the handsome linesmen from Scottish Power had left her his number with a view to having lunch sometime. He was in great physical shape and handsome too. She had supplied the workers with cups of tea as they worked at putting new cables up and was excited about having him in the house and might just call him if he really was single, which of course she doubted.

Lesley asked Jenny if she had made the decision to give up the caravan. Jenny surprised her by saying that she was thinking about buying a lodge instead. Lesley could not believe her ears as she thought Jenny had gone on her own with the purpose of selling up. Jenny took out her phone, selected the picture of Danny that she had taken previously and passed it over to Lesley. Lesley let out a very mannish wolf whistle and said 'My, is he not the handsome hot one? That is a very good reason indeed for staying on at the park. Is he available?' Jenny told her she was not sure; however, she loved her meeting with Danny, the way he spoke, his voice and the smell of his aftershave – she was totally smitten. Lesley had asked if there was any possibility of a romance for Jenny as Danny was so hot and could probably have his choice of a different girl every night and probably younger too.

They both laughed at this; however, Jenny explained that she felt some chemistry between them, but she was not sure if that was the salesman in him or in fact he was interested in her romantically and physically. He could, of course, be into older women. They both had another look at the photo and agreed to travel down to the park the following weekend, to investigate further on the pretence that they wanted to look at new lodges with the possibility of keeping her pitch down by the water's edge. Danny was right – it was a fabulous site to have a new swanky lodge. Jenny and Lesley finished their meals, had some coffee and talked about their trip to the park and Jenny called Janet to confirm that Danny would be available at the sales office that coming weekend. Janet confirmed that he would indeed be working that weekend and provisionally made an appointment in his diary for Jenny to see him at 11 am on Saturday morning.

It was 2.30 pm. Jenny kissed Lesley goodbye and they both headed off in opposite directions. Jenny and Lesley were more like sisters and knew everything about each other since day one; Jenny liked that and trusted Lesley with her life. Jenny walked round to The Rainbow Room to try and book a hair appointment before the weekend; she had a better chance of getting one if she went in person rather than calling, as it was always busy, and appointments were usually booked a few weeks in advance. The receptionist informed her that the only time to fit her in would be that day at 4.40 pm due to a cancellation; Jenny accepted the appointment, which was an hour away, and headed to Asda to do a food shop meantime.

Chapter 10

The Private Detectives

Ian, Mark, and Sue were sitting in the Glasgow office of Frank McMaster, private investigators. It was 6 am on a Wednesday morning. Frank gave them the target details, explaining that he expected it to be a straightforward job. The target today was a Mr Philip Hughes, a 45-year-old male living in the posh Castle Mains estate in Milngavie and working a few miles away at his businesses in Milngavie and Bearsden. Mr Hughes was supposedly involved in an affair with an unknown female. Ian had met with the target's wife the day before and had installed a tracker in the tyre well area of the boot of the target's BMW 5 Series.

The team would be Frank and Sue in the lead car, a Vauxhall Vectra, and Ian and Mark in the backup car, a Ford Mondeo. Start time on site which was Douglas Gardens in Milngavie would be 8.30 am as they did not expect their target to leave the house before then. Car one would follow the target as far as Milngavie Cross or Bearsden Cross depending on which shop he went to; car two would wait in the background. All being well with the tracker, they should be able to follow at a distance without being spotted, after which they would simply take turns to watch his work premises in case he left and did not use the car.

The two surveillance teams checked the tracking monitor, their radios and mobile phones and headed out of the office to their allocated cars. Frank was an ex-marine who was originally from Fort William. He had left the army in 1995 after seeing action in Northern Ireland and the Falklands and eventually in Kuwait. He had moved to Glasgow and started the business, employing ex-army buddies Ian Prentice and Mark Thomas; Sue was a rookie with no military training and had only been with them for two years. The cars stopped at Asda in Bearsden to fuel up and then headed for their individual positions.

Frank enjoyed his job; it was very diversified and changed from hour to hour; it also was paying very well – not so much the matrimonial work, because the money was much better in the commercial contacts. There were, however, some very long and uncomfortable days and cold ones too, especially if a surveillance job was in the middle of winter. Frank and Mark were sitting three houses up from Philip's house when a male subject exited the house, and from the photograph Frank had in his hand it was indeed the target. Philip did his usual run which was expected and returned to the house. Frank moved the car to a different position and sat and read his paper, it was another forty-five minutes before Philip drove out of the drive in his BMW. Frank called Ian and Mark to let them know he was on his way. As expected, Philip drove to one of his optician practices, the one at Bearsden, and entered the premises. There was a tearoom opposite his shop, and they decided to take it in turns to have breakfast – one at a time only as it was difficult for all four to spend more than a couple of hours in the café if they all sat together. They would also risk losing their target if they were not in their vehicles ready to go.

Sue went first and sat down at the window with some tea and toast, and the Daily Record newspaper. She stayed in the café until Ian walked in about an hour later and headed back to the car. Ian stayed in the café a little longer than that until the look of the proprietor convinced him it was maybe time to have Frank take his place. It was now nearly twelve noon and Frank's turn to sit in the café. He had just sat down to a cup of tea and a roll and sausage when Philip exited the optician's. Shit, he thought, as he texted Mark, Ian, and Sue to let them know that Philip was on the move. Sue picked him up outside the café with his roll and sausage in hand. The two men waited until Philip's car had left the car park and followed him, two cars behind. Mark and Ian stayed in radio contact; however, their car was nowhere to be seen. The detectives followed Philip as he drove out towards Duntocher and then headed northwards to Dumbarton; he then took the Erskine Bridge cut off and crossed the Clyde before exiting at the Bishopton cut-off. Frank called Mark on the radio and instructed him to take the lead; Sue and Frank then continued on towards Gourock, watching the BMW as it disappeared down the ramp. Frank and Sue had pulled into a layby overlooking the River Clyde and across the water from Dumbarton Castle. They were there for a couple of minutes when Ian called. 'Stop, Stop,

Stop, Target has come to a full stop at Ingilston Country Club Bishopton.'

Frank started up the car and continued driving towards Gourock until he found an exit which would allow them to double back to Bishopton. On their arrival some ten minutes later, they met with Mark and Ian. Ian had managed to take a photograph of the other half of this alleged affair. She had exited a white Range Rover, registration number K 11 LY and was immediately photographed kissing and hugging Philip. The target was of average height with a nice figure and long blonde hair, probably around 25 years old. Frank decided to enter the Country Club and have lunch with Sue, who was wearing a buttonhole video on her jacket. They went inside and were approached by a young girl who asked if they had a booking. Sue explained that they did not but were hoping for a quick lunch. The young girl confirmed she had a table available and walked them through to the restaurant. There were about twenty people sitting for lunch, all at window view seats. Frank thought the window view was unusual as all the windows looked into two horse jumping arenas. Neither Frank nor Sue had ever been here before but as far as they could tell one arena was a practice or training area and the other, which was much larger, was for horse shows or more experienced riders wishing to practise jumping, as it had jumps set out all around it.

Philip and the yet to be named blonde were sitting about six tables away and Sue had positioned herself to allow the video to film the target who also sat facing in Sue's direction with only the back of Philip Hughes' head and shoulders visible. Frank had left Mark to run a check on the Range Rover, which would have provided a name and address for the mystery blonde. A text from Mark was a shocker as the Range Rover was actually registered to Philip's company and was paid for by it. Did this girl work for Philip? Was this her company car?

The couple were all over each other during lunch and were providing plenty of proof that they were indeed more than just friends, or work colleagues. Frank and Sue ordered lunch and watched the couple as they ate their own, in between cuddles and kisses that is. The lunch, as you would expect, was very mundane and normal apart from the obvious flirting, and Philip and the blonde, who Frank now referred to as Killy, paid their bill and left the building. Ian and Mark were outside in the Mondeo and were instructed to follow the blonde. It was important that they put a name to the face and hopefully she would be heading home. There was too much of a risk to leave lunch uneaten and chase after Philip; both Frank and Sue expected him to return to work or follow the blonde. They sat and discussed the case as they finished their lunch; both were convinced that the blonde was indeed the lover. Meanwhile Ian and Mark had followed the blonde to a hairdresser and beautician's in Partick from which she emerged about an hour later. What she had done they were not sure; she did a grocery shop at Sainsbury's and then drove to a penthouse flat on the Clydeside where she vanished inside number 120.

Mark called Frank and gave him an update; Frank would join them soon to discuss the next move. Frank and Sue left the country club and headed for Partick, not the penthouse, however; they went straight to the post office sorting office on Great Western Road. Frank sent Tam an email to say that he was outside his work, He emerged ten minutes later and climbed into the car. Frank gave him the address and fifty quid and Tam said that he would get back to him asap. They both drove round to the Transport Museum and texted Mark to drive round and meet them; it would be too suspicious for them to sit outside the property as they would be easily seen from all properties in that block. Frank's tracker confirmed that Philip had returned to his business in Milngavie and not Bearsden – a quick call which was hung up before Philip could take it from his receptionist confirmed that he was indeed at his work. The blonde's address was too exposed to monitor from the car park in a normal vehicle, so Ian returned to base with Mark to pick up a more suitable form of surveillance vehicle.

Frank took a call from Tam the postman who had sent him the names of everyone in the block via email. The detectives had already confirmed that she lived in a penthouse on level seven and surmised that her first name could possibly be Kelly. Reading the list, the only K on the top floor was a Miss Kelly Stuart and through experience Frank reckoned that was their girl. Mark had returned to the Transport Museum in a Ford Transit van kitted out in BT livery; it was one of their best vehicles that never got any attention from anyone. It was fully fitted out to enable two operatives to spend up to five days inside with food and water, a microwave and fridge, and even a portaloo. The van also had every gadget available for covert operations including state of the art tracking and recording equipment. This allowed the detectives to carry out a complete surveillance on a target without ever being seen.

Frank sent Mark and Ian back to the penthouse address to start the surveillance on Kelly Stuart while he and Sue headed through the Clyde Tunnel towards Govan and the shipyard that overlooked the penthouse on the opposite side of the river. Frank took a return call from his contact in the Scottish Police force who had the intel on Kelly Stuart; she was a 24-year-old business owner with one previous conviction for possession of a class A drug.

Chapter 11

Los Angeles

Carolyn had said goodbye to the children the night before as she was on the 7 am flight from Glasgow to Los Angeles on the Dreamliner and would be leaving home at 5 am. It was Wednesday morning, and she usually enjoyed her trip to Los Angeles, a two day stop over and a great area to visit. Carolyn and the family holidayed in the States every year either in Florida or Las Vegas; one of the perks of the job was the free flights which made a saving of about £4k on their holiday every year. She was not in great form that morning as this was the day the detectives would find out if Philip was indeed having an affair and if he was, she had decided that their marriage would be well and truly over.

She had given everything to Philip over the last twenty years; they had two great kids, a beautiful home and a secure future. Was Philip really that reckless? If so, it was not the Philip that she thought she knew. Carolyn was concerned for the children who both loved their Dad very much and Jonathan just adored his father, spending a lot of time with him on the golf course. Emma was also a Daddy's girl. Philip had a tendency to be lenient with the children in regard to just about everything.

The flight time today was 10 hours and 46 minutes – they would fly over Iceland and the Southern tip of Greenland before turning southwest over Newfoundland, down over Canada and then west into Los Angeles. As usual the flight was full, and Carolyn and the rest of the cabin crew started to serve breakfast about twenty minutes into the flight. She was not in the best of moods but tried to smile and be happy in front of the passengers. Three hours into the flight she took her break and headed into the OHCR, the crew resting area on the 787. The resting area had beds where you could kick off your shoes and go for a nap. Carolyn grabbed some food, took off her shoes and searched for her mobile phone buried deep in her handbag. She had a text from both Emma and Jonathan and, as she was replying to the children's texts, there was one from her sister too.

There was, however, no loving text from Philip, no 'safe journey honey, hurry back, miss you, love you baby'; this convinced her even more that something was wrong. She tried to have something to eat and drink before going for a short nap and was woken an hour later by Marion, her crewmate, who was just about to take her break. Carolyn was back in the cabin for another five hours. God, she wished she was back on the ground safe in her house with the kids. The flight was uneventful apart from every member of the cabin crew and the captain asking if she was alright; she made the excuse that she was fine, just tired.

They landed on time; 5.50 pm local time and 9.50 am back in Glasgow. When everyone had disembarked, Carolyn left the airport on the crew bus which dropped them off at the Hilton LAX. Carolyn was exhausted and poured herself a small wine from the mini bar. There was a knock on the door. 'It's me,

Jessica.' Jessica was a work colleague on the same flight; they had worked together on and off over the last ten years or so, but never really socialised at home as they lived about 70 miles from each other. Carolyn unlocked the door and let her into the room. 'Hi, honey, are you okay? I am sorry, I don't want to pry but you did not look happy on the flight, is it something you want to talk about?' When Carolyn instantly burst into tears, Jessica ran over to her and held her in her arms. She sobbed for what seemed like ten minutes before she was able to blurt out the story of Philip's behaviour and how she thought he was having an affair.

Carolyn told Jessica the entire story while working through the booze in the mini bar. She explained that she asked the detectives not to contact her with any news until she had returned. Carolyn was happy that Jessica was there and although she had her sister and Dad at home to confide in, she still felt lonely and stressed at work. The girls lay on the bed and continued to empty the bar. Carolyn promised to join the rest of the crew on a trip to Universal Studios the next day. Both had been before, but the new girls had not, and it was a fun way to spend part of their two-day stop over. It was now 3 am and both girls fell asleep, fully clothed, on the king-sized bed.

Carolyn awoke the next morning with a slight headache. Jessica lay naked under the quilt beside her; Carolyn was still fully clothed but also under the quilt; she got up and headed for the shower. As she walked back into the room Jessica had got out of bed and was now dressed. ‘Morning, honey, how are you feeling?’

‘I am slightly hung over and really looking forward to breakfast – I am totally starved.’

‘Me too.’ They both laughed. Carolyn was smiling probably for the first time since leaving Glasgow and feeling much better after having confided in Jessica; they both agreed to meet downstairs for breakfast in an hour’s time.

The breakfast buffet at the Hilton was fabulous and both girls ate a hearty breakfast before meeting the rest of the crew outside the hotel at 12 noon. Bobby, also known as Biff, the first officer on the flight, had just driven up in a minivan; the rest of the eight crew were standing outside eagerly awaiting a fun day out. The van headed west on the 105 to Harbour gateway north, before turning north on the 110 towards Downtown Los Angeles and then northwest on the 101 to Universal Studios. Carolyn’s mind drifted back to her worries back home as she looked out of the window. Downtown Los Angeles loomed in the distance, its tall glass skyscrapers glistening and shimmering in the midday sun. The thump thump thump of the tyres sounded like the aircraft’s nose wheel as it ran over the lights on the centre line of the runway. She tried to put everything to the back of her mind but still felt alone and a million miles from home and the kids and she was scared of what the outcome would be when she got back to Glasgow. The weather in LA was hot and the freeways busy but they managed the drive in about forty minutes which was not bad considering the traffic.

The two new cabin crew, young girls in their twenties, were excited about the day trip and chatted and laughed continually and Carolyn could remember when she once did the same. She must have looked glum as she exited the minivan, as Jessica was once again by her side 'Hi, chick, you made me a promise.'

'Yes, sorry Jess, I was miles away, yes, you're right, look at this place, we are in LA for God's sake, let us have some fun!!!'. She could, however, not help but think about home; it was 11 am in Los Angeles so it was only 3 am in Glasgow and everyone would still be in bed. Reluctantly, Carolyn followed the rest of the group into Universal Studios.

Chapter 12

The Teenager

It was Wednesday morning. Danny awoke at 6 am and headed for a shower, got dressed and then made himself some boil-in-the-bag kippers with some bread. He had packed his bag the night before and loaded it into the 4 x4; by that time breakfast was ready. He made another coffee and headed out to the patio to have his breakfast in the sunshine. He would leave at 7.20 am giving him enough time to catch the 8.30 ferry from Gourock; it was a nice morning and Danny would have preferred to stay at home rather than work at the caravan site. The swallows were busy chattering away as they flew around the eaves of the house and four red deer were munching away on the heather on the other side of the river.

Danny's thoughts were on finding a rich mark this year. He wanted and needed the money and did not intend to be working at the park the following year. Breakfast finished, he washed up the dishes, grabbed his jacket and keys and set the alarm. The CCTV Amazon Blink system was linked to his mobile and allowed him to watch all eight cameras from his phone from anywhere in the world. The system also alerted him if anyone came near the house, a deterrent to anyone wishing to invade his beautiful Scottish home.

Arriving at the barn Danny swapped the Toyota Amazon for the Audi A5 which was covered in swallow poo, very much like the Amazon every time he came home. He made a mental note to kill the pesky birds on his next trip home as the poo was not good for the Audi's paintwork. The drive to the ferry was uneventful and he arrived in time for the 8.30 crossing. If he ever missed the ferry, he just texted Gordon who did not seem to bother anyway.

He arrived at the park and headed straight up to the lodge, unpacked his suitcase and headed for the office. Janet was standing at reception dealing with a queue of departing weekend holidaymakers; she was on her own and looking flustered and so Danny decided to give her a hand, a favour that he could always call in later. After the rush Janet gave him his telephone messages and went over his diary appointments for that weekend. 'You have four enquiries – one enquiry sounded hopeful and that was a Jenny Gunn.'

Brilliant, Danny thought, looks like Mrs Gunn has taken the first hook and would probably buy a lodge. This in turn would be a means for Danny to get closer to her. Danny made Gordon a cup of tea and sat in his office.

'How were your days off, Danny boy?'

'Just the usual housework, gardening and booze.'

They both laughed. 'Sounds like my days off except miss out the booze and add a moaning wife and baby poo to that list.' They both laughed again. Gordon walked over to the T-board in the office and took two cards from their alloy slots.

'Well, while you were away, I bought two vans from

owners who are leaving. One is Mrs Sharp's van on Eagle one; it's a 1998 Cosalt 28x10 selling at £9995 – a bit of a fucking dog but some fucking mug will buy it. The other is up on Bute 23 and is a lovely 32 x 12 Willerby Vogue, selling at £24,995. When you are ready go and have a look at them and put the price boards in the window.' He gave Danny both keys.

'Will do, Captain.' Danny got up to leave.

'And, Danny.'

Danny stopped just short of leaving the office and looked back at his boss. Gordon was smiling, 'Don't get caught shagging Natcha on company time,' he said, 'even if it is lunchtime.'

'Sorry Captain,' Danny smiled. Fucking prick, he thought, and left Gordon's office; how fucking dare he tell him what to do on his time. Danny went to his own office and wrote out the two sales boards in black ink, grabbed his jacket and the golf cart keys from reception and blew Janet a kiss as he left. The green and white golf cart was parked outside under the canopy and was the best transport to get oneself and potential buyers around the park. Danny went to the Cosalt first, a shit van on a shit pitch but it would be in someone's budget and some mug will buy it; they always did.

He always wondered why someone would want to come to a caravan park which was reachable in a couple of hours from their comfortable homes. He found the answer while working on this very park. He once had to go to a customer's house in Glasgow, and it was pretty much on his way home and worth leaving work early to collect the cash deposit. Danny could not believe his eyes when he turned up at the customer's house. It was a shit hole in a bad area, a council house similar to where Danny grew up. It was then that the penny dropped. Coming to the park was their escape to get away from their miserable existence in a council estate. Another time was when a customer bought a van when he only lived across the water in Greenock. Danny asked the question why he wanted to buy a van so close to home. The customer explained that he lived in a council tower block, and this was the only way his kids would ever see sunlight. It was also an escape from the neds hanging around the tower block. Financing the caravan was as cheap as buying a car on hire purchase.

Danny headed up the drive to the Vogue on Bute 23; it was a nice van, the Willerby, and this one was on a nice pitch. He stopped at the junction, checked his mobile for texts and looked up in time to see a beautiful blonde girl about 17 years old cycle past. She was hot and looked like trouble when she smiled at Danny as she passed the golf buggy. The girl was wearing a white halter neck top which revealed her ample and firm bosom; she was also wearing cutaway blue denim shorts. The shorts revealed her long legs and fine ass and left nothing to the imagination. A pair of white socks and white trainers finished the sexy young look. Nice, he thought, as he carried on his journey towards the Bute pitch. Danny had a quick look about the caravan, placed the for-sale sign in the window and stood on the decking looking out over the park and down towards the loch side. It looked like he was in for another good week's weather for selling caravans.

It was lunchtime when he left the van and Danny headed for the restaurant and bar for some lunch, leaving the buggy outside and calling Janet to let her know where he was, just in case a walk-on turned up and wanted to see the caravans they had for sale.

The restaurant was nice, with slate stone walls and an open gas fire in the centre of the room. Danny ordered macaroni and cheese and a glass of milk from a new waiter he had never seen before. He people watched as he ate his lunch. They were mostly parents and children and nobody that interested him. He finished lunch and walked out of the building; the sun was still shining and so he took his sunglasses from his pocket and put them on. Sitting on a bench beside the golf buggy was the blonde teenager.

'Hi,' she said, 'What's your name?'

Danny replied, 'Did your parents not tell you to never speak to strangers?'

'But you're not strange.'

'I might be.'

'Do you work here?'

'Yes, I do.'

'It's boring.'

'Depends on what you're doing.' Danny could feel his cock growing in his trousers; he could not keep his eyes off the hot little cheerleader-looking babe.

'I am here with my Mum and gran, but they went into Dunoon to buy groceries. If you leave your work, you can take me for a run in your black car and show me the sights?'

Danny would normally avoid someone so young, but he had been home for the last two days and this one was maybe just worth the risk. How did she know he had a black car?

'How old are you?'

'17,' she replied.

'And how do I know that?'

She went into her rucksack, pulled out her passport and presented it to Danny. She was 17 years and six months old. Danny promised to meet her later at the same spot at 6 pm if she promised not to tell anyone as he would get into trouble with his boss. She agreed, put her headphones on and pedalled her mountain bike down the drive. Oh, to be a bike saddle, Danny thought, and laughed. He planned to take her to one of the empty lodges after work, and he had just the one in mind. He sold a caravan later that day to two English twats who were moving up from Bristol and were looking for somewhere to stay until they found a proper bricks and mortar residence that suited them and their budget.

Dan finished work at 5 and headed back to his lodge for a shower; he was excited about the possibility of fucking the young and hot cheerleader. He was also a little apprehensive about getting caught; young girls could be a whole lot of trouble for an older guy. Anyway, she was legal so fuck it. Danny drove up to the bar as agreed; she was sitting outside wearing a white top and a pelmet-sized mini skirt, white and purple like a little kilt which left nothing to the imagination. She had white ankle socks on, and a gold love heart hung around her neck. Her name was Nicola, and she was every pervert's dream.

'Where are we going?' she asked.

'I thought I would show you one of our nice lodges.'

'Does it have a bed?'

'Yes, it does.'

'Okay, cool, let's go.'

Danny took the young chick to Loch View one, a lodge at the end of the row, which was well secluded and not overlooked. He unlocked the door; Nicola walked in and headed straight for the fridge in the open plan kitchen/living room. She opened the door, realised it was empty and turned around with a petted lip, a look of disappointment on her face.

'Where do you keep your booze?'

'There isn't any. I have a couple of beers in the car, do you want one?'

'Yes please.'

Danny walked out to the car and removed the six pack of Peroni from the boot. When he got back inside Nicola was not where he left her, and he thought she might have gone to the bathroom. He walked up the hall and saw that the bathroom door was ajar, but the room was empty. He walked into the master bedroom.

Nicola's clothes were on the floor. That is a pity he thought; he fancied lifting her tiny kilt and bending her over a chair and fucking her first with it on. She pulled back the cover to reveal she was not wearing anything; she looked fabulous, her long legs tanned from cycling around with her tiny shorts on and the tan showing the small blonde hairs that ran from her pussy to her belly button. She had great nipples which also had tiny blonde hairs round them. Danny started to undress, his cock making a tent shape in his boxer shorts. Nicola watched him strip off his blue jeans and t shirt. 'How old are you?' she asked.

'I am forty,' Danny replied as he climbed into bed beside her. She instantly rolled on top of him; her skin was soft and smelled young. Her breasts were solid – she could get away without even wearing a bra as they would just have stayed in the same protruding position without one.

'Do you want to fuck me?'

'What do you think?'

'Do you have a condom?'

Danny never wore one and never would, especially with this young chick; she was getting fucked bareback whether she liked it or not.

'It's fine, babes. I was married once and got the snip.' She was wanking him as they kissed, her kisses sweet and fresh like she tasted new. Danny was rock hard as he fingered her tight wet pussy. He wanted to taste her and rolled her over onto her back. He went down on probably the youngest sweetest pussy he had ever had. She tasted fabulous and Danny licked and sucked her clit as she moaned and screamed with delight, running her fingers through his thick hair, and pulling his face further into her pussy. She had come four times before she returned the favour, but the favour was a disappointment. Nicola was a bit naïve in the bedroom and her blowjob was average. She would let Danny fuck her in every position but would not let him fuck her ass. Danny bent her over she could handle his 12-inch cock in her pussy which was nice and pink and tight. However, when Dan took his cock out and tried to put it in her ass she would just wriggle away and complain. Nicola was probably more accustomed to being banged in the front or back of a 19-year-old mechanic's Corsa and was seriously lacking in the sexual experience category.

Danny was holding her hair back as she wanked and sucked him off; he liked to see her pretty face and she was watching him with her big blue eyes. He was just about to dump a big load of cum in her mouth. He thought he had held her down enough, but she rolled her head to one side just as he was coming. She kept wanking him and watched as the cum pulsed out of his cock, squirting eighteen inches above his belly, her hair and all over the sheets. Danny was by now totally pissed off with the girl; she had spoiled what could have been a really nice sexual encounter. He wished he had stuck to his rule of no teenagers. He felt weak, a slave to some fucking young pussy; he had lost control and did not like it one bit. He could have forced her, but that's rape and Danny had no intention of going to jail for some stupid little tart. If he wanted a wank, he would have done it himself. Fucking bitch, he thought as he got dressed. He threw the teenager's clothes on the bed. 'Come on, you need to leave.'

He stood outside until she emerged from the lodge. They did not speak as Danny drove her to her bike which was chained to a bench outside the leisure club. 'See ya,' she said, but Nicola did not unchain her bike and headed into the leisure centre instead, probably to tease some horny male teenagers. Danny was really annoyed and headed back to his lodge for some JDs and a shower.

Chapter 13

The Girls

Jenny and Lesley did a grocery shop for the weekend ahead and sat in Waitrose in Milngavie having coffee and cake before they set off on the one-hour drive to Dunoon. The sun was shining, and it looked like it was going to be a nice weekend to be down at the caravan. Jenny had bought some champagne in case she had something to celebrate, like a new lodge! Her thoughts about leaving the park were dismissed as she had now found a reason for going, even if it was just to look at him or flirt or even just lunch. Lesley was chirpy enough, but Jenny knew she was hurting about Simon the linesman who turned out to be married with two kids. Like her she just craved some male attention and sex now and again as a reminder that they were both still women and attractive enough to get a man into bed. They had both got drunk on holiday last year and had sex in the same room with two gents from the Borders whom they had met while on holiday in Portugal. Jenny and Lesley had never discussed that night again and probably never would.

The drive down was pleasant, and they now sat at the ferry terminal at Gourock. A lot of visitors, believe it or not, thought Dunoon was an island simply because you got a ferry to it. Dunoon is, in fact, on the mainland; the distance from Glasgow to Dunoon via the ferry is about 30 miles. The alternative – driving the long way round – is at least an additional 50 miles, hence most people opted for the ferry. There were two ferries running every day and one can watch them as they leave their docks on each side of the Clyde and pass each other somewhere in the middle.

Jenny drove the Bentley onto the ferry and parked where instructed by the man wearing a high viz vest, probably so he did not get run over. He also had a little leather bag like the ones bus conductors used to wear, where he kept his tickets and money. Jenny bought a book of ten return tickets from the little conductor. It was a nice day and both girls left the car to sit upstairs in the sunshine as the ferry started its short journey over the water. Jenny was excited about being back on the park and to seeing Mr Charming once more. 'I take it one has made up one's mind to stay on at the park,' said Lesley.

'What do you mean?'

'You have just bought a book of ten ferry tickets,' she laughed.

'OMG, you're right, I was not even thinking, it's just habit.'

'Or just a Danny infatuation, more like,' said Lesley and they both burst out laughing.

The 20-minutes crossing was smooth. Jenny and Lesley sat on the viewing deck just above the car deck and watched the various ships on the Clyde – a combination of commercial ships and the paddle steamer the Waverley steaming behind the path of the ferry, heading west, its decks full of day-trippers on a trip down the Clyde to Dunoon or maybe even to the Isle of Bute and

Rothesay. It was dwarfed by a massive cruise ship heading up the Clyde to the cruise terminal at Greenock.

In fact, Jenny had sailed on that same paddle steamer many times herself back in the 60s and 70s. In the days before package holidays the Island of Bute was a popular holiday destination. Every summer, in the first fortnight in July, the shipyard workers and all the workers from The Singer Factory would down tools for the Clydebank Fair Holiday. Many of these workers would spend the entire fortnight on Rothesay with their families. Jenny could remember these family holidays well. She and her Mum and Dad would travel by taxi to Princes Dock on the river Clyde where the steamer was berthed right in the heart of Glasgow. Hundreds of shipyard workers and their families stood waiting on the quay to board the paddle steamer for their trip to Rothesay; this was the start of their two-week holiday and the dockside buzzed with excitement.

The Waverley could hold a thousand passengers; she was a beautiful old ship painted white and black with a dash of red on her two big funnels. She was narrow along her length with large round sides sticking out, each housing the large paddle wheels that propelled the ship forward. On one of these trips when she was about four years old Jenny remembered her father taking her down below to the engine room to see the large steam-powered pistons rising and falling, quite a frightening sight for a four-year-old and it scared Jenny, a memory to this day. The ferry crossing was pleasant and quick, and the ferry docked at Dunoon Quay, a twenty-minute drive from the park. Jenny was excited as she drove up the long drive past the sales office, but Danny's black Audi was not in his parking slot in front of the office.

She felt disappointed as she drove past and continued up the driveway before turning back down towards the loch and her caravan at the water's edge. 'Well, here we are,' Jenny said to Lesley as they pulled up at the side of the caravan. 'It is lovely, isn't it? I haven't been here since last year, about August, remember, when I came down with Kim?'

'Yes, that was a fab girly weekend, wasn't it?' Jenny, Lesley, and Kim had had a fantastic weekend eating, drinking and being merry at the owner's ball in the big hall at the leisure centre. Robert had been in Spain with his mates on a golfing weekend; sometimes you had more fun when it was just the girls.

The girls emptied the bags of shopping into the fridge and the relevant cupboard space before sitting out on the deck with a glass of wine. The view over the loch was beautiful and spring was in the air. The girls chatted about previous visits to the park before the conversation eventually turned to Danny. 'You're really taken by this guy, aren't you?' said Lesley.

'Yes, I am,' replied Jenny. 'Don't get me wrong, I know he is trouble with a capital T, but he is so irresistible. If we ever got together in a relationship, it would only be because he was after my money, and that is something that he will never get. He probably has a string of women chasing after him every day and I doubt he is the faithful sort. I think I will enjoy a little fun with him but that will be all.'

Lesley agreed. 'You are bad,' she said.

'No, Lesley, just horny for a hot hunk,' said Jenny and they both laughed as Jenny poured another glass of wine. It was Thursday evening and the girls planned to stay till about 6 pm on Sunday.

Chapter 14

Aston Martin Day

Philip got up early that morning, excited about collecting his new car but disappointed that Carolyn would be home later. He went for his usual run before returning home and heading for the shower. He was crazy about Kelly and was thinking about leaving Carolyn; she had just become too boring; he enjoyed the sex with Kelly; it was always exciting and different every time. Philip had just grown out of his relationship with Carolyn and felt more like her brother than anything else. The business was going great, and he planned to open further branches in Clydebank and Dumbarton. The DB9 was a gift to himself and well earned. After all it was himself that had built up the business over the years without any input from Carolyn. All Carolyn did was look after the kids and they were now old enough to look after themselves. Carolyn had only worked part-time, but as soon as the kids were old enough, she decided to change back from part-time short haul to full-time long-haul. Her excuse had been she was bored all day on her own – how selfish could she be? Philip not only had to run the business when she was away but also feed himself and the kids, while Carolyn was jetting around the world having fun on her stop overs. He had worked hard and built up the business single-handedly and he now intended to reap the benefits.

He headed for work; both shops were about ten minutes from the house. He went to Bearsden this morning to see how the week was going there. This branch was run by his shop manager Calum, a 28-year-old optician who also lived in Bearsden. The two men went over the monthly figures, appointments and stock and staffing details. Philip was not really in the mood for work but had to be there nonetheless, He was desperate to meet Kelly for lunch. He loved her smell, her lips, her skin, in fact absolutely everything and he could not wait to see her. Actually, thinking back, he did not think that he ever felt that way about Carolyn, not ever.

The time from 9 am to 12 noon took forever to pass. Philip headed for his Beamer and drove to Ingliston Country Club to meet Kelly. He saw her car as he drove into the car park and parked a couple of spaces away; he headed towards her car, excited like a loved-up puppy. Kelly sat inside texting on her phone and smiled when Philip opened the door. 'Hi, lover,' she said with that beautiful smile. 'I am starving, and did you miss me?' 'Of course,' said Philip. 'I miss you every day.' Kelly gave him a huge hug and a kiss as they walked into the restaurant hand-in-hand. The Country Club was not a place he expected to see anyone he knew. Lunch was average but Philip did not really care; he was more interested in Kelly than eating and they had a nice two hours together before Philip had to get back to work. They stood in the car park embracing and kissing each other – she smelled awesome and looked gorgeous and Philip could not wait to see her again.

Reluctantly, he drove back to Bearsden and checked in to see all was well at the branch before heading back home to pick up the paperwork for his car and change into something more suitable. The Aston Martin dealer was in Edinburgh, and he was due to pick up his new car at 3.30 pm. He had not told Kelly that he'd ordered it, as he was keeping it as a surprise and intended to let her drive it when they were out together. Philip drove the BMW to Edinburgh for the last time. On arrival, his new shiny DB9 was parked outside as he drove in; it looked sleek and sexy. Philip signed the lease, paid the remaining balance by card and was shown around the car and the controls by the product genius, which took about an hour and made him impatient. He just wanted to drive this baby home. He eventually said farewell to the genius and drove the DB9 out of the dealership and along the M8 motorway towards home, its 6-litre engine roaring like a lion as he gave it the odd boost when he thought he could get away with it. He paired his MP3 player and listened to Duran Duran as his big muscle car purred effortlessly along the motorway.

He imagined what it would be like to be married to Kelly. She kept her flat immaculate, although she was not much of a cook. I guess you can't have everything, he thought. Was it really time to move on, because his marriage was the same old stuff every day? He found Carolyn boring after being with Kelly. Carolyn seemed content with the job, the kids, her Dad and her sister. Philip was going to have to think seriously about dumping his marriage. He would talk to Kelly first and he would also have to look at how much this was going to cost him. He drove back home and parked the new car in the driveway. Carolyn was going to be really pissed off when she saw this. Both Jonathan and Emma came rushing out when they heard the sound of the engine. ‘Whoa, Dad, what a cool ride,’ said Jonathan. ‘Yes, get you, Mr Top Gear,’ said Emma. He hugged the kids.

Usually, it is the mother who gets the children, but Philip thought there was a good chance that if he kept the house in Milngavie, he might just get custody of the kids. He took them both for a spin out towards Carbeth Inn and then back. He spent the rest of the evening in the study, reading the handbook for the new car while having a small dram or two. He did not go to bed until midnight and could only think of Kelly.

Chapter 15

The Boyfriend

Frank and Sue approached the nightwatchman as he locked up the gates to the shipyard, his Alsatian dog barking loudly at them until he told it to stop. They both flashed their IDs and tried to look official; the watchman was not impressed.

'I was wondering if you would let me climb the big blue crane,' Frank said as he shoved £100 into the night-watchman's hand. The old boy counted the money – his name was Pat and £100 was a lot of money to him.

'What the hell do you want to climb that thing for; you could fall off and be killed.'

'We are private investigators,' explained Frank, 'and want to take some photographs of someone in the flats at the opposite side of the river.'

'I could lose my job if you got caught,' Pat said as he looked over at the crane.

'We will be long gone before anyone turns up in the morning; it is just for tonight,' said Sue.

'It's not worth it for a hundred quid. If it were two hundred quid, then I would think about it.'

Frank took another £100 out of his wallet and showed it to the watchman. 'Thank you,' said Pat as he tried to take the money from Frank's hand. Frank held the money out of the watchman's reach.

‘We can’t just now,’ he said, ‘we will be seen. We will come back after dark and pay you the other £100 then. Do you have a mobile number?’

‘A what?’ asked the watchman, looking puzzled.

‘Never mind, can you meet us at the gate at 10 pm. I will give you the other hundred then, okay.’

‘Aye, I will but don’t be late; I have my rounds to do.’

The watchman and his old German Shepherd shuffled off to his wooden hut, probably to have a cup of tea and count the money again. Frank and Sue drove back round to the operations van parked at Kelly’s flat. It was now 6 pm and time for dinner and so Frank and Sue drove round to Byres Road where he found a chippie and a parking space, the latter being unusual on Byres Road at the best of times. Frank purchased two fish suppers, a pie supper, and a smoked sausage supper, along with four cans of Irn Bru and they both headed back to the surveillance van. Frank was starving and the smell of the suppers on Sue’s lap was making him even more so. The four detectives devoured their not-so-healthy dinner as they watched the various people enter and exit the flats.

Ian was taking note of any car registrations that came and went. It would be at least another three hours before dark and before Frank and Sue would head back to the shipyard. It was agreed that Frank would take on the surveillance from the crane with Ian and Mark staying in the van. Sue would drop Frank at the yard and return to a point not far from the flat and wait in the car in case Kelly went out. Sue and Frank left for the shipyard at 9.40 pm. Frank was now dressed in his black North Face outfit, consisting of black climbing boots, black climbing pants and a black fleece and jacket. The white logos on his clothes had been blackened out with a felt pen so as not to reflect in the dark. Frank was also carrying a black rucksack, North Face, of course. He resembled a Ninja warrior without the mask. They both arrived at the shipyard gate just as the nightwatchman and his smelly old dog were walking towards it. Pat let Frank in as he stood with his hand shoved out in front of him. 'I did not see you, mind,' he said as he closed the gate. Frank gave him the outstanding £100 as the Alsatian rammed its long nose between his legs and sniffed his crotch. 'Thanks, old-timer and don't worry; no one will ever know I was even here.'

'The men start at 8 am so you better be back at my hut long before then,' Pat shouted. Frank waved, and walked towards the towering black crane, the flats opposite with their glass balconies looking very much like a cruise liner sitting on the Clyde; maybe that was what they were meant to look like, he thought. Frank climbed the stairs of the large gantry crane, which must be at least a hundred feet high. The view across to the flats was perfect as none of the residents seemed to close their blinds because the shipyard was closed at night and there was no-one around to look inside their homes. Frank reached the top of the crane. The lights from the flats cast a dim light on the structure making it possible to see where you were putting your feet. As he edged his way along the steel boom, his radio burst into life with Ian's voice confirming they were all set and in position.

There was a large steel plate three quarters of the way along, exactly right to lie flat on. He took out and laid down his bed roll before setting up his video and film cameras. Frank was well hidden by the steel cross members of the gantry. A pigeon, startled by Frank's arrival, flew away in fright. The night was calm, and he had a fantastic view of the apartments across the water. He enjoyed this part of the job and found it interesting and exciting watching and filming people who were totally unaware that he was there. He scanned the apartment windows opposite with his sigma lens nicknamed The Bigma – it was big and heavy it had a lens range from 50 - 500mm. It was attached to a Canon 70D mark two, a very effective camera which reminded him of looking through his sniper scope from his army days, minus the cross hairs of course.

There were two penthouse suites on the top floor; the one on the right was Kelly's. The one on the left was occupied by two men who were in the lounge. One was sitting on a stool playing the piano, butt naked and in his thirties, while his friend, also butt naked, and probably in his fifties, stood beside him with what looked like a brandy in his hand. Frank assumed they were gay and would be shagging each other before long. Kelly's lounge was empty, and she was nowhere to be seen; the only other room you could see was the bedroom which was also empty. The flat below had a guy playing on an Xbox or similar gadget, and the one below the gay guys was empty.

Frank zoomed back into Kelly's flat where was still no sign of the little chick though her TV was now on in the lounge. Frank set up the video camera and settled back for what could be a long wait. They planned to end the surveillance when Kelly went to sleep for the night and resume the surveillance on both subjects in the morning. Frank was lying on his belly on top of his bedroll and a sleeping bag; propped up on his elbows he was watching Kelly's TV through his binoculars. A figure passed in front of him; it was Kelly, dressed in a bathrobe and drying her hair with a towel. Over the next half hour of exciting surveillance Kelly finished drying her hair and sat on the sofa, naked, painting her toenails. It looked like she was expecting company – hopefully it would be Philip. It was now 10 pm and it seemed strange that no one had yet turned up. As if on cue, Kelly headed for the intercom on the wall and looked like she buzzed someone in. Frank picked up his two-way radio. 'Falcon one to Falcon two.' Ian's voice crackled in the earpiece in Franks ear, 'Go ahead.' 'Can you tell me who just entered the building?'

'A fireman. I've logged his car details,' came Ian's reply.

'He has just entered Kelly's flat, stand by.' The man, dressed in a Strathclyde fireman's uniform, was about thirty years old, tall and handsome. Kelly went over to him, jumped up and wrapped her legs around the mystery guy's waist; they kissed for a couple of minutes before Kelly went to the bar. The fireman headed for what Frank thought was the hallway leading to the bathroom. Kelly had poured a couple of drinks at the bar, and she was now disrobing in the bedroom. Frank could see what the interest in this girl was – she had a knockout pair of legs, flat tummy, awesome butt, and beautiful breasts and she was also very pretty. She was dressed in black stocking and suspenders and lay on the bed as Mr Fireman came in. He was handsome with a six pack and rippling biceps; he obviously worked out. As he walked over to the bedside cabinet to his drink, Kelly grabbed him onto the bed and sat on top of him.

The fireman grabbed her breast before flicking her over onto her back. He removed her panties and gave her oral sex, she was completely shaven and ran her fingers through his hair, squirming in delight.

'Falcon one, I can confirm the fireman is our target, get me a name please.' Frank checked his video was recording and focused on the bed. Kelly was now returning the favour and was working the fireman's quite large cock with both hands as she sucked and licked on it. Frank zoomed in on the couple and took photographs of the two as they continued to please each other. Frank was aroused as he watched the couple, his hard cock pressed against his belly as he lay on the gantry floor. There was always something exciting about watching people who did not know they were being watched and these two were providing a xxx-rated porn show. Frank's earpiece burst into life; it was Ian from the surveillance van.

‘Falcon one.’

‘Go ahead,’ replied Frank.

‘Paul McBride is the fireman’s name; he is 31 years old and from Cumbernauld.’

‘Roger, copy that.’ Frank was fixated on watching Kelly; her lust for sex was intense, there was nothing this girl would not do, and Frank watched as she was fucked hard in both her vagina and ass by the well-endowed porn star fireman now known as Paul. Kelly finished off Paul by wanking his cum all over her face before exiting to the en suite. Paul went back to the bar and returned with a couple of drinks and what looked to be a joint. Frank could see Kelly wash her face, her perfect ass in full view as she was facing the sink; he could then make out her legs as she sat on the toilet. Paul was back on the bed watching the pop-out TV that had risen from the base of the bed, as he lit up the joint. It was now 12.40 am and Frank was starting to feel tired. He was relieved when, after the joint sharing and another blowjob, the porn stars switched off the lights and went to sleep.

‘Falcon one, it’s a wrap,’ Frank said into the mouthpiece, ‘can you come pick me up please.’ He packed his stuff into his rucksack and gingerly climbed down the ladders of the crane in the pitch blackness. He approached the hut where the old-timer was – the light was on, and Frank knocked on the door. The big Alsatian barked as Frank entered the hut; the old boy and the dog were sitting on an old sofa watching an old episode of Taggart on a 1990s style television; he was drinking out of a tin teacup, a bottle of Glengoyne whisky and a rollup fag tin were sitting on the table in front of him. 'That's me finished, old-timer, but I need to come back tomorrow night.' The old man's face lit up. 'Same deal as tonight.'

'Yes,' said Frank, 'I will be back at the front gate tomorrow night, at 9 pm.'

'Have you got the money with you?' the old man asked.

'No,' said Frank, 'I will bring it with me tomorrow.'

'No money, no entry,' said the old boy as he walked Frank to the gate, the Alsatian walking ahead as if it knew where they were going. Frank bade his farewell as he walked over to the Mondeo parked outside. Sue was leaning on the bonnet. 'I take it the fireman is the boyfriend?' she asked.

'Looks that way,' said Frank, 'let's go home; I am knackered; we will go over it in the morning.'

Frank called both Ian and Mark on their mobiles and arranged a meeting at the office for 6 am.

Chapter 16

Janet, Jenny, and Lesley

It was 7 am on Friday morning; Danny had just finished a workout at the gym and headed back to the lodge for some breakfast. He made coffee and scrambled eggs on toast and walked out onto the decking. He sat down at the table on the front of his deck and ate his breakfast while enjoying the pleasant morning sunshine, his iPad in front of him. He checked out the seven-day aviation Met Office weather for the following week. It was his intention to fly Jenny to Mull for lunch, a start to his campaign to seduce her and hopefully con her out of a few hundred grand. The great thing about Google is you can just about look up everything.

Jenny was indeed very well off, having been left a fortune – 1.1 million in cash and property by her late husband, she was also wealthy in her own right and worth at least another million from her farm and horse breeding business. The lovely Jenny was worth a massive 2 million bucks, well worth the risk, the chase, and his body; Danny hoped to get his hands on a least a small portion. Working on the park was a great place to fuck chicks of all ages, but Danny wanted to spend more time between his home and Zermatt; fuck this working for a living. He was getting tired of it. He had a meeting with Jenny the following day and planned to ask her out to lunch on his next day off; a flight over to Mull was a great way to impress her. He headed down to the office in the Black Pearl. Willie was nowhere to be seen and neither were the three amigos. He leaped the three steps and entered the reception. 'Morning Janet.'

'Morning, handsome,' she replied as she leaned on the reception counter, her chin cupped in her hands, watching him with lovey dovey eyes. Janet was married; Danny intended to fuck her this season and maybe add her to his little collection of sex bitches; she looked like she would do anything he asked.

'Are you on this weekend, honey?'

'Yes, Danny, its myself and Lindsay.'

'Excellent. I love it when you're on.' (a lie)

'Ooh, I love it too,' she replied.

Danny planned to invite her ugly mug up to the lodge over the weekend and fuck her to death. The rest of the day was completely boring. He sold a caravan to a Mr & Mrs Young who were anything but young and must have been in their 80s. Mrs Young had more lines on her face than a map and still wore makeup; there was nothing worse than an old hag with makeup on. She looked ridiculous and would be better spending her money on a coffin. It was now 5 pm and Danny headed for reception to give the girls a hand at booking-in. This was a busy and special weekend as it was the annual Junior Disco dancing weekend which meant the park was going to be full. Full, that is, of horny mums looking for fun. Danny stood behind the counter; the stream of mums and young girls was endless; minibuses and coaches were arriving, filled with pussy. Danny checked a few of them out as they checked in. Janet was not happy at the girls flirting with him especially two girls from Newcastle, who were definitely up for some fun.

Janet put them in the crappiest hire fleet van on Glen View 6 and Danny made a mental note to look them up later. They worked until 10 pm, Karen having left them both to lock up.

'I hate it when these stupid bimbos flirt with you; it's quite nauseating,' said Janet. Danny was shocked at her statement. 'Why?' he asked.

'Because I know you want to sleep with them, and you probably will.'

'Why would that bother you?' said Danny, 'you're married!'

'Because I want you and have done for the last two years and you don't even notice me. I could satisfy you better than those two.'

Danny smiled 'Well why don't you show me.'

He had already locked the front door and Janet had lowered the steel shutters at reception. Danny took Janet's hand and walked her through to the back office. He sat her down on Gordon's chair and stood facing her. She unzipped his fly, took out his cock and put it straight in her mouth. Janet wanked and sucked him, moaning in pleasure – she was like a woman possessed. Danny was horny as hell, his cock huge, hard, and throbbing for pussy. Janet did have a fabulous body under that summer dress and Danny intended to use it. He lifted her onto Gordon's desk and pens, paper and files flew everywhere.

Taking her panties off, Danny licked and sucked her surprisingly pretty vagina until she came. She was soaking wet and wrapped her legs around Danny, pulling him closer. 'Fuck me hard,' she whispered. Danny had every intention of doing exactly that and pulled her closer to the edge of the desk. She was very agile, and Danny pushed her legs forward until her ankles were touching her cheeks. He fucked her hard as she screamed and moaned in ecstasy, multiple orgasms flowing from her body

'Fuck's sake,' she screamed, 'stop, stop, stop; I can't take any more.' Danny pulled his hard wet cock from her warm wet pussy. 'Sorry Danny, I have gone all sensitive; can we stop for five mins? I have never had so many orgasms. Jesus.'

Janet made Danny lie full length on the desk and sucked and licked his balls. 'I will do anything you want honey, anything at all.' Danny smiled and lifted his legs and made Janet lick his ass. Pushing her head down hard, he decided there and then that he would make Janet one of his sex slaves. Danny returned to fucking her again, this time over the chair. She was kneeling on the chair as Danny fucked her hard from behind; he licked his finger and pushed it into her tight ass hole. Janet tried to stop him and let out a cry. 'You did say anything, darling,' Danny laughed. He decided not to ass fuck Janet and fucked her pussy hard as he fingered her ass; he would save fucking her ass for a more appropriate time, something to look forward to later.

Janet came a couple more times before Danny head fucked her until he exploded in her mouth; she swallowed it all. He must have worked her hard – her hair was a mess from Danny pulling on it; her body was covered in angry handprints, especially her ass which was bright red, and you could clearly see Danny's hand and fingerprints emblazoned bright red against her white skin. Janet looked totally fucked and totally happy.

'That was the most amazing sex I have ever had,' said Janet as she collected her discarded clothes from the office floor.

'Glad you enjoyed it,' said Danny.

'Not sure about your finger in my ass though,' laughed Janet.

'Well, you did say anything.'

She laughed. 'Danny, you will keep this to yourself, won't you? I don't want anyone finding out, especially my husband.'

'Of course I will, but only if you agree to become my lover and let me play with you whenever I want.'

'I agree, honey and look forward to it, preferably in a bed though,' she laughed. 'I need to go; I should have been home an hour ago.'

She kissed Danny on the cheek and groped his groin. Danny left her to lock up and headed back to his lodge. He was originally going to check out the bar after work, however that was before the surprise sex with Janet. He was content for tonight and the talent would wait and be in full swing in the bar tomorrow night anyway. Danny arrived back at his lodge at 11.30

pm, poured himself a JD and switched on the TV. He thought about watching *Breaking Bad* on Netflix but decided he was not in the mood and headed out on to the decking instead. The encounter with Janet, the ugly duckling, had been better than expected; he would have fun sexually abusing her over the next ten months while he was on the park. Her being married was also a bonus – that and the fact that she was totally smitten should allow him to sexually punish her and push her a little further. He also had the weekend to look forward to; he would tease Jenny tomorrow and leave her at a reasonable time. This would serve two purposes; it would leave her hanging and interested and also give him time to head back to the bar for his choice of disco mums.

An owl hooted away in the woods, He hoped it would fuck off soon as it would keep him awake. He lay back in his chair, looking upwards at a vista of stars. He seemed to be in awe of the planets above him but was not sure why. Maybe he wanted to be an astronaut, he laughed to himself. He decided to have another drink before bed and watch the stars some more. The TV was on with the volume down as he poured himself a drink. The news was all about immigrants and the Eurotunnel; what a fucking mess England was really in; Danny would kill the fucking lot of them. He went back out on the deck and lay with his head back, watching shooting stars and drinking JDs, wishing he were at home. The immigrant situation made him more determined to reach his monetary goal because Switzerland did not have the same problem.

He could see the lights of Jenny's lodge and a fire burning on her deck; he would leave her till tomorrow. Jenny and Lesley were also sitting outside on their deck drinking champagne; it was getting chilly, and they had lit the chimenea. They both lay back in the loungers watching the fire and the stars. The subject, after a few bubbles, was of course about the handsome Danny whom they would meet at 12 noon tomorrow. Jenny confirmed that she intended to let herself be seduced and bedded by the handsome hunk, probably only once and certainly not this weekend. Lesley thought it might be the drink talking.

'Certainly not,' said Jenny. A chance to sleep with such a handsome man ten years her junior was a rare opportunity.

'Yes, Jenny, but he probably shouldn't be trusted,' said Lesley.

'I agree, my darling friend; we will simply both use him for our own pleasure.'

'BOTH?' shouted Lesley, startled.

'Lesley, let's face it, we are both in our sixties; tell me the one thing that is missing in our lives.'

Lesley thought about what Jenny was saying, 'I don't think much is missing Jenny. We are both financially secure; we have our health as well which is important; we are both attractive despite our age.'

'Lesley!' Jenny shouted, 'when was the last time you felt like a real woman? In fact, when was the last time you had an orgasm?'

'Jesus, Jenny, steady on. Too much champagne perhaps.' They both laughed.

'Sorry, Lesley. What I'm trying to say is we both have everything but L.O.V.E which for us is difficult to find considering every man we meet wants to use us for a quick shag or is simply trying to get close to our wealth. What I propose to do is turn the tables – we become the hunters, the alphas; we take control of the likes of Danny boy, and we have the fun!'

Lesley was stunned; she had never heard Jenny talk like this, even with a drink. The more she thought about it, the more excited she got. 'So you want to have fun with Danny and then pass him over to me?'

'No, darling, we share him,' said Jenny. 'I will date him one week and you the next'.

'I think you're forgetting one thing, Jenny.'

'What's that?'

'He might not want to.'

'Oh, Lesley, you are so naïve, of course he will; he is a womaniser who is governed by that thing in his trousers.'

They both laughed and had some more champagne as the fire crackled away in the still night. Jenny felt alive for the first time in ages; she lay back in her lounger watching the millions of stars above her head, Lesley did the same. They were both thinking about Danny and were still doing so when they retired to their separate rooms for the night.

Danny's alarm woke him at 5.30 am; he had had a good night's sleep and was stacked about the weekend. He donned his gym gear and jogged down to the gym. It was 6 am. There were a couple of new faces around, one an attractive looking blonde in her twenties; however, she was with her boyfriend and the two were all over each other. The other female in the gym was a woman in her forties who looked like she had been trying to lose that extra 50 lbs all her life and was not worth looking at. Danny worked out for two hours before heading back to the lodge; it was a fabulous morning; the sun was out again, and it was already getting warm. Danny had an omelette and coffee out on the deck. Today was Jenny day and Danny was ready to play his role with her. He passed Willie on his way down to the sales office. Willie shouted his usual good morning phrase and went about weeding the patch of earth he stood in. There were a couple of hot jogging girls who gave Danny approving smiles as he drove past; he made a mental note to find them later. He walked into the office where Janet looked at him and smiled, careful not to let her colleague Karen see her.

'Morning, handsome.'

'Morning, girls,' replied Danny, 'it's a beautiful day.'

Janet followed Danny into his office. 'Last night was awesome, I can hardly walk.'

'I hope that's a compliment,' said Danny.

'Of course,' said Janet 'and I want to do it again tonight!'

'Whoa, steady on girl; you need to take it a little slower than that.'

'Sorry, Danny it was just fab; when then?'

'Soon,' Danny promised. 'Soon.'

Janet scuttled away disappointed; she could not wait to fuck him again, and she was wet just thinking about it. She had left his appointments on his desk. He was only interested in the one at 12 noon, Mrs Jenny Gunn. That morning Danny upgraded Mr & Mrs Thompson to a new van and by the time he did that it was 11 am; he popped into Leisure and headed straight for the big hall; the noise was unmistakable as 500 young disco dancers competed for the top prizes. It was a paedophile's dream as hundreds of scantily clad girls caked in makeup pranced about the great hall with hardly any clothes on. Danny of course was not interested in children and loathed the people who were. He was there for their slut mothers who were always up for some fun; he had already got his eye on a few. He was impressed as he walked across the hall – there were some really hot looking mums in the group and Danny hoped to bed at least a couple. The admiring mums nudged and whispered to one another as Danny passed by them.

He stopped at the two girls he had seen in reception. 'Good morning, ladies.'

'Lol, get him, how did you know we were ladies?' said the prettier of the two.

'Just a guess,' said Danny, 'how is your accommodation?'

'It's okay, we have seen worse.'

Danny laughed; obviously Janet had given them the crap van right enough. 'How would you like to buy us ladies a drink later?' said the blonde one.

'Oh, I don't know, I don't even know your names.'

'I'm Tricia,' said the pretty one 'and this is Sharon, and we're from Newcastle.'

'Hello, I'm Danny.'

'We know,' the girls laughed again.

'Where will you be after nine?'

'In the bar,' they said at the same time and laughed.

'Might see you there then.' He left them to watch his cute ass as he walked back towards the entrance; there were another couple of girls that also looked up for having some fun and Danny smiled at them as he walked past. It was now 11.45 am and fifteen minutes before his meeting with Jenny, He headed back to the office; Janet was on her own; Karen must be on her lunch. Danny grabbed her hand, walked her to the ladies, sat her on the toilet and took out his cock. Janet knew exactly what was required of her as she took his cock in her mouth and sucked him until he came right down her throat. She gagged at the amount of cum. Danny quickly zipped up his fly; there was no time for anything else, just Danny's pleasure. He had an appointment and Gordon was not far away either. They both returned to their workstations just in time. Two minutes later Danny's desk phone burst into life.

‘Hi Danny; Mrs Gunn is here.’

‘Thanks, Janet, show her in please; I will try to catch up with you later.’ Danny knew that Janet did not have a hope in hell of seeing him this weekend, what with all these eager girls about. He had just finished spraying some scent on himself when there was a knock on the door.

‘Come in.’

Janet entered with Jenny Gunn and another woman, whom he did not know. Danny thought to himself that this would put a block on his intentions tonight with Jenny, as the woman was probably on the park and spending the weekend with her. Danny extended his hand. ‘Good afternoon, Jenny, nice to see you again.’ ‘And you too, Danny. This is my very good friend Lesley.’

‘Nice to meet you, Lesley.’

Lesley was equally attractive, and Danny took her small hand and shook it gently. The Girls both looked fabulous; they looked like they had both had their hair and nails done and they both looked great for their age. A possible threesome popped into Danny’s head, but that was highly unlikely with these two. Anyway, the money was more important than sex with a couple of oldies. Lesley smiled at Danny, her breath taken away; now she really saw what all the fuss was about. This guy was one handsome fellow, an Omar Sharif, Clark Gable and Brad Pitt all rolled into one. Lesley wouldn’t mind a few years on a Caribbean island with this guy; hell, a few years on a Scottish island would do.

'Can I get you ladies a tea or a coffee?'

'I'm fine thanks, Danny,' said Jenny.

'I wouldn't mind a water,' said Lesley, Lesley was feeling all hot and bothered; even his sexy Scottish voice and the smell of his aftershave would make you weak at the knees.

Danny buzzed Janet who brought in a bottle of chilled water and two glasses, giving Danny a warning glance as she left the room.

'Right,' Jenny started off, 'I have decided not to keep the caravan.'

Danny interrupted, 'Well I…'

'Let me finish,' said Jenny. 'I have decided to replace it with a lodge, but only if the price is right.'

'That's great news, Jenny.'

'There will be a few stipulations.'

'Certainly, what do you have in mind?' Danny was over the moon. Not only was he due £2k commission on this deal but more importantly it meant Jenny Gunn was going to be around more.

'I don't want to deal with that foul mouthed manager of yours. I want £35k for my caravan as part exchange and I want the new Beachcomber 47ft.'

Whoa – make that £3.5k commission, Danny thought. 'Let me have a chat with Gordon; I won't be long,' said Danny, smiling at them both as he walked out the room and headed for Gordon's office.

'Well, girl, what did I tell you?' said Jenny.

Lesley was fanning herself with her hand. 'He is one handsome man, and he knows it.'

'Yes, I know. Do you now think he is worth having some fun with?'

'God yes, Jenny, he is gorgeous, and he looks really fit under his clothes. But don't you think it's a bit tarty to seduce a younger man to the point of using him for sex?'

'Lesley, you are your own girl. I am going to do my best to bed this guy; what you do is entirely up to you.' Both girls were unaware that Danny had started his Dictaphone to record as he left the office; it was taping their entire conversation as they both sat and chatted awaiting his return.

'I am the best salesman you have ever had,' said Danny as he breezed into Gordon's office.

'Pray tell me Danny, what makes you think that?' asked Gordon, curtseying as he did so.

'Well, young sir, I have just sold Mrs Gunn a new Beachcomber Lodge!'

'Fuck's sake, Danny boy, you're shitting me, right?'

'Nope, straight up,' said Danny as he high-fived Gordon. 'Thirty-five for her p/x; £105k to change.'

'Jesus fucking Christ, Danny boy, you just made my fucking weekend! What is the fucking catch?'

'None, except she wants it up in 14 days – can we do it?'

'Danny boy, I have just been told I have a display lodge on its way which will be here on Tuesday. You must be psychic; what a job well done; you can bloody well fuck Natcha every lunchtime for the rest of the season; now go and sign her up.'

Danny walked back to his office, order form in hand. The little filly he fucked earlier in the week was at reception with what must be her folks; she looked round at Danny as he passed. It looked like they were checking out; good fucking riddance, Danny said under his breath. He walked back into the office.

'Good news, Jenny, we can go ahead with the new lodge, and have it in place in the time that you have requested.'

Jenny smiled. 'Fantastic, I suppose you will want some money from me then,' as she took her cheque book out from her bag. Danny was delighted. 'That's great news; I am happy that you have decided to stay with us. Why don't you both let me take you out to dinner this evening.'

The Girls looked at each other. 'Yes, why not, 'said Jenny, 'I hope you're paying, Danny boy,' as she gave him a look from under her glasses and handed him a cheque for £105k.

'Yes why of course, dinner is on me, Italian okay?' said Danny. The ladies both said yes at the same time and laughed. 'Excellent. I will book a table for 6.30 pm and pick you up at 6.' Danny showed the Girls out, shaking their hands as they left. Lesley held on to Danny's hand a little longer than Jenny did, obviously impressed with his good looks and charm; he now expected to sleep with both ladies, Lesley looked as if she would be easier to bed than Jenny.

Janet was busy in reception, but still managed to give him a look; she had overheard Jenny's parting comment of 'see you at six'. Danny returned to his office, took the Dictaphone from the plant pot on his desk, rewound it as he phoned the Italian restaurant; he made the reservation, hung up the phone and pressed play.

Chapter 17

Surveillance Day 3

It was 7 am on a wet city centre morning. Sue was mesmerised by the rain running down the window; she started to daydream of her holiday to Turkey in two weeks' time with her man. Frank walked into the boardroom. 'Morning all,' he said as he placed a folder and his Costa coffee on the table. 'Right, let's get started. We have a busy day ahead of us and hopefully a result for our client. Play back last night's footage, please Ian.'

Ian had already lowered the screen from the ceiling and was waiting for Mark to finish closing the blinds before he pressed play. He forwarded the footage to Kelly's apartment and the arrival of the fireman. It was obvious from the footage that little Miss Kelly was in a relationship with the fireman and possibly Philip too. Frank hoped that Kelly and Philip were just friends, and that Carolyn did not get hurt; however, he had his doubts. He gave a brief on the days' surveillance, reading from the A4 board in his hand. 'Right, Mark and Ian will follow Philip for today. Sue and I will be on our very own porn star Kelly. Ian can leave the surveillance van along at the retail park on Great Western Road; it will be quicker to reach it there. We can reposition it at Kelly's later if required. I will return to my pigeon's nest in the crane for the second night of filming Kelly does Partick.'

They all had a laugh at that one. Frank went on to say that they expected Philip to have a normal day at work; however, in this business you just could not tell. Depending on the day and night's outcomes they should be prepared for another day on this if nothing materialised from the next 24 hours. The surveillance team headed for their vehicles, Ian boarding the BT van with Mark waiting behind him in the Ford Mondeo. Frank and Sue took the Golf GTi and headed for Kelly's penthouse pad. Ian dropped the van off outside B&Q at the Retail Park and then he and Mark drove the ten minutes to Philip's house in Milngavie, arriving there at 8 am.

'Déjà vu,' said Mark as they settled into another long and possibly boring day stuck in their little steel box. A half hour later a local police car drove past. 'Crap,' Ian said, 'and its only 8.30 am.' The police car returned about two minutes later and this time it stopped. There were two young cops inside, a male and a female; the twats put on their blue and reds before stepping out of the vehicle. Ian and Mark both got out of the Mondeo and presented their ID to the young female officer who returned to the police car to run their ID and their plate. The young police officer was concerned that they might have been staking out a house to burgle. After checking their ID and running the vehicle plates, they were both happy about why Ian and Mark were there. The smug little blonde female officer's parting words were that they should next time maybe inform the local police office of their intentions. Now that was never going to happen thought Mark; you just can't trust the local police force.

Ian and Mark decided to move from the now compromised position and instead wait along the end of the road next to the park. They called Frank and informed him of the new position. Ian also checked the tracker was working. 'Fuck me,' he said, 'the Beamer's not here; it's in Edinburgh.' Startled, they drove past Philip's driveway. There was a new shiny Aston Martin in the drive. It was clearly Philip's as it had his personal plate on it, which was PH 23.

Mark informed Frank of the changes. They would also have to get their tracker back from his previous car. Mark got a mobile phone from the glove compartment while Ian logged on to a web site called Locate a Phone on his iPad. They would attach the mobile to the Aston Martin via a magnetic box, which would allow them to find the car if they lost it in traffic. The rest of the day was uneventful, and the four PIs had a pretty dull day as Philip and Kelly only went about their daily routines. Philip spent the entire day at work in Bearsden, only popping out to the deli for a sandwich.

Kelly went to the gym where she flirted with every male she came across before going to Braehead where she bought clothes and did a food shop. She also had lunch with another female before visiting the Anne Summers shop and returning home at 4 pm.

The two teams had their dinner at 6 pm. Frank and Sue had pizza, while Mark and Ian did slightly better with a Chinese takeaway. Both teams managed to eat their dinner in peace as there was no movement from either party. Ian now sat in the car at the end of Philip's road; Mark was asleep in the front seat and had just started to snore. 'Bloody hell,' Ian said, waking up Mark, 'our target's on the move; you better let Frank know.' They watched Philip as he drove out of the road end, turning right onto Stockiemuir Road and then left at the Ski Club. The car was heading back to Bearsden Cross where Philip's optician's was located. Ian hoped he was not heading back to work as he had had enough boredom for one day.

The car, however, did not stop and instead headed west towards Anniesland Cross. Mark informed Frank that it looked like Philip was heading their way. Ian stayed well back as the roads were quiet and they did not want to be seen; the phone attached to the underside of the car was there as a backup. Philip was unaware of the car following him as he headed for Kelly's. She had promised him a night he would not forget. Jonathan and Emma were both out and had promised to be back by 10 pm and were under the impression that he was going to the golf club.

Ian was five cars and about three hundred yards behind Philip; he could just see him ahead as he headed for the expressway and Partick. Ian did not follow Philip when he took the exit for Partick and carried on, before taking the next exit and doubling back. Frank confirmed that Philip did arrive at Kelly's and asked Ian and Mark to collect the van from its current location and bring it back to their position. Frank needed to get back round to the shipyard asap as it was now 8.30 pm. Mark returned in the Mondeo, quickly followed by Ian in the BT van. After a quick chat and a change of clothing in the back of the van, Frank and Sue drove round to the yard. The watchman was nowhere in sight as Sue dropped Frank at the gate; it was a good fifteen minutes before he appeared.

'You're early, you said nine o'clock,' said the old watchman; he was stinking of whisky.

'Yes, sorry about that, look I am in a hurry.'

'Have you got my money?' Frank gave the old man his two hundred pounds as the smelly old Alsatian sniffed his crotch, the dog's long matted hair looking like it had not been washed in years. 'Don't get caught up that crane,' said the old man 'because I don't know you if you do.'

They both went their separate ways, Frank sprinting for the crane. He looked like the Milk Tray man as he climbed the steel ladder with his backpack. He was careful to stay out of sight as it was still light and decided to stay in the control room of the big crane until it got dark as going out on the gantry would expose him; the view from the box was sufficient for now. He set up both the video and film cameras just in time as Philip and Kelly had just come into view. They both had been lying on the couch and were out of sight when Frank arrived, as the back of the couch faced the window.

Kelly, dressed in white stockings and suspenders, was leading Philip to the bedroom. Frank checked that the video was focused and pointed straight at Kelly's bedroom. The couple were now lying full length on the bed. Kelly had her back to the camera as she lay on her side, her fabulous ass neatly packaged in her panties. Frank felt himself getting aroused. The couple seemed to spend the next ten minutes talking as Philip stroked her hair. Frank felt sorry for Carolyn and was not looking forward to giving her the bad news. His attention was distracted by a yellow tennis ball bouncing along the ground 100ft below him. The Alsatian bounded along behind it; it had been thrown by its master the old watchman who was looking up at the crane. The old boy waved up to Frank, who waved back as the Alsatian returned the ball to the old boy's feet.

Frank returned to the job in hand and watched Kelly on the display screen attached to the side of the camera. She was now topless and giving Philip oral sex; he lay on the bed with his head back holding each side of her head as she blew him. Frank fired off some photos with the Bigma, the shutter of the camera sounding like a machine gun as it shot ten frames a second. Frank was no longer aroused – he just felt sad for the poor woman whose life was just about to be turned upside down. The cheating pair continued to have a no holds barred three-hour sex session before having a few drinks together. They seemed to have a lot to talk about and spent the next half hour chatting.

Frank informed the team that they had enough footage and evidence and that they should all call it a night. He packed up his gear. He had hoped this job would have turned out differently but, instead, it was now all a bit of an anti-climax. Sue was on her way to pick him up; he climbed down the ladder and headed for the watchman's hut. As he approached, he could make out what he thought was a cat eating out of the dog dish outside the hut but could not believe it as he got closer when he saw that it was actually a large rat! Frank bade farewell to Pat, the old watchman, who was doing the exact same thing as the night before. Pat was hoping he would return tomorrow night, but Frank informed him he would not be, and thanked him for his time, leaving him with the dog and the big rat. Sue picked Frank up at the gate to drive him home. She informed him that Philip and Kelly had left the flat to go joyriding in the new car. Frank could not care less; he was not happy that the information they had for Carolyn was bad news and was really not looking forward to letting her know on her return from LA.

Chapter 18

Doubles

Danny was outside Jenny's caravan at 6.30 pm sharp. The two ladies emerged from the caravan, both dressed casually but smart; they drove the short distance to the restaurant. Massimo was a fine Italian restaurant with excellent food. Danny and the girls took their seats at a table by the window overlooking the Clyde. He ordered a bottle of Villa Antinori which was poured as they browsed the menu. 'What would you recommend?' asked Lesley.

'The food here is excellent; it really depends on your own taste.' He was looking forward to having fun with these two middle-aged women, he thought. More so as they had no idea he had heard their conversation. The meal was delicious with both women loosening up as the wine flowed. Danny would go back to theirs after dinner for a nightcap, but a quick one as he had plans for later. It was obvious that both women fancied him, and as they said themselves on the recording, they were both willing to share him, which suited him fine as it would save any difficulty later, as jealousy could sometimes creep in and spoil things.

It was 9.30 pm when Danny drove the Girls home and, as he expected, was invited in for a drink. He accepted. It would be senseless not to, but he was in a rush to get to the disco mums in the bar. Trying not to be rude, Danny suffered an hour of flirting and boring chit chat before thanking both Jenny and Lesley, who were both disappointed that he was leaving.

'Going so soon?' said Jenny.

'I am afraid so, dear, I have work in the morning.'

'That's a shame,' said Lesley, 'I was just starting to enjoy myself.'

Danny was now torn between staying with the oldies and establishing a future relationship or risking it all going pear-shaped by heading to the bar to meet the two Newcastle girls.

'Surely you are not bored with our company already,' said Jenny.

'No not at all,' said Danny. 'However, if I am to remain in such lovely company, I must nip back to my lodge and collect some proper drink!'

'Excellent,' said Jenny and squeezed Danny's hand as he opened the door to leave.

'I will not be long,' he said as he kissed the now tipsy Jenny on the cheek. He raced round to his lodge to collect a litre of JD and two bottles of caffeine-free coke. He then headed to the bar to locate the two females and spotted them as soon as he walked in. He spent the next ten minutes chatting to the girls before giving them £100 and the key to the Osprey lodge where he had fucked the little bitch teenager. He instructed the girls to buy some booze and he would meet them at the lodge later; they were both half-canned and both looking forward to seeing him.

Danny was walking back to his car when Sharon shouted on him; she had run out behind him. She pressed him against the Audi and kissed him, with her tongue down his throat as she groped his groin. 'How long will you be?' she whispered as she bit and sucked his ear. 'I want you,' she said, rubbing herself against him. Danny explained that he was at a company dinner and would be with them as soon as he could. He felt like a stupid teenager as he rushed back round to the oldies. Danny was now horny and would have probably fucked all four on the same night; he was having a ball this weekend but was more interested in fucking the two disco mums than spending any more time with Jenny and Lesley. The following two hours at Jenny's were a combination of light accidental touching and flirting; it was obvious they were both playing games with him, but he enjoyed it anyway.

Danny made the excuse that it was now midnight and he had work in the morning. Jenny walked him out to the deck. 'It was a lovely night,' she said, 'we both enjoyed your company very much.' Danny gave Jenny a hug and a kiss on the cheek. 'I enjoyed your company too, hopefully we can do it again sometime.' He left the two oldies who would probably spend the remainder of the night discussing the evening they had spent with him. Danny did not know if the girls would have gone to the lodge or if they would still be there. He was delighted when he pulled up in the drive to see both of them sitting on the chairs out on the decking, drinking champagne.

He walked on deck to be met with another tongue-in-mouth kiss from Tricia who was obviously wanting a good fucking and had both hands on his ass as she did so. Sharon was in the lounge pouring Danny a Jack Daniels and coke which he had brought back with him from Jenny's. It turned out that this was the girls' third time at the championship, and they had seen Danny last year in the bar. They did not have any fun time to themselves as Tricia's husband had been present and he was in fact Sharon's husband's best friend.

The girls were pretty drunk and ready to party. Danny put on some music and sat with the girls chatting on the sofa. It was Sharon who again started fooling around with him. Tricia got up and danced by herself while Danny snogged Sharon who opened up his shirt and started kissing his chest before reaching for his belt. Tricia was watching as she danced. 'You are one dirty bitch, Sharon Tate,' she said as she drank champagne from the bottle. 'I know I am. You're just jealous.' She plunged her hand down Danny's trousers, grabbing his now erect cock. 'Oh, my god Tricia,' she said, 'look at the size of this!' as she put Danny's throbbing cock in her mouth. Sharon moved her mouth up and down sucking on it hard; Tricia put her glass down and moved onto the couch.

Danny kissed Tricia as he pushed and pulled Sharon's hair to the movement of her head. He slipped his hand into Tricia's blouse; she was quite small breasted and the prettier of the two. This looked like becoming a long night of sexual delight. Danny pulled Sharon from his cock and shoved Tricia down instead; his cock was large, its head swollen; it looked like a peach as Tricia licked and sucked it. He pushed his hand down the back of

Tricia's jeans; she was small and petite enough for Danny to be able to reach her wet pussy from behind and finger her till she came. Sharon had stood up and stripped down to her undies; she was of medium build with an average figure and medium sized tits. The girls both stripped off. Tricia's small tits were complemented by their ski slope shape and delightfully dark nipples; she had black hair and was unshaven. Sharon was of a lighter perfection and had a butterfly tattoo on her hip; her pussy was clean-shaven. Danny lay Tricia on the couch, her feet on the floor – he spread her legs, took a drink from her champagne glass, and dribbled it on to her clit before licking it gently. She ran her hands through his hair as she had her second orgasm. Danny turned his attention to Sharon who was wanking his cock as she watched Danny lick her friend's pussy. He made Sharon kneel on the couch where he bent her over and fucked her hard from behind while he pulled her hair and played roughly with her tits. Tricia poured herself more champagne and watched Danny as he lay Sharon on her back, lifted her legs up to her neck and fucked her again. Her pussy was soaking from three orgasms before Danny took his cock out and Sharon fell on the couch exhausted.

Sharon looked like Janet did the other night. She was covered in bite and slap marks and looking like she had just been involved in a fight. Danny grabbed Tricia and made her kneel at the end of the couch and positioned Sharon over her friend. Now with Tricia and Sharon's pussies and asses above and below each other he now took it in turn to fuck them both, taking his cock out of one pussy and placing it in the other at his leisure.

Tricia refused to take Danny's cock in her tight little asshole, complaining each time he tried. He double decked the girls, slapping and pulling at them like pieces of meat. He liked to take his cock from Sharon's pussy and put it straight into Tricia's pussy. Finally, exhausted, Danny sat down on the couch, Tricia escaped from beneath Sharon as she now lay over the arm of the couch, her hair touching the floor. She kept repeating the words 'Fuck, fuck, fuck. I swear I have had a least a dozen orgasms and some of them were massive. Fucks sake Danny.'

The trio took the booze and moved into the bedroom, and more champagne and JDs followed. Danny tried to get the girls to play with each other but they both refused. He fucked them both again in the comfort of the bed before having his first massive cum in Tricia's mouth. This was followed up with fucking both girls, side by side, eventually pulling his cock from Tricia's wet dark pussy and wanking it into Sharon's mouth. The trio were now exhausted, Danny thought it was too good an opportunity to end and decided to spend the night in the bed with his two princesses for round two in the morning.

Chapter 19

Tell Me

Carolyn tried to relax on her trip to LA; the girls were great and did their best to help her over the couple of days they had spent on the stop over. Carolyn, however, could only think of what was going to happen now; it was Friday morning in sunny Los Angeles, and she was heading home. To what, she thought? She had a meeting with Frank on Saturday morning to find out the results of their surveillance. Carolyn was again sick with worry and could not get the thought of her two beautiful children being confronted with the news that their perfect life was just about to be shattered, and that she and Philip would be splitting up. Was this really going to happen – would she and Philip really be splitting up; is he having an affair? How would she cope and where would they end up living? Carolyn could not afford to stay in the house in Castle Mains Estate on her salary. The kids also had exams coming up; she did have the backing of her Dad and sister and was grateful for that, but she still felt scared and alone.

The flight home was a nightmare with two heavily pregnant women in her section along with four babies under twelve months. The babies seemed to take it in turn to cry the entire length of the flight. The girls all worked hard and were supportive to Carolyn's circumstances; even Captain Josh came up to the crew rest area and offered her a shoulder to cry on. The flight seemed to take forever, but now at last she was strapped into her jump seat as the aircraft continued its descent over Loch Lomond. The view to the north was beautiful and you could see Ben Nevis near Fort William in the distance. The flight landed on time and Carolyn said goodbye to her colleagues, receiving hugs from everyone along with wishes of good luck. Marion walked her to her car. 'Don't stress too much sweetie, it will be fine,' she said as she hugged her in the car park. 'You might find you have been worrying needlessly,' she said as she wiped tears from Carolyn's cheeks.

'I am sorry; it's just a relief to be home but I am scared nonetheless.'

'Don't be, and don't forget you can call me any time.'

'Thanks, Marion, and thank you for trying to cheer me up in LA.' The girls hugged for a little longer before they both headed their separate ways. Carolyn really did feel physically sick; she called Sarah on her hands free but she never answered; she was probably at work and could not. The journey home was silent; she was not in the mood for the radio. She would normally be over the moon to be heading home, and looking forward to seeing Philip and the kids, but today she was just looking forward to seeing the kids.

Carolyn parked in the driveway and let herself into the house. There was mail on the floor in the hall, mostly just the usual stuff. She walked into the kitchen, poured herself a large glass of rosé wine and went to sit down in the lounge, when there was a knock at the door. She walked over to the window and saw a local florist van at the kerb. My god! she thought, has Philip sent her flowers? She rushed to the door. The bouquet of flowers held in the young lady's hands was beautiful. 'For Philip Hughes,' the girl said, as she handed Carolyn the flowers. Carolyn was confused. 'You mean, from Philip?' 'No, ma'am – for him.' Carolyn was gutted. Who sent flowers to a guy? Was Philip gay?! She took the flowers, thanked the girl and closed the door behind her. Carolyn stood with her back against the door; the card with the flowers had the Aston Martin logo on the back and was indeed addressed to Philip, from the dealership where he bought his silly car; how stupid was she? Her whole being was lifted when she saw the flowers, now the drop back down to reality was just another painful blow to her. Carolyn placed the bouquet on the hall table before returning to her glass of wine. She sat in the lounge staring at the wall; the house used to look beautiful and homely, now it just looked and felt empty. She managed to drink the entire bottle of wine before the kids came home. Emma breezed into the lounge. Has Daddy bought you flowers?' she screamed. 'What's the occasion?' as she hugged her mum on the couch, her hair damp and smelling of chlorine.

'They're not for me, darling, they're for your Dad.'

'Who sends flowers to a guy?' laughed Jonathan as he took his turn at hugging Mummy on the sofa. Emma returned to the sofa clutching the envelope from the flowers. It's from Dad's car people,' she said.

'Yea,' Jonathan yelled, 'you should see Dad's new car!'

‘I will see it soon enough,’ Carolyn said, trying to smile. ‘Have you been swimming, Emma?’

‘Yes, mum, we were at the sports centre, how did you know?’

‘You smell of chlorine,’ Carolyn said as she laughed. ‘And you, mother, smell of drink,’ said Emma and gave her Mum another big hug. They all sat together and chatted, before the children both headed for their rooms and homework. Carolyn was not in the mood to cook but made dinner anyway; she heard Philip’s new car arrive in the drive. He appeared in the kitchen clutching the flowers.

‘Hi Carolyn, these must be from the dealership,’ he said as he opened the card. ‘I will put them in the car; they will brighten up the office. Do you want to see the new car?’ he asked as he walked out of the kitchen, flowers in his hand.

‘I’m not really in the mood, and I’m in the middle of cooking dinner.’ ‘Suit yourself,’ he replied and disappeared back outside. Previously he would have given the flowers to Carolyn; he often got freebees through his work, and she found it very selfish that he had not even offered, not that she would have taken them anyway. Philip returned to the kitchen. ‘Don’t make me any dinner – I need to go out,’ he said as he headed for the shower. He would normally have told her where he was going and ask if she was alright about it. Carolyn was quite happy that he was going out and decided not to challenge it. She would ask the kids if they fancied staying in with their Mum tonight and if they had plans, she would get Sarah round and get drunk instead; she was halfway there anyway.

Carolyn had lasagne and chips with the kids, and they all chattered away like budgies. Philip walked into the dining room and interrupted dinner, 'Don't wait up, I might be late,' he said as he disappeared back into the hall. 'Yea, see ya,' Carolyn wondered where he was going in his shiny new car with a bunch of flowers! Fuck you, she thought and decided that she needed something stronger than wine and headed to the kitchen to pour herself a stiff brandy! Emma and Jonathan both had plans for the evening, so she called Sarah after dinner, but decided just to chat on the phone rather than have her round. The rest of the evening was spent looking at old photos which became depressing and so she watched catch-up TV instead. She thought about where Philip was right now, and it was tearing her apart – it burnt into her heart and her mind. The kids came home at 10 pm by which time Carolyn was well drunk and had fallen asleep on the couch. Carolyn had supper with the kids, just a cup of tea and some toast, before they all toddled off to bed just before midnight. She decided to sleep in the spare room, so locked the bedroom door and lay in bed thinking about what tomorrow was going to bring, other than a hangover!

The next morning at breakfast Carolyn felt a tad fragile after the amount of alcohol she had consumed. Philip did not mention the fact that she had spent the night in the spare room which ground on Carolyn's nerves even more! They all chatted away like a normal family at breakfast before Philip left for work and the children went to school. Carolyn was now all alone on D-Day, well for a short time anyway. Both Sarah and Dad would be round before the PI guy Frank was due to arrive at 10.30 am with the good or bad news.

Sarah and Dad arrived early at 10 am and Carolyn made them both strong coffees as they chatted about work and the last couple of days, before Sarah said, 'Are you sure about what you want to do if it's bad news,' as they all sat down in the lounge with a coffee.

'Yes, Sarah, if Philip's been unfaithful, it's well and truly over.' Her father agreed. 'Do not worry about the kids. I will take them out to dinner and then the cinema to see the new 007 movie tonight. They will be fine.' 'Let's wait and see first,' said Sarah, 'we don't know the result yet.'

It was 10.30 am exactly when Frank drove into the driveway. Sarah let him in and brought him through to the lounge; she offered Frank a coffee before they all sat down. Carolyn felt sick and could hear her heart beating in her chest; she just knew this wasn't going to be the news she wanted to hear.

'There is no good way of doing this,' said Frank as he took an iPad from his leather satchel.

'I know' said Carolyn, 'I just need to know if Philip is having an affair or not.'

Frank looked at both Sarah and their father before turning back to Carolyn. 'Yes, I am afraid he is.'

Carolyn could feel the words burn into her chest – her heartbeat became louder and was all she could hear. Her mouth was dry; the sick feeling she had earlier intensified, and a new sense of pain washed over her. It was a horrible feeling, something she had never experienced before. All of a sudden, tears welled up in her eyes as Sarah rushed from her chair and sat beside her on the sofa. Carolyn thought she was prepared for this, but she was definitely not; her world as she knew it had exploded into a cauldron of pain and fear.

'I think we all need a drink,' said Sarah as she walked over to the drinks cabinet and poured three large brandies, giving one each to Carolyn and her Dad and offering the other to Frank which, to Sarah's surprise, he accepted, saying that he also needed it and had a driver outside anyway.

Sarah returned with a fourth glass for herself; she was gutted for her wonderful, beautiful, loving, caring sister. Carolyn stared at her glass, the smell of it actually making her vomit a little into her mouth; the taste was acidic and rancid. Carolyn knew now that her wonderful life, and that of her children, as they knew it, was over. She stood up and excused herself and ran to the downstairs bathroom.

Frank, Sarah and the girls' father sat awkwardly in silence as they listened to Carolyn crying in the bathroom. Tom, her father went to the bathroom door and rapped gently on it, but

Carolyn did not open it. He decided to leave her for now and returned to his seat beside Sarah. After five minutes or so, Carolyn composed herself enough to emerge from the bathroom, her face red and her eyes bloodshot. She sat down next to Sarah and her father and eventually composed herself enough to ask Frank, 'Who is she?' Frank looked at her father for approval to continue; Tom nodded, and Frank then explained that her name was Kelly Stuart, 24 years old and from Partick.

'Twenty-four!' Carolyn screamed, 'how could he, what about me and the children, does he know what he is doing? Oh my god, Sarah, how am I going to tell the kids?' She started sobbing again. 'Do you have evidence?' she asked, looking at Frank.

'Yes,' replied Frank,' however I suggest that it's maybe better that you don't see it, for now anyway.'

'No, I want to see it.'

'Are you sure, babes?' Sarah said, 'maybe another time.'

'Yes, I agree,' said Tom, 'maybe another time would be better.' He passed Carolyn some tissues.

'How bad is it?' Sarah asked Frank. The look on Frank's face said it all.

'I don't care. I want to see who this bitch is. I need to know, show me please.'

Frank switched on the iPad. 'I must warn you that this footage is of a sexual nature and will cause you a considerable amount of pain and heartache; it would be better if you did not view the footage.'

'I don't care,' screamed Carolyn, 'I need to see!' She suddenly realised that the feeling of pain had now turned to anger and apologised to both Sarah and Frank and insisted that Frank press play on his iPad. Her father Tom excused himself, stating that he did not need to hear or see any more; his son-in-law was finished as far as he was concerned, and he took his brandy and headed for the kitchen.

Frank cleared his throat and took a stiff shot of his brandy, informing the girls that the female in question, Kelly, resided in a penthouse flat on the Clydeside in Partick; she owned a hair and beauty salon also in Partick, and drove a Range Rover registered to Philip's company.

Carolyn took in a breath. Frank reached into his satchel and produced a dozen 8 x 6 glossy photographs of Philip and the girl having lunch, kissing in a car park beside the Range Rover and, worst of all, at various stages of undress in a bedroom. Carolyn felt unwell; this was worse than she had ever imagined. There was no going back from this; she felt betrayed and a fool, embarrassed for not seeing this coming. How can someone you love to be so blasé with your love – your feelings – your heart – your children? She was absolutely gutted, confused, and shocked! She had not expected this and was sick to her stomach. She went to the kitchen, poured her brandy down the sink and grabbed a bottle of wine and a couple of glasses, pausing to accept a warm strong hug from her Dad. 'I am sorry,' he said. Carolyn kissed her father on the cheek and returned to the lounge.

Sarah was sitting in the armchair, as white as a sheet. Taking control, Carolyn asked Frank bravely, 'What else do you have for me? Is this the only time you saw them together? Is there more?'

Frank looked at them both before taking another stiff one from his brandy glass. 'Yes, I am afraid we have actual footage of them having sexual intercourse, but I would suggest not viewing that content; nothing can be gained from it.'

'I want to see it,' said Carolyn interrupting.

'Now wait a minute, sis, maybe…'

'No, Sarah, this is my decision; I need to see it.' Carolyn had to see it. This was the end of her marriage, her life, and her kids' lives as they knew it – it had to be final. She had to be sure that this was the end and that there was no hope for her marriage and that it was really over for good. Watching this would make things final; she had to be strong for herself and the children.

Frank protested profusely but Carolyn was determined, and the footage was played. Both sisters could not believe what they saw. Sarah watched only a couple of minutes before excusing herself and joining her Dad in the kitchen. She wanted to stay with Carolyn, but she was uncomfortable seeing her brother-in-law having sex with the young female. Carolyn felt numb as she watched the footage; it was almost like she was watching someone else, not Philip. He was lying in bed stroking the blonde's back. The blonde was dressed like an expensive hooker in stockings and suspenders and started to give Philip oral.

Carolyn asked Frank to pause the footage as she raced to the bathroom again. She locked the door behind her, threw up and started to sob uncontrollably; the recording had made her physically sick. Sarah had seen her go into the bathroom and knocked on the door. 'Are you okay, honey?'

'I will be out in a minute, I am okay,' said Carolyn. She was however not okay; watching the once love of her life's total disregard for her and her children left her heartbroken. She felt drained and exhausted – her life with Philip was well and truly over and she felt bizarrely sad for him; he was just about to lose his entire family and most of his friends. She tried to think back, how long could this have been going on, where did they meet? They looked very comfortable together, should she get an STD test or something? Pain was not what she was feeling, this was worse than that, her entire relationship with her husband was a lie. She did not know this man in this video. He was a disgusting cradle-snatching pervert, a liar and a cheat who had abandoned his loving family for a cheap fucking WHORE!

Sarah and her Dad were only in the next room but she felt alone, very alone and very afraid but trying to keep focused; she had to be strong for Emma and Jonathan. She composed herself and returned to the lounge. She was going to beat this! She had herself, Emma and Jonathan to think about; they still had a future together even without Philip. Sarah and her Dad were still in the kitchen, leaving Carolyn and Frank to continue watching the footage alone; the entire footage was humiliating and disgusting and Carolyn was glad when it was finally over. Frank looked embarrassed, 'If it's any consolation, Philip is not her only partner,' said Frank as he pressed stop. 'You mean she is seeing someone else? You're kidding me.' Carolyn was shocked. 'Nope,' said Frank, 'she did the exact same thing the night before with a guy called Paul McBride, a fireman working out of the Bishopbriggs fire station; they look like they know each other pretty well.'

Great, Carolyn thought, depending on how long Philip was seeing this little tart he had probably passed on a bunch of STDs straight to her. My life is not over, she thought, I am not going to take this. Carolyn felt the worst she had ever done in her entire life, but she had to keep it together. Sarah and Dad had both returned to her side. 'What do you suggest we do next, Frank?' asked her father, 'you know about these things, right?' Frank suggested Carolyn changed the locks immediately; they all agreed, and Frank gave the locksmith he had on standby a call. He also suggested that Carolyn transfer as much money from their joint bank account into her own account as soon as possible. Carolyn was reluctant to do so at first, but after Frank had described a few previous cases where people had not done this and what the outcome was, she soon changed her mind. Carolyn's world was now spinning, and she was very glad that Sarah and her Dad were there for her; it helped her from becoming a victim and helped her take control of this disgusting mess that Philip had put them in.

Everything was now happening very fast. The locksmith had arrived and was busy changing the locks, Carolyn and Sarah went online and transferred money as Frank suggested. Carolyn decided to tell the kids when they got home before sending them out with their grandpa, and then to confront Philip with the photographs when he came home from work. She would allow him to collect some belongings before banishing him from the house forever. She thanked Frank for his time and advice. He left his mobile and home number which he said she could call any time.

Carolyn called her work and told them that she would be off sick for at least the next week. It was now 2 pm as both sisters sat at the dining table with their Dad, photographs and paperwork spread out on the table in front of them. It looked like three generals planning an attack during a war. Carolyn had already consumed a bottle of wine and four Co codamol 500mg tablets and was feeling light-headed. Sarah told Carolyn that she would be staying with her at least until the next morning and their father would keep the kids overnight and bring them round for breakfast the following morning. The children got out of school at 4 pm and Carolyn decided that they would both be told the truth as soon as possible. She did not have a clue how they were going to react, and it scared her. The next twenty minutes felt like hours before they heard one of the kids trying to open the door with their key. They both looked at each other before realising the locks had been changed and they both raced for the front door.

The kids were delighted to see them all and both ran in and gave Carolyn, Sarah, and grandpa huge hugs. 'What's up with the door, Mum?' asked Jonathan. Carolyn and Sarah looked at each other and Sarah asked both Emma and Jonathan to take a seat in the lounge. The children sat together on the two-seater brown leather Chesterfield; Carolyn and Sarah sat on its twin couch opposite.

'Is Dad okay?' asked Jonathan, 'has someone died?'

'Mum, is everything okay, is Dad okay?' asked Emma.

'Everyone is fine. No-one has died or is in hospital.'

'Then what is wrong, Mum?' asked Emma.

Carolyn just came right out and said it. 'Your father is having an affair.'

'WHAT!' Jonathan shouted, 'Dad, yeah right, who said so?'

'Oh Mummy, who would say such a thing? how do you know? are you sure? did he tell you? is he coming home?' cried Emma as she rushed over to Carolyn and hugged her so tightly that she nearly passed out.

The children looked frightened and there was much sobbing and hugging, crying and tear-wiping.

'It can't be true, Mummy. what will happen to us?' said Jonathan, the reality of what was about to happen to their own lives beginning to hit home and self-preservation kicking in. 'Are we going to have to leave?' said Jonathan who was still sitting on the couch in disbelief.

'No, we are not leaving, we have done nothing wrong, it will be your father that will have to leave.'

'Oh Mummy,' cried Emma and raced out the room. Sarah went after her.

'I love you, Mum,' said Jonathan, 'and want to stay here with you; I can be the man of the house and I can look after things when you're away working, I know how to do it; I've watched Dad when he looks after us; we can get jobs to help.'

God love him, Carolyn thought. He was sitting on the edge of the couch, rubbing his hands over each other. She went over and held him in her arms, and he hugged her back hard. 'That is a lovely thought,' she said over his shoulder as they hugged each other, 'but I have already decided I will no longer work long-haul; I am going to stay here with you and Emma.'

'Really?' screamed Jonathan as he pushed her away; he re-hugged his Mum as Sarah and Emma returned to the study. Jonathan told Emma the good news about the end of long-haul flights for Mum and Emma joined the group hug, as did Sarah; they all held one another.

Carolyn was the first to break the group hug. 'Listen, I need you both to go with your grandpa, just for tonight and stay there because I need to talk to your father when he comes home.'

'What is going to happen, Mum?' asked Emma.

‘I am just going to ask him to leave until we get something sorted out.’

Jonathan was trying not to cry, but it was coming. ‘Will we still see Dad?’ he asked.

‘Of course you will, now please go and pack an overnight bag.’

Emma and Jonathan both headed out of the room. Emma turned and asked Carolyn, ‘Do we know her, Mummy?’ Jonathan had also stopped in his tracks. ‘No, honey, we don’t.’

They both left, their eyes puffy and red as they headed upstairs to their rooms. Carolyn turned to Sarah, ‘what do I do now?’ she asked.

‘I do not think you should let him in the house for starters, so packing him a bag would be a good start.’

The children appeared back in the lounge with their grandfather and overnight bags. Carolyn hugged and kissed them both before they left, and the girls headed upstairs to the bedroom. Carolyn felt sick; her heart was beating so fast; it was thirty minutes before Philip would arrive home. She handed various shirts, ties, socks, and boxer shorts to Sarah who was packing them into a suitcase. She felt sick at touching his underwear which she had just noticed were all designer and new – it made her skin crawl. Carolyn and Sarah packed a full case and a suit carrier, along with a sports bag of shoes.

They had barely sat down in the lounge when they heard the now unmistakable sound of the DB9 as it roared up the driveway. Carolyn went to the door and opened it, a photograph held behind her back. Sarah was positioning the case and bags in the hall.

Carolyn's heart was going like a train. She was scared about his reaction. Philip had got out of the car and was taking his jacket from the hook behind the driver's seat. 'Oh, hi babes, it's not often you open the door on my arrival, is everything okay?' He looked puzzled. 'Have you been drinking?' His words trailed off as he realised that the look on her face meant that something was not right.

Sarah's appearance at the door with a suitcase was adding to his confusion. 'Are you working tonight?' he asked, looking foolish until Sarah brought out his sports bag and suit carrier and piled them in the driveway. Philip was just about to ask what was going on when Carolyn thrust a photograph into his hand, one of him and Kelly kissing at The Ingilston Country Club.

'Go live with your fucking bitch whore! You are not getting back in this house, Philip Hughes; we are finished!' Philip's face was chalk white as he stared at the photograph in total shock.

'Now wait a minute, this is my house! You cannot throw me out for an innocent peck on the cheek! Have you lost your mind?' he shouted, as he crumpled up the photograph and threw it on the ground. 'Let's talk this over, Carolyn, before you make a big mistake; there was nothing to this, you must believe me! You have got it all wrong!'

Carolyn was livid that he could actually stand there and deny it, lying to her face. 'Is that right?' she screamed as she thrust more photographs into his hand, 8 x 6 glossies of Philip and Kelly having sex in the penthouse. Philip's face went chalk white.

Carolyn screamed 'Her name is Kelly; she owns a hairdresser's and lives in a penthouse in Partick, where you go most nights to fuck her! You even pay for her FUCKING CAR! YOU'RE FINISHED, LEAVE US ALONE!'

She ran into the house and Sarah quickly closed the door behind her as she ran upstairs to her room. Philip came to the door and tried to open it with his key, which did not work. He looked at it, puzzled, until the penny dropped. He then rang the bell and battered the door with his fist, shouting for Carolyn to let him in; he wanted to know where the children were. The ringing of the doorbell was interrupted every now and then by Philip calling the house phone from his mobile.

Carolyn sat on the bed crying; she could hear Sarah shouting to Philip that if he did not go away, she would call the police. Philip eventually left when he realized there were also a few neighbours watching. He picked up the photographs and put his belongings in the car. The roar of the Aston Martin could be heard throughout the entire estate as Philip screamed away. It was a noise Carolyn would never forget.

Chapter 20

Second Thoughts

Danny sat in his office at 9.20 am on a Sunday morning; he was troubled and thinking about part two of his con on Jenny. He somehow thought that this might just be a waste of time. Lesley was definitely not worth bothering about apart from a one-off sexual encounter to add to his total. Jenny was, however, well off financially but their conversation about them both using him sexually was playing on his mind. They were both attractive but too old for him to keep as playthings, and after what Jenny said to Lesley it looked like Jenny's money would not be easy to get.

His mind drifted off to the South of France, Switzerland and Italy which were three of his favourite places. Big scores were available from mega-rich old ladies looking for that handsome gigolo. Wealthy old broads who would hardly miss a couple of million. He needed to get his cash balance into the big one million mark. Switzerland was calling. He loved the entire Zermatt thing – the trains, the electric cars and taxis, the cafés, bars and restaurants, the mountains, and the skiing. Most importantly no-one gave a second look to a handsome single guy living the rich high life on the slopes. He blended in well there; the Swiss asked you no questions when you had money. It was very expensive, however. The chalet where he stayed cost three grand a week! It was, however, well worth the money. The chalet was set over three floors with stunning views of the Matterhorn;

the master bedroom was in the basement and boasted a jacuzzi bath and a glass power shower – it was total luxury. The entrance hall and bedroom number two were on the first floor and the kitchen with its German units and Bosch appliances was on the second, as was the dining room.
Danny's favourite was the top floor with its stunning views of the Hornli Ridge The property had expensive furniture, a wood burner, the Bang and Olufsen TV and hi-fi; he had copied a lot of its features into his own house.

He once asked the owner Danielle how much it would cost him to buy the chalet; her reply was a whopping 1.5 million Swiss francs. Out of reach at the moment, but you never know. Danny had spent four months there two years ago and had learned to ski at the Klein Matterhorn; his Italian female instructor who was incredibly beautiful had become his lover. He got tired of her after a couple of months and still managed to bed five other females during his stay.

His thoughts were rudely interrupted by Gordon's voice, 'What you up to, ya cunt? Do you have any appointments for today?' Gordon swore in a non-aggressive manner, but it was still annoying, Danny decided that this would probably be his last season here right enough, working with such retards was becoming boring, and Danny new he was much better than this. He decided to continue with the Jenny con; if it failed, he would be gone by the winter. Danny followed Gordon to his office and went over his weekend appointments and the stock list. He managed to sell a 2003 Cosalt caravan before 2 pm. Before closing up he led Janet into the ladies' toilet where he fucked her stupid before making her sit on the toilet and suck his cock again, finishing off by dispensing his huge amount of cum in her mouth; she dutifully swallowed the lot. Danny was on fire – he was the one in control of everyone. All that mattered was his own gratification and how well he lived his life; he hated everyone, man woman and child.

At 5 pm Danny headed for his lodge; he was satisfied sexually for now and fancied a night in on his own. He would love to have Natcha round to stay some nights but that was impossible because she could never get away from her perverted, possessive old wanker of a husband who only allowed her out to work. Danny cooked himself steak and chips, poured himself a cold beer and sat in front of the telly; it was Sunday night and Jenny and Lesley were due to leave tomorrow. By 7 pm Danny was on his first JD when his mobile vibrated on the table. One of his sluts no doubt; he felt in an abusive mood – some lucky lady was about to be fucked.

He picked up his phone; it was a text from Jenny. **Hi Danny, thanks for everything. It was fab to spend some time in your company; we both enjoyed it very much and we should have dinner on my return next week, my treat!**

Danny was angry because he knew she was playing him, and he did not like it one bit. He was more used to being in control; these bitches were not going to use him; he was going to take control of bedding them both before taking everything they own. **Yes Jenny dinner would be nice, I will see you at the lodge at 11am, next weekend for the hand over Danny x** Jenny replied **Fabulous see you then x**. He had to somehow gain back control quickly or he would have no chance of seeing any money. He was angry and aroused now, so he texted Barbara to see if she was on the park; she texted back that she would not be down until tomorrow and could see him then if he was free. Fucking great – this was turning out to be a real crap night, Danny turned on the TV, grabbed the JDs and spent a very boring night watching the box. Things had to change; he was getting fed up with this. If he could not extract any money from Jenny or Lesley, this summer could turn out to be a total waste of time. He was in bed by 10 pm and masturbated before falling asleep. His sleep was interrupted by bad dreams, none of which he had forgotten about by morning.

Chapter 21

All Fucked Up

Philip drove like a lunatic out of Castle Mains Estate, narrowly missing a badly parked Ford Focus on Castle Mains Road. He was livid, how dare she throw him out of his own house and keep him away from the children. He called Kelly on his hands-free, but her mobile went straight to voicemail. He drove straight to her penthouse; her car was there but she did not pick up the phone to buzz him in. Philip called both Emma's and Jonathan's mobiles again and their phones went straight to voicemail. What the fuck was going on? He called the house and Sarah answered. 'Thank God,' he said, 'let me speak to Carolyn.'

'FUCK OFF PHILIP,' was the reply from Sarah and she hung up. How fucking dare she! He dialled Carolyn's mobile which rang but was not answered; he sent her a text **Please answer your phone, we need to talk!** He tried Kelly's phone again, again – no answer; he placed his phone on the seat beside him and sat in his car outside her apartment, his head in his hands; this was a total fuck up! He would stay at Kelly's until this got sorted out; staying there might not be a bad thing short term but he would have to get Carolyn out of his house. He wanted it back and had no intention of living in Partick; Kelly could move in with him. His phone vibrated on the seat beside him. Thank God, thought Philip as he grabbed his phone and typed in his password. It was an e-mail from Carolyn – at least she was communicating, he thought. The e-mail read 'This is what your slut was doing the night before she slept with you, YOU'RE A FOOL!'

Philip waited for the attachment to open and when it did, he could not believe his eyes. It was Kelly squatting in front of her bed sucking a guy's cock; he was in his 30s, handsome with a tan and a six pack and very well endowed. Who the fuck was this? Philip stared at the picture, his heart racing; the shock, however, was short-lived. Kelly would not do this to him, why would she? It was a fake, it was nothing. Carolyn's warped and jealous mind had done this. She had obviously taken an image of Kelly and photoshopped it to look like she was cheating on him. Nice try, bitch; if it's hard ball you want, then hard ball you will get. You only had to look at the guy to realise he was a porn star or a model.

He felt better and dialled his mate Kenny's number. They both agreed to meet in Òran Mór, a converted church in Byres Road, which was now a pub. Philip drove out of the parking lot just as Kelly and Paul walked out of her penthouse arm-in-arm heading for a local restaurant before going to a club for some cocaine and champagne.

Philip drove past Kelly's salon, but it was already closed; he then drove up to the top end of Byres Road where he parked the Aston Martin; he would hang out here with Kenny till Kelly got back. The Aston always got admiring looks from males and females alike; he was beginning to feel better, and the shock was now wearing off. Philip smiled as he walked over to the cash line. It was a Friday night; £500 should just about cover a few drinks and a meal with his best friend, maybe some champagne to celebrate his future with Kelly. Kenny was a good mate and had provided many alibis of nights out at the golf club or golfing weekends away so that Philip could be with Kelly even when Carolyn was not working. Philip had sent Kenny away on a few expensive trips that Philip did not go on; instead, he would go with Kelly for a weekend or even longer. He had, of course, paid for Kenny's trips, once even to Spain.

Philip punched in his password and pressed a withdrawal of £500. The card was immediately spat out by the machine, the message reading 'INSUFFICIENT FUNDS'! What the FUCK!!

He put his card in again and pressed display balance; it read £10.20p. Jesus Christ, that bitch had taken the entire £36,000 from their joint account. Philip was raging. He managed to use his credit card for a cash withdrawal, this was granted, and he headed for Òran Mór. Fuming, he needed a drink and some food. He sat at the bar talking to a couple of girls in their late twenties while he waited for Kenny – he still had the charm and the looks. Kenny appeared around a half hour later; both ordered food and a couple of drinks and sat at a table. Philip filled Kenny in on the day's events; he tried Kelly a few more times and left her a message. She must be busy he thought, maybe at her Mum's.

After their meal the boys headed for the bar again which was full of male and female talent; a few local celebs were around, TV stars, footballers and the like who liked to hang out in the West End area as it was a cool place to be seen. Philip drowned his sorrows with more booze. Carolyn was messing up his life and he did not like it; he would report her to the police for stealing the £36k, not tonight though as he was too busy knocking back gin and tonics and having a good time; there was always tomorrow. Philip and Kenny had a great night and got drunker as the night went on.

About 12.30am Philip noticed Kenny had disappeared with a girl and Philip was left with her twenty-something friend who he would have slept with if he was not so drunk. Kenny was probably doing exactly that with her pal; he had been chatting her up all night. Philip decided he did not fancy spending the night with the twenty-something whose name he could not remember. It was time for him to call it a night and head to Kelly's. He walked out of Òran Mór and headed straight for the Aston. He was a little bit tipsy but was not going to leave the car parked on Byres Road all night for some jealous prick to key it for sure. Anyway, it was less than a mile to Kelly's. He arrived there after driving the short distance without incident. Her car was there but there were still no lights on in the penthouse. Philip decided to walk over to the entrance and press the buzzer again anyway, He opened the door of the car and fell onto the tarmac.

'OOPS,' he said as he tried to get back on his feet. 'I must have drunk more than I thought,' he mumbled to himself as he sat upright on the cold ground facing his car door. He got his mobile out and called her number, again – it was switched off.

Philip was angry that the one and only time he needed her she was nowhere to be found. He was very drunk and very angry. Fuck Kelly, he thought. 'I am going home to my fucking house!' he shouted to himself. He called Carolyn but she was still not answering her phone. Kelly must have decided to stay the night at her Mum's, as she often did when she took her mother to the bingo. But why not take her car, he thought. Fuck it, Philip decided he was going to confront Carolyn about the money she stole and about the picture she made up of Kelly. Bloody bitch, he thought, she could sleep in the spare room. Philip would talk to the children in the morning and throw Carolyn out on her arse.

Philip's drive on the way home was a blur of Deacon Blue music and people shouting abuse at him and the sound of car horns. Fuck them, he thought, just because he drove an Aston Martin did not mean he should take abuse from people. At last, he swung the powerful car into the drive. He could see the bedroom lights were still on; good, he thought. Suddenly there was an almighty crash and the airbag deployed; it hurt his face and burnt his arms. Fuck's sake, he had driven the car straight into the double garage doors, hitting the brick pillar in the middle; there were bricks all over the bonnet.

'Jesus,' he roared as he fought off the airbag, nearly in tears, cursing. He fell out of the car for the second time that night. He was helped to his feet by Bill Porter or Mr Goody-two-shoes, who lived next door. Someone behind him shouted they were calling the police. 'Fuck you,' he yelled at the top of his voice, 'and fuck my wife and fuck the police, in fact fuck you all!!!! Except my children. I want to see my children.'

'Please that's enough Philip, look at what you have done. The children are not here; you didn't think I wanted them to stay in the middle of all this, did you?' Carolyn had appeared at the front door.

'Look what you've done to my new car, you thieving bitch,' he screamed as he tried to push Carolyn out of the way.

Carolyn somehow managed to push him back; he fell over the paving between the driveway and the lawn and landed back on the driveway. He could smell engine oil as he landed back on the drive; it was wet with fluid. He was trying to get up when a male and a female appeared at each side, and both helped him to his feet. 'Thank you,' he said as he tried to focus on their faces.

'Sir, you're under arrest. You're coming with us; anything you say or do may be used against you in a court of law,' said the police officer who was now hurting his arms which were being pushed and held behind his back.

'Leave me the fuck alone, I want to see my kids and she says they're not here. This is her fault; arrest that bitch, not me. She stole my money! Get these fucking things off me!' The officers emptied Philip's pockets before walking him to the police car sitting at the kerb with all its flashing blue and red lights. He was man-handled into the back of the car and the door slammed behind him. Left alone in the back of the car, Philip noticed the street was full of people on the pavement and even in the drive, looking at his car.

'What are you all staring at?' he shouted, 'go home, you fucking boring weirdos, get a life, go on, fuck off!' Philip could see Goody-two-shoes Bill and Carolyn talking to the two police officers in front of the bay window in the lounge. 'This is all her fault,' he shouted, 'I fucking hate you, Bitch! You will be left with nothing! You're a fat ugly old cow and a thief!' The two police officers swiftly returned to the car, and both took off their hats and sat in the front.

'You should arrest her, not me; she stole £36k from me!'

'You can make a complaint at the station, Sir,' said the male cop.

'What about my car? You can't just leave it there!' screamed Philip.

'Your car will be collected and taken to the police pound,' replied the officer.

'What police pound; where are you taking me?' he shouted at the two officers.

'To Maryhill police station,' came the reply from the female officer.

The car reversed into the driveway and headed back the way it came. Philip could see more people on the street. Nosey bastards, he thought. On the drive to the police station Philip was beginning to realise what a fucking mess he was in; he could not believe that 24 hours ago he was living the perfect life and now he was in a clusterfuck from hell; he needed Kelly.

His thoughts were interrupted as the car had arrived at the rear door of Maryhill Police station; it had only taken twenty minutes to get there. Philip was marched up to the booking desk where a sergeant asked the officers the charges. He was charged with driving under the influence, criminal damage, and a breach of the peace. Philip asked to use the phone, which was refused; the desk sergeant instead took all his details, and his belongings included his belt. He was then taken to a cell where his shoes were placed outside, and he was given a blanket. Whilst waiting for the police officer to open his cell, he heard the person in the adjacent cell busy kicking the steel door of his cell, interrupted intermittently with the shout of 'Bastards!' Philip had never seen inside a cell as he had never been arrested before, and this one was not nice.

As he walked into the cell there was a toilet to his left-hand side with no apparent way of flushing it. On the wall facing the door there was a small window at ceiling height with steel bars, and below that there was a concrete slab about four inches thick, which apparently was the bed. The police officer said he would check on him every hour. Philip, exhausted, sat down on the slab and put the heavy rough blanket round his shoulders. He noticed the slogans scratched, and what looked like burned, on the walls and ceilings. TONGS YA BASS, FUCK THE POLIS, TAMS A DEAD MAN, MARYHILL YOUNG TEAM, SHAZ SUCKS

COCKS FOR FREE were just a few of the writings on the walls – were these people for real? How the hell did they burn things? What did they use to scratch the walls? Philip was confused and felt like shit.

He needed Kelly; he should not be here; he was now living a nightmare; this was all Carolyn's fault; they could have discussed this amicably, and why the fuck was Kelly not answering his calls? Philip lay down on the concrete slab and tried to cover himself with the hairy blanket which smelled of pee or vomit or something, but it was cold in the cell, and he wanted to keep warm.

He lay there, the bright light on the ceiling hurting his eyes. He was in a pile of shit and he knew it. He sat back up; he would have to sort things out, speak to a lawyer in the morning and then move in with Kelly short-term. How long before morning, he thought? He looked at his wrist – no Rolex; the police took it; he had no idea what time it was, but it must be at least 4 am. He lay back down on the cold slab and closed his eyes; he was tired and wanted to sleep. Philip doubted if he would get any sleep as the lunatic in the next cell had started kicking the door again and had changed his chant to THE MONSTERS ARE COMING! THE MONSTERS ARE COMING!

Chapter 22

The Morning After

This was probably the worst Sunday Carolyn could ever remember; her entire world was in disarray. The police had called to say that Philip was held overnight at the Maryhill police office; he had been charged with driving under the influence and much more, was now free to go and would appear in court at a later date. He had also accused her of stealing from him. The police were coming to the house later to take a statement about the alleged theft.

She first phoned Kenny who sounded as if he was still drunk and still in bed and told him that his buddy needed a lift from the police office and informed him not to bring Philip back home as he was no longer welcome there and that it was probably best to take him to his slut girlfriend's place. She then texted Frank to ask his advice; he informed her that due to the bank account being in joint names she had nothing to worry about and did not need a solicitor as there was no theft; the police were simply doing their job by taking a statement. Frank was happy to come to the house if she wanted some support, Carolyn thanked him but declined as Sarah was there and her Dad was coming round shortly with the kids. She sat at the breakfast bar with Sarah. 'I need to go round and talk to one of the neighbours and explain about last night,' said Carolyn. Sarah agreed; this whole thing had turned into a bigger mess than they had expected and seemed to be getting worse. 'I feel like running away,' said Carolyn. **'Why don't we!'** yelled Sarah, 'it's the Easter break next weekend; the kids are off school, and I am off work; it would do us all the world of good especially the kids. Dad won't come, but he can stay here and keep an eye on things.'

Sarah was right, she had the weekend to recover before consulting a lawyer about the divorce on Monday; she could also contact her work and request more time off to deal with the situation. 'Okay, Sarah, if you are sure it's a good idea, see if you can find anything online, but not anything abroad; I don't want to be too far away from Dad.'

The girls hugged each other, and Carolyn went out to visit her neighbour, leaving Sarah to ring her husband, Bob who was very sympathetic and told his wife to assure Carolyn that she was doing the right thing by divorcing Philip; he thought she deserved much better than this. Bob was happy to keep an eye on Dad and the house if they decided to go away.

Carolyn visited Jo, another close friend and neighbour, who witnessed the entire unfortunate episode. Carolyn explained the entire story from start to finish. Jo was upset and hoped everything would turn out alright; Jo was always there if Carolyn needed her.

Carolyn returned to the house about an hour later; she was feeling a little stronger after her conversation with Jo and learning about Bob's reaction and his offer to take care of their father.

‘What have you found, sis?’ asked Carolyn as she closed the kitchen door.

‘Unfortunately, there is not much available; most of the cottages and hotels are now fully booked but remember the Easter break we had in a caravan park in Blackpool?’

‘Yes,’ said Carolyn, ‘it was fun.’

‘Well, girl, there is a lodge available in a caravan park in Argyll; its only about an hour and a half’s drive from here and the park has its own gym, a pool and lots of activities for the kids – it looks fab.’

Carolyn joined her at the table and they both surveyed the photographs displayed on the web page. It did look good, Carolyn thought. Just then the kids walked in with their grandfather. ‘Hi guys.’ Hugs all around. ’How would you both like to go on a short Easter break?’ said Carolyn. ‘Yes please,’ replied the kids; most of their friends were going away and it would be nice to go somewhere too, they said.

Everybody was in agreement and their Easter break was quickly booked online; they would arrive exactly a week from today, ‘High fives all round, everyone,’ shouted Carolyn, ‘DUNOON HERE WE COME.’

Philip felt like shit as he lay in his cell, the monster shouter had eventually stopped shouting but not until 4 am; hopefully he had died of a drug overdose. Philip’s head hurt like hell, and he needed to use the bathroom, but he was not going to sit on that disgusting toilet. A police officer from the morning shift came round with breakfast which consisted of a bacon butty and a cup of tea.

Philip devoured it because he was absolutely starving. The officer informed him that he had been charged with drink driving and resisting arrest. He also informed him that Kenny was coming to get him in the next hour. Kenny! Philip thought, how does he know where he is, and where the fuck is Kelly? Philip asked for his mobile phone, this was refused point blank and would be returned to him on his departure. He had no idea how much time had passed that morning before the same officer returned; time passes so very slowly when you are locked in a cell and with no watch to look at every minute, it felt like an hour. He thankfully walked out of the cell and picked up his shoes, the removal of which was apparently to stop prisoners from hanging themselves with their shoelaces. The officer took Philip back to the booking desk; he could see Kenny was sitting in the hallway looking a little confused and the worse for wear. The sergeant behind the desk shoved a brown A4 envelope across the counter, giving Philip a stinker of a look as he did so. He started to read from the list written on the back of the envelope as he started to remove the contents. He shouted out, 'One Rolex watch, one brown leather wallet, one hundred and forty pounds in cash, one gold wedding band' and slammed the envelope down on the counter.

Philip collected his belongings and was escorted through the locked doors to the waiting Kenny. 'What the fuck is going on, buddy?'

'Let's get out of here, I have just spent the worst fucking night of my life.'

They walked along the corridor heading for the exit. Philip called Kelly's house phone, but she did not answer. 'Fuck, where the hell is she?' he yelled. They both got into Kenny's car. 'How did you know I was here?'

'Carolyn called me, she said you were not to go back to the house.'

'Brilliant, this is her fucking fault. I have wrecked the Aston, spent a night in jail, been robbed by my bitch wife and cannot even go and see the kids.'

'Jesus, Philip, where do you want to go?' asked Kenny.

'I don't have anywhere to go; can we go to yours, just for today? I need some sleep and I need to find Kelly. Do you mind if I crash in your spare room until I can sort something out?'

Kenny nodded, 'Yeah sure; let's go.'

On the drive over Philip told Kenny what had happened after Kenny had left the pub with the chick. Kenny was stunned at how quickly Philip's life was turning to shit. 'Bloody hell, Philip, I am so sorry, what are you going to do now?'

Philip explained he intended to stay at Kelly's for a short time and on Monday he would hire the best divorce lawyer he could find with a view to tossing Carolyn out of the house and getting custody of the kids. Both men had now arrived at Kenny's two-bedroom flat in Milngavie; it was above Philips optician's in the shopping precinct and was owned by Philip's company.

Their intention was to both go back to bed and get some sleep. Kenny showed Philip into the spare bedroom and left him to catch up on some much-needed sleep. Kenny also returned to his own bed which was now vacant of the horny little slut he had taken home from the pub last night. Kenny had dropped the girl off at Milngavie station after he got the call from Carolyn.

Chapter 23

Kelly's Night Out

Kelly was awakened by Paul, who was lying in bed beside her in a spooning position, and you know what girls say, spooning always leads to forking. He lay on his side behind her. One arm under her neck was clutching her breast while his other hand was on her hip. He slid his erect penis inside her; she lifted her leg to allow him easier access as they both lay on their sides facing the shipyard on the opposite side of the river. Paul started slowly at first before quickening up into a fast hard fuck and they both exploded in synchronised orgasms. Kelly sometimes loved being with Paul so much that she forgot about everything else. Philip was a nice sugar daddy who could give her things that she wanted, but sex with Paul was something else. Kelly lay in bed; this was a lovely way to start a Saturday morning. Paul was still horny and lay face down on the bed, groping between her legs. Kelly, however, had things to do and Philip to see later. She gave Paul a friendly slap on his backside as she leapt out of bed and headed for the shower.

Paul never gave up and joined her; she decided it was best to please him as she needed him out of here asap. She had to get the place cleaned up for Philip coming and she still had to go to the salon and the supermarket. Paul fucked her against the shower wall before turning her round and bending her over for some anal; they both finished by soaping and rinsing each other off.

Kelly stuck on a robe and made them both a coffee, after which Paul headed into the bedroom to get dressed. He started his three-day stint at the fire station today, starting at 2 pm and had to go home to get ready.

Thank fuck, she thought, some time to herself would be nice. Kelly turned on the radio and plugged her iPhone into the charger on the kitchen unit; her phone had died on her last night, and she was aware that she had not texted Philip since Friday morning. Her phone burst into life as soon as the charger was switched on. Kelly could not believe it – there were 16 missed calls from Philip plus five Voicemails. There were also a dozen texts. **Please call me asap x, / where are you x? /Kelly call me please/are you home yet babes xx/Kelly where the hell are you I need to talk to you! /call me when you get this x**

Bloody hell, Kelly thought, something's gone down, it was not like Philip to be so persistent when he could not reach her. She immediately dialled his number which went straight to voicemail. Kelly was concerned something was not right; this was so out of character for Philip and so she sent him a text **Hi babes hope you're okay, I left my phone at my mums, please call me when you can, I am worried, love you xxx.** Fireman Sam left shortly after breakfast leaving Kelly time to tidy up the apartment and then head out for some shopping. She checked her phone again. Still no word from Philip; what the fuck has happened? Kelly did the food shop in a trance she walked round Asda supermarket dressed up as if she was going on a night out.

She was unaware, as she always was, of people looking at her and thinking to themselves what a stupid tart she really looked, dressed from head to toe in designer clothes and accessories while doing the shopping.

Philip woke up in Kenny's flat wishing he could turn back the clock, Carolyn was finished, but he had fucked up big time. He was out of the house; he had wrecked his new car and would probably lose his driving licence. His mobile was charging on the floor; he unplugged it and turned it on; there was a text from Kelly. Reading the message, he thought thank God she was okay, but she could not have picked a worse time to forget her phone. Philip dialled her number and she answered right away.

'Jesus, babes where the hell have you been? I have been worried sick,' said Philip. Kelly explained that she had been at her Mum's and then went out with the girls, leaving her phone at her Mum's by accident. Philip told her briefly what was going on and they both agreed to meet at her flat. Kelly was worried Philip had been thrown out of the house, which could seriously impact her freedom and her relationship with Paul. She quickly finished her food shop and drove back round to her apartment. Philip was already there. He was standing outside and looked like shit; he walked over to her parking spot and threw his arms around her, practically crushing her.

'Jesus, Philip, you're hurting me.'

'Sorry, babes I just need you right now. It's been a living hell.' He helped her remove the carrier bags from the 4 x 4 and they headed towards the elevator. Philip started from the beginning, telling her what Carolyn had done. Kelly made him a coffee which he needed badly, and she suggested he take a shower. Philip did as she suggested, giving her time to think of what she was going to do next. Philip wanted to move into the penthouse with her and that was a huge problem! What the fuck was she going to tell Paul? Her mind raced. He was at the fire station for the next three days and nights, so it was not an immediate problem.

Philip emerged from the shower looking unshaven but a lot better than he did when she first saw him. He had suggested he stay with her until he got a divorce and got the house back and they could then move in together with the children. Kelly nearly died! Would rather die than move in with Philip; she was quite happy with her current life, thank you very much.

She made them both dinner and he spent the entire night talking about Carolyn, the kids, the house and himself while knocking back the booze! Kelly was glad when he went to bed and fell asleep. Something that did not come easy for Kelly that night; it looked like Philip – and their relationship too – was just about to come to an end. That would mean she would lose her car and lots of other goodies and that nice financial security she had. This weekend was turning out to be a fucking disaster. She tossed and turned the entire night.

Chapter 24

Blow off

Danny was getting fed up working on the holiday park. He would prefer to spend his time travelling or at home eating good food and drinking alcohol than working at the sales office. He would also like to spend more time flying around Scotland, especially when the weather was good. He liked to bunny hop the islands and fuck local lassies. He would promise to love them before leaving them, flying off into the sunset, promising to return, which of course he never did. Island girls were easy; they were usually bored and fed up with male chauvinist local boys and always welcomed a change. Sex and drugs were a welcome change from island boredom. like living in Alaska where drug crimes were high, as were suicides. It's a lonely existence.

Danny felt he was wasting his time here on this caravan park and time was what was running out, and fast! If he wanted to reach his millionaire status while he was still young enough to enjoy it then maybe this was not the place for him; the pickings were too lean. It looked like Jenny was not going to be a walk in the park and he was getting sick of fucking old bitches for money. This was the reason he had never became an escort as the thought of having to do that every day made him sick.

He got out of bed, showered and dressed. He had breakfast before driving down to the sales office; same old shit, different day, he said to himself. The words had hardly left his mouth when he rounded the bend to be met by a female jogger running ahead of him on the road. She had a cracking ass wrapped in tight black jogging pants with white stripes down the outside leg. Her blonde hair was tied up in a ponytail. Danny slowed and watched as her ass pumped away. The 5mph speed limit allowed Danny to draw up level with her. She was very pretty, maybe about forty, a little on the rounded side, but hot and sexy, nevertheless. The blonde looked across at Danny and smiled. He could not resist and powered down the driver's window. 'Morning,' he said.

'Good morning,' said the blonde.

'Are you here on holiday?' asked Danny as he drove down the hill with one foot on the brake and one eye on the road ahead, giving the blonde his full 24 carat smile. The blonde stopped running, bent forward slightly and with both hands on her knees. He could see down her vest top. She had a great pair of titties. 'Yes I am.'

Danny stopped, got out of the car and shoved out his hand. Blondie wiped her hand on her leggings and shook his. 'My name is Danny.'

'Carolyn.'

'I work down at the sales office; how long are you here for?'

'Just the week, until Saturday,' said the blonde.

'Would you like me to show you around, maybe buy you lunch while you are here?'

'No thank you. I am here with my sister, sorry, and besides, I am married.'

'I apologise,' said Danny, 'I did not see any wedding ring and just assumed you were unattached.'

'Look, if you don't mind, I would like to finish my run; it was nice to meet you, Danny; goodbye.'

The blonde bitch called Carolyn just blew Danny off as if he were nothing. He was left at the side of the road as the blonde jogged off into the woods that led to Pucks Glen. He was fucking fuming. The bitch practically told him to fuck off! He continued his journey and parked outside the sales office. Janet was on reception with Carol who was dealing with a customer. Danny signalled for her to follow him to the gents; he went inside and looked in the mirror.

Janet followed shortly behind; he grabbed her hair and walked her into a cubicle where he bent her over the toilet and lifted her summer dress and then pulled down her panties. Janet tried to object, but Danny was having none of it. He pulled out his erect penis and forced it inside Janet's pussy; she was not exactly wet and let out a stifled cry as Danny thrust his cock inside her. It was all over in a matter of minutes. Danny sipped up his fly, slapped her hard on the ass and left her to fix herself; he was enjoying having a sex slave at work, someone to fuck at the office when he felt like it.

He headed for the kitchen and put the kettle on, watching Janet as she walked past the doorway looking a little flustered;

this amused Danny – she was, after all, one of his sex bitches whom he would treat whichever way he liked. If she did not like it, she could fuck off. He made himself a cup of tea, Gordon was off today, and the freedom was welcome. He walked into reception behind the counter, gave Janet a cheeky smile and took out the identity card box sitting next to the laminator Every holidaymaker had their picture taken when they arrived which was then put onto an ID card. This was to allow them entry through the barriers and on to the park and it was also ID for the various venues in the complex.

Danny flicked through the various ID cards before coming to the one he wanted. Her name was Carolyn Hughes from Milngavie near Glasgow, an air stewardess, staying in Eagle lodge number seven with her sister and two children; the sister was average, but the daughter was cute. Danny took a note of Carolyn's mobile number before heading for his office. He sat down at his desk, looked at the number and immediately headed back out of his office. He told Janet he was heading out for ten minutes, grabbed the keys for number 6 Eagle row and headed in the direction of the lodges.

Danny did not drive his car into Eagle row, instead parking in number 12 Osprey which was behind eagle 7. He let himself in just as Carolyn appeared back from her run; she looked sweaty as she sat down outside on the decking. Her sister came out and passed her a bottle of water. Danny stood at the open window of the lounge; the blinds were partly closed, but he could hear them quite clearly.

'How did your run go, sis?'

'It was fine, honey, yeah it was good, and my time was good over that distance.'

'So there is hope of you getting fit, losing a few pounds and finding a new man,' joked her sister, laughing as Carolyn flicked water at her from the bottle and disappeared inside. Danny watched Carolyn from the window as he masturbated standing up. He watched his cum spurt all over the curtains. He smiled, put his cock back in his pants and headed back to the Black Pearl. He did not return to the office, but instead drove up the hill to his own lodge. He texted Janet and told her he would be at his lodge; if anyone was looking for him, she was to call him on his mobile right away. Carolyn chatted to Sarah before going for a shower. The children were now up and out of bed, and they all had breakfast together; this break was a great idea and just what they all needed. The foursome planned their day ahead. First on the agenda would be to pick up their ID cards before they left the park; they had been told that failing to do so would mean the hassle of getting past the security barrier on their way back later that day. They were heading into Dunoon to do a food shop and look around the various curio shops in the town. Carolyn had seen one online called Doon The Watter where she saw a bracelet she wanted to buy for her sister.

Sarah had been brilliant supporting her, as Philip and her divorce were always at the back of her mind, but she tried to keep it there and not let it spoil her trip. Dunoon was fabulous and she managed to leave Sarah browsing in a charity shop, something Sarah did often. This allowed her the time to pop into the shop and purchase the bracelet without Sarah even noticing she was gone. The girl who served her was chatty and, after finding out she was staying at the caravan park, told her to watch out for Danny. Carolyn never let on that she had already encountered him, and the sales lady's comment made her laugh. Carolyn was well used to dealing with handsome pilots who loved themselves, and she would be able to handle the handsome sales guy easily.

She returned to the Barnado's charity shop where Sarah was still browsing. The girls and the kids later went for a fish tea and a chip butty on the pier, something they had not done for years. They all looked on in wonder as the Waverley docked and unloaded its cargo of happy day trippers from Glasgow; everyone was having a fab time. The girls' holiday was turning out just fine. Carolyn's thoughts turned to the handsome Danny; she was a bit hard on him and he was fabulously good looking and sexy, well dressed and well mannered. He just drove up at the wrong time, just as she was thinking about Philip's adultery. She thought male company and lunch would not be proper at this time, especially with a hot hunk, but if she saw him again a light apology might be in order.

Back on the park, Danny meantime lay in his lounge. He had closed all his curtains and lay on the sofa. He had removed his tie and had his arm now covered his eyes. He could not understand why he was so pissed off, perhaps because nothing was going right, and everything was standing still and not moving fast enough. Jenny looked like she only intended to use him for sex; parting her from her cash looked like it was not going to happen. The teenager was a mistake, something which Danny did not usually make, and it riled him that he fell into her honey trap. It could have turned out badly if he had been caught with the youngster; thankfully he had not been, but he was mad, nonetheless. The blonde Carolyn had also brushed him aside as if he were nothing. He would watch for her tomorrow morning; he was not finished with her. Fuck it, he thought, pick yourself up and get back to work.

Chapter 25

Katie

Danny sat in his office watching a squirrel do squirrel things on the grass beside a tree; he had no idea what it was doing, and he was not much of an animal lover anyway. He had once drowned a cat just for the hell of it; he actually enjoyed watching it die. There was a knock on his open office door; a young female stood in the doorway wearing shorts and a Fred Perry style short-sleeved shirt bearing the company logo; she obviously worked in the leisure center.

'Hi Danny, is it?' She walked, hand extended, towards him. She was about 25 years old with jet black hair, nice perky tits, small waist and long legs; she had fuck me written all over her. Danny stood up and shook the girl's hand.

'My name is Katie, and I am the new lifeguard at the pool. Today is my first day and I am going around everywhere introducing myself.' Happy Fucking Easter, Danny thought, His day just went from ground zero to outer fucking space.

'Hi Katie, I'm Danny in sales; do you live locally or are you living on site?'

'Lol, no, I live in Dumfries, so I am sharing a caravan with another lifeguard from Poland.'

'God, you're just a baby; you don't look old enough to be away from home. How old are you?'

'I am twenty-five and old enough lol.'

Danny liked this slim pretty little chick very much. 'Listen Katie, in fact give me your mobile number and when I get a chance, I will call you and show you around.'

'Yes, I would like that.' She smiled her lovely smile. 'It's 07788991011; I look forward to my tour,' she laughed.

'Me too, Katie, me too.' His cock was starting to grow in his Calvin Kleins. This young vixen was flirting with him; there was no time like the present; this girl was asking for it.

'Katie, actually, what are you doing tonight?'

'Nothing,' she said, 'not found my way around yet; that's your job, Danny boy.'

'Cool, what time do you get off?'

'Nine.'

'It's a bit late for dinner; do you fancy meeting for a drink? I can pick you up and we can head into town. I can show you some local pubs.'

'Yes, that would be great. I am in the caravan behind the leisure club.'

'Okay, Katie, I will pick you up at 9.30 pm?'

'Okay,' she said and smiled that beautiful smile. 'Thank you; see you then.' She shook his hand and held it. She was petite and sexy, and Danny watched her cute ass as she left the office; he could not wait to taste it. He was now on a high. Where the fuck did she come from? He walked out of his office; Janet was off today so no chance of a blowjob, and Carol on reception was a stuck-up cow. He decided to leave for the day, very excited about spending time with the smiling Katie and much more.

Carolyn, Sarah and the kids had a great day in Dunoon and had returned to the lodge. Both the children had retired to their rooms to do teenager stuff in private. The women sat in the lounge planning their next trip, for the following day. They decided that after Carolyn's morning run, they would drive up to Inveraray, visit the castle and gardens and have lunch in the small coastal town. The Vital Spark and old Clyde puffer were there which they wanted to visit. They sat on the sofa watching the evening news. 'How are you bearing up, sis?' asked Sarah.

'I am fine, babes, just hurting and a little numb but not as scared as I was at first though, and I really think we will be fine after it's all over.'

Jonathan burst from his bedroom clutching a leaflet, a look of excitement on his face. 'They're showing *AVATAR* tonight at the centre! Can we go?' He passed the leaflet to Carolyn.

'I don't see why not; it starts at eight and you are both capable of walking there; if you don't mind, I think we will give it a miss.'

Sarah jumped up next and ran to the dining table, also returning with a leaflet. 'You can come with me for a pamper and spa!'

'Yes,' they all agreed and returned to what they were doing.

Danny went to the local Chinese takeaway and bought a beef curry with boiled rice for his dinner. He had been trying to bed the Chinese girl at the counter since last year but without success. He loved her femininity, her high-pitched voice, the way she dressed, dark hair in pigtails, knee-high socks and short skirt like a mini kilt and a short, cropped blouse that showed off her belly button – like a schoolgirl but legal. She was about 19 years old, sexy as hell and Danny imagined his large cock sliding into her tight small dark wet pussy. He imagined Katie would be equally as tight as the girls were both about the same size. He drove back onto the park and headed for his lodge. Katie was now back at the pool. She had seen Danny the day she came for her interview and knew then she wanted to fuck him; he was so hot!

When she got the job, he was the first thing that came into her mind; everyone talked about how handsome and sexy he was. Katie would lie in bed thinking about him until she was wet and could not stand it anymore and would masturbate until she came. Danny did not know it yet, but Katie was insatiable in bed and could fuck for hours. She often thought of getting into porn and loved all sorts of kinky stuff; she had countless lovers and lost her virginity at fourteen with her Dad's friend Kevin. Katie's small build and bone structure meant her pussy was as tight as the day she first accepted Kevin's lame excuse for a penis inside her; he had been a total disappointment and came in seconds.

It was now 8.30 pm as Katie sat on her high seat above the pool; every male in the place had hit on her as soon as she arrived which was to be expected as she was the prettiest girl in the place.

For now, though, her skills and body would be for only one man and that man was Danny; she could not wait to see him. He was hot and sexy, dangerous and rough, just exactly what she wanted; he did not know it yet, but he owed her big style. The next hour seemed like a week. Katie stopped work at 9 pm and headed straight for the showers, then to the caravan and looked out a pair of boots, a very short skirt, no panties, no bra and a white top. Glass of wine in hand, she waited for Danny who eagerly arrived right on time. He got out of the car. Little Miss Hottie Katie was out on the decking and dressed to kill.

'Hi, Danny,' she said. This was his Easter Bunny, and he was going to eat it all up. 'Listen, Katie, you look fab, but its 9.30 and a Monday night in Dunoon; by the time we go out it will be time to come back; do you fancy a drink at my place instead?'

'Yes, Danny, that will be fine.'

Danny was gobsmacked this was so easy. He held the door open for her and got an eyeful of her shaved pussy as she got into the front seat. He could not believe his eyes – she was not even wearing panties; he could not wait to get this honey pot back to his place. She looked awesome as she sat next to him, no longer looking like a cheerleader as she did earlier, but more of a purring sex kitten. He opened the door of the lodge and showed her inside. 'Wow,' she said, 'I need to get into sales; this is way better than my accommodation.'

'What would you like to drink, young lady?' 'Anything, Danny.' 'JDs and coke okay?' 'Yes, fine, thanks.'

Danny poured Katie a drink, walked over to her as she stood in the lounge, handed her her drink and immediately ran his hand over and under her skirt, his hand reaching her neat little pussy, Katie spread her legs. She was tight – very tight even for Danny's finger. He removed his hand just as quickly as he had put it there and put his fingers in his mouth. Katie's eyes were alive; they both put down their drinks and started undressing each other, Danny's cock popping out of his boxers as soon as Katie had lowered them – it was rock hard. She squatted and took it straight in her mouth, deep throating his entire cock all the way to his balls. He could not believe after all the lovers he'd had – at least 200 – he was mesmerized by this fit 25-year-old sex goddess.

He lifted her up and slipped his cock into her tight warm pussy. She wrapped her legs around him as he carried her over to the kitchen worktop where he set her down. They both watched his massive hard cock slide in and out of her pussy. Danny was wrapped in her smell, her taste, her look. Her hair was draped over his head and her top lip had little beads of salty sweat on it. She came all over his cock and his balls, her juices soaking the base of his erect penis. They both kissed and fondled each other, and Danny sucked her nipples as she dug her nails into his tight hard ass. She had four orgasms before Danny walked her over to the sofa where he lay her down.

'You are an amazingly dirty girl,' he said. Katie just lay there and smiled; she was perfect in every way. 'Where is the bedroom?' she asked. Danny smiled, grabbed the booze and took her to the bedroom. The entire night was a marathon of no holds barred sex; they were both fit and both highly sexed. Four hours later they both slept entwined together, exhausted – this was the closest Danny had come to being in love and Katie missed her second day at work.

Chapter 26

Softly, Softly, Catchee Monkey

Danny awoke the next day to find his bed empty. Katie must have gone to work; she did mention she started at 6 am; it was stupid of him not to notice she had left. He would have to add her to his little list of playmates, which was growing by the day. He would normally be at home today; however, he had an important task to do. He got out of bed and dressed in black Nike shorts and vest top. For the first time in a long time Danny did not go to the gym; his other agenda would not be in the gym that morning; she would hopefully be out running.

Runners and joggers usually adhered to a time, a pattern and a route. Carolyn was staying at the park for the week so he imagined she would run every morning. He had not been on a run for ages, usually preferring the treadmill at the gym with its ease of use, TV screen and the talent using the other equipment. Today was an exception, today was the start of a relentless campaign of charm and wit to convince the blonde jogging Carolyn how fantastic he really was and why she belonged to him and belonged in his bed.

Danny walked out on the decking. It was another beautiful morning at the park, and he was having mixed emotions which were worrying and confusing; he should really see a psychiatrist but knew he would not. He had lived with his demons this long on his own and could never confide in anyone about what he had done. He was, however, completely confused as to how he was either on a massive high – usually when he was fucking chicks and making money – followed by a massive low when things were shit, like the teenager for instance.

He would have to do something about this and soon, but he had no idea what, though. He saw the blonde pigtail bounce and bob just above the hedge and heading in the same direction he met her last time. Danny sprinted off the deck and headed in Carolyn's direction, catching sight of her as soon as he got to the end of the road where his lodge was sited. She was about two hundred yards ahead, oblivious to the fact that the devil himself was just about to pull up beside her.

She was thinking about her future and Philip when the handsome Danny appeared beside her. She got a bit of a start as she was listening to music on her iPod and had earphones in her ear. He waved at her, and she removed her earphones.

'Good morning, Carolyn,' he said, fixing her with a look from his beautiful eyes.

'Good morning,' she replied and stopped running, taking a long drink from her bottle.

'Do you mind if I join you?' he asked.

Carolyn did feel as if she was a bit hard on him the other day and she did enjoy male company and this male was as good as they get, so she decided there would be no harm in it.

'Sure, why not,' she said. Danny smiled a gorgeous smile and they both set off on a medium-paced run. Danny explained that he normally ran this route out to Pucks Glen and, once clear of the woods, ran out across the moor before returning the same way. Pucks Glen was enchanting with its bubbling stream and waterfalls meandering through the forest of great firs and Caledonian pines, very much like the ones near Danny's house. He informed Carolyn that the reason the area was so enchanting was the fact that the beautiful gardens of a nearby castle had extended and grown over the years. The Glen had benefited from exotic plants, ferns and trees, either grown from windblown seeds or planted by the gardeners many years ago.

Carolyn enjoyed his chat and found him not only very pleasing to the eye but very charming. They stopped halfway up the Glen where there were various logs at stages of the path which were cut into charming wooden seats, mostly where waterfalls formed pools on the stream. Carolyn thought it was very lovely.

Danny walked along the trail to the edge of the waterfall. He was truly a magnificent looking man. If things were different, she would not hesitate in dating this hot hunk. Dating, however, was the last thing on her mind. 'Is it safe to drink that water?' she asked. 'Yes,' he replied,' it comes straight from the nearby hills and is very pure.' He offered her a sip which she took. 'Mmm, yes, it is very refreshing.'

'Until you find a dead sheep further up,' he said with a wicked smile and they both laughed.

'So, what about you, have you worked here long?'

Danny explained that he started to work on parks a few years ago, that he was single without children, came originally from Perth – a lie; he was cautious not to reveal to much about himself. Carolyn felt comfortable in his company and started to tell him the entire story of Philip's adultery from start to finish. She felt at ease, the peaceful surroundings adding to her calmness. The trees above were still, and sun shone through the gaps in the canopy; vapour was rising from the stream and the sound of the water was also very soothing. She found herself telling Danny everything. Time seemed to stand still. She could hear her own voice and the sound of running water.

Danny was an excellent listener, very attentive and very understanding and it was about an hour later when she finally ended her story. Danny gave his advice, thoughts and views and was beginning to grow on Carolyn. She would have enjoyed their encounter even more if not for the circumstances. Her mobile vibrated; it was a text from Sarah asking if she was okay. She excused herself and walked away from Danny, called Sarah and confirmed she was fine and had just decided to run longer and that she would see her shortly.

When she turned round, Danny was on the ground doing sit ups; he was incredibly fit-looking. They both continued the run and got back to the site about thirty minutes later. Danny stopped at the end of his drive. 'Thanks for letting me tag along,' said the handsome man beside her.

She really had warmed to him. ‘I am glad you did,’ she said,’ it was really nice talking to you and thank you so much for listening to me.’ They shook hands. ‘You have my card,’ Danny said,’ you can call me any time.’

‘What about tomorrow morning, we could run again if you like’

’I would much rather have lunch or dinner.’

‘Me too,’ she said, ‘but it is not the right time for me – sorry.’

They both agreed to run together the next day. Carolyn decided that now was not the right time to introduce a new man into the already screwed up situation she was in. She preferred to keep their meeting under wraps; it was unlikely ever to become anything as she was still in love with Philip.

Chapter 27

Jenny Does Danny

Danny and Carolyn ran together for the rest of the week. He had asked her out on a couple of occasions during their long chats in the Glen, but she had refused. This, however, did not faze him because he was enjoying the chase and this one was in the bag. She would, of course, pay for all the extra work and running around – pardon the pun, he laughed to himself – that she made him do. Carolyn left for home on the Saturday morning but did not go before giving him her mobile number, which he already had, of course. He stood at his office window watching Carolyn and her little family leave. She had taken up a lot of his time and would have to be punished for that. He had deliberately avoided contacting any of his playmates in case Carolyn turned up at his lodge. He had, however, fucked Janet during the day at work on her lunch hour, both times in an empty lodge on the park; this was not enough, although it saved him having to wank himself off all the time. Janet was now a fully hooked sex slave, and he was enjoying treating her roughly; he had lots more to teach her.

His mind turned to Katie. He was slightly confused that he had not heard from or received any texts from her. It was only three days since their night together, but he thought she might have sent or answered his text. He did like to play hard to get and had kept low key but had never heard a word from her. He decided to go and see her at the pool.

She was nowhere to be found at the swimming pool. A spotty-faced teenager was sitting in the crow's nest seat watching the weekend holiday kids swim around pretending to avoid floating turds in the water; good game, he thought. Danny went round the back to her caravan; a wee lunch time sex session would be good right now, he fancied taking Katie to a movie or dinner tonight. He did not see her at the caravan and there was no reply to his knock on the door. Danny then went into the office where another teenager and Gordon were drinking coffee.

'Morning, boys.' They both looked up, disinterested.

'Gordon, I met one of your staff the other day; is she around?'

'If you mean Katie, she's gone,' Gordon snapped, without looking up from the computer screen. Danny was stunned. 'Thought she had just started?'

'Yes, Danny, she did, and she was late on her second day, late by a mile, which caused me a whole day of pain trying to sort it out. I sacked her and she went back to the Borders.'

Danny could not believe it – again he was on a high only to be slammed back down again. How the fuck did she leave without telling him? He walked out of the leisure complex and dialled her mobile number which went straight to voicemail, meaning that she was either out of signal or had blocked his number. His mind was doing overtime; why had she left without saying? Who was she? Really! He had just been fucked and dumped for the first time in his life! Danny was annoyed and confused. He went back to his office, closed the door and the blinds, and sat with his head in his hands.

Janet texted him and asked if he fancied some fun tonight, but he ignored her, his head hurting, his mind spinning. He decided to take the rest of the day off; Gordon could deal with any enquiries. He made his excuses at reception and left. Janet looked none too pleased, especially when he had not answered her text. He spent the rest of the day in bed although he did not sleep much because visons of his past were haunting him.

There was a knock at his door. He could hear Janet's voice. He ignored her and the text she sent when he did not answer. He later managed to nap and got up at 5 pm. He still had to meet Jenny. While he slept, his phone had received texts from Janet, Natcha, Barbara and Jenny, all wanting the same thing, Sex! He felt better, wishing he could invite them all round and play with them all together. He could be the Hugh Heffner of Scotland!

He texted them all except Jenny and explained that he was feeling poorly and would give them a call tomorrow. They all texted him back within seconds; how sad and pathetic their little lives were. He had looked out a white shirt and a pair of blue cotton trousers, brown belt and shoes; aftershave tonight would be Johnny Depp's Dior Sauvage! He intended to blow Jenny away with his look, charm, and smell. He masturbated in the shower; this would help him control his lust later; he needed to keep Jenny keen. She thought she was in control, but she was not. DANNY WAS ALPHA! He played them; they did not play him.

He had a JD and listened to the Killers on his iPod; it was only 6.30 pm and a table was booked for 7.30 pm at a local sea food restaurant.

Jenny had insisted on taking him out to dinner to celebrate her new lodge. He was quite happy just to meet at the lodge and have a few drinks. She, however, wanted to parade him in the local town, her trophy – a bit of eye candy. This made him more determined to reach his financial goal soon and then get the fuck out of Dodge.

He tried Katie's number again; he could smell her off the towel in the bathroom; the whole thing confused him. Who was she really? Was she police? He doubted that after their night together. He would have to find her address from the office, maybe fly down to Carlisle airport as it was the closest to Dumfries, but his flight would be recorded and that would be risky if she had to be dealt with – he did not take risks. He grabbed his jacket and keys and jumped into the Black Pearl. Like himself, his car was immaculate inside and out, always in showroom condition.

Danny might be a bloke, but he was house and car proud; everything he had was in pristine condition; his philosophy was, if you had nice things and did not look after them, then you did not deserve them. He grew up with nothing, though once he got a toy cowboy gun as his only present on Christmas Day, which his sister stood on, breaking it just three hours later. He respected everything he owned.

He arrived outside the new lodge on time and knocked on the door, Jenny answered, looking good in just a pair of tight jeans, boots, and a white blouse, showing a healthy amount of cleavage. He might never part her from her money so he might as well enjoy the free dinner and anything else that was going. Danny drove them the short drive to Dunoon; they were booked in at the Mussel Bar, a well-known seafood restaurant right on the seafront. Its location and ocean views added to its charm.

Jenny explained that Lesly was unable to join them this weekend as she had another engagement; Danny knew that this was just an excuse so that Jenny could sleep with him.

The food was great, and she was not bad company, but his mind was still troubled. Katie's sudden departure was annoying him and although he tried to put it to the back of his mind, it just kept on popping up again. He decided to look her up on his day off and find out what it was all about.

'Are you still here, Danny, or is your mind elsewhere?'

Jenny was smiling but you could see she was not happy.

'Sorry, I was just thinking. There is a seafood place on the Island of Mull called Cafe Fish; it is right on the harbour with stunning views and fantastic food. It's very much like here but better. I thought I could fly us over in the Cessna one summer's evening.'

'Yes, Danny, that sounds wonderful.'

The rest of the evening was pleasant, and they left the restaurant at about eleven and headed back to Jenny's lodge.

Danny stopped the car outside the lodge. 'Are you coming in for a night cap?' She was more or less telling rather than asking.

'Yes Jenny, that would be lovely.'

She showed Danny into the new lodge which looked pretty awesome. The last time he was here it was not completely furnished but she had good taste and could afford nice things, right down to the new fifty-five-inch smart TV.

'Do you like it?'

'Yes, very much, the place looks great, and you have wonderful taste.'

Danny thought of the Bothy which he had missed going to this week because of Katie. There she was again; he had to find out what that was all about.

Jenny appeared with JDs and sat beside him on the sofa; he turned towards her smiling, 'Are you glad you did not leave?'

'Yes, actually I am,' she replied, 'and thank you.' She placed her drink on the side table and suddenly swung her leg over his; she was now straddling him and bent forward and kissed him on the mouth. Danny responded and kissed her back he lay her down on the sofa and opened her blouse. She was tugging at his shirt, pulling it out of his trousers. She opened his shirt, running her hands over his chest. Danny buried his face in her bosom, kissing, biting and sucking her nipples.

Jenny was like a woman possessed and before he knew it, she had his cock inside her before you could say the word. She had an orgasm in the first five minutes, whispering 'I love you' which gave him the boak. She lay quivering beneath him.

'My god Danny, that was beautiful; I knew it would be.'

She lay beside him, holding on to him as if he was going to run away. Danny excused himself and headed for the bathroom, locked the door and headed for the sink. He washed her wetness from his cock, feeling sick and angry and disgusted at what he did to survive. He decided there and then that he would not be playing Jenny's little games as he was convinced that he would have more chance of winning the lottery than getting that tight bitch to part with any money.

He returned to the living room. Jenny had taken the time to gather up her clothes and was sitting back on the couch drinking champagne. She was smiling like a Cheshire cat. Danny smiled back but he felt disgusted, cheap and nasty, the more so because he knew that she was toying with him, playing with him, using him like a piece of meat.

Jenny had folded his clothes neatly on the arm of the sofa and he felt stupid standing there naked. He started to get dressed. 'Please say you are not leaving?' Danny laughed. 'Not at all,' he replied, 'just feel awkward sitting around naked when you are dressed.'

'Good. I was actually hoping you might spend the night.' Danny was expecting this and had a readymade excuse. 'You, Jenny, are here at your leisure, whereas I am not and will be in the gym by 6 am and then spend the rest of the day at work. It is,

I might add, also company policy not to fraternise with owners; being caught here with you could result in instant dismissal.'

'You will stay a little longer?'

'Yes. Let's sit outside and enjoy the wonderful view you have.'

She agreed and Danny got dressed, thinking that he had more chance of leaving if they were both outside on the decking and less chance of getting dragged into bed. This scenario was strange for him as he was more used to being in control. Jenny had turned the tables on him, and he did not like it one bit. It was also made so much worse because he knew it. They sat outside in silence, Jenny sipping her champagne as she lay on the lounger. He spent another hour out on the deck with Jenny, had a few more JDs before saying good night and heading home.

Chapter 28

Rejection

Danny went to work the next morning and was disappointed to find that Janet was on a day off as he fancied a quick fuck before work. He would need to find Natcha for some fun instead. Work was the usual crap – same shit, different day. There was no word from Katie, and this was still troubling him. Normally after spending time in bed with a female they would never be off the phone, pestering to see him again. Katie, however, had just vanished into thin air and seemed to have blocked his number; he could not go through the staff files to find her address as he needed Janet there for that.

Natcha was also not at work that Sunday, but he got a text from Barbara whom he arranged to meet later on; she always brought him gifts and he liked that. It was lunchtime and Danny headed up to the centre for some lunch. The park was buzzing with Easter holidaymakers, but he was too busy to chase any new meat. He ordered a baked potato with tuna and sat in a cubicle, his phone vibrating and buzzing around the table, stopping every now and then. Danny picked it up.

Well, well, he thought – it was a text from Carolyn. Softly, softly, catchee monkey. **Hi how are you x** He smiled and texted her back **I am fine, how's your weekend? X** Danny's mood changed immediately; he was now in hunting mode and Carolyn was his prey. **It's okay I suppose back home and all is quiet**

which is a bit worrying, are you working today? X. Danny was pleased that she had taken the bait but getting annoyed as he was trying to have his lunch; he hated texts that went back and forth; a text conversation was stupid and unnecessary. **May I call you x, YES x** was her prompt reply. She answered the phone on the first ring.

'Hi Danny.'

'Good afternoon, Carolyn, how is life in sunny Milngavie?'

'Fine thanks, but I do I miss our daily runs and chats.'

'You can always come back,' said Danny, knowing that it was a really stupid thing to say.

'Ahh, that might be a tad expensive and practically impossible.' He liked her voice over the phone and was getting aroused talking to her.

'Can we meet for dinner sometime perhaps, like tonight?'

'I am sorry, Danny, it's a bit short notice and with everything that is going on I don't think I am ready yet.' Danny was raging. How dare she toy with him. Why call him in the first place? He calmed himself enough to ask, 'How about lunch then next week; I have a day off on Tuesday. I can come to Glasgow.'

'Can I let you know tomorrow, would that be okay?'

'Yes, that would be fine.'

'Thanks Danny, talk tomorrow, bye.'

'Bye.' He hung up, as fucking mad as hell; who the fuck did she think she was? Danny could have anyone he wanted, and this bitch thought she could lead him a merry dance. The rest of the day was shite and he was in no mood for anyone. His head was splitting, he took two 500/30 Co codamol tablets and spent the rest of the afternoon in his office. 5 pm could not have come quickly enough. He left the office, oblivious to the hot babes standing at reception who were eyeing him up and headed straight back to his lodge and lay down on the sofa. His mind was racing as he lay there looking at the ceiling. His head still hurt, and he took another two tablets chased down with a Jack Daniels. He had still not managed to get in touch with Katie. Janet was not back in the office till tomorrow morning and would be punished for not being there when required. Carolyn was another issue, she infuriated him and was now the chosen one for this year. Blondie was about to have the worst day of her life – she just did not know it yet.

Danny got up, had a shower, and sat naked on the sofa listening to music while he waited for his slut to arrive. He thought of what he was going to do to Carolyn and slowly masturbated to his evil thoughts. There was a knock at the door; it was now 7 pm and the slut had arrived right on time. Still naked, he opened the door. Barbara shrieked in delight, 'Oh my god, you are a naughty boy, Daniel, could you not wait, darling?' He removed the bottle of Jack Daniels from her grasp and placed it on the dining room table, grabbed her hair and marched her straight to the bedroom.

'Oh, steady on Danny, you're hurting me.' Danny slapped her on the face and pushed her against the wall; he bit her on the cheek and ran his hand up between her legs. She was not wearing any panties and Danny was beginning to wonder if she had any. 'Jesus, Danny, try not to be too rough and please don't leave any marks.'

Danny slapped her again. 'DANNY!' she protested. He strapped her to the bed and tied a gag round her mouth. Over the next two hours Danny fucked her in every position and every hole hard! She protested and often struggled, making screaming noises from under the gag. Danny finished with her and now lay on the bed exhausted. Barbara had been crying and her mascara was all over her face. He did not give a fuck. He removed the gag. 'Fucks sake, Danny, you hurt me.' She looked pretty beat up and ran to the mirror in the bathroom. 'DANNY!' she screamed.

Danny walked in behind her. She was looking rough, with a cut lip and a bite mark on her check; she was naked and covered in welts and bruises. 'How am I going to cover this up? You're lucky hubby has just left for two weeks.'

'Not at all, darling, it is you that is lucky.'

Barbara gave him a killer look. 'Not happy, Danny; that was unnecessary, far too rough.'

Danny watched her get dressed. She did not say another word and disappeared into the night, sneaking home to lick her wounds. Danny poured himself a drink and, naked, sat out on the deck; his lodge was very secluded, and no-one could see him. His skin was alive, the cool air causing goosebumps; the hair on his arms stood erect as he lay on a lounger looking at the millions of stars in the night sky. Danny thought of Carolyn and masturbated. It was time – and time had come early.

Chapter 29

If you go down to the woods today

It was Tuesday morning. Danny sat on the train. He was travelling to Glasgow to steal a car for his trip to Milngavie. Carolyn told him she ran every morning after the children left for school. He had left early, not wanting to miss his prize. He would visit Katie soon and deal out his justice on her also. When he was in this state of mind, he only saw the task ahead and never deviated from his intended path, no matter what. He planned everything down to the smallest detail; nothing was left to chance; no risks taken. Before leaving, Danny had spent the rest of Monday night going over his plan. He had got Carolyn's and Katie's addresses by accessing their files at work while Janet was at reception. She did not mind him snooping in customer files, thinking he was just trying to get a sale. During the night he studied Google maps on the area surrounding Carolyn's house and the local area in general.

He looked out of the window of the train as it sped towards Paisley Gilmour Street. A fat lady sat opposite him; she looked fucking disgusting, fat lazy cow, he thought. Sitting next to her was an old bag who looked like she had no teeth in; again, fucking disgusting! They both sat and stared at him; he could see them watching him in the reflection on the window as the train entered a tunnel. They both looked away when he turned round. Danny was used to people watching him; he was, after all, stunningly good-looking and very manly, every girl's dream in fact. This had its downside; he was easily recognisable and very distinctive. He did stand out in a crowd, and this had hindered him in the past.

Danny hailed a cab and headed for Glasgow airport where he got out at the main terminal building. He did not go inside, however, and instead walked round to the long stay car park. As he walked, he put on a grey wig which made him look ten years older. He selected a dark blue Mondeo 2 litre diesel, placed his Slim Jim down the side of the window rubber and hooked the wire of the door lock, pulling it up swiftly. He waited until a 757 was lifting from the runway before he opened the door. The alarm went off as soon as he opened it. He quickly popped open the bonnet; the siren from the alarm was deafening as he leaned into the enclosed engine compartment, where he quickly disabled the alarm. He had a quick look around.

There were two other people in the car park, neither of whom turned round; the sound had been covered by the noise from the departing aircraft's engines. Danny slid into the driving seat and used a slide hammer to punch out the ignition barrel in one easy go; his petty crime skills from his days in Faifley had never left him. He put his bag and tools in the boot and headed for the exit. This was the tricky bit. He sat in the car at the exit waiting for a car to leave. A short time later a Vauxhall Astra arrived at the barrier and a young girl leaned out of the window, inserting her ticket in the machine.

Danny drove right up behind her, practically touching her bumper. As soon as the barrier lifted, he stayed right behind the Vauxhall; the barrier did come down slightly as the car in front passed but raised again as he went through. It was that easy! He smiled as he exited the airport and headed for Milngavie. Look out, Carolyn here I come. It was only 7.45 am and he was beginning to enjoy himself; it had been a while since he had done this. Stealing the car was fun.

Danny was in Milngavie in twenty minutes and parked in the Clober Road Car park, reversing the Mondeo so it faced out the way. There was no-one around as he took his binoculars and went for a walk. Sitting in the car would only attract attention if someone were to see him. He waited, watching birds fly about the woods doing their morning business; he even saw another squirrel. Twenty minutes passed when, out of nowhere, he saw her, her blonde hair visible from a long way off. Danny saw the look of shock on her face as she appeared over the small hillock. She stopped running and walked the rest of the way, looking at her watch as she approached him.

'Hi Danny, what brings you up this neck of the woods – not me, I hope? This is a bit creepy, you turning up like this.'

'Hi Beautiful. I was in the neighbourhood and thought I would look you up.'

'How did you know where to find me?'

'Why, you told me of course.'

Carolyn thought back to their chat in the Glen. 'Yes of course I did.' Silly me, she thought.

'I brought you something,' he said as he reached into the boot. There was no-one about as he poured the chloroform onto the medical cottonwool hidden inside. He quickly scanned the area and was on Carolyn before she could blink. She tried to move away but Danny was far too fast for her; he was overpowering and very strong. The chloroform worked quickly and, as she collapsed into his arms, the last things she heard were the sounds of little birds in her ears and the sound of a passing car in the distance.

Danny quickly threw her in the boot, wrapped duct tape round her head, leaving just her nose clear so she could breathe. Two cable ties were quickly tied round her wrists and ankles; he shut the boot and headed out of the car park, whistling to himself. He would have to drive round the long way to the park as driving a stolen car on the ferry with a trussed-up woman in the boot would not be a good idea.

The drive back was relaxing, and Danny felt good with himself. The Loch Lomond part of the trip was pretty. He would have loved to take Carolyn to his house, but you know what they say, you should never shit on your own doorstep. The car left the Loch Lomond road and now twisted through the glen towards Arrochar, a small village on the shore of Loch Fyne. The road continued west past the Cobbler before climbing steeply to a mountain pass aptly named The Rest and Be Thankful. Danny stopped the car at a car park at the top overlooking what was now known as the old military road. He looked in the boot.

Carolyn was still out cold but breathing nicely; he got back in the car and texted Jenny. **Hi babes how are you, when are you down next?** He started up the car. Jenny texted back immediately, **not sure Darling, why don't you come here instead, I can make us both dinner, Lesley would love to see you too.** Danny smiled, **yes that would be wonderful thank you, when? Friday Night? Yes sounds good, see you then, please text me your address.** He drove out of the car park and hummed to himself as he headed onwards towards the park.

Chapter 30

Hell

Carolyn woke up; nothing felt right; she was confused. She felt like she was choking and felt dizzy and sick; her head hurt like hell, her arms felt as heavy as lead. The ceiling? She stared up at the ceiling, it did not look right. There was something in her mouth; she tried to get up and then she remembered! Danny! Please, no, please, she thought. SHE WAS TIED TO A BED!

She tried to scream but choked instead. He appeared in the doorway totally naked and aroused, holding a glass of what looked like coke.

'Hello, my little whore,' he said, smiling; his eyes looked different and scary.

Carolyn tried to scream but could not get it out and started to choke again; Danny sat beside her on the bed. Carolyn was more terrified than she had ever been in her entire life. She did not know where she was but knew this was dangerous – very dangerous. Danny looked like the devil himself. She could not understand his eyes; he looked evil. His once fabulous eyes had changed. His penis looked silly as it stuck out from his lap and rose past his belly button.

She was sick with fear. He looked mad, crazy even. She was naked and the tiny blonde hairs on her body shivered. She struggled to free herself from the restraints. Danny made a silent sign by placing his finger to his lips. He took out the gag and had just turned to place it on the bedside cabinet when she started to scream and scream loud, 'HELP Me!!!!' before Danny was on her in a flash, his hand over her mouth before she could get the words out. He sat on top of her legs and punched her full force in the stomach. The pain was unbelievable.

'Somebody please help me, please please, please.'

Danny started to place the gag back in her mouth. 'No please Danny; let me drink with you,' she said, hurting with the pain. Instead, he threw the drink in her face; it was not just coke – it was bourbon or whisky too. Danny leaned over and licked the wetness from her face, his eyes wild. 'You are a fucking bitch cunt, that is the last drink for you,' he hissed.

He pushed his fingers inside her, taking them out and smelling them before putting them in his mouth and tasting them. Carolyn thought she was going to be sick. She tried to focus. Where was she? Was she back on the park? He was keen to keep her quiet; there must be people nearby.

'You really think you're special, don't you,' he whispered, 'well, my little fuck, tonight you are going to wish you were never born; tonight, you are going to be mine to do with whatever the fuck I please.'

He was stroking his penis as he touched her. He lay on top of her, slipping its full length inside her. It hurt, she struggled, and Danny swung his hand back and slapped her full force in the face. Her ears rang, her head was spinning. He hissed 'Ride with me, Bitch!' It was hurting her, but she did as she was told. She started to move with him, there was nothing else she could do; she did not want to die. Maybe after he raped her, he would let her go. 'Untie my arms; I want to hold you.' Danny slapped her again. 'SHUT UP!' and put the gag back in her mouth.

God, please help me; she felt the warm tears run down her face. He bit her lip hard as he raped her; she could taste blood in her mouth. She had to survive this; she might have a chance of getting away. He was aroused and very big, he was hurting her, and she was trying not to cry. He suddenly stopped, untied her ankles and flipped her over on her stomach, pulling her backwards and forced himself inside her rear. Pain, Pain, Pain. She bit down on the black rubber ball in her mouth and sobbed as he raped her anally and hard; he was slapping her bum and hips and she could hardly bear the pain. He eventually came inside her, turned her over again and sat astride her, taking the gag from her mouth before forcing his cock down her throat; she nearly resisted but thought better of it. She could smell and taste blood and faeces – her own and it made her gag.

'Take it all bitch, every inch.' She gagged and choked as Danny forced his manhood down her throat, eventually pulling his cock out of her mouth and slapping her face with it, laughing 'looks like you need a little practice, missy; you need to get it all in before you can go home.'

HOME! She thought, was he really going to let her go? 'Can we have a drink, Danny please; we can chat.' Danny punched her in the stomach again; she tried to curl up but could not.

'I can go on top, even; would you like that?' Danny slapped her hard, splitting her lip wide open this time and knocking her head to the side. He came up close to her ear. 'Do you think I am fucking stupid? Danny boy is calling the shots today, missssssy!!!' he shrieked.

'Yes of course you are. Sorry Danny, please forgive me.' He put the gag back in her mouth and leapt off the bed, picking up his glass as he disappeared out of the room. Carolyn lay on the bed; she did not deserve this; she thought that her divorce was the worst thing in the world. All she could think about now was the children; she wanted to be home. She sobbed uncontrollably and could hear the sound of her heartbeat in her head.

She was terrified – fear and terror engulfed every fibre in her body. She wanted the detectives to burst down the door and untie her; she was shaking and shivering, bleeding and sore. Danny returned to the bedroom clutching a drink, he then left the room and returned with a razor and soap and a bowl of water. 'Danny is going to give you a little trim, can't have you looking like a German whore,' he laughed. Carolyn had not bothered to keep herself trim as Philip was not showing any interest in her. She thought about Philip and the kids and started to cry, tears running down her cheeks. If he had not done what he did, then she would probably not be here. She closed her eyes; she desperately wanted to leave and did not want to suffer another second.

Danny gently applied shaving foam and shaved her. 'Don't cry, my dear. Danny is going to make you all nice again.' He finished shaving her and sat on the chair looking at her vagina as he drank from his glass. 'Good job Danny Boy, good job,' he said, smiling at her. He removed lingerie from a bag, put it on the bed and untied her ankles and wrists. 'Put it on, slut.'

'It' was a pair of panties and a bra, black with red lace, and a suspender belt and stockings to match. She did not argue and dressed as he watched her every move. 'You look just like a fucking whore.' She felt like it too and looked like a whore in the mirror. The bra and pants were also a little on the tight side and were cutting into her.

Danny sat on the chair slowly masturbating.

'I need to go to the toilet please.'

'I want to watch you.'

She was desperate to get away and did not need at all. 'It's not that kind of toilet.' He stared at her for a while before standing up, grabbing her and dragging her into the hall. Carolyn could see they were in a lodge, probably on the park, but different from the one her family had been in. This was a lot bigger and posher than the one that she and Sarah had rented; she could see down the hallway to an open plan lounge and kitchen. She thought it might be his, but probably not as it looked too feminine. She could also see the front door.

He opened the bathroom door for her and stood there watching.

'I can't go while you are standing there.'

Danny looked angry but walked away from the door. 'I forgot your shoes.' He turned right from the bathroom door: the front door and exit were to the left. 'Don't try to run, bitch, it will only cause you more pain,' he said as he walked away towards the bedroom at the back of the lodge. Carolyn sat on the toilet, her legs shaking. She looked around. Someone lived here – there were women's toiletries in the bathroom, cotton wool, nail varnish remover, shampoo; everything was female and there was no man stuff anywhere to be seen. She was confused.

Danny was singing something in the bedroom. She sprang off the toilet seat and turned left down the hall, bouncing off the walls as she went, knocking a picture down. She could see the front door only twenty feet away – ten feet – five feet – she looked round. Danny was walking down the hall, a pair of 6-inch black stilettoes in his hand. He was shaking his finger at her. 'Naughty, Naughty, Naughty.'. She tried the door; it did not open! It was locked. He came up behind her very fast, grabbing her by the hair. She spun round and he threw her, uncontrollably, across the room.

'Fucking whore!' he screamed. She crashed into a glass coffee table, smashing it into a thousand pieces; glass and ornaments flew everywhere. She got up and raced towards the patio doors; she did not want to be here a second longer and launched herself at the right-hand door, covering her face as she shouldered the glass at full speed. She bounced right off it! She hurt her head and there was a sickening noise as her arm broke. Danny was on top of her now, punching, kicking and slapping her. He was enraged now and slapped her repeatedly.

Then he choked her. She could not breathe. Everything went black.

Chapter 31

God Help Me

Carolyn woke up for the second time that day; she was tied back to the bed and her left arm hurt like hell. There was not a bit of her body that did not hurt; her lip and face were swollen. Danny was sitting opposite in the chair picking bits of glass from his feet. 'Like your new shoes, dear?' he asked. She looked down. Her feet hurt. They were now encased in the stilettoes. He came up beside her. 'Who do you think you fucking are, I told you not to run!' He hissed it like a snake. 'You really think you are it, don't you! Living in Milngavie.' He pronounced it MIL-N-GAV-IE. 'Living the dream with your posh house, your posh life and your posh job, jetting all around the world. You are nothing but a fucking slut. I have news for you, my cute little puppy, that life for you is fucking over.'

She tried to mumble under the gag, but nothing came out. He sat on the chair masturbating slowly. 'Open your legs, bitch.' Carolyn did as she was told; he got more excited and now kneeled on the bed in front of her, stroking himself slowly while fingering her, putting his fingers inside and playing with her roughly. She was sore and extremely scared and thought about previous girls who had been murdered and sexually abused by monsters like him. She realised she never even gave a second thought to what they must have gone through.

Danny grabbed the inside of her leg, his nails digging into the meaty soft flesh; she winced as he screamed at her, 'Naughty girl, pay attention, cunt!' He continued to play with her while he masturbated. Carolyn was exhausted; she wanted to be home; she feared for herself and wanted the children. Carolyn wanted her Dad too. She started to cry as he thrust himself inside her and closed her eyes tightly. Danny slapped her again hard; she could taste blood in her mouth, and up her nose. He started to choke her. 'Watch me, darling, this is fun, don't you think.'

He was very strong, and she could not move from under him; he was choking her until she nearly passed out and then he would start the process over again. Carolyn knew she was going to die. She tried to struggle but it was in vain; she lay there while this monster violated her. She was drifting in and out of consciousness as Danny's hands were getting tighter and tighter round her neck. He started fucking her hard in a frenzy – she could not breathe. His grip was even tighter than before; he started to come inside her; she pleaded with her eyes that she wanted him to stop. Please God, no please, my children, Philip, Dad, Sarah, please.

He started to go wild. His eyes were crazy, he arched his body and threw his head back as he came, applying more pressure on her neck. He was smiling in a grimace, his eyes wild; he was enjoying this!

His face was the last thing Carolyn ever saw.

Chapter 32

Knock Knock

Danny thought long and hard on the drive south; this was turning into a howler of a year and was disappointing as it started well. Jenny, Carolyn, and Lesley had all been great disappointments and it looked like he would have to move on quicker than was first planned. He did not like this; having his yearly schedule disrupted because of three selfish bitches was annoying to say the least. Having to deal with them, though, was challenging and exciting; he loved the hunt for the cunt! He had left his mobile at home, one sure way of getting convicted for a crime being to use your own mobile phone going to or near a crime scene. He had instead brought another burner phone, purchased at Asda, which he might use later.

The drive was two hours long – all motorway – none of which he could remember. He arrived at his first destination at 8.30 pm where he set up shop, so to speak, before heading to Katie's address which turned out to be in a small private estate which he had already looked at on Google maps; it was bound to have lots of nosey neighbours, though. He drove along the street of neat houses on one side and woods on the other; this was ideal for him as there were no watching eyes on the opposite side of the road.

According to Google maps there was a path in the woods that ran the entire length of the road. He slowly drove past no 46

Beech Drive. Katie's Mazda 4 x 4 was parked in the drive behind a BMW traffic police car!!!! Danny was stunned; her husband or boyfriend must be a cop and that was a disaster. His mind was in turmoil, and he felt sick. Was she a cop or a detective? He had killed before; were the police on to him? He had to find out as soon as possible.

He drove back to the end of the road and turned left to a small, empty car park in the woods and parked the car. It was now 9 pm and he walked along the wooded path until he was in line with Katie's house. It was still light, but a confused owl hooted in the woods anyway; silly bird, he thought. Just then she was in view; in the kitchen in front of the drive, she was busy making a cup of tea when a tall dark man walked in behind her and cuddled her as she leaned against the counter.

Danny was livid; this was all the confirmation he needed that a third female in one month had made a total fucking fool of him, something he was not going to stand for. He walked back to the car and got dressed from top to toe in black. There were no stars tonight, which suited him; he hoped it was not going to rain and lay down in the grass, keeping the path between him and the house. He decided about three o'clock would be a good time to visit Katie; it was 11 pm now so not long to go. Suddenly the porch light went on and Katie and the police officer were at the door. Adrenaline flowed through his veins; he was pumped up and ready for action. What luck – the cop was leaving! He lay down in the grass as the BMW reversed out of the driveway –

this was going to be easy. Danny watched the house for a further fifteen minutes before making his move. He grabbed his rucksack, leapt the fence and ran into the driveway.

His previous young life of stealing cars and of carrying out house breakings stood him in good stead; there was not a vehicle he could not steal; cars, boats, planes, and trucks were easily stolen by such a talented thief. While married to Gillian he had taken a one-year course on alarm engineering, domestic and commercial on the pretext that he hoped to start an alarm company; he also took a one-week locksmith course and what he had learned, he had used many times in the past.

Danny ran and leapt onto the flat garage roof that was attached to the east gable end of the house. The alarm was within easy reach, and he disabled it in a matter of minutes. He lowered himself onto a bench which was conveniently situated at the rear of the garage on the patio, probably a sun trap when the weather was nice. He moved very quickly and quietly, had the back door open in seconds and moved quietly through the kitchen towards the sound of the television. He removed the vial of chloroform and the medical cottonwool from his pocket. Katie was watching television, sitting on a chair, her back to the kitchen door with only the top of her head visible.

He moved quickly. The chloroform was pressed against Katie's mouth before she could move and she slumped forward, her head resting on the arm of the chair, her hair trailing onto the carpet. Danny swiftly removed duct tape and cable ties from his bag which he quickly wrapped around her wrists and ankles. The entire assault took less than five minutes. He moved quickly through the house; every room was nicely decorated and very neat and tidy; there were photos of the cop with Katie but no obvious signs of him actually living there. Danny checked out the bathroom; there was no shaving gear or aftershave anywhere, which meant the police officer did not live there after all; he smiled to himself. He moved back downstairs and opened the front door, walking up the driveway which was separated from next door by neatly trimmed leylandii hedges.

He looked left and right – there was no-one around. What a lovely quiet place to live, he thought. He had only a short distance to cover and sprinted back to the house, lifted Katie over his shoulder and walked out of the house, closing the door behind him. He paused at the end of the drive, looked both ways and sprinted across the road, dropping Katie's limp body over the fence. He leapt over and lay in the grass beside her. Danny was always careful and meticulous in all his planning; he waited for five minutes before picking Katie up and heading for the car; he walked through the woods, avoiding the path as he went.

Katie awoke just as he popped her into the trunk; her eyes were wild with fear, and she was screaming something under the tape. Danny gave her another little sniff of the chloroform. 'Ching Ching Cheerio,' he said as she passed out again. He removed the ninja clothing and was now smartly dressed as he drove the five miles to his destination. This was the dangerous part, driving late at night in an unfamiliar area. He did, of course, have an alibi – that he was visiting a girlfriend; he knew Katie's address so he should be okay. He had checked out the police station on the way in; it had only two 4 x 4s parked outside and would probably have only about four police officers at most. Police very seldom left the police station during the night, doing so only if they had too. The drive was uneventful, and Danny arrived at the disused airfield about twenty minutes later, driving up to two large gates where he picked the padlock open on one of them and drove in. He got out and closed the gate behind him and locked it again. Driving with his lights off, he parked behind an old Nissan hut and, again, picked the lock and walked inside. The building was empty apart from chairs – lots of old chairs, like the stuff you saw on American Pickers. The hut was long, about sixty feet, with the entire end taken up by a single wooden stage. Danny went back outside and checked his watch; it was now 1.02 am. He opened the boot. Katie was still out cold as he tossed her inside.

Chapter 33

Stage Fright

Katie woke up with a blinding headache and could not figure out where she was. She was tied to a chair on a wooden stage, a small lamp lighting up the space around her; the light hurt her eyes. Katie knew it was Danny who had abducted her, and she knew why. He must be hiding in the shadows. She tried to shout his name and jumped up and down on the chair which made a lot of noise on the wooden stage.

She suddenly felt pain on her left side and fell over onto the floor; her ear was ringing. Danny stood over her, grabbed her and the chair and sat her upright again. 'STAY STILL YOU BITCH!' he screamed. He had slapped her and rubbed the back of his hand as he spoke. 'Tonight, my pretty friend, is the night you die!' Katie tried to shout, tried to plead, but Danny was like a man possessed. He undid his fly and pulled out his erect cock. Katie struggled again and Danny slapped her hard, again. Huge pain in her head; her ear was ringing; she fell over again, and yet again Danny picked her and the chair up; he was immensely strong and fast.

He ripped the duct tape from her mouth, taking skin from her lip with it; she winced a little at the pain and could taste blood in her mouth as he swung at her again.

'I KILLED JEFF THOMSON!' she screamed. Danny stopped mid-swing, picked her and the chair up and threw her off the stage. He knew who Jeff was but was confused at her statement. Katie flew about ten feet into the rows of chairs. She had no way of protecting herself and landed heavily; every bone in her body ached and she was scared.

'Please, Danny, let me explain, I beg you.' Danny was coming down the stairs towards her. 'Can you untie me, please.' Her wrists and ankles hurt like hell, bound to the chair with cable ties. He sat the chair upright; her weight was causing the cable ties to cut into her skin. 'Now start talking.' He slapped her hard again, this time holding on to her, so she did not fall over again. He still looked mad as hell and Katie was afraid, really afraid.

'He was on to you at the park,' she screamed, 'he had a photo of you that his wife had taken. I killed him and destroyed it; he was going to give it to the police.' Danny's eyes burned into hers. 'Who was the cop at your house?' he asked. 'My brother,' she blurted out, 'he knows nothing.'

'How do I know you are not lying?'

'Danny, please, I know it all; I can show you; please untie me; let me show you, would I not have handed you over to the police by now? I know you killed Sandra Thomson.'

Danny's head was in a spin – this was not going to plan. 'How do I know you killed him?' he asked.

'It was in the paper – you can look at it on your phone.'

Danny could not as he did not have his phone with him and neither did Katie. He watched her face, her eyes. He should kill her now but was not sure anymore.

'Danny, I want to be like you, very like you, please let me show you, come back to mine.' He took a knife from his pocket and cut the ties from her wrists and ankles. Katie tried to stand but sat down again; there was no blood in her feet. Danny grabbed both her legs and sat back down again. He rubbed both her feet and her wrists. she started to have feeling in her feet and could walk. Danny's mood had changed – he was still cautious, but curious. The words 'curiosity killed the cat' were on his mind, but she was different, and he needed to know more; he might still kill her anyway.

'If you are lying, I will kill you. I will bring you right back here and fucking kill you slowly,' he said.

'I know you will.' She was still frightened.

With her help, Danny quickly returned the chairs back the way he had found them, collected his things and left, with Katie now sitting in the front seat. The car drove off the disused airfield at exactly 2 am; it had started to rain. The car travelled along the dark winding country roads towards Katie's house as they both sat in silence, the car's window wipers moving silently back and forth over the windscreen; there was only silence.

She was the first to speak. 'I am telling you the truth, Danny. I worked with her and her husband in the Co-op supermarket; we both worked side by side on the checkout and that is where you met her; he was the manager of that same Co-op. He knew that she was having an affair but not who with. I did because she told me; she showed me your picture and told me all the sexy details of fucking you in your lodge on the park. She herself was a total bitch, her and her vile husband stole thousands from the shop and treated everyone like shit. We were all happy when she disappeared. I knew it was you right away. After she vanished, he went through her locker and found that photograph of you and he also discovered a hundred grand was missing from her bank account. He thought she had run off with you and was going to the police but was hesitant because that money was stolen from his work. He was a dirty old pervert, always trying to get into the checkout girls' knickers. I asked him to give her one more week to come home, acting like I was her friend and he agreed, but only if I came to his house for a drink.'

They had now arrived back at the car park in the woods, Danny did not want to park the stolen car in her driveway. 'I thought you were taking me home.' 'I am but this is as far as the car goes.' They walked along the street together in silence; the rain had stopped, and the pavement shone wet under the streetlights. She had no keys, but he had left the back door open previously so they both walked round the side of the house to the back door and went inside. The silence between them was deafening, an intense mixed feeling of fear, suspicion and attraction.

Katie poured them both a drink, He was starting to believe her, and she could have gone to the police a long time ago as she knew where to find him. 'I went to his house that night, even though he made me sick. He kissed me and groped my breast the moment I went inside. I asked him to slow down and pour me a drink. While he was doing so, I asked him to show me the photograph as I might recognise him. He asked me what his reward would be. I told him I would suck him off till he exploded in my mouth. He could not get the photo quick enough and handed it to me as he unbuckled his trousers. He stood in front of me with his trousers at his ankles; he wore Y-fronts that looked stained and disgusting. I took one look at your picture, removed the ice pick from my bag and stabbed him once through the heart. The look on his face pleased me. I watched him die, and I wanted to fuck you, and wished you were there. I then set fire to the house and left; it burned to the ground and left no trace.'

'Did anyone see you arrive or leave?'

'No, he lived in a smallholding in the middle of nowhere; I went there on my mountain bike.' Katie took his empty glass and refilled it; he was impressed with her story of protecting him; it aroused him; his cock was hard as she returned with his glass.

'Let's go upstairs,' he said, 'unless your brother is coming back, of course.'

'His weekly visit is over; he won't be around again until next week.'

The following sex was intense. Katie could take it and give it back and for the second time Danny found himself spending the night holding Katie in his arms. The next morning, they both sat in silence at the breakfast table in the kitchen. Danny had to be back at the park by nine and it was already past six. The silence was interrupted by Danny. 'I need you to kill someone else just to be sure.' She did not waver at his request. 'Who?' she asked as she drank tea and ate her toast.

'I have not decided yet; I will let you know.' Ten minutes later, Danny was back on the M8 Motorway heading north.

Chapter 34

DCI John McLeod

John McLeod sat at the stern of his 28-foot sloop moored in calm waters at the head of Loch Scavaig on the west coast of Skye. Seil Island sheltered him from the rest of the loch, and the towering mountains of the Black Cuillin cast a dark shadow on the calm water behind him. John had dropped anchor here the previous day, part of a weeklong trip around the waters of the Western Isles, eventually finishing on the island of Hirta St Kilda. John was a 56-year-old retired detective with Police Scotland. He had worked the last 20 years in Partick in the West End of Glasgow. John could not say he enjoyed the life much, maybe because he was involved in its dark side of murder, drugs, theft, and prostitution; he had never been a city person at the best of times anyway.

John and his wife Heather, a secondary school teacher, had lived and worked in the city their entire lives. Whenever they got the opportunity, they would leave the city behind and drive out to the country. They would visit places like Killearn, Drymen, Luss, Balmaha and Callander. They both loved and enjoyed the countryside; hillwalking was something else they both enjoyed and had climbed many of Scotland's Munros together. John's other passion was his 38ft yacht JIP which he sailed mostly round the west coast of Scotland and mostly on his own, as Heather hated being on the water. She had never set foot on his boat for that very reason. A year earlier Heather had been offered a head teacher position in which they both decided would be a great chance to escape the city life and its streets. John applied for early retirement and got it; they quickly sold their house in Hardgate, Clydebank and bought a three-bedroom cottage in Connel not far from Oban. John kept his boat moored in the bay in front of the cottage.

It was also only fifteen minutes' drive to Heather's new school. Their two sons, Ben aged19, and Steven, who was 21, were both studying aeronautical engineering at Glasgow University and were both content with the culture and city life. They had decided to buy a flat together in the West End of Glasgow, which allowed them to remain at Glasgow University after their parents moved. John had set sail from the Crinan Basin two days earlier, sailing north towards Oban before turning west down the Sound of Mull past Urquhart Castle. Tobermory's colourful houses, painted in pinks, yellows and blues, could be seen ahead. John then turned north-west towards the island of Skye.

John had felt the need to make this trip after a previous visit to Skye had left him disturbed, the reason being that as a child John had read a book about an otter, *Ring of Bright Water* written by Gavin Maxwell. The book was later made into a film starring Bill Travers and Virginia McKenna. John had loved the book and the film; it was and always had been a fond memory from his childhood. He had now returned to Skye with the intention of visiting Soay Island and going ashore to study its dark past. Its dark past was exposed by the captain of a boat that John took a trip on the previous year. Three hours after passing Tobermory he was sailing past the very island that brought him back. He was on his way into Loch Scavaig, sailing past the east side of Soay Island now visible over his left shoulder.

It was a Tuesday afternoon as John dropped anchor in Loch Scavaig, a loch he was visiting as part of a solo trip which would take him to the most westerly island of Scotland, and hopefully help him get over his initial trauma of Soay Island. The wind was light and the view stunning. A yacht, the Stardust a 48ft Sun Odyssey, appeared around Seil Island and dropped anchor in the bay, not far from JIP. John had just rowed back to his own yacht in the tender after taking his lovable black Labrador Jed for a walk on dry land and give him a chance to do his business, so to speak.

Jed loved the water and very often would simply launch himself off the side of the boat and swim to shore by himself. John had fancied stretching his legs and decided to spoil his loving and much-loved Labrador and best friend by rowing him to the beach. He was back sitting on his yacht with a cup of tea and bacon butty and Jed was watching the seals swimming in the bay. He waved to the couple on the Stardust as they dropped anchor, a male and a female probably in their late sixties; they waved back and carried on about their business. That afternoon John lay on his bunk listening to Dave Gilmour on his iPod and reading '*Into the Wild*' by John Krakauer. Jed lay upside down on his back on the floor below him, balancing himself between the floor and the bunk; the dog just loved sleeping on his back. They were interrupted by a shout from the stern of the boat 'Permission to come aboard, Captain?'

Jed was up on his feet and heading up the steps towards the voice, barking at its owner as he went. John climbed out onto the stern. The visitor and owner of the voice was the captain and owner of the Stardust. 'Good morning, Captain. My Name is Stuart Dixon from the Stardust yonder.' 'Good morning, Stuart; my name is John McLeod and the Captain. of the JIP.'

'Pleased to meet you, John.' They shook hands and Jed was wagging his tail so hard it looked like his bum might fall off; he got a pat on the head from the new visitor. 'I hope you don't mind,' said Stuart as he lifted a bottle of 18-year-old Talisker that was by his side. Jed barked his approval. 'Distilled on this very mystical island,' said Stuart. John smiled, 'Allow me to grab a couple of glasses,' he said as he disappeared down to the galley. John came back with two whisky glasses sporting little stags on the side, and Stuart poured them both a drink. It turned out that Stuart and his wife Margaret were from Helensburgh and had sailed their yacht from Rhu Marina via the Crinan Canal. Dixon explained that his wife had gone for a nap as she was not as young as she used to be and had found the trip tiring.

Stuart was a retired bank manager who, at every opportunity over the last 30 years, had sailed round Scotland in his beloved yacht. He explained that he had boarded the JIP to invite John to dinner that evening, John accepted and arranged to be on the Stardust by 7 pm. They both finished their drams; Stuart rowed back to the Stardust as Jed watched, wagging his tail. John spent the rest of the afternoon reading his book; he also called his wife from his mobile and took Jed for another walk round the coast, walking as far as the Bad Step, a rocky part of the path that ran from Elgol to Couruisk. John then had a shower, grabbed a bottle of wine and the Talisker left by Stuart and jumped into Nipper, the name of the little shore tender that he towed behind JIP. He rowed over to the Stardust, feeling guilty as Jed looked on with his big sad eyes. 'Stop it,' he said, 'I won't be long.' Jed whined back at him. 'Permission to come aboard?' he shouted to Stuart and his wife. 'Aye aye, captain,' came the reply from Stuart.

John climbed aboard the beautiful boat which was a tad more luxurious than his. He was introduced to Margaret who was a slim and attractive woman for her years; she had short grey hair which she obviously did not colour, and she suited the look very much.

Margaret introduced herself to John, asking if he liked seafood, to which John replied yes, he did. Margaret scurried back to the galley, smiling. 'Dinner will not be long,' she said as she disappeared below. John and Stuart sat in the stern watching the seals and talking mostly about boats and Margaret brought dinner a short time later, consisting of mussels in a white wine sauce to start. followed by salmon and scallops on a bed of black pudding for the main; it tasted delicious. More so, as the only seafood John had eaten on this trip was toast and sardines two days previously. The setting for dinner was stunning as the dark and moody Black Cuillin towered above them, the setting sun casting shadows along the ridge. There was just a very light breeze which was enough to keep the midges at bay but left the water in the bay flat calm.

John thought of Heather and wished she was with him now; she missed a lot of beautiful things because of her fear of the water. After dinner and coffee, they sat in the stern with a dram, admiring the view and chatting about life in general. Stuart had a great knowledge of sailing in Scottish waters and had many a sailor's story to tell. Margaret filled John in on her family as John did on his. During their conversation, the Misty Isle, a tour boat from Elgol, arrived at the jetty in the bay to pick up the last tourists and climbers from the steep jetty which hung over the rocks on the opposite side of the bay.

Stuart explained to John that the boat visited Harris and Soay island and was getting a reputation as one of the must dos on Skye. John replied that he actually had taken that very same trip the year previously in October and that was part of the reason he was on this particular trip.

'Pray tell,' said Margaret, 'are you planning to start up a boating business on Skye perhaps?'

‘No not at all,’ replied John as he went on to explain that while on a previous climbing trip to Skye with his wife Heather, he had fancied a wee boat trip round Soay, Rhum and Canna, hoping to see whales and basking sharks. Heather was not going to come along and instead had arranged to go to Portree by bus for lunch and a wee look about the shops with a view to John joining her later.

John had driven to Elgol and boarded the Misty Isle which ran the wildlife trips from the harbour there. The setting was stunning with the Cuillin’s jagged mountain range visible at the head of the loch. John, dressed in his all-in-one survival suit, looked like a North Sea oil worker about to depart for the oil rigs. He was looking forward to the trip out to Rhum and Canna with the hope of seeing some wildlife and the red deer on Rhum.

The Captain of the Misty Isle, however, stopped first at Soay Harbour, a narrow and shallow sea inlet on the north-west side of Soay Island. As he edged his boat into the shallow water, he explained that the island was once owned by Gavin Maxwell, the author of the book *Ring of Bright Water*, the book that John had read before he saw the film. He went on to explain that many people actually thought that Gavin Maxwell was a conservationist. In fact, he was not; the truth was that before he wrote *Ring of Bright Water*, Gavin Maxwell and his business partner and friend Tex Geddes were responsible for nearly wiping out the entire basking shark population from Scottish waters.

John could not believe what he was hearing; he was a fanatical lover of all wildlife and, being a seafarer himself, had a soft spot for sea mammals. The captain explained that the ruined building on the jetty in front of them was the old whaling station used to process the basking sharks; you could also make out the old steam engine that was used to haul the basking sharks up onto the quay to be cut open, for the oil in their livers, by workers.

This revelation ruined his entire stay on Skye and was made worse by the fact that after his boating trip and while collecting Heather from Portree, he spotted a book in the bookstore window '*Harpoon at a Venture*' written by Gavin Maxwell. The book had a map of the island on the front cover and a picture of a basking shark being hauled into a boat, with a harpoon in the foreground. Heather had begged John not to buy the book, saying that it would only upset him; upset him was putting it mildly. That night over a few drams John sat at the bay window overlooking the jagged peaks of Sgùrr Nan Gillean and Am Basteir in the snug bar of the Sligachan Hotel. He read the entire book from cover to cover; it not only ruined his entire trip with Heather, it traumatised John very much and still does to this day. The book depicted the entire story of how Gavin Maxwell and Tex Geddes inhumanely murdered and killed these beautiful and harmless creatures. Gavin Maxwell did not have a clue of what he was doing or how it should be done. He had experimented with different types of harpoons, many of which failed, resulting in a great number of sharks suffering trauma and pain unnecessarily.

The business eventually went bust and the whaling station was abandoned. John was disgusted.

Gavin Maxwell and his friend were responsible for the killing and suffering of over 200 basking sharks over a two-year period; they also killed whales, porpoises and other sea mammals, their ignorance resulting in the suffering of these poor creatures. Stuart and his wife were both stunned and had never known that Soay Island had such a dark and evil past. Retelling the story upset him and John had enough for one night. He bade his farewell to the Dixons as he was planning on leaving early in the morning for the island of St Kilda. He thanked them both for a lovely meal and exchanged contact details with a view to arranging to meet in a few weeks' time for dinner and an opportunity to meet Heather.

John was just about to row over to JIP when there was an almighty splash from behind him; it was Jed! The dog had done a doggy dive from JIP into the bay. The lovable mutt was now swimming to shore, obviously having decided it was time to do his business before having his customary digestive biscuit and going to bed. John turned the tender round and followed him as the Dixons looked on in utter amusement.

Back on JIP, John dried Jed before giving him his much-awaited digestive. Jed liked to sleep on the bunk beside him, and now snored and farted in his sleep, keeping John awake with the noise and the smell. John eventually fell asleep but was woken at dawn by Jed doing the usual dive bomb off the side of JIP and heading ashore for a sniff about. John put on the kettle and sat and watched Jed walk along the shore. Jed peed at intervals on the rocks, looking up every now and then, casting a look out towards the JIP to make sure John was not sailing without him.

John made up the dog's breakfast for his return, made himself a cup of tea and put some bacon on; he sat in the stern watching the seals who had all taken to the water to avoid the dog. Jed plodded around the beach some more, doing more doggy stuff, including a back roll on the seaweed before heading back to the boat. John hauled him back over the stern which was no mean feat considering he was wet and heavy; Jed was quickly dried again before they both had breakfast. After checking the weather John decided to leave; he lifted the anchor, started the 40hp engine and they left the bay quietly, passing Seal Rock which had about 70 grey seals sleeping on it, some of which would open their eyes to see who was passing by before closing them again, deciding that the passing boat was of no threat to them.

The seals were probably happy that Jed was leaving, as his jaunts to shore had often disturbed them, causing them reluctantly to take to the water. John enjoyed the beautiful surroundings before him as he sailed from Loch Scavaig, the towering mountain of Bla Bheinn looking mean and moody with a misty cloud wrapped about its summit. The dark Cuillin ridge was looking less moody with sunshine lighting up its summits; a sea eagle flew high overhead, looking for a fish breakfast from the loch below; it was apparently nesting round at Heaste. On leaving the loch John turned west along the coast of Soay island passing Soay Harbour itself, which made his skin crawl – what a terrible misuse of a beautiful island.

He decided not to go ashore and steered JIP westwards towards Rhum before turning north-west and heading towards the island of Barra. John intended to stop off at Barra for a few hours before heading out over the open sea for the 41-mile trip to St Kilda. He planned to anchor at St Kilda for a couple of nights, giving him and Jed time to explore the island. St Kilda was a place that John had always wanted to visit as it was the most westerly island of Scotland; it was a destination that was missing from his ship's log and had always been on Johns 'things to do before you die' list.

JIP cut through the calm water between the islands of Soay and Skye and Jed was up in the bow posing like something from the Titanic, his ears lifting and falling on the slight breeze. The dog actually looked if he was smiling. Jed started barking wildly at the water in front. John walked along the deck to see what all the noise was about. He would never forget the vison in front of him – a basking shark and her calf were swimming just ahead and to the right of JIP. John ran back to the stern and grabbed his Go Pro video camera. He wanted to shoot some video to show Heather on his return. He slowed the engine and gently cruised alongside these wonderful mammals. Who would have believed it, he thought? He filmed the shark and calf for a couple of minutes and then took some photographs with his camera before leaving them in peace to continue their journey. There were more sightings of dolphins and a Minky whale before an hour later JIP sailed into Castlebay harbour on the Island of Barra.

John tied JIP up and went for a stroll round the village with Jed. They stopped at a café for lunch and sat outside people watching, Jed enjoying the many people who stopped to pet him as he sat at John's feet. John took Jed for a walk on the beach, which was soon interrupted by a man who approached them in a Land Rover. He introduced himself as the air traffic controller from the Tower overlooking the beach. Barra airport had no runway and aircraft landed on the hard packed sand instead. John and Jed did as they were asked and sat on the dunes to watch the aircraft land, the blue and white Twin Otter, painted in the Scottish saltire flag, spraying salt water all around itself as it touched down on the still wet but hard-packed sand. It was met by the guy in the Land Rover who emptied its belly of bags and boxes, while passengers disembarked and headed for the small terminal building. Time was now getting on and, although it was pleasant sitting watching the aircraft land, it was now time to continue on their journey.

John and Jed headed back to the village; The walk back in the warm sunshine was pleasant; little birds were busy in the sand dunes chirping away excitedly. Jed must have stopped about a hundred times to sniff interesting doggy smells and pee short squirts of pee at every opportunity. Back at the village John bought some fresh supplies before returning to the boat and setting sail for St Kilda. It was after 2 pm and John planned to make the 41-mile crossing by dusk. The rest of the trip was full of adventure with sightings of various sea birds, porpoises and even a humpback whale; the wind was in John's favour as they sailed under clear blue skies and emerald-green waters towards St Kilda.

He called Heather to let her know he had posted a few pictures and the video of the basking shark on his facebook page whilst in Barra; she was delighted to hear from him again and wished she was with him as she missed him very much, and Jed too of course! John was starting to enjoy his early retirement. Being a detective in Glasgow was not a nice job and had left some mental scars on him. He had only joined the force because of his father who had also been a police officer in Glasgow, and it was expected of him. He also thought he could maybe help people and make a difference; however, he doubted if he did.

At first, he enjoyed being a police officer but that soon changed as the years went by, more so after he was promoted to Detective and his work became harder and more unpleasant. Dealing with the murders of prostitutes and Glasgow's drug culture soon took its toll. The sight of a murdered and mutilated person is something that will haunt him his entire life – a body, which was once a person, someone's loved one, a son or daughter, mother or father, brother or sister, its life ended prematurely. John had always had a problem with death, never good at funerals and always saddened by the passing of friends or relatives. He had an even bigger problem of dealing with animal fatalities such as hunting or roadkill. He was traumatised by seeing roadkill: foxes, pheasants, badgers and deer lying on the roadside as people casually drove past in their cars. People could not care less that these poor animals who, like us, had families or partners, were dead. These animals felt pain and joy just like we do, like for instance the swallows at John's house who flew all the way from Africa and stayed with the same partner for their entire lives. John also hated the senseless killing of sharks and whales for commercial gain. The murder of rare animals like elephants, rhinos and tigers was disgusting and continually upset him.

John was known throughout the Glasgow police force as DCI Doolittle and even known by the local vets by that very name. The vets who looked after Jed had often seen John arrive at the surgery with injured owls, cormorants, foxes and deer. He even called them during the night about an injured animal he had found. John's difficulty in dealing with fatalities had, in fact, ruined a month-long family trip to Australia. John had insisted that he Heather and the boys visited a kangaroo sanctuary just north of Sydney. There were lots of baby kangaroos at the sanctuary. The vet had told them they were there because their mothers had either been shot or even killed on the roads and that they were now orphans, requiring 24-hour round-the-clock care. John learned that female kangaroos were pregnant for only six weeks before they gave birth to a tiny one-inch-long baby joey. It then had to crawl up the mother's fur to reach its pouch, after which it stayed there for months feeding off its mother's milk.

As they left the sanctuary John and Heather had been placing a donation in the box on the counter in reception. A young Aussie girl, who was holding a baby kangaroo wrapped in a blanket in her arms, walked by and said, 'Joeys Should Never Be Orphans.' Those words rang in Johns ears every day for the rest of the trip. Heather knew very well about John's pain and had asked him after the Aussie trip and on many other occasions to seek medical help, but he had always refused as he felt and knew at that time that it would seriously affect his career in the force.

John thought about his wife as he sat on the deck, a dram in his hand. He loved Heather dearly, she was the most loving caring person in the world, and he missed her and wished again that she was with him now. JIP was about three hours out of Barra and John could see St Kilda on the horizon about 25 miles to the west. He could also see the great sea stacks off Boreray and the island of Boreray itself. John dropped sail and started the outboard as the JIP headed into village bay. There were a few yachts in the bay, one of which was moored to the buoy belonging to the tour boat The Hirta belonging to Angus Campbell which left from Levenburgh on Harris. The tour boats and the fishing boats had little time for yachts and often referred to their crew as WAFIs (wind assisted fucking idiots) which, to be fair, was true as many of them were clueless idiots.

John finally dropped anchor in Village Bay on the Island of Hirta at 11.15 pm. Jed immediately jumped in the tender with the 'let us go ashore before I pee myself' look on his face. They both headed for the jetty in the little dinghy, the water lighting up in the dark with every stroke of the paddle, due to the plankton in the water. It was a lot of extra and hard work having Jed with him sometimes, but he was a lovely dog and John's best friend, intelligent and great company and John loved the dog to bits.

On their return to the boat, they had a drink of tea, and both had a digestive biscuit before going to sleep, well sort of, as Jed snored again loudly which kept John awake. The next morning brought another beautiful day; the island looked mystical and spiritual, just as he had always imagined it. John watched Jed swim ashore for his morning pee; that dog just loved the water, he thought, as he headed to the galley to make breakfast. John had only time to pop some bacon on before he heard shouts from ashore; he headed back on deck and saw half a dozen people pointing to Jed and shouting. John saw the problem right away There were at least 30 Soay sheep and lambs running around, startled by Jed who, of course, was not in the least bit interested in them. John turned off the cooker, jumped into the tender and headed for shore to pick up his beloved pet. Mary was the first one to approach him on the jetty; she was livid. 'What the hell do you think you are doing?' she yelled. 'Do you not see that the sheep are lambing?' She was a feisty little thing from Scottish

Heritage who managed the island, and she was not at all happy. John had sadly just become a WAFI!

Once calm, Mary was very pleasant as she explained there were no dogs allowed on St Kilda which scuppered John's plans of a long walk up to the highest peak and the viewpoint at the top of the island or of spending any time ashore. Jed, now under control and, reluctantly on a lead, was escorted back to the jetty from which they both left with their tails between their legs.

Chapter 35

Claire

Claire was proud as punch to make CID at such a young age of 24; she was, however, not happy with her posting to Oban, but hey ho, it was not forever. It was a long haul from her time at training college at Tulliallan Castle, Alloa to her long stint at Pitt Street in Glasgow; she had only been in the Scottish police force for seven years and had now made Detective in the CID.

Claire was missing the girls back in the West End; she had gone to Glasgow University and spent a lot of time in the West End and of course Byres Road with its array of fabulous clothes shops, bars and restaurants. Most of her friends still stayed in the West End, except for Pam who now lived and worked in Canada. Claire sat at her desk which faced the window and looked out over Oban Bay; it was a beautiful day and the view out towards Ben More on the Island of Mull was quite spectacular. She supposed that working there had its good points even though it was sometimes a bit boring, especially over the winter months as Oban was mainly a fishing and tourist destination.

Sergeant Millar shoved his head round the door and asked if she could come and chat to a young female at the booking desk. Her name was Katrina and she wanted to talk to someone female. Claire thought it might be a sexual or other personal matter and agreed to have a chat with her as she was the only female in the station at that time.

Katrina, a pretty, dark-haired girl, stood holding a young infant about 2-years-old and looked extremely nervous and scared. Claire introduced herself and walked her back to her office. As she closed the door, the young girl immediately burst into tears. Claire managed to calm the girl down after much crying. She was from Latvia and was living with her baby and boyfriend in rented accommodation in Oban. She explained that her boyfriend had developed a drug problem and got into a lot of trouble with fellow Latvians and some other people from Romania. She explained that they had left in a white van, had boarded the ferry for Mull that morning and intended meeting a boat off the coast of Mull with the intent of bringing drugs into Scotland. Katrina wanted assurances that the police would help protect her boyfriend from the gang and from prosecution.

Claire thought to herself that the girl had more chance of winning the lottery than this chick risking a brilliant career prospect like this by becoming soft for the likes of her. Depending on the number of drugs, this could be a great opportunity to get back – promoted – to Glasgow! Claire contacted the Chief of Police, the Coast Guard and the Drugs Squad and held Katrina in custody, telling her it would be better for her and the child's safety, and also, under protest, confiscated her mobile phone in case she had a change of heart and wanted to call her boyfriend.

She got together a mini task force, the best she could at such short notice, telephoned the Chief and explained it might not be that big a haul, but it was best not to take any chances. The Chief did not see the need to get involved and told her to go ahead. She called in a few of the officers who were on leave or days off and, armed with maps and as much intel as she could gather, held an emergency briefing. She had also contacted and briefed Hamish and his merry band of four officers stationed in Mull. The Coast Guard had sent a fast cutter from Greenock which would track, from a distance, any vessels in the vicinity. She had also organised the local police launch which now sat down at the harbour ready to go.

Claire also sent Margaret and Ronald, both of whom were police officers, over on the morning ferry and in plain clothes to keep an eye on the van and its driver. Whoop, she thought, this chick is ready to kick ass! After the brief she headed out with her fourteen colleagues, full of adrenalin and hyped to the hilt. Claire had decided to keep the launch in the harbour meantime and to head over to Mull on the 2.20 pm CalMac sailing to Craignure.

No chances were being taken and there was not a single police uniform in sight. The sailing took forty minutes during which all uniformed officers had to stay in the van and lorry down on the ferry deck –wouldn't she be popular? The benefits of being a CID officer and in plain clothes meant that she could sit on deck and enjoy the sunshine as she looked out towards the island as the ferry passed Duart Castle. She was a tad nervous at the thought that this might turn out to be a wild goose chase and it would then have the opposite effect on her career, but the girl seemed sure, so nothing ventured nothing gained.

She also thought about sex and could really do with some physical fun in the near future, something to think about later.

The ferry docked at 3 pm. She had arranged to meet Hamish and his officers at a secluded forest walk car park near Ben More and she had already positioned officers in various locations over the island. A radio call came, confirming that the van and another 4 x 4 had been spotted stopped near the shoreline at Fidden and that they did not look like leaving any time soon. Claire recalled the officers and re-grouped them not far from Fidden. She and Hamish headed for a vantage point in the same area; they drove up through a commercial forest on a steep winding track before Hamish pulled over and parked the Land Rover a short way from the top, explaining that if they drove any further, the gang might be able to see them from below. Claire liked Hamish; he was tall and strong with ginger hair and a ginger beard, and just like her – the ginger hair, that is, not the beard.

He was married to Morag, a Gaelic teacher on the island and they had identical twin girls, Rebecca and Charlotte, both with the same ginger hair. They lived on a pretty croft near Croig, along with some sheep, pigs, and geese. Hamish had, like his father before him, been a police officer on the island for over twenty years; his father had since retired and still lived in the police house next to the police station in Tobermory. One of Hamish's officers, Stephen Little, approached them; he too had left his 4 x 4 further down the forest track and was in communication with the Coast Guard and a Royal Navy frigate which were both sitting just north of Islay; they had reported a Spanish fishing vessel as the most likely target, about 50 miles off the coast of Mull and heading in their direction, probably reaching them before nightfall.

Claire scanned the beach below. There were the two vehicles parked on the roadside – the Iveco double wheel-based van and an Isuzu pick-up. There were four men on the beach; she could make out Costin as the guy on the beach – she had a passport picture with her that she got from Katrina. The four men had erected tents and it looked like one of them was talking on a mobile phone. They did not seem to be armed, but it was hard to tell; they were not likely to have any weapons on view. The other two were standing at the tent, chatting. Claire was thinking they were in for a long wait and arranged with officer Little to bring food and water for herself and the other officers. Officer Little handled the task well and did a grand job of fetching sandwiches and soup from the deli in Tobermory; the food was excellent and after the late lunch, Claire really had to pee, and she was not leaving her vantage point for a public loo miles from her goal, so she made her excuses to Hamish who had a chuckle to himself. Very funny she thought – not! It's all very well for male cops with their dicks, being able to piss against trees at random.

Claire walked into the pine woods for about a hundred yards and, making sure she was out of sight, took down her trousers and panties and squatted in the heather. She felt like she had been peeing for hours; however, she was staying in the same place for too long and was being attacked by a ferocious swarm of midges. She tried swatting them away as she was being eaten alive! Eventually losing her balance, she cried out as she fell over and partly peed herself. Claire was rolling about in the heather with her trousers halfway back up when Hamish and Stevie appeared; she screamed at them, and they both immediately turned their backs. She knew that they had both seen her bare butt and ginger pubes and was mortified. Hamish was a decent cop, but Stevie was just a young cop, and she was sure this would be all round the station before she even got back.

She returned to the Land Rover where Hamish had put a Tesco carrier bag over the seat to keep it dry. 'Very funny,' she said. 'Sorry, ma'am,' said Hamish and laughed. The remaining three hours were a combination of more midges, radio, and phone calls to the ship, the Chief and the Coast Guard and daydreams of being back in the West End with the girls.

Her mobile interrupted her dreams; the call was from Commander Todd Steel, who was big boss on board the HMS Reliant. The ship to shore call informed her that the Spanish vessel should now be in view in her 2 o'clock position. How he knew that the boat was in her 2 o'clock position was baffling; how clever, however she would not ask in fear of making a twat of herself again! Claire had asked Boss Todd if, when they arrived near Mull, the ship would not show up on the Spanish trawler's radar and scare them off; he simply replied no, that their transponder would be switched off. The ship would anchor behind Iona so the trawler would not see them. What the fuck is a transponder? she thought.

Captain. Todd sounded hot and sexy; she imagined him in his white trousers, shirt and cap, like Richard Gere in *An Officer and a Gentleman* (but taller). She watched the fishing trawler from the hillside; her heart was pumping, and she needed to pee again. It was black and white and a lot larger than she had imagined, more like a smaller version of the ferry they had sailed over in. Claire could see the name clearly on the side of the vessel – it was called The Santa Maria, a bit girly for a fishing trawler, she thought. She radioed everyone to standby. The Coast Guard cutter was lying in wait out of sight around the opposite side of Iona, probably with its transponder switched off, she thought. The police launch was also on its way across to Mull; nothing had been left to chance. The Santa Maria was suddenly launching a fast rib from its port side, and everything started to happen at breakneck speed.

Claire, Hamish, and Stevie started driving down the forest track at a great rate of speed, the drive made more difficult due to the fading light. Claire arrived at the wooded area and joined her team of fellow officers; there were 21 police officers in total, practically the entire Oban Police force which included two armed officers. The neds in Oban would be running riot by now, she thought.

All roads had been closed, well just the one and only road actually; this was really looking like the real deal – if they were landing kippers or a couple of spliffs, she would fucking die!
The rib moved swiftly to shore – there were also four men on the boat. Claire spoke to her firearms officer Robert and his fellow firearms college Toby. They both agreed that it would be best to let the Navy and Coast Guard pick up the entire Spanish crew because if they were armed and a gun battle broke out, the police would be badly outgunned. It was unlikely that the European thugs would be armed, but you never know.

The entire area was silent; even the men working frantically on the beach were in complete silence. They worked in a chain, feeding the double wheel-based Iveco van with packages and there looked like a lot of them. Claire notified the waiting ships that the drop was complete and gave the order to move in.
'Go! GO! GO!' she shouted at the top of her voice.

All hell broke loose with lights, vehicles and men appearing from all directions. The criminals on the beach tried to make a run for it and one of them even dived into the sea – was he going to swim to the trawler? Claire had Stephen radio the police launch to pick him up before he drowned. Another had managed to run back up to the single-track road and was heading for Tobermory at great speed with Ajax the police Alsatian, and three of her officers hot on his tail. Claire knew who was going to win that one.

A short time later all three were safely cuffed and in the back of separate police vehicles, one of them being treated in the back of the ambulance for a few serious dog bites. Claire rushed to the Iveco van. Brian, her drug techie, was already there smiling, holding up a Sure Screen amine-colour-metric test, showing the colour purple – a positive sign for heroin, and lots of it! There were also half a dozen bales of marijuana. Claire asked Brian what he thought it was worth, and Brian's reply was 'Millions'!

'YABBA DABBA DOO!' she cried out. She called the Chief, as requested, on his mobile and gave him the good news; he was absolutely over the moon, so much so that he was heading back into Pitt Street even though it was after midnight. The Spanish trawler had upped anchor and was heading for the horizon; it would not get very far. Colin called to say the police launch crew had picked up the transatlantic swimmer, wet, exhausted and angry. Claire asked him to pick her up at Craignure jetty for her return trip to Oban. She was now sitting in the Land Rover, shaking, when Hamish appeared with a hip flask and two glasses; she could not resist, and both knocked back a glass of 18-year-old Tobermory whisky straight. 'Well done to us both,' she toasted. She was exhausted and sat slumped in the passenger seat of the Land Rover as Hamish drove her round to the jetty, singing at the top of his voice.

En route, sexy Todd had called her from his big muscle ship to inform her that all eight crew from the trawler were in custody without anyone being hurt, and both ships were on their way back to Oban Harbour. Claire's phone went into meltdown on the trip back; this was bigger than she ever had imagined, and it could have well turned into a disaster. If it had gone wrong, her career would be over as, due to its magnitude, it should have been handled by Glasgow and probably the Chief himself. Claire had, however, managed to pull off a large drug bust with very little notice and practically on her own; the end result looked very good for her career.

She was exhausted as the adrenaline was now wearing off and the dram was kicking in; she sat in shock on the stern of the boat as it headed back to Oban. It was now 1 am and she had been working since 7 am the previous morning. It was a beautiful boat trip back; the stars were out and if it were not for the noise of the boat's diesel engine, it would have been quite pleasant; she was now totally pooped and wanted to go home to bed.

On her return to the station, she spoke to the booking sergeant; a total of twelve people in custody, four on land, and eight from the boat. She held a half hour debrief with her team who all looked as knackered as she did; she also spoke again to the Chief and confirmed she would be back at the station later that morning. She left the station at 4.30 am, exhausted but very happy indeed and was sound asleep as soon as she hit the pillow.

Claire awoke the next afternoon. Bloody hell, it was 1.20 pm. There were six messages on her answer machine. One from the Chief, one from her Mum and Dad and one from Hamish. Hamish said she should check out the papers online. There was also a message from the team at the station, and one each from two of the girls in Glasgow.

Helen plugged in her iPad, put on the kettle and a croissant in the microwave, went back to her iPad and googled 'drug bust Mull'. She nearly had a heart attack when she saw the headline. 20 MILLION DRUG BUST ON MULL! BIGGEST EVER DRUG BUST IN SCOTLAND! Fuck's sake! That was HER! She headed for the shower; she had to get down to the station tout de suite as she was missing all the action; she was a fucking hero!

Claire arrived at the station where there were TV vans outside with satellite dishes on their roofs. She walked in, to be met with rounds of applause from everyone she passed; there were messages galore, and the Commander-in-Chief was in her office. She did a stupid salute and the Chief walked from behind her desk, shook her hand and gave her a huge hug! Claire tried to stay calm as she discussed the previous night's activities, starting with Katrina's visit to the station that morning. She also gave Hamish a short mention but missed out the peeing part!

There was another press conference later that afternoon which she would hold accompanied by the Chief. Scottish television and the BBC wanted a statement from her for their evening news. Claire's heart was pumping along at a hundred miles an hour. She thought it might be too early to ask for a transfer back to Glasgow, but it was exactly what she was going to do, just not this week. She was sitting in her office with a coffee when a journalist from STV walked in. His name was

Colin Robertson, average height, nice build and very charming; he was here to do a story on the bust. Colin was from Lenzie near Glasgow and asked her if he could take her out to dinner that evening. 'Yes,' was her reply; she had not been out much in Oban as there was not really anywhere to go. They arranged to meet at EE-USK (Gaelic for fish), a seafood restaurant on the pier, to discuss her story in further detail.

Later that day, and after what can only be described as nonstop, Claire headed home to get ready for her date; she did not date anyone at work or locally, for professional reasons, and was in need of some male company, and more! Her mobile rang in her pocket; it was the Chief again – maybe she was heading back to Glasgow!

Chapter 36

Gone

Sarah got a call from the kids about ten minutes past four, just after they had come out of school; they had arrived home to find Carolyn was not at the house and was not picking up their calls or texts. Sarah had also been looking for her sister as she had not returned her calls or voice mails since that morning. She had also called her Dad, who was now also worried and who had also not seen or heard from Carolyn; she had even called Philip who said he had not spoken to her that day. There had been no contact or sign of her since she left the kids that morning.

Sarah drove round to Carolyn's and sat with the kids; her Dad was there, too and they both decided to call the police and the private detectives; something was seriously wrong.

Mr McMaster was at the house within the hour; he too was concerned about her whereabouts. He picked up her iPad first of all, as he had insisted that Carolyn left her tablet password with him. That meant the private detectives could locate her phone if they wanted to, and if it was still switched on. He was surprised to find it was switched on and was located just a mile from this very house.

Frank McMaster spoke to the detective taking notes from Sarah, explaining that he knew where Carolyn, or maybe her phone, might be. The Police detective and the private detective, along with a police officer, drove the short distance to the location shown on her iPad. A female walked past with a dog which barked wildly at the trio as they searched the grass up and down the pathway. The kids said that Mum went for a run in the morning and would have come this way for sure.

The police detective, a Ronald Blane, found the phone and house keys as he walked back towards his police car; the items were just off the path and lying in the grass between the car park and the path. The detective checked the phone, but it was locked; he bagged it and sent the police officer straight to Pitt Street to have it examined. He then called in an investigation team before sending officers to Philip's work to collect him and bring him to the house.

The two detectives then searched the surrounding area; two local police officers arrived in a police van and cordoned off the area with police tape. When the area had been secured, they both walked back round to Carolyn's house; it was obvious she was not still in the area where her keys were found.

Philip had arrived and was giving a statement to a female police officer; he had an alibi as he had left Kelly's by taxi and had not left the optician's all day. They all stood around the house – Sarah, her Dad, Frank, Carolyn's next door neighbours Bob and Margaret, and the children, who were now in tears. There was also a police officer outside and two police detectives inside; no-one had now seen or spoken to Carolyn for fifteen hours and it was getting dark outside.

Due to the current situation and it being totally out of character, the police were now in the process of contacting everyone she knew and questioning those that could be suspects in her disappearance, like Kelly and her boyfriend who, along with Philip, were their main suspects. An alibi for Philip from Kelly was just not good enough. The two detectives were relatively young and inexperienced, Carolyn's father asked them to call their boss at Pitt Street; they both replied at the same time 'Chief Inspector Murdo McLellan.'

'Can you call him please.'

'Yes, sir,' said the detective and walked outside with the mobile pressed to his ear. The detective returned shortly after and handed the mobile to him. The Chief had been an old friend of his, they swapped Christmas cards but did not really socialise as such; they attended each other's weddings and family funerals and suchlike but were really just two people who knew each other from way back in the day. The Chief had moved on to University; Tom had not. Regardless of this, Murdo was at Carolyn's house within forty-five minutes. He took control immediately, giving them new hope.

Chapter 37

MV Titan

The 78-metre service and supply ship MV Titan slowly cruised into the Clyde. The ship had left Stornoway in the Hebrides earlier that day. It was cruising slower than normal due to a Royal Navy class 2 submarine about three miles ahead. The submarine was being shadowed by a Royal Navy frigate, a police launch, three smaller ribs with powerful outboards and a Lynx Helicopter which had flown past the ship twice now. The helicopter was now circling above the frigate like an angry wasp. The submarine was probably returning from a three-month trip at sea and was now heading to the Faslane Naval base on the Gareloch. The captain was complying with the MOD police launch's radio request to keep a three-mile distance between the MV Titan and the submarine.

Calum was standing outside on the deck, watching the Naval ships as they steamed on up ahead; he was the ship's diver on this trip. He could hear the captain speaking to someone on the radio, probably the police launch as the MV Titan now changed its course and turned port. The lights of Port Bannatyne could be seen as they neared their destination – Loch Striven. Calum could see a massive structure in the middle of the loch up ahead which was ablaze with lights. He knew instantly it was an island of six Maersk B-class container ships which were on a cold lay-up in the sheltered anchorage of the loch. The huge ships were moored together like a big blue and red floating platform; one, three and five were facing north and two, four and six were facing south. The ships had now been anchored in the deep-water loch for several years. The Dutch shipping company who owned them had asked the Clyde Port Authority permission to moor the ships there because of a worldwide downturn in demand for oil. The loch was deep and well protected by the surrounding mountains. The ships' presence, however, did not go down well with the locals as they blighted the surrounding landscape, an area of natural beauty, and because of the constantly running generators and the light pollution.

Calum and Brian, his dive mate, were aboard as part of a dive team of four who were there to replace a navigation buoy and also to recover two Highball prototype bombs lying on the seabed. The bombs were designed by Sir Barnes Wallis. When recovered, they would be displayed at the Brooklands Museum in Surrey and the de Havilland Aircraft Museum in Hertfordshire. The prototype bombs, which were never used operationally, did not contain any explosives. Highball was the military codename for these weapons, a naval version of the "Upkeep" bouncing bombs used in the Dam Busters raid in May 1943. It was one of five bombs developed by Sir Barnes Wallis and was designed to be used against ships.

The crew bell sounded, disturbing him from his thoughts; the ship's crew appeared from steel doors in the hull as if by magic and were now heading to their various workstations to get the ship ready to dock alongside the pier. Calum stayed on deck watching the bustle of activity. Ten minutes later they were tied up, the gangway was lowered, and all was quiet. It was a nice night and he now stood on deck checking out the various fishing boats tied up in the harbour – trawlers and lobster boats of various shapes and sizes. A few of the crew disembarked, heading to the local pub located just along the seafront from the harbour. They would be looking for local lassies and if none were available, they would sit and tell Para Handy type sea stories to anyone who would listen.

Calum didn't join them but instead headed back to his cabin. He was unhappy this trip and he knew why. He lay on his bunk looking at a picture of his wife and his beautiful three-month-old baby daughter Morgan. Calum was for the first time in his life homesick. He picked up his mobile and called his wife; he was going to tell her that this was going to be his last dive. He had thought about it long and hard and had decided this after watching his wife standing on the pier with Morgan in her arms, crying as the ship left port.

Looking at things financially, they had enough savings to live on the croft quite easily. Calum would also buy a small dive boat and dive for scallops to supplement their income. His wife was overjoyed at the news; she missed him badly when he was away. Calum felt better after their chat and slept like a baby.

The next morning, he got up, had a shower and headed for the canteen for his 6 am pre-dive meeting with Brian. In attendance were the ship's captain, the ship's safety officer and Mike the crane operator. Also sitting in were members of the team from the maritime museum who were in charge of overseeing the recovery of the bombs, and two Royal Navy divers who were there to assist in the recovery of the bombs, but not the buoy exchange dive. He had worked with Brian and Mike before on the Titan, mostly in the North Sea and in Canada.

Brian was a professional diver's mate and Calum was happy he would be looking after him during his dive. Loch Striven was deep and dark and Calum's dive would take him to the sea floor where he would cut the navigation buoy free. This dive, like all others, had its risks. Even though the tides, weather and safety were all strictly monitored, there was still that element of risk. Calum was looking forward to spending more time at home; he already had a scallop boat in mind that was up for sale and the thought of working the croft and spending more time with his family warmed him inside. After a check-up by the ship's doctor, he was soon in his diving suit.

A common grey seal popped his inquisitive head above the calm water; it looked like a wet Labrador as it studied the strange figure sitting, with his feet in the water, on the diving platform attached to the stern of the ship. Brian was now giving Calum his last-minute instructions before he placed the diving mask on his face, crossing himself as he did so. A quick radio check and thumbs up and Calum was ready to go. The cage which held various tools and monitoring equipment was lowered into the water; this was his ride down into the murky gloom. Calum held onto the cage as the crane lowered it slowly towards the seabed. The depth monitor read fifty feet as the light from above disappeared completely. Powerful LED lights on his helmet illuminated the blackness. Sea creatures, that had attached themselves to the wire cable that now ran through his hands as Calum continued his descent, fell away silently to the darkness below.

The control room on the stern of the ship was full as the men watched the dive video from Calum's helmet. He checked the altimeter attached to his wrist which now read 102ft. This was not a deep dive as such, about 200ft, but it still meant he would have to spend seven days after the dive in the decompression chamber on board the ship before his next and last dive; this would also be his second last time in the chamber.

Calum soon reached the seabed and called Brian to inform him. A hermit crab popped out of its hiding place on the large concrete block to see what all the commotion was about, before hurriedly returning to its shelter. Calum fired up a flare which helped shed more light on the concrete block that was the buoy's anchor, the chains running from the block up to the buoy.

Suddenly, something hit him in the back; he half turned and screamed into the radio.

A grotesque zombie-like face of a woman filled his entire mask – her eyes, lips, and the skin around her mouth were missing. It looked as if she was grinning, tiny baby crabs spilling from her mouth.

Calum, for the first time in his life, panicked on a dive and pressed the emergency button which would immediately tell Billy to lift the cage. Straight away, the cage started to lift off the seabed, the disturbed silt dancing around the body as the cage headed for the surface. Calum's muffled screams could be heard from behind his mask as the woman's grotesque and ghostly figure followed him from below, an arm outstretched in front of her.

Chapter 38

Bring Up My Dead

Danny had been back to work for about a week; it was the usual boring shit, you know – same shit, different day. He had not seen Jenny or Lesley as they were at some Clydesdale horse competition in Calgary, Canada, which Jenny went to every year as a judge. She had asked him to join her, but Danny had told her he could not get the time off from work, because it was just the start of the season, which was probably true. He would, however, see her as soon as she returned. He still thought there might be a chance of some money, so he would keep hanging in there.

Danny had sex with another two newbie female holidaymakers on the park. He also had sex with both Janet and Natcha, but not at the same time. Barbara, however, had been absent and did not appear that weekend; she usually turned up on the Friday night. It was now Saturday; she was probably still licking her wounds from the last time.

He had just finished work and decided to head for the bar because there were a few new babes about that he wanted to meet. He was wondering what to order for his dinner as he walked into the bar. Just about everyone, except for a fat bitch with two kids who sat in the booth, was crowded round the telly on the wall near the bar. It was not the usual sports channels that was showing, but something else.

Once close enough, he could see that it was the STV news girl, Laura Miller, standing at the water's edge, microphone in hand.

Danny's heart started to beat loudly in his head. The camera panned away to a massive tanker which he recognised straight away. The news crew were at Loch Striven and so was the entire police force, by the looks of it. Danny could see that there was a body covered up on the slipway; he turned around and headed straight back to his lodge. Rushing in, he took off his suit and dressed in his running kit; he also grabbed his binoculars and a spare set of registration plates which he fitted to his car with double-sided tape over the original ones and then drove towards Loch Striven.

His mind was racing; was it her? He did not believe in coincidence; it was only a week since he took her from the lodge in the dead of night. He had used a lodge owner's boat to travel the twenty minutes round to the loch. He had also weighted her body down well with chains attached to her body bag with large industrial cable ties and dumped his burner phone in the water. There was no way she would have resurfaced. His thoughts were interrupted by a police road block up ahead. He stopped the Pearl and powered down the window.

'What's the problem, officer?' he smiled at the young policeman with the ill-fitting hi-vis vest.

'The road is closed, sir.'

'May I ask why?'

‘I am not at liberty to say sir, please turn around; I am sure the road will be open later.’

Danny did as requested and parked about a half mile further back from the road block in a layby at the side of the road. It was next to a forest track; he retrieved his backpack from the boot, locked the car and started to run. It took fifteen minutes to reach a point where he could see the slipway. He walked to the edge of the forest, careful to remain out of sight. He was now just above the slipway and pier and could see clearly. He removed the small rucksack from his back and removed a lightweight sheet which he lay down on the ground over the pine needles on the forest floor. His head and heart were pounding as he focused his binoculars on the scene below.

The place was heaving with police and other plain clothes personnel. He could not believe his eyes – there were press everywhere, photographers with cameras, and reporters. There was also a van with blacked-out windows and two men dressed in funeral attire – black suits, white shirts and black ties, talking to a uniformed cop.

Down near the slipway there were two men talking to what must be, and he was assuming, two detectives; one a female with red hair who was writing in a notebook. The other was an older guy with grey hair who had a black Labrador dog by his side. He walked over to a sheet and lifted it and Danny’s heart nearly exploded as he could see the chain he had used to sink her body, on the ground at her feet and which had been removed from around the body. It was her!

And with a body came DNA and that fucking bitch had lots of it on her and it was his. One of the guys talking to the redhead was wearing a diving suit. Danny at first thought that he was a police diver, but he changed his mind when the police underwater unit turned up; he must have been the one that found the body. Danny scanned the surrounding area with the binoculars. Parked nearby was a Ford Ranger 4 x 4, its back tailgate down. Because of its angle he could only make out Ion Buoy Solutions on the side; there was, however, a work boat tied up at the quay, which was called the Titan; a shiny new buoy stood on its rear deck.

Danny thought he had an idea what was going on; her body had not surfaced! It had been found! Which was really strange as the loch was so deep. He watched as the two undertakers removed a stretcher from the private ambulance, walked over to the body, placed the stretcher on the ground and spoke to the grey-haired guy. They then lifted the body, unzipped from its body bag, onto the stretcher, the chain remaining on the ground. Danny remained calm; he had to get her back and fast; he would have to follow the black van until it revealed where the body was going. They would not do an autopsy tonight, he hoped; if they did, he was fucked and would be leaving the park that night, never to return.

He had a Swiss bank account and two passports and could leave pretty sharpish if he had too. He packed up his belongings and headed back down the track towards his car; the black van passed him just as he closed the boot. Danny did a three-point turn and followed the van. He was unsure where it would go, possibly a local hospital, morgue, or local undertakers perhaps. Danny was wrong on all counts because the van headed for the ferry; it was heading across the Clyde to Gourock or Greenock. There was a main hospital in Greenock, which would make sense, as the hospital this side of the Clyde was only a day clinic, like a cottage hospital you would find in the Western Isles.

Danny kept his ferry tickets in his visor and promptly handed one out of the window of his car; he then went to the boot and removed a holdall with a change of clothing which he always kept in case of emergencies, and this was definitely an emergency, He returned a short while later dressed from head to toe in black. He was parked behind the black van and sat in his car; the bitch was maybe about seven feet away from him in the back of this private ambulance. He thought about what fun he had had with her, how she pleaded with him, she really did not want to die, but how could he let her live? He teased her constantly during their coupling and enjoyed every minute of it. She was a whore, she thought she was above him, and guess what? She was not, and she was now lying in the back of the van heading for the morgue.

The ferry ride was soon over, and he followed the van as it headed east towards Greenock; he was surprised when it did not take the hospital cut-off. Danny spent the next thirty minutes following the van to a large sandstone building with a slate roof on Hyndland Street, Glasgow. It was a big building with a circular driveway and stone pillars at the entrance with MORGUE cut into the stone. Danny stopped outside and leaned against one of the pillars; he could see the two men carry the body inside on the stretcher. Danny could not get any closer and sat outside in the car until both men left in the van. An old security guard walked down to the gates before locking them. Who the fuck guarded a morgue, he thought? He drove around the streets of sandstone properties, a mixture of businesses, dentists, accountants, banks, and a few residential homes, and quickly found what he was looking for. He then drove back to the morgue to check that the place was definitely shut for the night; it was in darkness except for the reception desk which was lit by a solitary lamp and what looked like the glow of a computer; the old security guy looked like he was settled in for the night.

Danny had a lot to do and had to do it quick. He drove straight home; it was a nice night – the summers seemed now to come early and then end early. He loved driving home but not tonight. Tonight, he was in trouble and lots of it; he had to get her back. He was not going to prison EVER! He had been before and hated every second; he would not survive even a week in jail, preferring to die instead even by his own hand; doing this would be far better than confinement in a prison full of scum. He was once held on remand in Barlinnie Prison because of some stupid cop's mistake of taking him to the wrong court. It was a bank holiday weekend, and the courts were not open again till the Tuesday, meaning Danny was then held for four days in a cell with a brainless Celtic football supporter whom he hated. That made up Danny's mind that he would never get caught and would take every step not to.

He collected tools from the house and a Smith and Wesson 45 semi-automatic and silencer, a gift to himself which he had bought in Russia, no questions asked and no licence of course; the gun would normally cost about £600; this one cost him £2500, a high mark-up, he had thought, but bought it anyway; this gun was clean and untraceable.

He put his things in a rucksack, took a long look around his amazing home and then headed back up the track. He wanted to spend more time at his house away from all this crap; he needed to get more money in the bank; life was for living, not working; he was also, for the first time ever, afraid of being caught. He raced the old 4 x 4 up the track before putting it back in the barn and swapping it for the Audi.

Danny then drove through Kinlochard towards Aberfoyle; apart from the current circumstances it was very pleasant. Kinlochard had some posh homes on the banks of loch Ard in some truly beautiful settings. He drove past the old Altskeith Hotel, featured in the film *The Forty Nine Steps* which was in a really nice spot with its boathouse on the lochside. Danny worked hard to be here and was not going to lose it, no matter what the cost.

He carried on through the villages of Aberfoyle and Blanefield before arriving at his destination – Milngavie train station. On the train to Glasgow, he was conscious of the CCVT which would now follow his journey from here on in, it was everywhere, even on the train. He wore a cap to cover his face and avoided the cameras whenever possible. He had abandoned the Ford Mondeo in Glasgow on his trip back from Dumfries; it still sat where he left it and he went into the alleyway opposite, watched the car and street for about half an hour before he approached it and jumped inside. He drove straight to the morgue where he stopped two streets away.

Danny was in a league of his own in what he was about to do. He was no fucking James Bond, but he was super-fit and intelligent, he had a huge knowledge of survival techniques, hand-to-hand combat, weapons, IT, mobile data, and forensics. He had once dated a forensics investigator who used to work for a police force in London but moved on to work privately for an insurance company. She taught him lots of techniques that were used in investigations to catch criminals and how to avoid getting caught by leaving forensic evidence behind. Danny dated her, soaking in tons of information on not only murder but arson, IT, bank accounts, and much more; he read books about it all. He could, in fact, even survive out in the wilds on his own for months, even years if he needed to, without leaving a trace or getting found.

He made the SAS, Bear Grylls and Rambo, the so-called survival experts, look like a bunch of fucking sissies. He worked quickly, opening the electric box on the side of the road; the two large cables coming out of the ground were cut with the insulated bolt cutters he had brought with him. The entire area went black; it was a dark night, and you could hardly see your hand in front of your face. There were no lights on in the buildings surrounding the morgue; there were also no streetlights, no stars; no moon.

Danny worked quickly. Driving straight to the front door of the morgue, he jumped out of the car, leaped up the steps to the front door and gave it a gentle tap with the 45. The old security guard stood at reception; the area was lit by something. He looked about sixty and had some kind of temporary lamp. As the guard walked towards the door, Danny saw it was a gas camping lamp.

The guard walked up close to the door, peering out, his eyes squinting.

Danny shouted, 'Electricity company' and gave him his best pearly smile.

The stupid old fool unlocked the door. He would probably not expect anyone to break into a morgue, even in Glasgow. Danny gave him an even bigger smile as he was let inside.

'What's happened to the power, sonny boy?' he asked. Danny pushed him inside. 'Hey, what?'

'Shut up, old man, or I will kill you right now.' He shoved the gun in the old man's face, causing his cheek to bleed.

'This is a mortuary,' the old man protested. Danny ignored him. 'Shut up and take me to the body that arrived earlier.' The old man was shaking. 'The medical examiner is coming to see her tonight,' he said. 'Well, he might just not find her here when he arrives. Now shut up and hurry up.'

The lamp lit the way as the old man took him down the stairs. 'The lift won't work; we have to take the stairs.'

It was spooky inside; why the hell anyone would want to work here, let alone by yourself and at night, in a morgue was beyond him. The lamp light bounced back from the pristine white wall tiles. They both arrived at the bottom of the stairs and went through a double door. They were in a large room. Danny felt like they were Burke and Hare stealing bodies for re-sale in Victorian times and he laughed. 'What?' said the shivering old man.

'Shut up and show me.' Danny pushed the old boy ahead of him, his gas lamp swinging from side to side. There were shiny operating tables, four in all; there was also an array of instruments on some type of racks against the far wall; on the opposite wall there were lots of small steel shiny doors that would no doubt hold the bodies; it was cold in the basement and even the tiled walls were uninviting.

'Which one?'

The old boy walked over and pointed to a drawer two up on the right. Danny pulled it open and pulled away the white sheet. It was her – slightly bloated and not looking so good. 'We meet again, bitch.'

Danny turned round to the old boy who was still shaking and shot him in the face at point blank range.

A bit of something, possibly his skull, shot across the room and landed in something metal, making a weird sound.

The old man fell to the floor, a dark pool of blood spreading out quickly around his head; it looked more black than red. Danny lifted her body out from the drawer, fuck she was heavy; he was careful not to step in the blood and sprinted for the stairs, the body swung over his shoulder, his legs straining under the weight as he climbed the stairs back up to reception. He placed the body at the top of the stairs and had a good look outside; it looked clear.

He carried his prize downstairs out to the car where he opened the boot and placed her on the ground. He took out another body bag, zipped it up and threw her in the boot of the car. He then drove away slowly; there was no sign of anyone on the streets outside and the power would be out for at least the next few hours.

Danny drove first to the Necropolis graveyard in the city centre, an old Victorian graveyard with huge tombs and graves, making it scarier than any modern graveyard. He parked the Mondeo on the street and climbed the gates. He spent 15 minutes searching around the old graveyard, but he did not find what he was looking for; he also felt uncomfortable as he was not on his home ground and was a little nervous. He drove straight to

Dalnottar Cemetery, where a lot of his relatives and friends were buried, including his Dad.

Danny found what he wanted in the first two minutes. There were two newly dug graves, easy to spot in the dark as the silhouettes of mounds of earth rose up from the ground at each side. He went back to the car and got a round mouth shovel and a pick from the boot.

Carolyn looked awful and smelled a little awful too. He slapped her once pretty and now grotesque face. 'You're still a bitch, even when you're dead. Never mind, you are going to have a proper resting place now, better than that wet one. Hey, your family can come visit you,' he laughed, knowing they could never come as they would never know she was there.

Danny removed the fake turf and boards from around the hole dug in the ground. He spent the next two hours digging the hole a full two feet deeper; it was hard dirty work, but worth it to keep his pretty face out of a long stint in jail and the loss of his freedom. It was also fitting that this stupid bitch had a proper grave; she was not the first he had buried, sunk, or burned – in fact she was the tenth. Aah, such lovely memories he thought. He stayed vigilant as he dug the hole deeper. Graveyards did not get many visitors at night, but you did get a few crazies like ghoul hunters, lovers, or just plain vandals.

He nearly got caught burying a young female in a grave in woods near Cambridge when he was disturbed by badger baiters out poaching with dogs; they sounded mean and had weapons.

There were four of them and three were big guys, their shapes clearly visible in the lights from their lamps – rough sounding fuckers too. He had tried to move away along the riverbank, but a small terrier type dog broke away from them and was on him before he could get away. He killed it quickly, driving his knife between its ribs and into its heart, before slipping into the cold river. He held on to the banking until they left, still looking for their stupid dog and he floated the still warm mutt down the river once they were out of sight.

Danny collected Carolyn from the car and placed her in the grave, carefully shovelling the earth over her before returning the graveside back to the way he had found it. He went back to the car, removed all his clothes and put them inside a polythene bag. He then walked, naked, across the graveyard towards the building that housed the gravediggers and their tools. Two diggers stood outside, a large JCB and a smaller Kubota machine; there was also a tap outside.

Danny stood under the tap and turned it on; the water was freezing. He noticed as he washed that his normally large penis had shrunk to half its normal size, causing him to laugh out loud, his voice carrying across the graveyard, probably scaring everything else that was out there that night. After washing, and still naked, he returned to the car, removed a black holdall from the back seat and removed the clothes from inside. He got dressed in black jeans, a black shirt and a black navy type pea coat, combed his black hair, gelled it back, and slapped some aftershave on.

He felt great and looked great even though he was pretty tired. He was not, however, going on a date with some lucky female, but instead would remain right there in the graveyard till morning. He moved back to a tree near the grave, where he stood in its shadow. The night was dark and quiet and would be a long one. It reminded him of his snow dropping days in Faifley when he was younger. Snow dropping got its name from the route through the woods that the gang would use to reach the posh houses in Bearsden and Milngavie; the floor of the woods was covered in the small white flowers – snowdrops – hence the name was born as the boys started snow dropping in spring when people started to hang out their washing in their back gardens. Danny and his band of thieves would go to the posh estates and steal designer clothes from washing lines and stuff from sheds and garages, scooters, motorbikes, even a few cars.

It was a good way of bringing in cash and kitting yourself out in the best designer gear for free, and also for dining on posh food taken from freezers that they kept in their lockups at the end of their gardens. It was also a good laugh with lots of nonsense in between. Danny remembered that on the way back from a raid in Blanefield, one of the gang that night was Duck Donaldson who saw a racing bike while looking in the window of one of the wooden huts. These huts were used as weekend getaways and owned mostly by families from Glasgow who spent their weekends there – freedom in the country and all that.

The stupid bastards who owned the huts spent most of their time in the Carbeth Inn, drinking, and never saw the fucking countryside anyway. During the week, the wooden huts, which were painted a shitty green, were empty and provided easy pickings for this young gang of marauders.

Duck broke a concrete slab in two pieces and lifted it over his head and threw it at the window, none of them realising at the time that it was a Perspex window; the slab suddenly bounced back off the Perspex at great speed hitting Duck in the face; it was really funny but did hurt his face and left a permanent scar. Danny had later learned that Duck once worked at this very cemetery as a gravedigger, no less, but had since died of a drugs overdose.

He watched a cat walk by, looking in his direction and he wondered where cats went at night; he hated them and had once drowned one in a sink. It belonged to the old witch who lived next door to him when he was a kid. He enjoyed killing it and enjoyed watching her as she tried to find it for weeks afterwards.

Danny spent the rest of the time in passing the early hours till dawn watching cars as they drove across the Erskine Bridge; it was close by and was well lit, and you could make out the types of cars that were crossing its long, arched roadway. An owl hooted not far away. Danny thought they were stupid birds and looked ridiculous. A fox appeared at Carolyn's grave. Foxes would smell her a mile away and that was the reason Danny had remained in the graveyard. He shuffled his feet and watched it sprint away, looking back at the fucker who had just spoiled a free meal; maybe it would catch up with the cat and eat it instead.

Many a body had been found after it had been poorly buried in a shallow grave; badly burned bodies were often dug up by wild animals including foxes or even domestic pets. To protect himself, Danny had stood there all night against the tree until daylight; walking away at this stage could cost him dearly. He did not move from his position until the first of the council gravediggers arrived at 7.30 am; he wondered if one of them was indeed an old gang member.

Danny did not want to be recognized and walked away. He picked up a bunch of fresh flowers from a recent grave nearby and placed them on the front seat of the car before closing his eyes. He had a power nap until 8.30 am when the crematorium opened. The times of the burials would be posted inside. He was in luck – the first one was at 9 am and the second at 10 am. He called Janet at 8.45 am and told her he would not be in that day as he had to go to the dentist after losing a filling and would swap his days off to Monday, Tuesday instead of Tuesday, Wednesday. She went to tell Gordon and returned to the phone to tell him that was fine, and could she come see him later after work at his place. He hung up without answering.

Danny had no idea which funeral to go to and ended up going to both; the first deceased was not buried with Carolyn, meaning he had to wait for the second, in which time he nearly fell asleep, the female minister being so fucking boring that he fought sleep for the entire duration. He followed the second coffin outside where it was placed on wooden beams above Carolyn's body. After another skull-numbing speech from the boring minister, and to the shrill of bagpipes, the coffin was eventually lowered on top of the blonde bitch. She now lay in a grave never to be revealed to anyone. People were crying and sobbing for whoever had died, Brian somebody; they all walked away after the burial, heading for the Radnor Hotel for tea and sandwiches. Danny hung around as the workers covered the coffin and the blonde's body. An hour later the gravediggers had moved on to digging another fresh grave for the next dead twat to be lowered into the ground that week. Danny drove out of the graveyard, smiling and relaxed, He drove the Mondeo the short drive to Peel Glen Road, a notorious back road that led into Drumchapel. Many a stolen car was found dumped and burned here; the police would not give the soon to be burnt out Mondeo a second look.

He drove the car into a nearby field and set it on fire, watching it burn before walking to the main road and catching a taxi back to Milngavie train station. Danny would collect his car, do some shopping and spend what was left of the next two days at home – something he was looking forward to. Two hours later he arrived back at the 4 x 4 and loaded it up with his holdall and rucksack; he had one more job to do before he got to the Bothy.

He stopped the Toyota at the side of the forest track and removed the 45 from his bag; he put on a pair of gloves and cleaned the handgun from end to end; he then removed the ammunition clip and the silencer and launched them into the loch. One sure way of getting caught for a murder was by keeping the fucking gun; you would not believe how many murderers have been caught that way. He would have preferred to have kept it, but it would have been silly to do so, and he reluctantly launched it into the deep loch.

Job done, he walked back up the banking to the 4 x 4 and headed for home.

Chapter 39

Body Snatcher

John was woken by his phone ringing; he rolled over and looked at his alarm clock, it was 4 am. Heather stirred beside him, 'God, John, I thought we had left this all behind.'

'Yep, sorry darling, so did I.' He picked up the ringing telephone. 'Morning.' He listened as the police officer on the other end of the phone told him there was another murder and it was at the morgue and that a body had also been taken, his murder victim. John took the details, scratched his balls, and sighed; he would have to call Claire. Until yesterday they had not seen each other for about twelve months; Claire had been doing well in Oban and he was, of course, meant to be retired. They were both, however, asked by the Chief to look into the death of his best friend's daughter who had been missing for a week and had now turned up very dead indeed.

John was now officially out of retirement temporarily; a retirement that did not last very long, he thought. He did not want to be, nor did he want to start dealing with death yet again – in fact that was the main reason for retiring early in the first place, but the Chief had been good to him over the years, and he felt obliged to help him.

He got out of bed, put the kettle on and dialled Claire's number; it rang for ages before she answered. 'Blimey, John, do you know what time it is?'

'Of course I do Claire, but this is important.' He told her about the nightwatchman's murder in the morgue and the missing body. 'That's a first for me, a stolen corpse.' 'Yes, me too, invasion of the body-snatchers for sure.' They agreed to meet at the morgue on Jocelyn Square in the centre of Glasgow, a place they had both been to many times in the past. John felt saddened to be involved in a gruesome murder and was not looking forward to the task ahead; the second body in two days he thought.

John arrived first. He did not go inside, instead he followed a police officer to a street round the corner where another officer was standing beside an electricity box at the far side of the pavement; it was about four feet tall and wide and painted grey. Blue and white police tape was wrapped around the two nearest lamp posts forming a no-go area; two cables about three inches in diameter and about three feet long and insulated in black lay on the ground. Scottish Power had already restored power to the area and replaced the cut cables with new ones, not realising of course that this was a crime scene and not just a theft. The police officer told John that he was waiting for the forensic guys who were round at the morgue to come and take photographs and fingerprints.

John left the officer and walked back round to the morgue. Walking up the steps to the glass doors you would not believe anything was wrong apart from the high volume of police officers, cars and vans that were parked outside, and the officer at the front door. Reception was also neat and tidy with the dead watchman's cup of tea, now cold, and a custard cream, and Daily Record newspaper still open and lying on the desk which was hidden from visitors by the high counter front. John went down the marble stairs to the mortuary where just about everybody was. The tech guys were busy taking pictures of what was now the primary crime scene. John shook hands with Malcolm Stevens, the medical examiner; he was originally here to examine Claire's body. 'Never seen this before John.'

'Me neither,' said John as he knelt beside the old watchman's body, keeping away from the huge pool of blood around his head and spread back from his shoulders to the wall behind. A large calibre automatic, by the looks of the entry and exit wounds and, judging from the burn marks, pretty close up to, in fact, practically touching his forehead when the gun was fired. John could hear Claire's footsteps coming down the stairs, her shoes and stride easily recognisable; she swung through the double doors clutching a Costa coffee.

'Morning Boss, morning Steve,' she said before walking across to the body. 'Jesus, what a mess, poor old guy.' She returned to the two men while sipping her coffee. John brought her up to speed, telling her about the power being disabled and there being no hope of any CCTV footage. He then introduced her to the rest of the team before taking her back upstairs where they stood behind the reception in the foyer.

'Whoever did this knows what they are doing,' he said as he flipped through the watchman's newspaper. 'Do you think the body being taken was for ghoulish purposes or do you think it's to hide the evidence?' John passed her a couple of photographs taken the previous day at the slipway; one was of a birth mark on a swollen ankle, the other was of a mole on a similarly swollen arm; she put them both in her bag. 'According to the M.E this was a violent and prolonged sexual attack. I think whoever it was knew we had found the body and he knew where it was being taken. That means the killer or killers are close. I think it's a solitary male sexual predator and I don't think this is the first time he has killed either. One thing that worries me, Claire.'

'What, boss?'

'He seems to really know what he is doing; I have never seen anything like this, not here in Scotland anyway.' They walked back to their cars. Claire opened the central locking on her car and John opened the door for her as she climbed inside. 'We need to confirm our Jane Doe is in fact Carolyn Hughes, and those photographs are all we have to go on unless our body turns back up, which I doubt very much if it will.' They both left the morgue car park in separate cars, John agreeing to pick Claire up at Pitt Street Police Station, the head office of Police Scotland. Claire would now be staying with a friend in the West End of Glasgow for the foreseeable future.

John collected Claire from the front entrance in Pitt Street and drove towards Milngavie. He and Claire worked well together and had enjoyed working together in the past. They discussed the case between them as they drove the twenty-minute drive to Castle Mains Estate in Milngavie to speak to the family and hopefully identify whether it was Carolyn Hughes or not. If it was not, then they were back to square one as they had no reports of any other missing female, and now no body in the mortuary. They arrived in the driveway of a smart detached house with a double garage and neat garden. The door was answered by Frank, a private detective who had been investigating Philip; he showed them into the lounge; present were Carolyn's father, her sister, and Frank's sidekick Sue.

Sarah asked if they would like some tea and then asked everyone else; their faces were drawn and tired, looking like people were when you were at a house after a funeral. Both Sarah and Sue disappeared into the kitchen to make tea and coffee.

John spoke first. 'I can't have you carrying out your own investigation, Frank, I am sorry.' Carolyn's father stood up, and intervened 'I have asked Frank to be here, not just as a witness to previous matters which I think might be useful, but also as a friend of the family.' John agreed that Frank and Sue could remain which they did, but without any other involvement. John hated this part of a murder inquiry and instead left it to Claire to show the photographs of the body. Claire explained to everyone the recent events, including the theft of the body from the mortuary; she then asked if anyone could identify a birth mark or a mole from a photograph.

Carolyn's father stood up from his chair and walked towards Claire who was sitting in the dining area of the lounge. She placed the two photographs on the table; he picked one of them up and stared at it before sobbing uncontrollably. Sarah ran over to him and held him; she too started crying. 'Oh, Daddy,' she cried. Frank buried his head in his hands but did not cry.

John hated this job for this very reason. There were beautiful photographs of Carolyn and her family around the house, an attractive blonde woman with a lovely smile and everything to live for, and now she had been violently murdered in the most brutal fashion. Just as sad was the fact that the family could not even bury their beautiful girl even if they wanted too. John wanted to discuss the case in more detail and asked if anyone wanted to leave. Sarah decided she did not want to know any details and would go and sit with the children who were at her house. She would have to break this awful news about their mother to the kids. John discussed the case with Frank, Sue, and Tom. 'Do you want me to go on?' asked John.

'Yes, you come highly recommended, detective; I want the person who killed my daughter, please go on.'

John went into more detail and asked Frank to provide any information he had. They would bring in Kelly and her boyfriend, and Philip, who were still all suspects, however John did not think that any of them were involved; this was different, very different, not something an enraged husband would do, not in this fashion; this was a hatred for women in general and a total disregard for the older generation like Billy Thomson, the old boy at the mortuary, who would never have thought he would be shot dead at his work at night.

Chapter 40

The Dark Past

Danny was having a blast. He was pretty well-oiled, having drunk a half bottle of Jack Daniels since he got home; he felt tired but good about the way he recovered from the potential disaster that would have happened if that bitch's body got anywhere near a medical examiner. There was a medical examiner at the slipway, but he would have been confirming a time and cause of death; the autopsy would have happened later if Danny had not removed the body. A total clusterfuck of pain had been avoided and he was safe for now; the thought of having to leave his home to become an abandoned one on You Tube upset him. There would, of course, be an investigation into her whereabouts over the past few weeks; the park would come into play at some point, but he would deal with that when it came. Meantime there was no connection whatsoever between him and Carolyn; the police had only found the secondary crime scene where the body was dumped, and he doubted very much if they would find the primary crime scene which was Jenny's lodge. He had broken the glass table but had cleaned it up and had an excuse ready for that when Jenny returned. He would tell her that he bought her flowers for her return and dropped the glass vase through the table; he would replace it if she told him where it was purchased. He had very much left the lodge the way he had found it, minus the table of course.

Danny walked outside; music from the external speakers was playing but the volume was very low. Two months ago, his year was looking good with a new mark on board – Jenny – who was now looking like a financial flop, plus the fact that she was playing him was concerning. Sex with her was also boring, mundane and dull and it was obvious he would have to ditch her. His bitches on the park were all good but he had fucked up with Barbara and it looked like she would not be back.

Danny could, of course, leave his house in less than ten minutes if he really had to. He learned this from a statement by Robert De Niro in the film *HEAT* – 'don't ever have anything you can't walk away from in ten minutes' were words stamped into Danny's brain He was well organised with an escape route; money and weapons were both at the house along with ID and passports, and a backup set was buried near the Cessna at Strathallan Airfield. Danny could be out of there before the cavalry even got to the barn. He had also installed an early warning system up at the barn, an Amazon Blink camera focused on the road and which he could view on his iPhone anywhere.

Danny had practised an exit from the Bothy many times, He would time himself and run out of the house, jump in the jeep and drive north-west on a very old forest track which took him back to the main road via a different long and winding track and a climb up and over the hills; the big Toyota could handle the route easily; it was a good escape route and you would need a 4 x 4 to follow him. Another alternative was to leave on foot through the forest and hike the eastern side of Ben Lomond and then descend by the west side into Rowardennan.

Danny was chilled as he lay on the lounger outside; the stars were amazing, and he felt small looking up at the billions of them twinkling in the night sky. He thought about the last few weeks' events and was not at all happy about his current situation; he felt concerned about his status for the first time in his life. He had come far too close to being found out and was unsure whether to kill Katie. He had strong self-preservation issues with letting her live; as a risk, he would normally not have hesitated to kill her, but this time he did not; he felt close to her. He wanted to tell her about his previous kills. It was lonely being him, and he liked to be with her. He could pack his bag and leave right now; his plane was always fuelled and ready to go at Strathallan Airfield and he could fly anywhere at the drop of a hat. Leaving now, however, would only cause suspicion and attract attention. He would have to ride this one out; he doubted it would come back to him. His previous killings had all gone well, with the bodies never being found apart from one burned one and his forensic cleanliness had never led a trace back to him.

His kills had always been carried out cleanly, apart from just that one time in a penthouse flat in the South of France. He was working his charm round the casinos where he targeted and bedded a fat ugly French slut called Madame Cerise Lemieux. He had killed her for money; he slept with the disgusting bitch before torturing her for the combination to her safe, and then strangled her and set her and the penthouse flat on fire. He watched her burn on the bed for a while and did not leave until Cerise and the flat were well ablaze and not before he had emptied the safe. On exiting the apartment, he crossed the hallway and pressed the illuminated down button on the lift panel; he could hear the lift leave the ground floor, and walked back to lock the apartment door. The lift arrived with a whirr and a ping. As the doors slid silently open, a gentleman in a black tuxedo appeared and exited the lift, his keys in his hand. He looked Danny right in the eye and said "Bonsoir, ou est-ce le matin?' as he walked over to his own apartment door and suddenly stopped. He was just about to go into his own apartment when he shouted 'FUMÉE', pointing at the bottom of Madame's door where smoke was beginning to pour out from underneath it.

Danny walked quickly up to him, spun him back round towards his own door, and slashed his throat. He left the smartly dressed gentleman gushing huge amounts of blood from the main artery in his neck all over his white shirt and bow tie and all over his front door and the very expensive carpet beneath. He lay dying, clutching his throat, eyes wide in shock and surprise, his keys still grasped in his hand.

Danny sprinted back to the lift and managed to catch it before the doors closed; there was no one in the posh lobby as he left the building. Looking up, he smiled as he saw billows of smoke coming from the roof. He walked a few streets away before catching a cab back to his hotel, and then he booked an

Easy Jet flight online and spent the next couple of days sightseeing. He visited the Eiffel Tower, The Louvre and Notre Dame de Paris, all sights he had seen before; he had simply gone to give himself an alibi in case it was ever needed.

He was back in Scotland three days later, where he intended to take some time off. At that time, he was crazy about flying and fed up hiring light aircraft from snooty flying clubs and arseholes running small airports and so decided to spend some of the money buying his own aircraft. He found and purchased a Cessna 172 for cash from a gentleman who had used the aircraft to smuggle drugs. He arranged to keep it at Strathallan Airfield from which he once skydived before deciding it was safer to stay inside the fucking plane.

The French thing was his first double killing; he did not enjoy killing men and, until recently, had only ever killed that one male. His tally now, after the nightwatchman, was up to two, with nine females – that makes eleven. Danny supposed that he was now a serial killer and enjoying it – and he laughed. His female kills were all sexual, brutal, and violent. He enjoyed the asphyxiation the most; it excited and aroused him; people would never understand the sexual thrill he got from it. Killing someone this way was known as asphyxiophilia and this is what gave him the kicks he desired – you would have to experience it to understand. Some men did this to themselves and some even died doing it while masturbating, but this was not for him. Danny loved doing it to the girls and the more he did it, the more he wanted it.

He was proud of where he now was to where he had come from; living in a housing scheme in Glasgow with a mother who did not give a fuck and a father in jail was hard. Danny's father was jailed for murder when Danny was nine years old and did the entire 25 years in Barlinnie. Danny had never seen him since and never visited him in prison; he died of a heart attack three years after his release. When his Dad was sent to prison, his mum became a bitch; she had lost her breadwinner and now encouraged Danny from an early age to lie, cheat and steal; she would then take everything that he stole away from him. He learned quickly not to give her everything and to hide money and stolen items from her.

When he was fifteen Danny's mother took him to a woman's house in Bearsden and forced him to have sex with the woman and her friend; this was the first sexual experience he had, and he hated it. His Mum remained in the house in Bearsden while he was abused by both women; they paid her well and his Mum gave him twenty quid for his efforts! One of the women later became his first victim. Danny walked into her bedroom and strangled her. The other bitch had died of natural causes before he could get to her. His life really was a world of shit; the council house where he lived was a dump. His Mum was a drug-dealing fat lazy cunt who abused her own son to the extent that she hired him out to sex-starved women for money, seriously! Sometimes they were nice, but most were fat and ugly. Danny had a few breaks away from his mother when she was jailed herself for minor drug offences and petty theft, when he would still stay in the house but with his aunt who also dealt drugs for his mother until she was released. His aunt was not as bad as his mother, but he still came close to being taken into care in his younger years, for many different reasons.

Danny had attended Braidfield High School in Clydebank, which is now demolished; schooling there was practically non-existent with teachers even going on strike for long periods of time. He was eventually expelled from school at the age of fifteen for fighting and striking a teacher, after which he got a job at Morelands farm in Hardgate, Clydebank, delivering milk and later, a paper round where he could really earn decent money. Both jobs, however, were eventually spoiled by his mother who made him deliver drugs, using the paper round as cover. Danny was later found out by the shop owner who then fired him, the farm following suit closely after. He then went back to hanging around with a young gang of neds called the Sticky Bandits who stole just about everything. Twenty young men, most of whom were now either in jail, dead or doing drugs and who later became known as the Faifley Mad Squad. It was not all doom and gloom, however, and they did have summers where they would go fishing or hiking and they spent many days in the countryside around Loch Lomond and its islands, a great way of escaping their city slum.

They often stole boats and would blast around the loch. Danny and the boys enjoyed hiking and climbed various munros to prove how fit and manly they were. As they got older the opposite sex would become apparent and they all started to think with their dicks instead of their heads. Danny, being the most handsome, fucked just about everything that moved and often escaped his Mum's grip by no longer needing to live with her full-time. Many of his girlfriends' mothers wanted to sleep with him and he often obliged; they rewarded him by letting him stay at their posh houses, sometimes in the same rooms as their daughters and sometimes for weeks, even months.

His mother, however, was ever present in the background and hellbent on keeping him around; she expected him to deal her drugs, have sex with her clients, and become her muscle as he got older. At seventeen Danny stabbed her to death in her own home; she was 42 years old. The thirty stab wounds were blamed on a robbery probably committed by a drug addict or other local criminals who, of course, were never found or convicted.

For the first time in his life, Danny felt free, liberated, and unchained but the nightmares and the darkness always came back – ALWAYS.

Chapter 41

Gone but Not Forgotten

Day one of the investigation saw the task force gathered in the briefing room at Pitt Street. John would head the team with Claire, with him as second in charge; there were twenty-two detectives and police officers assigned to this case. This was not only because Carolyn's father was a friend of the Chief but also because they had a violent killer to be found; someone had taken the lovely Carolyn's life and with great brutality and force, and it looked likely that he had also murdered an old man in cold blood.

Claire was standing in a large room on the top floor of the police headquarters; the blinds were tatty with slats broken or bent and the office furniture was also dated and well used. Strathclyde Police had now become part of and renamed as Police Scotland and were moving to new premises on Dalmarnock Road in just in a few months' time and the sooner the better. Claire stood at the front of the room next to a large white marker board and cleared her throat. The talking died down and stopped; someone at the back shouted, 'Let's hear it for John and Claire.' The audience of police officers and staff started clapping their hands and a detective standing on the left of her shouted 'Well done girl!' There were more shouts across the room. 'Welcome back, John.' 'Yeah, you just could not stay away.' 'You will be joining the FBI next, Claire!' 'She is the new Chief.' 'Naw, John is.' Lots of laughter went through the room.

Claire was smiling and did a small curtsey while John remained standing at the back off the room. 'Thank you all. Now please let us proceed.' Claire spoke clearly and firmly, 'I will start from the beginning as I know there are a few of you here who have just been brought in today.' The mood in the room instantly changed when Claire pointed her laser at the photograph of Carolyn; it was a nice picture of her at what must have been taken on a night out; she wore a short black dress covered in sequins; her hair was shoulder length and she looked a little like Cybil Shepherd, the actress.

'Our victim – Carolyn Hughes, a 40-year-old wife and mother from Milngavie. On Sunday afternoon Carolyn's body was found by divers carrying out maintenance work on a navigation buoy in Loch Striven; they were working on it that day as there would be little shipping movements to affect their work. Carolyn's body was found caught up on the anchor chain of the buoy; it was in a body bag wrapped in chains that were secured by industrial size cable ties.' She pointed to photographs on the board, of the buoy, chains and ties. 'We have not yet established how her body got to be caught up on the buoy, but it was most likely dumped into the Clyde and drifted here on that tide. We do not know where the body went into the water. Mark, you and your team get onto the tides, also the cable ties and the chain. I want to know where they all came from. John and I, along with the M.E., examined the body on the slipway on Sunday afternoon; it was established from that examination that she had been in the water for about a week and that she had also been raped and brutally assaulted.'

Claire moved over to a flipchart and flipped over the front page. There were a few whispers as half a dozen photographs of Carolyn's bloated and battered body were displayed on the second page. 'We think she was either kidnapped or knew who the perpetrator was but did not go voluntarily. Carolyn's mobile phone was found not far from her house on the path where she would have gone on her run, and we think she was taken in the morning during that run.

'There will be four teams on this investigation headed by John and myself. The Incident room will be run by Maggie, Bob, Ronnie, and Brian, and I want all information passed to them on an hourly and daily basis. Richard and Stephen, you will both work on the mortuary case with Melissa, Mitchell, and young David with us. That is all, folks, let's find this bastard and fast.'

The Chief, who had walked in and had stood at the back of the room, walked forward. He stood facing the now standing group of police officers and cleared his throat. 'Carolyn Hughes was the daughter of an old friend of mine, and I have known her since she went to university. I was at her wedding 20 years ago; she was not only a beautiful girl and a fantastic mother, but she was also one of society's wonderful people – a joy to be with and lovely to know. Carolyn was a girl who would do anything for you if you were her friend. She did not deserve to die this way. I want this evil person caught, not only because of who she was, but because of what he is. Good luck and dismissed.'

The Chief turned to John and Claire. 'I don't need to tell you both how I feel about this. I want this bastard found. Leave no rock unturned John, and when you do find him, I want a conviction – no mistakes, Claire.' Claire felt a bit miffed as it looked as if the Chief's parting comment was aimed at her.

She watched her boss as he left the room, the double swing doors rattling in their frame as he disappeared into the corridor. She and John walked into his office and closed the door and the blinds. 'Am I being paranoid or was I just called incompetent?' John sat down behind his old captain's desk in the green leather high-backed seat with its brass buttons. He had been given permission when he retired to take the seat and the desk when the force moved to their new headquarters.

'Yes, you are being paranoid, and you are not incompetent. The Chief just wants a solid conviction, plain and simple". There was a knock at the door. 'Enter,' shouted John; it was young DCI, David. 'Cup of tea, coffee?' he asked them both. 'Yes, David, that would be nice and thank you,' said Claire as she sat on the worn Chesterfield across from John's desk, notepad in hand. 'What's your verdict, John?' 'Claire, I think we have our first serial killer on our hands; I don't think this is a one-off and I don't think it is his last.'

'Do you think it's a definite that the body was stolen to cover up evidence?'

'Without a doubt; I don't see anyone wanting to recover a body in such poor state, nor do I think after the way he disposed of the body did he expect it to ever resurface. Have Mark's team go through the missing girls' file for, say, the last five years and get some divers back in that loch just in case there are any more surprises.'

David returned with a tea and a coffee. 'Thanks, David,' he said as he curtseyed back out of the door.

'Cheeky monkey,' laughed Claire. John stood looking at the OS map that covered the entire wall and the entire area of their jurisdiction. 'Why Dunoon and Loch Striven?' asked John.

Claire passed him his cup of tea. 'Does the perp live in Dunoon?' she asked. 'If he is as intelligent as I think he is, he would not shit where he slept.'

'Yeah, I think you're right, why would he? She could have been dumped from shore, but would it not be more likely to have been by boat?'

'Why do you think he choose Loch Striven?' John pointed on the map to the loch. 'In that area, there must be hundreds.'

Claire marked it in her notebook. 'Call her sister, let's go and have a chat with her.'

They both finished their drinks, grabbed their jackets, and headed out of the office. Claire stopped at David's desk, 'Have a look at any reports of boat thefts from the Greenock, Gourock or Dunoon areas, check out the marinas, boat clubs and so on, also find out if there is a register of boat owners in that area; we are going to Milngavie to talk to Carolyn's sister; you will get me on my cell phone.'

On the drive out to Milngavie they both agreed to live, eat and sleep on this case 24/7; they had a large and good team of officers with them and intended to leave no stone unturned in their task of finding the Striven Strangler, the name now given to the killer who had strangled Carolyn.

On arrival at Carolyn's house, they were surprised by the presence of just about her entire family. Sarah was there as requested, but also present were her father and her husband, along with her friend and work colleague Annemarie; the children were upstairs and best left there at this time. Sarah offered both of them coffee which they accepted and after pleasantries and introductions, they sat in the kitchen with Carolyn's father and Sarah only.

Carolyn's father spoke to them first. 'I know you did not know my daughter, detectives, but she was the most wonderful daughter in the world.' He looked over at Sarah, 'You too, Sarah.' The big man looked at his big hands clasped in front of him on the kitchen table. He looked straight at John. 'Have you found my daughter yet, Detective?' He looked tired and seemed to have aged ten years, as had Sarah since the detectives had last seen them.

'I cannot start to tell you how myself and my family feel at this time; we are in a living hell, detectives, and we need some answers. I want this person caught.' He slammed his big fist down on the table, startling everyone. 'I want him hung, drawn and quartered for what he did to my lovely girl.' Sarah stopped what she was doing and ran over to be beside her father. 'Dad, please calm down; this is not going to help.' He started sobbing, pinching the bridge of his nose with his thumb and forefinger while Sarah stood behind him, her arm around her Dad's slumped shoulders.

When he had composed himself, Sarah returned to making the coffee, her father apologised, and they all sat round the four-seat table. Sarah started the conversation by saying she did not want to know any details about Carolyn's death, she just wanted to know how she could help. Claire replied, notebook in hand; John also had a notebook and pen in front of him. 'We think she was taken from here in Milngavie on the Monday morning and held somewhere else during a 24-hour period. Her body was found in Loch Striven near Dunoon, and we have yet to establish whether the killer knew her routine or whether it was a chance meeting and abduction off the street, so to speak. As to her end location, we are working on how she got there.'

John spoke up at this point, 'Did Carolyn know anyone in that area; would she have any cause to visit someone there?'

'No, I don't think so,' said Sarah.

'Are you sure?' asked Claire.

'Yes, pretty sure; we went to Dunoon during the Easter break for a week's holiday.'

Both detectives looked at each other before John asked, 'Did she meet anyone there or talk to anyone?'

'No, we were always together with the children.'

'Where did you stay?' asked Claire.

'At the Mountain View Caravan Park, in a lodge,' said Sarah.

'Why Dunoon; was it Carolyn's choice to go there?'

'No,' said Sarah, looking worried. 'No, it was mine. I found the deal on Groupon and as Carolyn was having such a hard time about Philip, I thought it would be a good idea to get away.'

Carolyn's father had not said much, but now spoke, 'Do you think that the holiday was where Carolyn met her killer?'

'No, sir,' said John. He did not really know that but did not want to upset Sarah who was starting to sob quietly as she had been responsible for the booking. John and Claire interviewed them both for about an hour before John stood up from the table. 'I think that will do for now, folks; if you think of anything else, please call either myself or Claire, regardless of how insignificant you think it might be.'

Carolyn's father stood up and shook John's hand, 'I hope you find this bastard, Detective.'

'I do too, Mr Brand.'

'Call me Tom, please. I want you to meet the children before you go. Sarah, please call the children.'

'But, Dad,' Sarah protested.

'Please do as I ask.'

Sarah left the hallway where they all stood and went upstairs, returning shortly afterwards with two teenagers, a tall attractive girl and an equally handsome young man. Both had been crying.

'This is Emma and Jonathan.'

'Hello,' said Claire and shook their hands. 'It is nice to meet you both; we are so sorry about your mother.' John also shook the children's hands but did not say anything and all six of them shuffled down the hallway and said their goodbyes at the doorway. The children had gone back upstairs before the detective's car had left the driveway.

'A bit of emotional blackmail was served there, don't you think, John?' said Claire as they drove out of the estate.

'Yes, he is a broken man but very determined.'

Claire was driving; apart from the nature of the case she was enjoying being back in Glasgow. 'Do you think the holiday is of significance?' she asked as they headed back to Pitt Street.

'I think it might be, as far as where the body was dumped; the killer must have known that area and known it was one of the deepest lochs in Scotland, hence why the tankers are anchored there. Carolyn could have met her killer while on holiday and they could have communicated after she left. Let's go and have a look at her phone records.' They drove the rest of the way in silence, deep in thought about the case.

Chapter 42

Conal Fury

The next morning Danny was back on the park, he had enjoyed his three days off but would now have to catch up on sales and lost time. He walked into the office early because Janet would be on her own. He walked past reception and snapped his fingers, beckoning Janet to follow him which she did. Danny hung his jacket on the stand just as Janet walked into the office, closing and locking the door behind her. He sat her down on the couch in front of where he stood and pulled out his cock, Janet started wanking him till he was big and hard and then put his cock in her mouth and he head-fucked her. She gagged a few times but was getting better at taking his cock deep throat style, nearly getting down to his crotch but just not quite there yet.

Danny took his cock out and slapped her a few times in the face with it. 'Who's a naughty girl then?' he said as he slapped each cheek repeatedly with his manhood.' How many times did you text me when I was away?' 'Lots,' said Janet, 'I missed you.'

'Stand up.' Janet stood up; he looked at the clock, Gordon would walk in at exactly 9 am and the second receptionist would not start till ten. He had ten minutes to play. He bent her over the sofa, pulling down her panties; she was wet between her legs. Danny fucked her hard from behind, her face buried in the sofa cushion to muffle her cries. He exploded inside her tight wet pussy but not before she had come herself on at least three occasions. It was three minutes to nine; he did not have time to make her lick his cock clean. Instead, he zipped up his fly, opened the patio doors behind his desk and walked out onto the showground just as Gordon drove up.

'Morning, boss.'

'Morning, Danny, how are things?'

'Good, tooth is fixed, and I am raring to go.'

'Excellent; go and sell some vans then.' Gordon laughed as he headed for his office where he would spend the next few hours at his desk answering emails and making calls. Danny opened the Willerby deluxe caravan – the first one on the showground and went inside. He sat in the lounge with his feet up on the table and took out his mobile which had been switched off while at home as Janet's texts were getting annoying.

There was a text from Jenny who would be arriving back in Scotland on Thursday and hoped to see him at the weekend. There was another from Barbara who must have finished licking her wounds and was missing him; he texted her back and told her to be at his tonight at 11 pm. He also texted Natcha and asked her where she would be at lunchtime and to have her phone on, so he did not have to look all over the park for her. He stood at the lounge window and looked down the long, curved driveway that ran down to the park entrance and the foreshore. He was expecting a police visit at some point in the week but was confident he had covered all the bases. It looked like rain, but he decided to take a drive round the park anyway, so he headed back into reception.

Janet was pretending to be busy as he walked past her and nipped her ass; she jumped and looked flushed. He grabbed a walkie talkie from the base chargers on the reception desk, signed for it and the cart and told Janet where he was going. He also popped his head into Gordon's office where that fuckpig parrot shrieked 'Danny's a wanker.' He glared at the bird as Gordon pissed his pants laughing.

'That cracks me up every time,' he grinned.

'Yeah, fucking hilarious,' Danny replied. 'I am just going to take a drive around the park.'

'Yeah, no problem, just don't be visiting Natcha on company time.'

'I won't.'

Gordon laughed as Danny walked away to the parrot's call of 'Danny's a wanker' yet again. He walked outside and started up the silent golf cart and took it for a spin; he was looking for two things this morning. One was if there had been any police around; if they had, a caravan owner on the park would soon let him know – caravan residents loved a bit of gossip. He could not ask Janet or Gordon as this would only raise suspicion. He also wanted to check out Jenny's lodge one more time before she came back because it had been dark when he left it last.

He cruised around the park for about an hour and was just about to head for Jenny's when his walkie talkie burst into life. It was Janet to inform him that a couple had arrived and would like to view some caravans. Danny looked at his watch; it was 11.10 am. He would show them a few vans and then leave them to have some lunch in the bar; this way he could still fuck Natcha at lunchtime.

He walked into reception to be met by his worst fucking nightmare – a blast from the past. Conal Fury, a fucking low life taxi driver from Clydebank, was now standing in reception. The dyed blonde MILF, who was with him, was trying look sexy; she was a dog – fake tanned, fake blonde, fake fucking everything and well past her prime.

'Danny Boy, would you fucking believe it, what the fuck are you doing here? Last time I heard you were working on a cruise ship or something.' Janet looked on from reception. 'Conal, how the devil are you?' He gave the prick a hug. 'Come on into my office.' He had to get this prick out of earshot of anyone else in reception.

'Your office,' laughed Fury, 'what a fucking laugh. Babes, this is Danny, he ran with us when we were teenage bad boys, and now he has his own fucking office! That's a riot.' Danny was furious; this could not have come at a worse time. He sat them both down on the couch where three hours previously he was having fun with Janet. Just then Janet knocked on the door and offered everyone tea or coffee; they both asked for coffee.

‘Danny is a mad shagger from the old days,’ said Fury as he ran his hand up his tart’s leg; she had on a mini skirt and still had good legs.

‘I can see why,’ said the tart. Fury introduced her as Maggie. ‘The wife’s at home, all sixteen fat fucking stone of her.’

Maggie could not keep her eyes from Danny and looked like she would fuck him there and then, whether Fury was there or not. “What brings you both to Dunoon?’ asked Danny as Janet returned with the coffee. ‘We want to buy a lodge, cash deal, you know, a wee hideaway from the wife.’

Danny laughed. ‘You would be cheaper getting rid of the wife.’

‘Yeah,’ said Fury, ‘we can discuss that later.’ He laughed like a fucking chimp. Danny hated this fuckpig grease ball and his stupid bint tart. His whereabouts would be all over Clydebank and Faifley by the time this stupid cunt got home. He would have to get rid of them both and fast, either that or he would have to leave the park which would only throw suspicion on him for the blonde bitch’s murder.

Danny hardly took in what Fury and Maggie were saying as he was desperately trying to think of a way out of this. He was safer working further away from his past but missed home, missed Scotland. He decided they would have to go and today, but how the fuck he was going to manage that he did not know. They both laughed and chatted about the old days, while Maggie the slut walked around the office bending over and showing her cleavage or a bit of leg at every opportunity.

Fury told Danny he had spent five years in jail for drug offences before he took over the taxi firm; his licence for the firm was in his wife's name, hence why she was still around. Danny asked them if they would like to see a lodge.

'Yeah, sound, mate; I hope you are going to give me a good discount.'

'Of course, you bet, old friend.' Danny walked them both outside. 'Where is your car, Conal?'

It was obvious that it was the black G-Wagon with the tasteless wheels. 'It's right there, Danny boy, what a machine.' He unlocked the doors with the remote and Danny opened the passenger door for Maggie, who slipped her card into his hand before he had closed the door and mouthed 'call me'. Danny sat in the back and guided them round to Jenny's lodge. He unlocked the door and showed them both inside.

'Jesus, look at this darling, do you fancy weekends down here with your hot sexy baby?'

'It's gorgeous, honey,' she said as she looked at Danny. 'I need to pee, sweetheart, where is the loo?'

Danny showed Maggie the bathroom; she went inside and locked the door.

Danny showed Fury to the back bedroom. He immediately closed the door, rushed up to Fury and grabbed him by the throat and strangled the fucking life out of the little prick who did not see it coming and fought like fuck to live, but Danny was too strong for him – big time gangster my arse. You could be the fucking biggest tough guy in the world but if you bleed. you can be killed. He died just before Maggie started to wash her hands; Danny could hear the tap running in the bathroom.

He walked quickly back to the lounge, where he stood as the stupid tart emerged from the bathroom. 'Hi, sweetie, where's Conal?'

'He just nipped out to get a bottle of champagne; he won't be long.'

'We're all alone then,' she said as she walked up to him and grabbed his crotch. Danny took her hand and led her to the main bedroom where she threw herself on the bed. 'Conal must think I am daft; he is only away to get champagne so he can get me drunk and watch you fuck me.'

Danny straddled her on the bed, bent over and started to choke her. 'Kinky, baby, go for it,' she said and wished she had not as Danny strangled her to death. She struggled like hell, scratching his hand as she did so, her tarty eyes filled with horror and tears as her last gasp of air left her body.

Danny did not get aroused and left her lying on the bed, walked to the fridge and poured himself a Jack Daniels and sat down on the sofa.

These past few months were becoming a nightmare; his body count for the season should be one but it now stood at two and he now had another two bodies to dispose of and a G-Wagon with ghastly wheels that stood out like a sore thumb. He was beginning to doubt himself. Had his luck finally run out? What else would rear its ugly head? He had to pull himself together. He had had no choice but to kill Fury and his slut – if word got round and it would have, he would have been descended upon by every leech and parasite from his past that he had worked so hard to avoid. He could drop everything, but it would raise suspicion. If the police did come round about blondie's disappearance, he did not want to become their person of interest and he could not risk more time out of work – it would not go unnoticed.

Natcha would also need to wait until tomorrow. Danny went back to his lodge and washed, changing his shirt for another clean one; no-one would notice any difference. He drove back down to the sales office, waving to groundskeeper Willie as he went; he also took time to stop and talk to two regulars on the park who were out walking their small dog.

Danny had only been back to work for four hours, and he had already killed two people. He smiled at Janet as he walked back into reception; she smiled and blushed. 'Coffee, handsome?'

'Yes, that would be nice and a little cake if you have some.'

He walked into Gordon's office. He was not there and was probably at lunch. Moby shrieked 'Danny's a wanker' as Danny about turned, went into the kitchen, filled a cup with cold water and went back into the office and threw it over the bird who was standing on its perch in its cage. The stupid bird went berserk which amused Danny greatly. Janet came rushing in to see what all the noise was about.

'Jesus, Danny, you will get sacked if he sees you abusing his bird,' but she was laughing as she said it. Danny felt better; he still had to get rid of the bodies of Fury and his slut, but it should not take long; he had an idea where to put them, then everything should be back to normal. Sex was out tonight; it seemed to be that when he killed someone this way he lost his appetite for it, not for long though as he was usually back on form the very next day.

The rest of the day went slowly and was uneventful. At 5 pm sharp Danny left his office and went into Gordon's office. 'Bye,' he said. Gordon barely looked up as he and Janet tried to figure out where the water had come from. Gordon was raging and Janet was no good at keeping secrets – her face was bright red, and this made Danny laugh. He headed home and got changed into an old pair of black running leggings and a black short-sleeved Fred Perry type of golf shirt. These clothes were old and would be burned later. He would not leave the park until it got dark. He was going to have to drive Fury's distinctive G-Wagon with two fucking bodies in the boot. He would drive it round and over the Rest and be Thankful which was closed off due to a landslide and had been for a couple of weeks.

He sat in his lounge and watched the news; the blonde bitch was still making the headlines on STV news and so was the old-timer he had shot in the mortuary; there were photos of them both popping up on the screen. One was of the old boy with a kid – he was probably a paedo anyway, and one of Carolyn all glammed up on a night out. She looked hot. Gone but not forgotten, he laughed. Danny felt like he had fucked up on blondie's killing; her body's return was a shocker; that, and Katie's revelation, and now these two new bodies had rocked him a little. Bad things come in threes, he thought, and he had his three already. Yeah, things would get better. Fury's disappearance would probably be put down to gangland stuff and should not affect him.

He walked down to Jenny's lodge, a blanket folded under his arm, and went inside. The curtains were closed, as were many on the various other lodges around the park. Maggie's body was on the bed looking a little grotesque after her strangulation; he lifted her short skirt; she had stockings on and no panties – just another whore ready to go meet her maker in hell. Conal Fury never did have any taste and obviously still didn't.

Danny went over the entire lodge with a fine-tooth comb; he even hoovered the beds and every room, emptying and cleaning the hoover before wiping down every surface in the lodge. He went outside and reversed the G-Wagon round to the back of the lodge. It was now between him and the Holy Loch and he would hopefully not be seen from the other side of the water. Jenny had a huge decking out the back which you could access from the lounge patio doors. He sat outside at a large eight-piece outdoor dining table, very much like his own at home. He had his binoculars and was scanning the houses far across the loch; there was no-one about – coast clear. He opened the boot lid, collected both bodies and dumped them inside, before covering them with the blanket. He then drove out of the park without anyone seeing him; the G-Wagon had privacy glass, and no-one could see inside, not unless you walked up close and put your face against the glass. It was late and mid-week, so the roads were very quiet of traffic.

On the drive through the glen, he passed only two vehicles, one a Dunoon taxi and the other an Asda delivery truck. Even the villages he drove through were deserted. The big beast of a 4 x 4 drove well and he was well impressed with its performance. He arrived at the top of the Rest and be Thankful. The road had flashing orange lights and traffic cones across it and a large sign reading ROAD CLOSED which you would be daft not to have known, as there were signs at the side of the road along his entire route saying the same thing. Danny turned the big 4 x 4 onto the single-track road that led to Lochgoilhead, its Xenon headlights lighting up the entire road and the forest at each side.

Danny had spent many years hiking in the area and knew it well; he drove a further five miles until he reached a forest track on his right. He stopped at a barrier blocking his path and opened the gate and then got out and closed it again; it was really dark as the sky was overcast; this would hamper his long hike home. He drove slowly for another three miles until he arrived deep in the woods where it suddenly opened up. Danny had arrived at an old slate quarry which he had stumbled on years before while on a hike and had swum in it to cool down. It was deep, very deep and had been abandoned a long time ago. He drove the 4 x 4 to the edge of the quarry where he got out; there was about a twenty-foot drop from the cliff edge into the water. He had swum in this exact spot and knew it went straight down for at least a hundred feet.

He stood at the rear of the 4 x 4 and took a piss. Danny had a long hike ahead of him; he could have called Janet and made some silly excuse about how he had become stranded but could not take the risk and end up having to kill Janet to silence her – anyway, the run would do him good. He planned to hike round to the shoreline at Carrick Castle and run the costal path round Loch Long via Ardentinny – walk no. 464 if you were a hiker. It was a nineteen-mile hike which he could probably do in under four hours. He would then borrow a small boat from Strone Pier for the short trip across the Holy Loch which would bring him back to where he started from – at Jenny's lodge.

He walked over to the G-Wagon where he removed his rucksack and changed into his outdoor sports wear, placing the clothes he was wearing in the small black rucksack. Danny got both Fury's and Maggie's cell phones from the front of the 4 x 4; he had dismantled them as soon as he had killed the pair. He threw both in the quarry and walked back to the vehicle, jumped in, put it into drive and jumped back out again, leaning in over the driver's seat and releasing the hand brake. He stepped away as the 4 x 4 rolled towards the edge and watched it go over the cliff. He walked over to where it had vanished; it was still very dark, but he could make out the black water turn white below him as the big black vehicle hit it with a crash and disappeared below the surface. The noise as it hit the water was loud in the still night and echoed around the mountains but there was no-one around to hear it, except the animals and herds of deer scattered around the hills.

Danny picked up his rucksack and started his hike; it was 11.45 pm. He was clear of the forest within twenty minutes and was now hiking up the slopes of Ben Sgurr; the path was good, and he summited within the hour at exactly 12.35 am. It was now downhill all the way to the shores of Lochgoil before a brisk trot along the twisting shoreline to his destination. He ran in the dark, his head torch lighting his path before him; he felt good within himself and felt as if things were turning for the better. He reached the shore of the loch at 1.05 am; he was making good time and decided to take a ten-minute rest before he continued. The moon had come out and it was no longer necessary to wear the head torch. He sat on a rock and drank from a water bottle; the grey seals nearby were restless about his presence but would rather rest than take to the water. They watched him nervously, their backs looking shiny in the moonlight.

Danny checked his watch – it was now 1.20 am and time to go. He grabbed his rucksack and picked up a rock which he threw at the resting seals; it hit one of them on the side. They all took to the water, their heads appearing shortly after, looking at Danny and not happy that he had disturbed them. Danny set off on his run along the coastal path. He felt good, felt fit, and hoped to get back on to his money trail. This year was becoming a killing spree instead of a money-gathering feast. Jenny was still a con, and a good one; if he could not extract any cash from her, she would be dumped asap. Lesley did not have enough money for him to bother with and would be cast aside; he might fuck her once if it were both her and Jenny together. His mind drifted to Katie, and he wished she were running with him now. If she carried out her task that he was about to give her, then he would take her under his wing; it would be nice to share his work with her. He would enjoy teaching her his trade and maybe they would benefit from working together.

Her first task would be to kill a female judge. Why? Because she had sent a friend of his to prison when he was 18 years old where he killed himself. He was found hanged in his cell after only a month inside. Michael begged not to be sent to prison as he did not like to be shut away. His dad used to lock him in a coal cellar when he was a kid, and he was terrified of it. Danny and two of his young friends watched her jail him for a petty theft, despite his pleas. She was now retired, something she would not get the chance to enjoy. Danny ran the moonlit path in good time and had reached Strone by 3.20 am; it looked as if he might be able to get some sleep before having to go to work.

He chose a small sea tender from the dock beside the pier; it was called Dixie and was a 12ft rubber dinghy used to reach a yacht of the same name moored further out on the Holy Loch. The water was dead calm, and the water glowed green around it with every stroke, caused by little sea creatures that were bioluminescent and glowed when they were disturbed by his paddle; he crossed the distance in good time. Danny landed the small boat outside Jenny's lodge on her private jetty; he used one of the oars to push it away and threw the oar into the dinghy, watching as the tide carried it out to sea.

He did not enter the lodge, but instead headed back to his own lodge; it was now 3.50 am; he went out on the deck and had a JD. Even at forty, he was fit enough to join the green berets and felt as if he could run that distance again right now. This wee night cap after a hard night would help him sleep.

He felt good about killing Fury who was a prick, and his stinking whore was disgusting. Danny would have a shower before he slept and wash off their stench. He went to bed at 4.30 am; four hours sleep was about as good as he was going to get. He masturbated and left the spunk on his belly; his sheets were needing changed anyway. He would get Natcha to change the bed and clean the lodge tomorrow.

He switched off the nightstand light and was asleep in minutes.

Chapter 43

Here they come

It was now Thursday morning. The squad had been gathered since 7 am and the results of the past two days' work by the detectives was being collated together by the home bees. The detectives had decided that the body had been taken by the killer to hide evidence – there was no other logical reason. The old man's murder was also committed to prevent him from being a witness to the crime; whoever was responsible did not want to get caught.

Claire was up at 5 am and was not happy; her fanny hurt like hell after an awesome sex session with Colin, who was a typical Scots lad and well endowed. She had not had sex for months and had made up for that in one night, hence the sore toush; she also had a slight hangover from too much champagne.

On the subject of the body, it was established that it would have been dumped further down the loch or maybe out at sea as the tide would have carried it into the loch rather than out of it. The body, which could tell them lots of things, was unfortunately still missing. It was also established that the killer was either extremely strong, as carrying his victim up the stairs and out of the morgue would have taken some doing, or he had help. The gun used was a 45 and had not been recovered; the long task of fingerprinting the morgue and eliminating the hundreds of prints from their database would take some time. There were no prints or DNA on either the chain or the cable ties; someone seemed to know what they were doing, and the team was no further forward in catching him.

Claire and John left the briefing at 9 am; they were on their way to Dunoon where Carolyn had gone for her Easter break on the Mountain View Park. The park was only a few miles by boat from Loch Striven where her body was found. It was also only nine miles by road. Claire and John discussed the case in great detail as they drove west towards Port Glasgow, Greenock and then Gourock, from where they would catch the ferry from McInroy's Point to Hunter's Quay, Dunoon.

Claire had spoken to Gordon, the manager of the Mountain View Caravan Park where Carolyn and Sarah had spent their Easter break; he was expecting them both at 10.30 am. Claire was driving. 'I am stumped on this one so far,' said John as he studied the file in his lap; he was looking at the photograph of Carolyn. 'Do you think we have a serial killer on our hands?' asked Claire.

John studied the photograph more. 'I don't want to say it, but I think we do. He is too smart and too careful, and it does make me think that it is not his first time, but not here in Scotland – somewhere else.'

They were deep in their own thoughts as they continued onwards. The drive itself took forty minutes and even including the twenty-minute ferry trip they still arrived on the park in good time at 10.20 am. They parked outside a sign which read 'Reception and

Sales Office'. Inside, a woman named Janet asked them to take a seat and offered them coffee or tea; they both accepted tea.

On Janet's return, Claire asked her if she remembered Carolyn when she had visited the park. John showed her the picture they had with them. 'Yes, poor girl, I saw her on the news, so sad. She was here with her sister and children.'

'Where did she stay?' asked Claire. Just then a man came out of an office and entered reception. He was in his late thirties with blonde hair and blue eyes. Claire had him about six feet, two inches and he looked strong. Janet introduced him as Gordon, the general manager. 'Pleased to meet you both,' he said as he shook their hands; his hands were strong, right enough. Gordon showed them to his office. On entering, a parrot in a big cage told them to FUCK OFF! Gordon apologised, lifted the cage and stand and walked back into reception, returning quickly, without the cage. 'Really sorry about that,' he said, blushing.

Claire and John sat in front of his desk, in patio furniture that was obviously a substitute for proper office furniture, the office being more suited in the Bahamas, palm tree wallpaper and parrot included. 'Gordon, we are investigating the murder of Carolyn Hughes,' said Claire who was trying not to laugh about the bird and the decor.

'Yes,' said a very red-faced Gordon, 'we will help you all we can; it's awful.'

John spoke next. 'Did you meet Carolyn when she was here, Gordon?'

'No, I would only have met her really by chance or if she had wanted to purchase a caravan, or if there had been a problem perhaps.'

'Can you provide details of all staff at the park; we might want to interview them, and we would also like to see where she stayed during her visit.'

Gordon agreed to show them the lodge, which just happened to be empty, and to have Janet print off a list of all staff on the park, including their addresses and contact details. Gordon led them out the back way from reception where a golf buggy was parked.

Claire saw him first, a tall, dark-haired man, taller even than Gordon. He came down the steps of a lodge with an elderly couple, a clipboard in his hand. He was stunning, immaculately dressed, with the most amazing blue eyes. He shook hands with the couple before disappearing back inside the lodge. John looked at Claire and they both asked at the same time, 'Who is that, Gordon?'

'Oh, that's Danny Fleming; he is our sales guy.'

'Has he worked here long?'

'About two years now; he lives here on the park.'

Claire watched Danny. As they drove away, she was sure he was watching them in the shadows further inside the lodge but could not be sure. Gordon drove them the five-minute drive and let them both into the lodge. 'I can leave you both here, if you don't mind locking back up and it's only a very short walk back to the office.'

John took the keys from Gordon. 'I want forensics here to have a look, so from now on this lodge is off limits to everyone.'

'Yes, I understand.'

'I take it this is not the only key,' asked John.

'No, there are two others. I will have them ready when you get back to the office. We do have other holiday-makers here; if you could keep it as low key as possible it would be very much appreciated.' He looked sheepish as he left.

John burst out laughing as soon as Gordon left. 'What's so funny, John, is it the parrot?' asked Claire.

'Yeah, that and the whole Carry-on Camping, Hi-De-Hi thing, it's hilarious; did you see that office? I thought I had been transported back to the seventies.' They both laughed. It was unusual to see John display humour which made Claire laugh even more.

Danny had seen the red-haired bitch as soon as he had walked onto the decking of the Aspen lodge he had just sold to Mr & Mrs Allan. The sale was ruined by the sight of her and the grey-haired guy; they were here, and they were looking for him.

He went back inside the lodge and watched Red and Grey leave with Gordon, gathered up the paperwork and headed straight for Janet in reception. Danny grabbed her hair, walked her to the back office, threw her on a chair and made her suck his cock till he came in her mouth. She protested a couple of times but did the deed anyway. 'Jesus, babes, that's a bit risky, Gordon's not on his lunch; he is around here with the two cops,' she said as she sorted herself.

'Yeah, I saw that,' said Danny, trying to seem disinterested. 'That is what made it more exciting,' he laughed as he slapped her ass hard. 'Ouch,' she cried as the thin summer dress provided little protection from his hard slap.

'What were the police wanting?' asked Danny.

'It's about that girl that was murdered, you know the one that stayed here on the park; they want to interview everyone and have just gone to the lodge where she stayed; Gordon has taken them there just now.'

Just then Gordon returned, he was not a happy chappie and Danny followed him to his office. Gordon threw down the keys for the golf buggy before walking back out the office and returning with that stupid fucking bird. It started as soon as it saw Danny. 'Danny's a wank,' it shrieked, 'Dan the dobber, Dan the dobber.' Gordon usually laughed his nuts off when it insulted Danny; however, this time he did not, and put the bird straight into the walk-in stationery cupboard.

'Sorry, Danny,' he said as he sat down looking flustered, 'no lunch for me today and it looks like the cops are going to close that lodge off for the foreseeable future, plus there will be cops here as well, something we could do without. Did you sell the Aspen to the walking dead that came in earlier?'

'Yeah, the paperwork's next door.'

Danny left, went to his own office, and picked up the contract for the two old buddies who had bought the Aspen. Janet was talking to her dick of a husband at reception and Danny shouted hello and smiled; Janet's face was the colour purple.

Gordon was on the phone to his directors when two young police officers arrived in reception; they spoke to Janet before heading towards Danny and Gordon. The tall officer said they were looking for Detective McLeod. Gordon held his hand over the phone and asked Danny to show the officers round to the lodge.

'I will get you guys out front and you can follow me round,' said Danny

'Which lodge?' he asked Gordon, knowing full well which one it was. Gordon gave him two sets of keys for Eagle 7. Danny drove ahead of the cops who were in the white marked police van; it was now time to meet his next prey; it was always better to stand and fight than to run and hide, and these two fuckers would be no match for him.

He pulled the golf buggy up outside the lodge and opened the gate, holding it open for the two officers before knocking on the door which was opened by Red who was wearing blue surgical gloves, a grey suit and white blouse; she was pretty with really white skin, Danny thought about fucking her bright orange pussy and started to get erect.

'Hi,' he said, 'these guys are looking for you,' as he stuck out his hand. 'My name is Danny.'

Claire was looking at the most handsome man she had ever seen; he was electrifying with a body to die for and the most amazing face, but his eyes were what made him – he had the most amazing eyes she had ever seen.

'Hi Danny, Detective Stewart, nice to meet you.' She showed the officers inside and closed the door. 'Sorry but I can't ask you inside.' Instead, she led Danny round to the front decking overlooking the loch.

'Please take a seat. I need to chat with you anyway.' One of the officers was outside, running blue and white police tape around the lodge boundary.

'Do you mind if I ask you a couple of questions?'

'No, not at all,' replied Danny. He knew that he would have to kill this petite little busybody and knew he would enjoy doing it. Claire actually questioned him as if he were a suspect even though he knew she had nothing to go on.

Claire thought Danny was a bit creepy; he made her feel a little uncomfortable, like a guy who undresses you with his eyes. Danny was enjoying himself – the red cop looked uncomfortable. His fun was stopped when the patio doors slid open and out stepped the grey one. Danny stood up as the older detective stuck out his hand. 'DCI McLeod,' he said as he shook Danny's hand up and down. 'This is Jed,' referring to the black dog at his side.

'Danny Fleming. I work here in sales; your lovely colleague is just giving me the once over.'

John asked Danny a few questions before they both dismissed him as if he were a naughty little schoolboy. Danny got back in the golf cart and headed back to the office; he would deal with both of them and soon. 'What do you think?' asked John.

'I think he is well worth looking into; he gives me the creeps.'

John stood looking out over the loch. 'Yes, and you can reach Loch Striven from here by boat. Check and see if Mr Fleming or any other staff have a boat here on the loch; it might be worthwhile checking all these boats out. Forensics will be here shortly although it's very unlikely she was killed here in this lodge, as she was taken from home. We need to find evidence and fast and this is all we have to start with.'

'Do you think this park has something to do with it?' asked Claire.

'Do you?' said John.

'Yes. It's not a coincidence that her body turned up a short distance from where she had her last holiday.' Danny closed his office door. He was sure they knew, call it instinct, but he fucking knew it, the Red and the Grey were trouble and needed fixing asap. He was off tomorrow and would put his time to good use; the hunters were just about to become the hunted.

He spent the night looking at ads in Gumtree while killing a full bottle of Jack Daniels; he called a guy who was selling a Kawasaki Ninja and arranged to meet him the next day in Glasgow. He went outside, pulled up a chair and sat out on his deck; it was a lovely night and Danny surveyed the park below him. It was like a little city with its streetlamps and small roads, all the rows of caravans stepping down the hill till they reached the water's edge. He would be home this time tomorrow; it was time to move on, he thought; things were not going well, which was a pity as life here was not too bad up until he had killed that blonde bitch. Jenny, Lesley, Natcha and Janet had all called and texted, but they could all fuck off for now as he had far more important things to deal with; he sent them all short replies saying he was busy and would catch up with them all soon; he had other things to do on his days off, and it did not include sex.

The next day was very much the norm apart from the obvious police presence. Gordon was a bit touchy, and the park was buzzing with gossip. Danny left work as normal and caught the 5.30 pm ferry to Gourock, driving straight home and making sure he was not followed. He only drove as far as the barn where he collected the 4 x 4 and hooked up the trailer that sat beside it. He also opened a safe hidden in the ground and removed £3500 in cash before driving to Rutherglen where he met the guy called Steven Hicks whom he had called the night before.

Steven showed him to his garage where the blue, black and white Kawasaki Ninja sat; he had obviously polished it and the bike looked good. Danny handed him his keys as security and borrowed a helmet before taking the bike for a quick blast along the dual carriageway towards East Kilbride. It ran well, was mega-quick and covered the distance in no time. He returned ten minutes later and haggled with Steven before buying the bike for £3200 which was £300 less than the asking price. Steven helped him load the bike onto the trailer and Danny then headed home, where he unhooked the trailer and then parked his new bike beside the A5. He enjoyed the drive back to the house from the barn – it was a nice night, and the sun was setting in the west, the sky above Ben Lomond a mixture of oranges and reds.

He sat outside down on the parapet of the bridge listening to the water as it made its way to the loch. Danny knew he might have to leave his home, his prized possession, behind and move away for a considerable time; this annoyed him greatly because it was not what he had planned for this coming season. The blonde bitch's body being found was a major disappointment and was forcing him not only to flee but to kill again; both Red & Grey would have to be killed before he left, apparently.

Apparently, Claire was the up-and-coming female version of Taggart, and the old guy who had apparently retired but was obviously now back working, was the Scottish version of Columbo. The old detective was responsible for solving many murders in Glasgow before he retired. In short, these two were Glasgow's finest, and posed a major threat to his freedom. Unfortunately for Danny the more you kill, the more risk you took of getting caught; he would enjoy having some fun with Red before she met her maker, but there would not be much fun in killing the old guy.

Danny spent the next two days studying his next two victims. Claire had gone to Glasgow University and then Tulliallan Police College before spending a few years on the beat; her rapid progress to detective was quick and unusual, especially for a woman on the force, but she made detective at the very young age of 24 as she was super at her job. She now worked out of Oban and was recently responsible for a huge drug bust. This interested Danny as this could now be the reason she was killed, more like a gangland drug killing, which would take the pressure from him.

Her place of origin had been the West End of Glasgow, but Danny had never seen her before.

DCI McLeod was a beat bobby as was his father before him; he took longer to move up the ranks, being promoted to Detective at 36 years old, he was responsible for solving many high-profile murders in and around Glasgow and a few other cold cases, one a killer who had killed two prostitutes over a ten-year period.

Claire lived alone in Oban and John lived with his wife in Connel just North of Oban itself. John's wife was a schoolteacher in a local school.

Danny felt better – he now knew where he was going with this and might not have to leave after all. He always planned his movements in a military style fashion; the more he planned, the less chance he had of being caught. He went to bed at 3 am; he had a busy day ahead and would still rise at 6 am. He had plans for the rest of the day and had to be back to work as normal on Thursday.

Chapter 44

Dog Gone Day

It was another fine day, which pleased Danny; it was always a bonus when it was dry on your day off, especially if you planned to go out on a motorbike ride. The downside of living in Scotland really was the weather, that and the fact that it was infested with midges and the English, the latter having turned their own country into an immigrant-filled cesspit and who were now leaving it in droves to move to Scotland. Danny was not sure who he hated most – the immigrants, midges, or the English. As far as the weather went, if the winter was mild, which it had been recently, and the weather was good early on in the year, then the summer was usually crap.

He stood in the master bedroom admiring himself in the mirrored wardrobe doors. He looked fit and hot, and he was always proud of his manhood, his weapon of mass destruction; he had the body of a thirty-year-old athlete and he felt good this morning. His research into the two detectives had made him feel more confident of disposing of them both. He took out his leathers from the closet; he had not worn them for a few years, but he had not gained any weight since, so they should be fine; his black helmet and Sidi boots would also not be a problem.

He liked himself in his biker gear; he looked good, in fact he thought he looked good in anything. He locked up the house and drove to the barn; he did feel a bit of a twat driving a 4 x 4 dressed as a biker. He drove up to the front of the barn and unlocked and swung the big double doors open. The Audi and Kawasaki looked good sitting side by side, the sunlight streaming into the barn making his toys look even better. He had not been on a bike in a few years and was looking forward to his trip. He filled the bike's tank with fuel – petrol stations all had CCTV cameras and were a sure way of being seen in an area where he did not want to be seen.

He started the bike up; it thrilled him as it purred between his legs. His last bike was also a Ninja and Kawasaki was always his favourite make. This bike was, however, a road bike and would have to be driven slowly and carefully until he reached the first tarred road. He walked the bike out of the barn and closed the doors behind him. It was a slow, bumpy ride down to the road but once on tarmac, he let rip and raced round the many twisting and winding roads. He headed to Glasgow first where he walked round the Kawasaki dealer. He was approached by a salesman whom he quickly brushed off, took a photograph of a newer Kawasaki Ninja lined up outside; these were demos and should be registered to the dealer. He quickly left the dealership, next stop being a car accessory shop in Hyndland that made number plates for both bikes and cars.

Danny went inside, keeping his helmet on, and asked the guy to make up the rear plate: ST 60 GNS. Back outside he changed the plate and stuck the old one inside his leathers; he would dispose of it later. He started up the bike and headed towards the A82, destination Oban. His bike was not stolen but if the police did trace it back to who he bought it from via the registration number, the guy would easily be able not only to describe him but also identify him and so it was much wiser to change the plates. The bike, as it was now and if spotted by traffic cops, should show up as registered to the dealership and should be insured; if not, this was a risk he would have to take.

He drove through Dumbarton. He used to fuck a girl called Diane who worked in a vet in Dumbarton; he thought of looking her up on the way back and started to get aroused as he rode the powerful machine down the dual carriageway. Diane was always horny after being out on her horse. She had once told him that girls who ride horses got aroused while riding and that's why so many horsey type girls were all super horny.

He drove the new section of the A82 within the speed limits, only stopping once to throw the old reg plate into the loch. He arrived in Oban at 12 noon; first stop was Claire's house; he had found her address on the internet – it's easy if you know where to look.

He parked the bike in the Tesco supermarket car park, secured his helmet to the bike and walked quickly to a quiet lane next to the block of six flats where Red lived. He put on a boiler suit to cover his leather bike trousers and jacket. The one-piece set of overalls had the SSEB logo for the Scottish electricity company embroidered on the left pocket, and a baseball cap on his head had the same logo.

The flats had a controlled entry system; he pressed number 2, the door buzzed, and he let himself in. So much for security – it also only took him ten seconds to gain entry to Red's flat. Once inside he closed the door behind him; if Red or anyone else turned up, they would die that very day. It was a typical professional single girl's flat with a few more gadgets than he would have expected – a new Sony Bravia TV with sound bar sat in one corner with an iPod, iPad, and iPhone docket. A small remote-controlled drone, more likely found in a guy's flat, sat on the coffee table, a Go Pro camera attached to its underbelly. The kitchen was also clean and tidy with an out-of-date carton of milk from a week ago still in the fridge. It looked like Red was staying down in Glasgow and not coming home. The bedroom was female, modern, and nice, there was a picture on the bedside cabinet of Red and some other guy sitting in a restaurant – could be a brother or a boyfriend perhaps. This was his favourite bit – the underwear drawer; you could learn a lot from a girl just by going through her knicker drawer.

The top drawer was panties; lots of sexy lingerie, size 8, along with – surprise, surprise – a Roger Rabbit vibrator or, in Anne Summers' words, a Rampant Rabbit Vibrator. Little Miss Red was a naughty girl. The next drawer down was for bras and slips and some kind of massage bars from Lush, there were also other Lush products in the bathroom.

The bottom drawer was for a variety of stuff including suspenders, and three photo albums. Well, wasn't Red a naughty girl. Danny removed a pair of her panties from her drawer, lay on her bed, took out his hard throbbing penis and masturbated with the red panties on his face. He removed them just as he was spunking and discharged a load of cum into them. Fuck me, that was intense, he thought, as he straightened up the bed and put the cum-filled panties back in the drawer. He doubted if she would live long enough to wear them. He then made himself a black coffee and sat in the lounge; the view over the harbour towards Mull was nice; however, he would not like to live here. He had flown over Oban many times but a day visit by aircraft was enough. He flicked through the photographs, mostly dull and boring shite, a few birthdays and weddings, what must have been her parents and lots of Red when she was younger, some nice ones of university and a couple of her and some hot chicks in the West End. The very last photo was the same as the one in the bedroom. Danny had not noticed at first but the guy in the photo was a reporter on STV news; he could not remember his name, but it was him alright. He peeled back the clear film that held the photographs in place turning it over. Written on the back was 'me and Colin, 11/07/21'. It was dated less than three weeks ago and was taken here in Oban. Danny walked back into the bedroom and found what he was looking for in the wardrobe at the end of the rail; hanging there were two men's shirts; it looked like little Red had herself a celebrity boyfriend, a fucking reporter no less, whoopee fucking doo, this was all he needed and just added to his problems, now, after, and when he killed Red. Mr Numb Nuts reporter would, after his pain and grief, return to being a dickhead reporter and try and find out who killed his lovely girlfriend. Guess what, Numb Nuts – you're dying too!

Danny left the apartment the way he found it and returned to his bike, putting his overalls back in his rucksack which also contained a climbing rope, lock-knife with a four-inch blade and a serrated edge, black duct tape and a Beretta automatic 38 with two clips and a silencer – standard survival kit Danny-style. Next, he rode the bike round to old Grey's house at North Connel next to the airport. Danny had landed at Connel airfield on many occasions. The detective's house was a bungalow with a two-car garage; there was a Ford Mondeo parked in the driveway, a green metal gate and fence surrounded about an acre of gardens and there were chickens and a hen hut out to the rear. He rode past the house slowly on his bike; the ground at the back sloped away and backed onto woods. A black Labrador, the same one that the detective had at the park, was standing at the gate, a soft toy in its mouth; he looked stupid, wagging his tail as if Danny was his friend.

Danny rode about a quarter of a mile further on and stopped the bike at a small layby which had a picnic table and got off. It had a nice view and was close to a caravan park which was mostly for tourers. He took out the rope and sat at the picnic table, where he made a hangman's noose; it was perfect and, apart from the fact that climbing rope is made to stretch, it should still do the job. He learned to make the perfect noose years ago when he thought about hanging his mother; it would have been nice to see her swing and watch her die. That didn't happen because he stabbed her in a wild frenzy instead.

There was a blossom tree in the detective's driveway which would suit his purpose well. Danny drove back towards the detective's house; the car was gone but the stupid mutt was still there. He parked his bike further along at the Connel Bridge Hotel and walked the short distance back to the bungalow, without hesitation opening the gate.

The dog walked up to him wagging its tail, still with the soft toy in his mouth, Danny placed the noose round the dog's neck; it was still wagging its tail as he walked it towards the tree. The silly dog walked with him and still had the soft toy in his mouth when he threw the rope over a branch about ten feet up and hauled the mutt off his feet. The fucking dog was heavy, but he managed to get him five feet in the air; the dog dropped the toy and started to struggle but the more the daft mutt struggled, the tighter the noose got. He was jerking and bouncing about for a good five minutes. his paws clutching at the rope around his neck. He now swung back and forth, his big brown eyes bulging, a huge pink tongue hanging from his mouth, vapour rising from his now dead body.

The dog looked quite comical, actually; he watched the now dead dog for a few more minutes before walking back to his bike, whistling. He would have preferred to have hung around (no pun intended) until the detective got back but could not be bothered;

he was sure the dead dog deed would achieve the desired effect, and he had a long bike ride home.

Danny took the long way home and stopped in Glencoe for a selfie at the Three Sisters, mountains which towered side by side. There were a few mini coaches around; Rabbie's Tours was one and Discover Scotland another, apparently this was a great way to see Scotland.

Danny then had a thrilling ride down through Rannoch Moor, topping 140mph on the Ninja, eventually stopping at the Drovers Inn for some haggis, tatties and neeps and a beer. The Drovers was the oldest pub in Scotland and one of Danny's favourites; the bar staff always wore kilts, and the place had a good feel about it.

He was back home and in the shower by 8 pm; he masturbated and fancied having some fun when he got back to the park tomorrow. Janice and Natcha would be available during the day, but night-time was an issue. Barbara had still not returned after their last session got a bit rough. He decided to wait and see what tomorrow would bring.

John had spent the day in Glasgow and was looking forward to getting home; he did not leave the city until six and it was now nearer eight. He drove down towards the cottage. Heather had left earlier that afternoon; she was away overnight on a course and would not be back until the following evening.

John knew something was wrong as soon as he saw the house; the gate was open which it never was. Jed slept in the back porch when there was no-one home and could come and go between there and the garden as he pleased. If you left the gate open the old boy would wander off down the beach and further afield so it was always closed and had a sign on it that read **Please close The Gate.** He turned slowly into the drive. The sight before him would haunt him for the rest of his life. His best friend, his beautiful Jed, was hanging from the blossom tree, John screamed 'NO! NO! NO!' He stumbled and fell as he tried to get out of the car, tears blurring his vision as he ran towards the tree. His car rolled gently backwards as far as the gatepost where it came to rest with a crunch. He grabbed Jed and tried to lift him up; he was heavy. He tore at the noose with his other hand, but it would not loosen.

He ran to the house to get a knife, but the door was locked. He ran back to the car and removed the keys from the ignition and fell again as he opened the door, crying and screaming 'Please no! Please no! God, please help me.' He got back to the dog and frantically cut through the rope. He tried to hold the dog in both arms as the rope cut through, but Jed was really heavy, and they both slumped to the ground.

Jed's soft hair was warm to touch; his eyes bulged out of his head; the old boy was dead in his arms. John had never felt pain like it. He sobbed uncontrollably as he sat against the blossom tree. Holding Jed over his shoulder like a baby, he hugged and held him tight, his beautiful doggy smell making him cry even harder. John remained like that for the next two hours –

little birds sang their bedtime songs; he could hear the tide gently washing along the beach as it came in. He felt numb, sad and sick. What sick bastard had done this to his beautiful friend? John cried some more before finally getting to his feet and going into the house. He returned with a sleeping bag which he unzipped and lifted Jed inside, picking up his toy Daffy Duck which he also placed inside.

John removed his shirt and placed it under the dog's head, zipped it back up again and carried the dog inside. He placed the sleeping bag on the cushioned seats that wrapped around the bay window. Jed still felt warm inside the bag. John thought of calling the vet, but knew he was gone, and he was just being silly. The phone rang, startling him; he nearly jumped out of the seat. He walked over, picked up the phone and placed it under his chin, balancing the phone on top of his shoulder as he poured himself a whisky. It was Heather. 'Hi, John, how are you?'

'I am fine, darling, are you okay?'

'Yes, just wishing I was home with you.'

'Me too.'

They both chatted for a while, He decided not to tell her about Jed until she got back; he knew it would upset her very much. It would probably be better to spare her the details; however, there was a threat to both her and John, probably from someone he had arrested and who might now have been released from prison. That person obviously knew where he lived and so Heather had to be told the truth.

John called Pitt Street incident room and reported the incident to a young detective whom he asked to look into anyone who had recently been released from Scottish prisons.

He sat back beside Jed, a third whisky in his hand, looking out over the sea; the tide was in, and the seals were on the rocks for the night, looking just like Labradors. John was feeling sick and tired when the phone rang again, this time it was the Chief.

'Is it true?' he blurted down the phone, 'did someone really hang the dog?'

'Yes.'

'Jesus fucking Christ, John, what sick bastard would do such a thing? I have a car coming round from Oban. 24/7 round the clock until we find out who did this. Are you okay, John?'

'Yes, Chief, I will be fine, and thanks.'

Shortly afterwards, two police officers arrived at the house. John could do without the company right now but invited them in anyway. The two officers introduced themselves and gave John their mobile number. The officers said that they did not want to intrude and declined his offer of a cup of tea; instead, they went back outside to their patrol car. John managed to finish the entire bottle of Talisker whisky before curling up on the bench sofa beside Jed where he fell asleep.

Chapter 45

Happy Days

The next morning it was raining but Danny felt good; he was horny as hell and was looking forward to having some fun with his bitches on the park. He had spent the rest of the night watching back-to-back *Two and a Half Men*, one of his favourite programmes and he thought that Charlie Sheen was one lucky dude; he went to bed about 2 am where he masturbated while thinking about Red again.

Danny deliberately arrived half an hour early as did Janet who had been told beforehand to be there early and wear stockings. Danny took her into his office and locked the door. She looked nervous as he lifted her dress and slipped his hand down inside her panties. Her pussy was wet as he slowly put one, then two, then three fingers inside her. He played with her until she came before sitting her down on his office chair where she took out his cock and sucked, licked and wanked him to the brink of orgasm.

Instead, he made her kneel up on the office sofa and fucked her hard from behind. Janet came a further three times before he finally came inside her. Happy days and what a way to start work! Janet's face was all red blotches, you know, the way fresh faced kids are when they have been playing outside. She scurried away to the toilets and Danny wiped his cock with baby wipes from his drawer before he went out to reception to open the shutters and doors.

Gordon arrived about ten minutes later. 'Morning, boss,' said Danny as he stood in the doorway of Gordon's office to the sound of 'Danny's a wanker', courtesy of the soon-to-be dead Moby.

'Cup of tea?' asked Danny.

'Yes, you bet,' said Gordon.

Danny went to the kitchen and made them both a cup of tea; passing Janet in the corridor, he groped her as she passed. 'God, Danny, you're so romantic,' she said, scowling at him.

'I take that as sarcasm,' he said as she walked on, her face still red; her pussy would still be wet. Danny returned to Gordon's office and handed him his cup of tea. 'Did I miss much on my days off?' he asked. Gordon was now standing looking out of his window. 'Not much. The fucking cops have gone for now and they have removed that fucking scare-the-holiday-makers-away tape from around Number 7. They have still to interview people, your fucking-self included, but I don't think it will come to fucking much; the girl only came here for a break for Christ sakes! It's not as if she fucking died here! Anyway, thank the fucking Lord they will be out of our way in a day or so.' Moby was busy attacking something white that he held in his claw as he sat on his perch. Danny hated the fucking bird. After some idle chit chat with Gordon, Danny returned to his office; he was meeting Natcha at lunchtime for more fun.

The rest of the morning was quiet; he went to chat to Janet a few times, but she was a moaning pain in the arse. She complained that Danny had never taken her to his lodge, nor had he ever taken her out anywhere; all he ever did was fuck her in the office. Danny explained that he could not as she was married. Apparently, they could, according to Janet, meet in Glasgow for lunch. Danny could not be bothered listening to her whining and was glad when Gordon stuck his head round the door to inform him that he was going for his lunch. Danny left the back way and drove the golf cart round the park until he found Natcha's van. He walked inside the lodge, but she was nowhere to be seen. He walked towards the master bedroom; inside he was confronted by the most beautiful sight. Natcha was lying on top of the bed, legs wide open, fingers inside her shiny wet pussy, He slid onto the bed face down, cupping her tiny butt in his hands as he took her sweet pussy in his mouth. Happy days, he was back, he thought.

Danny licked, sucked, and fucked Natcha in every hole, amazed at how she managed to get his entire cock down her throat. It was amazing, it was quite a feat considering its length and girth; she could also take it in both holes, and she loved it. The entire hour was total ecstasy followed by the customary wash and dry. Natcha was definitely his favourite, and he did enjoy her best. Barbara had still never been in touch and that was four weeks now. Danny had driven past her caravan a few times, but it looked like she had not been back since their last encounter.

Danny refused to call or text her; if she wanted to come out and play, she would do so on her own.

He went back to work – he fancied a bit of fresh and decided to have a spin round the park in the buggy before he went into the office. The park was still quiet but there were a few bits of pussy about that he had seen earlier. He visited the leisure complex, where there were a few couples around and some families, but no interesting singles, so he decided instead to head back to the office.

Groundskeeper Willie was doing his usual hobo gardening and Danny stopped for a chat.

'Hi, Sir Sean, how's business?' he asked. Danny stuck a twenty in his hand. 'Oh, thanks Danny, every little helps,' he said, smiling and sucking air between his teeth as normal.

'All is well, kind sir, all is well,' said Danny.

Willie chuckled. 'Bit of a mess about that poor lass that was killed,' he said as he continued to hoe the earth at his feet. 'Police were asking me questions just last week.' Danny was now more interested than he was previously; the idle chit chat now had some meaning.

'What kind of questions?' asked Danny.

Willie shuffled up close, not there was anyone around to hear him. 'They asked if I saw her with any men.' He stank of bad body odour and booze. 'And did you see her with anyone?'

'No, sir, she went jogging a couple of times, but she was always alone. It's a real shame; she was quite a looker.'

'Did you tell that to the cops? Did they ask you anything else?'

'No, the girl with the red hair asked if I saw anyone or anything unusual; she left me her card.' He took the card from his pocket – it was dirty and creased and looked as if it had been in his pocket for years. Danny took it from him. 'Can I keep this?' he asked.

'Sure, Danny, sure.'

Danny squeezed the old man's shoulder, thanked him and put the card in his pocket, got back in the buggy and headed back to the sales office; he decided he would have Janet round tonight – she would be Barbara's new replacement, without the fab tits of course.

Janet was standing in reception. There was no-one around and he grabbed her from behind. 'You need to find an excuse and come to mine tonight; can you do that?'

'Yes, I will think of something.'

He slapped her in the ass and walked into his office. There were no customers around, so Danny made a cup of tea and texted Katie; she had also been quiet of late. She responded immediately – **call me please** read her text. Danny did so; he thought it would be nice to have her around for a couple of days and intended to find out if she was available.

Katie picked up the call on the first ring; she was beginning to grow on him and the more he had contact with her, the more he liked it. 'How are you, my deadly little kitten? You have not been in touch for a while.'

'And neither have you, my hot sexy master. I thought you would rather be left alone as you were busy with more important stuff.'

He had been preoccupied, what with the blonde bitch clusterfuck and then that prick Fury and his whore turning up. He thought about telling her, but would not over the phone and, in any case, he still wasn't sure if he could trust her. 'I want you to come and see me, can you do that?' he asked.

'Yes, when?'

'Say tomorrow.'

'Yes, I can come tomorrow; can I stay over?'

'Yes, kitten you certainly can.'

Excellent, he thought, that's tonight's and tomorrow's sex sorted out. His next text was to Jenny who had also been put on the back burner; her last text was when he was despatching Fury and the whore (sounds like a double act, he thought). However, he had told her he was very busy, what with a murder near the park, the police and just work in general. She had been patient and Danny sent her a text asking if she was coming down this weekend; he was never one to quit and did have enough confidence in himself that he could part her from at least a little cash. Jenny texted back quicker than even Katie. **Yes Darling that would be great, I have missed our chats, and you! Dinner would be lovely, may I bring Lesley?**

Danny had missed the part of when he had become her darling and was not bothered about Lesley tagging along. So yeah, a three-way tag would be fun with the old chicks, they usually got hooked after he had pleasured them. Older ladies never got laid much or were paid as much attention as they were used to when they were in their prime. Over 50s were always looking for that love and excitement that they once had but now did not get, either from their boring husbands who were not interested, or who were dead. **Yes, Jenny that would be fine, I will book a table where and for what time?** Jenny fancied an Indian meal and texted Danny if he was fine with that and could he book a table for 8 pm at the local Indian restaurant. Danny did as was requested and felt like everything was back in order. He took out the scruffy card that he had got from Willie – DC Claire Stewart, Strathclyde Police; both a mobile number and office number were on the card. Danny would leave them both breathing for now, but if they showed up again, he would have to take care of them and of Red's boyfriend. He wondered how old Grey was getting on with his dead doggy and smiled; it is nice to be wicked, he thought and sat whistling in his chair, his hands clasped behind his head.

Danny was horny but was keeping Janet for later. Gordon was not around, and Danny decided to head up to the leisure centre for a swim and a sauna. He had missed working out during the last two weeks due to the circumstances, but he intended to return to normal as of from tomorrow.

Danny told Janet of his intentions and collected his gym bag from the Black Pearl, deciding to leave his car outside the sales office and walk up the path to the swimming pool. Once changed, he managed 30 lengths of the pool. The female and males present consisted of one fat ugly fuck who should never have worn a bathing suit; in her sixties or older, she was with a girl about fifteen and possibly her brother and an old guy (Danny could not remember his name) who lived on the park – in other words nothing that was of any interest to him.

Swim over, he decided to head for the sauna, hoping the fat cow would not follow him and spoil his time there. She did not, however, and Danny had the sauna to himself. He enjoyed the sauna, hence why he had put one in his home; it was a relaxing pleasure and good for you.

He was back in his lodge by 6 pm. Janet was already gone when he went back to collect his car; this was her night, and he was going to push her further than he had previously. Barbara had obviously been pushed too far and had maybe decided not to come back for further sexual abuse and torture. Janet, however, was growing on him. She did have a cracking body and she was very submissive which he liked; he would find out tonight how far she was willing to go.

Danny would have sat out on the deck, but it was now raining, and he sat in the lounge instead and watched the STV news. There was a short mention of the blonde bitch's death, but it was short, and now old news. and not high on the agenda of the reporting journalist. Neither was the dead pooch; he did not even get a mention which was not surprising – after all he was just a fucking dog.

Janet arrived at 7 pm looking shy and nervous. 'I got a taxi,' she said. 'I could not bring my car.' This amused him; she was taking risks for him, and he liked that. She had on a black dress which Danny lifted slightly to reveal black suspenders, his favourite. He offered her a drink, something he had never seen her do and she accepted a Jack Daniels. This pleased him as it might loosen her up; tonight was anal night whether she liked it or not. He put on some Angus and Julia Stone and sat beside her on the sofa. 'Do you mind closing the blinds, please Danny, just in case.'

'Of course, how silly of me.' Danny got up and closed the blinds.

'I can't believe I am here,' she said as she raised her glass to his. 'I am really nervous, please don't be rough. I still sleep in the same bed as my husband and have been trying to cover up the bruises from having sex in the office; I am covered in them.'

'Don't worry Janet, I will be careful, and we have a real bed to play in this time.'

They both laughed. He placed his drink and took hers, putting both of them on the coffee table. He kissed her mouth. She had her tongue down his throat and he lay on top of her as he reached inside her dress. She had great legs, smooth and silky, no panties and shaved; she was wet, and moaned as he slipped two fingers into her pretty vagina; it was perfectly formed, and he already knew it was very tasty.

She fumbled with his belt; he was erect and throbbing and could not wait to fuck his new playmate. He sat back up allowing Janet to unbuckle his belt and kicked off his trousers as Janet wanked his impressive cock. 'Jesus, Danny, you are huge,' she said as she bent down and took him in her mouth. He pushed her down harder, but she just gagged and pulled up; she had not mastered the art of getting all of his manhood into her mouth, but she would, and soon. Danny watched her suck his cock as he sat with his drink and made her lick and suck his balls. She complained about getting pubic hair in her mouth, so Danny promised to shave next time. He fucked her slowly on the couch, first on her back and then kneeling up; he would save the anal till last.

Janet had little beads of sweat on her forehead and had come at least eight times. They both stopped and charged their glasses. Janet stood at the drinks bar; apart from her face she looked pretty hot. It's a pity she covered up so much at work, Danny thought. He sat on the sofa as Janet stood across from him. 'I love you, Danny, I can't stop thinking about you.'

'Let us not forget that you're married.'

'Yes, I know but I can get a divorce.'

'Aw, sweetheart, you would do that for me?'

'Yes, but only if you were serious and stopped sleeping with other girls.' She laughed as she said it and threw an ice cube at him as he sat wanking his hard cock. He launched himself off the sofa and was on her in seconds, spinning her round and sliding his erect throbbing cock between her cute buns. He fucked her hard from behind. 'I want you to myself,' she gasped as Danny pulled her head back by the hair, his other hand playing with her cute little soft tits, and he slid his hard cock in and out very fast until she came, again and again.

She must by now have had a dozen orgasms to his zero. He licked her face and neck and bit her erect nipples before taking her hand and heading for the bedroom. The next two hours were intense, He was surprised at how supple and willing she really was – she even gelled his cock for her first try at anal. Danny lifted her legs onto his shoulders as she looked down and pushed his slippery cock into her very tight asshole.

Janet actually enjoyed it so much she came again as she masturbated, as his cock slid slowly in and out of that cute little brown hole. She then wiped his cock with a towel before wanking an enormous amount of cum all over her face. Danny was stunned that a boring and dull-looking female from work, someone who he had worked with all last season with and had not noticed turned out to be a whizz in bed and who was now not so plain and one of his sexy keepers for future fun.

Janet headed for the bathroom; she had wiped his cum with a towel, but it was everywhere, including her hair. He went through to the bar to recharge their glasses; this was much better, he thought. He placed the drinks on the table and headed for the shower, slipped inside and fucked her one more time before she left.

Chapter 46

A Bad day at Pitt Street

Claire sat with John and the Chief in his swanky office on the top floor. John looked like shit and was still dressed in casual clothes – jeans and a checked shirt – and had not even bothered to shave. This was very unusual as he usually wore a suit and was pristine; the Chief also looked troubled.

'Thank you both for coming,' he said as his secretary placed three coffees on the desk in front of them. The Chief took his cup and walked over to the window; it was raining outside which it seemed to have done for the last three days. The Chief spoke first. 'Claire, there has been an incident at John's house.' He turned and faced them both. Claire looked at John, a puzzled and concerned look on her face.

'It's Jed,' John said, 'someone hanged him from the blossom tree in the garden.'

'Hanged him? You mean like a hanging? A dog? God, who would do such an evil thing?'

This was bad, unbelievably bad, she thought. John loved – in fact, adored – his Jed and just about every other animal on the planet. No wonder the poor guy looked like shit; he must be gutted. 'Do you want to tell me more about it?' she asked.

The Chief spoke as John buried his head in his hands. 'It was last night when John arrived home about 6 pm; poor Jed was still warm and hanging from the tree. John managed to cut him free, but the poor dog was dead.'

Claire was stunned. 'I am so sorry, John, I know he meant the world to you.' And he did. John took the 10-year-old lab everywhere with him and he was a very lovely dog.

'We are checking anyone who John has put away who has been released from prison, anyone that has threatened revenge and such. We are also keeping a local police presence around the clock; if this person is capable of doing this to a dog, then he is capable of much more. I suggest you go home, John, take care of Jed and Heather and we will carry on here until you return.'

John stood up, as did Claire and she gave him a really tight hug; he smelled slightly of BO, and his stubble was sore on her soft skin.

The Chief closed the door as John left. 'Poor John,' he said as he leaned against the front of his desk.

'What are your thoughts, Chief?' asked Claire.

'Not so sure; it looks like a revenge attack,' he said as he sat back down and clasped his coffee cup in his hand. 'We will keep an eye on things for now; meantime, can you run this one on your own until he comes back. I know it's only a dog as such, but you know what he was like with that dog; that mutt was his best friend in the world; it might have as well been human.'

Claire agreed. And yes, she would handle things on her own for now. They both decided that whoever did this really wanted to hurt John and knew either what he was like with animals, or how much Jed meant to him; he had brought the dog to work many times and the bad guys would have known that – this was done for maximum effect and, God help us, it had accomplished the desired effect and then some. It was also decided that it was highly unlikely to be related to their current case, about which the chief was looking for an update. Claire explained that the task force was working hard on both the murder and the body theft. Claire thought that whoever killed Carolyn also stole the body back from the morgue. Due to the sexual nature of the killing, DNA would have been on her body.

'My thoughts are that the killer did not expect to see the body again and was probably alerted by the TV coverage of its reappearance. His DNA may be on file, and according to the lengths he went to retrieve her, I am guessing it might be. This could have led us straight to the killer. I think the need to get that body back was well worth the risk to him. I also think that our killer is close to the dump site.' She flicked through her pad. 'He would have had to be there when the ambulance took the body to the morgue – there was no way of knowing otherwise, not unless he was told by someone who knew, which I doubt very much.

'I think the ambulance was followed back to Glasgow, sir; there was a black Audi seen at the scene by a local officer and the same type of car shows up again, not once but twice, on CCTV cameras on the route to the morgue. However, the plate is not recognisable – all we know is its colour, black. I have officers checking shops and offices on the route to see if we can come up with a plate.'

'What about the ferry boys; did they remember anything that night?'

'No, sir, they see a thousand cars a day and more often than not simply go into auto mode and don't pay that much attention to vehicles; once the ferry is loaded, they go back inside and play cards during the crossing. They remember the private ambulance, but nothing else.'

'I need this guy found, Claire; we have managed to keep this as low key as possible but it's getting hotter around here and I am depending on you.'

They both got up and Claire shook his hand before leaving. No pressure there, she thought, as she closed the door behind her. She spent the rest of the morning in the operations room; they really did not have much to go on. The press was still unaware of the missing body, but they were aware of the old boy's murder at the morgue, so it would only be a matter of time.

This black car was all they had to go on; without the body it was difficult to come up with answers. Claire sat in her office, closed the blinds, texted the love of her life and then also sent a text, just a love heart and a x to John. Poor guy she thought. He once said to her, when she asked him what he was going to do when he retired, that he was going to spend every minute possible with Heather and Jed; how hurt he must be right now. She took a bottle of water from her bag and started reading through the files that had been left for her and John. His chair was empty across the office, his suit jacket hanging on the coat stand; the whole place felt like it had lost one of its own.

She started looking through the piles of research and wishing that the officers investigating the killing of Jed would find the sick bastard and return his sad ass back to jail. There were 27 boat owners at the caravan park who were now being investigated by her officers; there was also a whopping 1700 registered boats of various sizes located at Dunoon, Gourock, Port Glasgow, Wemyss Bay and Rothesay, all capable of reaching Loch Striven. Her best hope was this bloody Audi; there were 178 black, two-door Audi A5s registered in Scotland and, again, the list was being worked on by the team who would work on the Milngavie and Dunoon areas and work their way outwards.

More often than not, victims knew their killers who often would live not too far away from them either.

It was 1 pm and Claire had a lunch appointment; she was meeting Colin in the West End. She was now not really in an eating mood and had as little food as she could; the sick killing of Jed was beginning to sink in. She felt bad not telling Colin, but if she did it would probably be all over the papers and would only hurt John more.

Colin was always on the lookout for a story; he was either investigating a story or what was in her pants, the latter of which she did not mind as he was good between the sheets. Lunch was spoiled nonetheless, and she returned to Pitt Street an hour later. One of the young officers, Jordan Mitchell, eagerly awaited her return; he was pacing up and down outside her office. She also noticed that she had missed a call from him during lunch.

'Afternoon, ma'am,' he said as he walked into the office behind her.

'Yes, Jordan, what has you all excited?' she asked.

'It's the car, ma'am. I spoke again with the police officer in at the cordon where the body was found; he remembered a black Audi parked in a layby not far from the crime scene and he also remembered that a local man owned such a car but did not know his name. BUT GUESS WHAT! HE WORKS ON THE CARAVAN PARK!'

Claire nearly wet her pants. Could this be that easy? Was this car going to lead her to the murderer?

'Who is he; how old is he?' she said as she riffled through the papers on her desk

'His name is… – Jordan looked at his wee black book – his name is Daniel Fleming; he is 40 years old…' 'Stop!' she said. She was pumped and grabbed her jacket as the name came out of Jordan's mouth.

'You come with me,' she said to the young cop. Jordan actually skipped behind her as they left her office; he ran for his jacket which was over his chair in the main office and sprinted back to catch up with her.

'Are we going to visit Mr Fleming?' he asked.

‘You’re damn right we are. This is the best break we’ve had, young man.’

Claire updated Jordan in regard to her first sighting of him at the caravan park; she had never seen a black Audi, but an interview was definitely required for just the car alone. It was still pissing down as Claire called the Chief with a quick update; she remained calm and unexcited on the phone as this could be a total duck egg and she was conscious of not wanting to look stupid.

The trip was dismal, what with the rain and the dog thing. Jordan also talked non-stop and kept looking at the little gap in her blouse while she was driving, which she kept trying to close and could not. She drove off the ferry now aware that a little bit of breast was available for all to see. Twenty minutes later they were driving up the long driveway to the sales office at the park and – guess what was in the car park – a black two door Audi A5. Claire parked her car beside it; they both got out and looked at it, not really knowing what they were looking for.

Danny walked out of his office. Gordon was gone and even though he had Katie coming tonight he still was up for a quickie with Natcha. He walked through to the kitchen, washed his cup and left it on the dryer. He was on his way back towards the reception desk when he looked outside to make sure there were no customers in the sales area. He saw Red and someone else at the Black Pearl and his heart raced.

He had taken a chance the other day following the ambulance to Glasgow, but he had had no choice.

Ignoring Janet's comment of 'You off to get some lunch, sexy?', Danny walked out on to the small terrace and steps at the front office, placed both hands on the railing and shouted, 'May I help you?'

Both Red and the young man looked over at him and the young guy took something out his pocket while Red fumbled in her bag. They both walked upstairs showing off their ID – DC Claire Stewart and Officer Jordan Mitchell.

'May we have a chat,' Claire asked as Danny held open the door for them.

'Of course. Can I get you tea or coffee?' he asked. Claire asked for a coffee and Jordan, water. Janet headed to the kitchen to oblige, as Danny walked them both to his office. He closed the door and showed them to their seats. Claire might have ginger hair, but she was remarkably pretty, with gorgeous long legs, an ample pair of bombs bursting out her tight blouse, and the clearest and lightest complexion he had ever seen.

'How can I help you? he asked, staring at the gap in Claire's blouse. She in turn still thought he was amazingly handsome, like the guys you saw on aftershave adverts or in the movies, none of whom she had ever met of course. What the hell was he working on a caravan park for? It was a massive waste of talent; he should have been a model. His eyes were unbelievable and were his most striking feature. But even with the charm and the looks and the body, this guy still gave still her the creeps; he was staring at her breasts, not that they were big, but she decided this blouse was going in the bin.

'Mr Fleming…'

'Please call me Danny.'

'As you are already aware, we are investigating the murder of one Carolyn Hughes, who spent some time here on the park, immediately before she was killed, and whose body was later found not far from here in Loch Striven.'

'Is this an interview or am I under investigation, Detective?'

Danny looked at them both. Jordan was obviously out of his depth and was starting to sweat.

'No, not at all, Mr Fleming; we are just trying to eliminate you from our enquiries,' replied Claire as she crossed her lovely legs, which suited the short skirt she was wearing. 'There were reports of a black Audi A5 near the scene at Loch Striven; can you confirm that this was your car.'

If he was guilty of anything then he certainly did not show it. Claire wished she had John with her instead of the easily spooked Jordan. The creepy and smart-arsed Mr Fleming was trying to turn her interview inside out.

'Yes, I was there, and, like many others, I was curious about what had happened; it also affects my job here if the tourists stay away.'

'Were you at the slipway?' asked Claire.

'No, I was not allowed to drive that far and walked up the hill for a better look instead. I think I actually saw you there.' He smiled, trying to be charming, but was more of a dick than anything else.

Claire consulted her notebook. 'I already have a statement from you with regard to whether you ever met Carolyn Hughes when she was on the park. You said that you had met her briefly. Do you have anything to add?'

She took notes, as did the nervous Jordan. It was a pity that Danny was so creepy and smug; a lot of her pals would have eaten their own vomit to get a date with this hunk.

'Just one more thing, Mr Fleming. Can you tell me where you went after your little jaunt round to Loch Striven?'

'I came back here, had my dinner and watched the news. I think I would have stayed in my lodge for the rest of the night.'

'Your lodge?' asked Claire.

'Mr Fleming lives here on the park in a lodge,' piped up Jordan for the first time. Claire gave him a dismissive look. 'Well thanks, Mr Fleming; it was good of you to talk to me.' She gave him her card, the same one he had taken from Willie, but a fresher one. 'If you hear – or remember – anything else, please let me know.'

They all got out of their seats. Danny shook their hands, his handshake hurting them both. Jordan winced and so did Claire. It looked like Mr Smart-arse sales guy had a strong grip; he also was fit and muscular- looking under that suit – and way over six feet tall.

Danny asked Janet to show them back out and returned to his office where he closed the door behind him, held out his hand and watched it shake. 'FUCK! CUNT! BASTARD! HERE WE FUCKING GO AGAIN!' Red was onto something. It was the car trip to Glasgow behind the ambulance, he thought, but he had had no choice, and was careful and had used false plates. Danny was fucking raging. Gordon popped his head round Danny's office door and hooked his thumb back at the two departing cops.

'Everything okay, sport?' he asked.

'Yes, just some routine questions.' Gordon nodded, 'Yeah, they said they wanted to talk to everyone.'

He nearly knocked Janet over as he backed out of the door, apologised, and headed for his own office. Janet now standing in Danny's doorway. 'Everything okay, honey?' she asked. Danny tried to remain calm. 'Yes, babes, everything is fine, just asking if I saw anything strange on the park when that girl was here.'

Janet mouthed 'I want you' and left, closing the door behind her. It was only 3.40 pm and Danny could not wait till he got the fuck out of his office. It looked like Katie had a job to do and it was going to be in Glasgow. Danny decided there and then that he was not remaining here for much longer; the sheriff was coming, and it was time to get the fuck out of Dodge.

He was in a foul mood and wished now that he had not killed that fucking blonde bitch. The killing stank to high heaven and could send him straight to hell; there was no body, but people have been convicted without one in the past. Katie was due here at 5 pm but sex was not on his mind. He had to get rid of Red. Just the way she looked at him convinced him that she knew that he was involved, and she looked like she was going to turn over every fucking rock till she found out.

The phone rang on his desk it was Janet. ‘Hi, babes, that detective is on the phone; you know the one that just left, she wants to speak to you, will I put her through?’

Fuck me, he thought, here we go. ‘Yes, Janet, please put her through. Hi, Detective, what did you forget?’ She was on the ferry; you could hear the automated woman’s voice announcing the safety brief as the ferry left its dock.

‘Sorry to call you,’ she said, ‘I just have a quick question. Do you have another address, apart from your lodge, that is?’

Danny replied that he did not, and she thanked him and hung up.

Fucking bitch has now got a hard-on about him being guilty; Danny would have to leave, and soon. Leaving his home, at least for the time being, looked inevitable; he had to protect himself and his home. Being put in prison for even a day was not an option; he would kill again to keep from going to prison.

The next two hours dragged by and were punctuated by visits from Gordon and Janet and a couple who were thinking of changing their caravan for a newer model. Katie texted him from the ferry; she would be arriving at his lodge in twenty minutes.

Danny said his goodbyes. Janet was hoping for a quickie. but saw by the look he gave her that that was not going to happen.

He left the office and drove round to the lodge. A JD was in order. Danny felt rattled and for the first time in his life he was scared and worried. The ginger bitch was on to something, he was not sure what. Sometimes it was better to run and hide and live to fight another day, than to stand and fight and bleed. Or in this case go to prison. Danny's whole attitude his entire life was his self-preservation and he intended not to spend the rest of his life behind bars – he could not do it. That in mind, he poured himself a drink and stood outside on the deck. Killing Red and her boyfriend could bring down more heat on him, but so would leaving; he was really stuck between a rock and a hard place.

Katie arrived in her SWB Shogun. She looked hot and sexy, but Danny was in no mood for sex, well not right now anyway. He went back inside and poured her a drink, before going back outside.

'What's up, lover?' Katie asked as she straddled him on the chair; she smelt fabulous, and Danny could feel his cock growing between his legs.

'Quite a bit,' he replied, 'we have a problem, and it looks like it is going to need fixing.'

'Well, I am sure we can fix that,' she said as she rubbed his now erect cock. Danny could not resist, and they headed for the bedroom – his problem could wait until later.

The sex with Katie was intense and lasted for hours; it was dark by the time they emerged from the bedroom. Danny phoned in some Chinese food and they both sat back out on the decking. Katie lay back in the lounger looking at the stars visible in the black sky.

Danny spoke first, 'There are two detectives investigating me about this murder, and they are getting on my nerves. I think they know something.'

'What makes you think that?' asked Katie.

Danny leaned back and thought to himself, is she trustworthy? Should I tell her before she's proved herself to me?

She would be a good ally, and his was a lonely path. He had always wanted a Bonnie to his Clyde, ever since he saw the film of the same name. But…what if she wasn't to be trusted?

'What's the matter, lover?' she asked, with a puzzled look on her face. 'You are very quiet. What do you think the detectives know?'

Oh fuck it. Just tell her, he thought to himself and so he did; told her the whole story from start to finish.

'So, you see, I think it's just the way that bitch looks and talks to me; that body reappearing caught me by surprise, and I had to use the car to go to Glasgow. I changed the number plates, but I think they might have seen the car on CCTV.'

Katie was quiet; didn't say a word but just lay back on the lounger with her eyes closed.

Fuck's sake, thought Danny, I've made a mistake. I'll have

to kill the bitch.

Then, slowly, she opened her eyes and looked at him. She smiled, and he saw that her eyes were glittering. He recognised the kindred spirit and realised that all was well – very well – in the world of Danny Fleming.

Just then a car swung into the drive; it was the food and Danny went to the door and paid for their meal as Katie set a table outside. It was a nice night and they both decided to have their meal on the deck. They ate in silence. Danny liked his new apprentice – she was young, pretty, a dream in bed and keen and she was loyal. It was never in his mind to have someone like Katie who knew of his killings; however, she did save him from popping up on the police radar in Dumfries which could have resulted in him being caught.

It was a good feeling to have some backup now and again and someone like her that he could talk to. He was capable of looking after himself and used to being on his own, but a killer's mind was a lonely one. Danny decided to keep his house and aircraft a secret for now, though – no point in giving all his secrets away too soon. They chatted through the night, and he decided that he would drop his pursuit of Jenny's wealth as it was a dead duck anyway; he had more serious issues to deal with. He would keep Natcha and Janet under wraps for now because girls can get jealous when you are playing with other chicks.

Danny and Katie lay in bed. It was now 3 am and the moon was out as lay side by side. He could see her small erect nipples in the moonlight. Katie rolled over and lay on him, kissing his lips. 'You not tired, lover,' she said as she kept kissing him.

Danny moved her off and put his hands behind his head. There was a short silence until Katie spoke the words he was wating to hear. 'I will kill her for you.'

'Are you sure? Don't forget she is a cop.'

'Yes, I will, but can you help me?'

'Course I can; how would you want to do it?' he asked.

'I don't know. I could stab her I suppose.'

'Do you know how to use a gun?'

'No, Danny, I am a girl, remember.'

Katie leaped back on top of him. 'Do you have a gun?'

'Yep, and I can teach you how to use it.'

'Will you really?'

'Yes, I will.' Katie smiled, slid down under the sheets and took Danny in her mouth. They decided afterwards to kill Red as soon as possible; the other detective was not a problem for now as he had other things on his mind like his doggy funeral. It was now 4 am and the birds had started to sing as they fell asleep in each other's arms.

Chapter 47

Suspect

Claire was back at Pitt Street at 6 am; she had a feeling about this one, a feeling she was close. Mr Handsome could be her killer, but she needed much more than a gut feeling; she needed evidence and evidence that would hold up in a Scottish court of law. It was obvious that he was in a relationship with the woman at the front desk which was strange as she was not only married but also a bit of a plain Jane. He was possibly seeing a few other girls at the park. Her Dad would have called him a shag nasty, but she hated that description – he was certainly a womaniser but was he really a serial killer? He did not fit the usual profile, which was usually a loner and much creepier; this guy was confident, outgoing, handsome, and dating women who were very much alive. What better place to pick up women than on a holiday park? Single women were usually looking for romance on holiday, married ones too, and Mr Handsome looked like the type to give it to them all.

She had been digging into Mr Hunk's past; his mother had been murdered when he was 17 years old, and his father died in prison of natural causes, while serving a sentence for murder. There were a few minor scuffles when he was younger, mostly at school from which he was expelled at just fifteen years old for striking a male teacher. Danny lived out his teens in a tough housing estate and did well to get out of there, she thought. There was a ten-year gap of what looked like no job, no bank account, or address but this could be explained if he worked casually or lived with a friend, or on parks. He later appeared on the voters' roll in Newton Mearns where it looked like he got married to a solicitor and had a son.

Claire finally had someone she could talk to about his past, someone who knew the real Mr Danny boy. Jordan, her appointed junior detective on the case, was meanwhile trawling through the hours and hours of CCTV that had been gathered from the route of the mortuary van. Claire decided to leave him to it as she did not see a problem visiting Danny's ex-wife who was at home only until the following day.

She left the office at 10 am and made the short drive to see her; she was excited – no one knew a man better than an ex-wife. The sat-nav took her to what only can be described as a posh house in a posh place. The previous Mrs Fleming came out on the drive to meet her; she was older than Claire had thought she would be, but extremely attractive.

'Hi Claire,' she said as she extended her hand, pumping Claire's hand vigorously. She showed her inside. The house was immaculate with lots of white, even the carpets! Gillian asked her to remove her shoes and showed her into the lounge before disappearing into the kitchen to make some coffee. Claire could not imagine how she kept the place so pristine; it looked as if no-one had ever set foot in the place, and everything was brand new. Gillian returned with the coffee shortly afterwards.

'Your house is beautiful.'

'Thank you,' she said.

Gillian sat across from her. 'Is Danny in some sort of trouble?' she asked as she poured them both coffee. 'No, not that I know of; we just need to eliminate him from our inquiries.'

'What do you need to know?'

'Just the truth, why you got divorced for starters.'

'I caught him fucking my best friend in our house the day before our anniversary.'

'Do you still have contact with him?'

'No, never.'

'What was he was like to be married to?'

'At first, he was very loving and caring, I later found out that he had just about fucked everyone I knew. Look, I am sorry for my language, but Danny is a cheating serial liar, shagger, and con man. The man came from the gutter, and I hope that is where he is now.'

'When you say con man, in what way?'

'I also found out later that he had conned £30k from a lady I know who was supposedly teaching him business studies; she owned a company that fitted electronic gates.'

Claire was writing this in her notebook. She looked at Gillian, 'How did you find out?'

'She came to me after we were divorced, confessed everything and apologised. I was shocked as she was not Danny's type and a lot older than him.'

'When you say a lot older, how much older?'

'About twenty years, I would say.'

'Can you give me a name?'

'No, I am sorry, I promised not to mention it. You see, she is still married; she was just one of many of his married lovers whom he conned money from.'

'Do you know of others?'

'No, but I am sure there were many. I am just not interested anymore and am happy that we are no longer married.'

It was as Claire had thought – Mr Charming was indeed a naughty boy. 'Would you say Danny was capable of murder?'

'MURDER? Are you serious?'

'Yes, I am. Did he ever hurt you?'

'No, he did not.'

'Can I ask you a personal question?'

'Go ahead although I am not sure if I will answer.'

'Did he ever do any weird stuff in bed?'

'When you say weird, what exactly do you mean?'

'Like was he rough, did he hurt you or try to choke you?'

'No, never.' Gillian looked flustered and worried.

'I am sorry Gillian. I had to ask those questions and I might have to speak to you again.' Claire took a card from her bag. 'I'll leave you my mobile number; if you think of anything else, please let me know.'

Gillian walked Claire to the door and, pausing before she opened it, placed her hand on Claire's arm. 'Claire, there was once when we were making love. He had a look in his eyes that frightened me, but it was only for a brief second.'

'In what way did it frighten you?'

'I don't know, just the way he looked. I am sorry, I really can't explain it, but it did put a dampener on the moment, and I did not orgasm either, which I always did with Danny.'

They shook hands and Claire started to walk to her car. 'You won't tell him I told you, right?' called Gillian. 'No, Gillian, he won't know I have been here; thanks again.'

Claire headed back to the station, convinced more than ever now that he was her man. Most of the lads at the station laughed when she had a hunch, even John, but she felt strongly about this one, and anyway there was no-one else in the frame for Carolyn's murder. But she wished she had a body. She didn't go back to the police station, driving instead to the housing scheme where Danny grew up. She parked her car outside a hairdresser's which was next to the local pub. This was probably not a good idea, but she had to keep digging, John had always told her to keep throwing shit at the wall until it stuck. Detective work involved lots of leg work and lots of data-crunching which was the shit.

She walked into the pub and regretted it immediately; the bar was a dive. Everyone stopped what they were doing; there was not a single female in the place. The men playing darts and the others playing pool had all frozen and turned to stare at her. The barman asked if he could help. Claire about turned and left and could hear the men laughing inside.

She returned to her car at a quicker pace than when she got out of it. A man, probably in his late thirties, sat outside the hairdresser's where she had parked her car; he was catching the sun and had his eyes closed. He looked like the drummer from the band The Black Keys and wore the same type of black-framed eyeglasses. There were two girls sitting inside the shop. He spoke without opening his eyes, 'You can't park here when you go to the pub.'

Clare explained that she was on official police business and could park where she wanted. He opened his eyes as Claire flashed her police ID card. 'You still can't park here; this car park is for my customers only.' Claire asked him his name. 'It's John, John Fenner.'

'Hi John, my name's Detective Claire Stewart. Can I have a chat with you?'

'What about?' He looked at his mobile. 'I have a wedding to plan.'

'About a guy that once lived locally; his name was Danny Fleming.'

'Oh yeah, Mr Handsome himself; he used to come here for a haircut but would only let the girls cut his hair. He slept with most of them, a right mad shagger. He was right up his own arse, really loved himself; rumour was he killed his own mother.'

'Seriously?'

‘Yep, that was the word going around; he disappeared soon afterwards.’

A man walked into the barber’s shop and John stood up. ‘I gotta go, see ya,’ were his parting words as he showed the guy to his barber’s chair and threw a cape round him.

Claire got back into her car and locked the doors; this was the first time anyone had mentioned Danny in a violent way. She decided to head to the local nick to update her info from a more reliable source. She showed her ID to the desk sergeant at Clydebank police station and asked to speak to any of the detectives who were on duty. The sergeant showed her the lift and told her it was the third floor. On exiting the lift, the first detective she met was Eddie McCabe, a veteran of 30 years who was, by a lucky chance, the detective who had worked on the murder of Danny Fleming’s mother.

Claire explained why she was there and what her thoughts were. Eddie was confident that the killer or killers were never caught and that it could not be Danny. He went on to say that the murder was the most ferocious he had ever come across; the woman had her throat slit and was stabbed more than forty times. Danny had an alibi which was confirmed by many witnesses. Claire thanked him for his time but was more interested in the words spoken by Mister John Fenner. It was time to call it a day, and Claire decided to head home to mull over the recent intel.

Chapter 48

Plan B

Danny was in good spirits. It was Monday morning, and he was off on Tuesday. He had left Katie at the lodge and told her not to show herself; they planned to go to Glasgow the next day; however, he had to collect a gun and the motorbike. Katie would lie low until Danny picked her up on Tuesday.

The rest of the day went well, Danny fucked Janet in his office before selling two caravans and Gordon was on his day off which allowed Danny to do as he pleased. He called Jenny and lied that his mother had died, and he would have to put any future meetings on hold meantime; she was upset for him but very understanding. He had Katie, Janet and Natcha to keep him satisfied meantime; he seriously had to see Natcha, as they had not played enough, and she was his favourite fuck.

He left the park at 5 pm; his ferry left at 5.30 pm and he would not come back on the same route, as he would be on the bike and did not want to be seen with it. It would have been much simpler to take Katie home with him, but he was not ready to reveal where his bolthole was – not now and maybe not ever. Danny arrived home at 6.40 pm, put on some Kasabian music, poured himself a drink and sat out on the patio. Katie's agreement to kill Red was perfect; he would make sure he had an alibi.

The hard part was finding out where Red was staying; he hoped it was not a hotel with CCTV. He would use Katie, as the risk of him being recognised by the police was high. He looked out spare one-piece Negeri leathers which would be a little big for Katie but would have to do. The boots would also be too big but buying a new set or riding the bike without the proper gear would be a mistake. He walked back inside to a wall in the office, where he removed a set of books, to reveal a door handle which he pulled.

The heavy bookcase swung out to reveal a small 8 x 8ft room with a huge heavy safe on the ground. On the left wall was a collection of shotguns, pistols, and an UZI and AK47 automatics; the other wall was covered in metal shelves and held an array of boxes of cartridges, bullets, two stun guns and some C02 gas, pepper spray and a multi-shot Adder crossbow. It was a bit James Bond but necessary to hide the weapons and keep his cash safe.

He chose a small snub-nosed 38 pistol which should be okay for Katie to use as it did not have a huge recoil, although it still gave a kick, and a silencer. He placed it and spare ammo in his backpack along with the leathers and boots before locking up and heading up to the barn for the Kawasaki Ninja. He drove the long way back to the park, taking his time, being careful not to break any speed limits. He was back at the park by 11.20 pm. Katie was glad to see him, and they sat down to plan their next move; she was keen to please Danny and loved the gun. The next morning, they headed out on the bike to a remote forest about five miles from the park for some firing practice. The 38 would not be heard because of the silencer anyway; it was really just for privacy.

Danny let Katie fire a few rounds at the trees; she was a good shot and loved the power. He then showed her how to load the gun and fit the silencer. Lesson over, they sat on a log and chatted about how they were going to carry out their termination of Red; Katie was more than willing. They agreed to visit the police station on the bike to find out what car she drove and fit it with a tracker. She had shown up in a Ford Mondeo, but it could have been a pool car. Danny was convinced tailing her was not a viable option. 'When you say a tracker, what do you mean?' asked Katie as she handled the gun in her hand, as if she was guessing its weight.

'I can attach a mobile phone under her car and track her that way; it's called Locate a Phone.'

'That easy huh? I thought you were ex-SAS or something,' she laughed and pushed him backwards over the log, jumping over it and quickly straddling him. Leaned over, she pressed the gun to his temple, kissed him and said 'kapow!' before blowing on the barrel, laughing.

Danny took the gun from her and kissed her back while tugging at her clothes. He stripped her naked before bending her over the log and fucking her from behind. It was a very pleasant ride in the warm sunshine. The following morning, when they woke up, it was raining. Danny made breakfast for Katie which he served up in bed. Janet and Natcha were texting him like crazy and it was becoming annoying. He was trying to stay focused on the job ahead and sex with Katie was good enough for now.

By 4 pm they were both walking along Pitt Street. Red had twice previously been driving a grey Ford Mondeo on a 65 plate and that same car now sat on the street. Danny stopped to tie his shoelace, while fixing the magnetic tracker under Claire's car. Katie commented on how clever she thought he was. The couple continued hand-in-hand towards Blytheswood Square. Two fat Ladies was Danny's choice for dinner due to its location and he also loved seafood. The meal and the company were, of course, excellent; they looked like any other couple enjoying a meal in the city centre. Danny now saw light at the end of the tunnel and felt good.

It was now 7.05 pm. Danny and Katie were having coffee and planning to go to the cinema. He had his iPad in front of him and logged into 'locate my phone'. The car had moved! The phone was now parked in Danny's old haunt, The West End; they would carry on with their plan and watch the movie chosen by Katie, which was *The Revenant,* a movie which was enjoyed by both. It was now 10.30 pm and according to the tracker the car had still not moved. They both drove in silence to Hyndland Terrace near Park Circus; it was perfect for what they intended. The car was there right enough. Park Circus was mainly offices converted from the original town houses, set in curving crescents with a large crescent shaped garden separating one side from the other. The garden, with its high hedges and mature trees, was great cover. No-one could see you from the opposite side of the street.

There were a few flats still used as residential properties, fetching over £350k for a two-bed as it was a well sought-after area to live. The bottom two premises had decals on their windows – one an architect's, the other The Royal Society for the Protection of Birds. That left two flats above. Considering only one had its window open on a balmy night, it was likely that Red was in the flat on the right and, as if on cue, she confirmed that as she passed the large bay window. They couple walking hand-in-hand round the crescent went completely unnoticed.

Danny suddenly squatted beside Claire's car and removed the magnetic box from underneath it. The pair headed back to Dunoon and managed to catch the last ferry. They were back at the lodge just after midnight after a successful night in town; it was time to plan their next move. It was agreed that he would return to work as expected tomorrow morning, Wednesday. Katie would return home and meet him back at the lodge on Thursday night and later that night Danny would take her to Park Circus.

Danny was no longer the hunted, but the hunter.

Chapter 49

Park Circus

On his way to the office Danny was thinking it was maybe time to leave the park; he could probably lie low at the house, or possibly go abroad, maybe live in Switzerland with Katie until everything had died down. It was just getting far too dangerous to remain. He had never been close to getting caught, but killing blondie had started a whole new clusterfuck of unwanted police activity. He had no intention of going to jail for the rest of his life and was seriously thinking of moving, with or without Katie. He arrived at the sales office for 8.30 am and had screwed Janet over his desk before 9 am. Janet, at this stage in her life, had just discovered multiple orgasms and could not get enough of them; she was mad for sex constantly. After sex, the remainder of the day was dull and boring; he didn't even sell anything. He left at 5 pm and headed to his lodge. The weather was surprisingly good so far with only a couple of wet days, and the park was alive with people; yep, wildlife, the birds, bees, and the babes had suddenly appeared, and the park was buzzing. He, however, was preoccupied with the cops and the other shit that was going on.

He was both resigned and worried about leaving for new pastures. Leaving his house was not an option so he would have to work around it. His house was not the only issue; he would not sell it, nor did he want to leave it empty for any length of time. He might have to trust Katie more than he wanted to and never had before in a relationship. Katie gave him a hug as he entered the lodge. Danny poured them both a drink and switched on the TV; he had the illegally downloaded Kodi and could watch any film, TV, or sports from around the world and in HD, even movies that were currently in the cinema. He settled down and watched *Swiss Railway Journeys* with Katie. She was surprised at his choice, a programme he said he secretly enjoyed but would never admit to.

He wondered about Barbara who still had not appeared back at the park and had not answered his texts. Was the sex that night really too rough? Possibly. Danny chatted to Katie about Zermatt before going to bed at 11.45 pm. He was up by 6 am and in the gym for 6.30 am for a good workout and a swim to set him up for the day. The rest of the day, however, was at a much slower pace and it seemed as if every minute were an hour. Danny did not sell anything again and Janet was on a day off. Gordon was also missing due to a family bereavement. Katie stayed at the lodge keeping a low profile; they planned to finalise their visit to Red after dinner.

Danny left work early and on his own; he was on the ferry by 4.30 pm, leaving Katie behind, with strict instructions to stay out of sight. After much thought he was beginning to feel good, and confident that once Red was dealt with and when he had taken care of the Grey one, his troubles would be over. He had reached Kinlochard in good time and parked the Black Pearl in the barn. The Toyota Land Cruiser and the Kawasaki Ninja were both covered in bird shit. The bloody swallows were back alright.

Danny would have to take the bike down to the house – a very uncomfortable ride that was going to be. He drove the bone-shaking ride and nearly fell off twice; he then washed the bike down before getting kitted out in his leathers; he put a spare jacket in a backpack for Katie, and a spare helmet was attached to the bike. He was back at the park for 7 pm. Tonight was the night – how exciting, he thought.

Neither Katie nor Danny was nervous; they were both excited, how cool is that. Danny would have preferred to do the same to Red as he did to the blonde bitch, but he had to know how committed Katie was; if she didn't kill the cop, he would have no choice but to kill them both. Danny hoped Katie would. 'When you kill the bitch, tell her it is from me, tell her it's from Danny.'

Katie smiled. She could not explain it, but when you kill, you feel different – special, and powerful; she loved it and loved Danny and could not wait to pull the trigger for him. They were both silent as the Kawasaki Ninja purred quietly as it made its way slowly out of the park unnoticed, its riders pumped with adrenaline as the bike took the long way round to Glasgow. Death was coming to the city for the second time that week.

Danny rode the Ninja out towards Cairndow and then onto the A83 and the Rest and be Thankful. The roads were quiet, and they were soon cruising along the A82 on the banks of Loch

Lomond as it started to get dark; a low ground fog a few feet above the loch enhanced their silent journey towards their victim. It took an hour before he finally turned the bike into the row of immaculate Georgian mansions of Park Circus and switched the engine off. A bird, disturbed by their presence, flew startled from its perch in the trees. It was a fine night as a quarter moon shone a weird light on the white buildings. Katie felt pumped as Danny handed her the gun. She checked the mag. was fully pulled back, the lever putting one in the chamber. She then screwed the silencer on as Danny had shown her.

They both walked across the road, Katie sticking the gun in the back of her leather trousers as she walked towards the front steps. The flat was in darkness. Danny made light work of the lock on the entrance door. The stair lights were on a motion sensor and Katie was startled as the light burst into life. He opened the door to flat 4D with ease and kissed Katie on the forehead; she was sweating and looked nervous.

'Do not worry, I will be waiting for you outside.'

He really would have preferred to kill the detective himself, but he had to know if he could really trust Katie, and there was no better way than this. This was her chance to prove she was who she said, and that she was committed to him. Danny descended the stairway quietly, the lights going out as he left the doorway and walked back onto the street. He sat astride the Ninja but did not start the engine; he waited, watching and listening.

Katie's heart was pounding; she could hear it beat in her ears. She could smell perfume; there was a small blue light on a table, it was coming from the wi-fi router and lit the hall enough to see. A cat walked towards her; it meowed and rubbed itself against her leg. She opened the first door she came to; it was a bedroom but was empty. Slowly pushing open the next door, the smell of perfume was suddenly a lot stronger, and she could see the shape of someone lying on the bed. The floor was tiled in black and white; the bed was brass, like something from the film *Bedknobs and Broomsticks*.

Suddenly a girl in the bed sat up, her red hair visible in the moonlight shadow. She was very white and pretty. Katie shot the redhead in the face; the gun made a different noise in the room than when she had fired it with Danny. Katie pulled the trigger again. 'This is for DA!.......' she tried to say but did not finish the sentence as she was slammed hard from the side. The pain was immediate as she was propelled through the air.

Danny was outside sitting on the Ninja, a helmet over each handlebar. He saw the flashes of shots in the window just to the left of what he thought was the lounge. Suddenly there was an explosion of glass, and wood, extremely loud in the still quiet of the night. The sash window had disintegrated and two figures, one of which, he could see, was Katie fell towards the ground, their landing hidden by the hedge in front of him. A white Mercedes car alarm burst into life as lights started to come on in some of the buildings.

Danny pushed the electric start on the Kawasaki and put it in gear. He drove slowly towards the entrance to the building. There was no sign of the other person, but Katie was impaled on the wrought iron railings at the front of the building. Her back was arched, her beautiful dark hair touching the pavement; her body looked like it was floating in mid-air. Three black railings wet with dark blood pierced her chest. Danny gunned the bike from the crescent, its rear tyre struggling to get a grip on the damp cobblestones.

Claire lay on the floor in her bedroom. The cat had woken her from a light sleep when it had jumped on the bed. Where was Colin, she thought, just as the bedroom door opened. There was someone walking into the room, and it was not him. There was a bright flame and loud noise. The first shot hit her under the chin as she tried to dive to the other side of the bed. She could feel the bullet tear through her mouth, taking her teeth with it before the bullet tore an exit hole through her right cheek. The second shot caught her on the right shoulder. The shooter was female and spoke the words 'This is for Da…!'

Claire hit the floor on the other side of the bed hard; there was an almighty crashing sound of glass and something breaking.

'Colin,' she whispered as she held onto the bottom of the bed and tried to stand up. The window was gone and the room now much colder. Claire took the phone from the nightstand and dialled 999 – that was the last she remembered.

Danny was forced to stop at a red traffic light at the junction of Great Western Road and Hyndland Road; a large dog fox crossed the road in front of him; it paused its trot and gave him a look before disappearing into the hedges opposite; he watched it as he waited for the light to change. He could see blue lights lighting up the night sky near the tower block at Anniesland Cross – they were heading his way. No sirens until the police BMW X5 reached the traffic lights and they turned on their siren, the noise deafening even with a helmet on. The cops didn't give him a second look and sped past him. An ambulance could also be heard from somewhere behind him. He was in control and not worried about the police, fuck them. If a chase ensued, they would never catch him.

Danny continued his journey, heading west towards the Cross. More police cars appeared ahead of him, all heading in the same direction from where he had just come. He headed home, taking a longer route through Drumchapel. It was alive with street people. Gangs of youths, druggies and rats controlled the streets here at night. They watched him as he rode the bike along Kingfauns Drive. Danny then headed out towards Carbeth, stopping at the Queens View and removing his helmet.

Katie was gone for sure but was the detective dead? He fucking hoped so. He was not worried about the gun; it was clean and could never be traced back to him. Danny was sure it was not Red that fell with Katie – it looked more like a man. Possibly the boyfriend perhaps? There was nothing he could do. Katie could not be linked to him either. Yet again he found himself knee-deep in shit. He was cursed by that bitch for sure.

He rode home and decided that he was having the worst fucking year of his life and that Blondie was his worst kill – his biggest mistake. He arrived home at 1.17 am and put the bike in the barn. He put both helmets on a shelf and climbed into the old 4 x 4. He drove slowly to the house, parked it behind the wood pile and headed for the shower. Thank fuck he was off tomorrow; he would have to drink himself to sleep tonight. Half an hour later he sat on a chair outside on the patio, a drink in his hand. There was still a quarter moon and a zillion stars in the night sky. The hills and forests were awash with the sound of night animals. The red deer could be heard snorting and grunting. A haunting squeal of something being killed, probably a rabbit; they sounded like babies crying when you killed them. There were bats everywhere, attracted to the moths that were in turn attracted by the lights from the house.

He was dressed all in black and anyone would be hard pushed to make him out in the dim light of the patio. Danny sat with his head in his hands; he was fucked right off. Plan A went to shit; Plan B (which you should always have) was a total clusterfuck of gigantic proportions. There was not, and had never been, a plan C. He found himself in limbo. Was Red dead? Did they have anything on him? Was there any chance of the now dead Katie leading back to him or would she be the opposite and lead them away from him? If he ran too soon it would look too suspicious. He decided he had no choice. He had to stay and fight; there was no way he was giving up his life as he knew it, nor did he think he would work for much longer. Killing and conning was the best way forward and he loved it.

He poured himself another drink; tomorrow would bring news. He drank an entire bottle of Jack Daniels before going to bed, absolutely canned. His sleep was riddled with nightmares – the beatings from his father, the physical and mental abuse by his mother, the years of abuse, physical and mental from them both. Visions of the now dead Katie freeing herself from the railings and walking towards him like a zombie. The ghoulish eyeless bodies of Conal and his bitch. But, worst of all, the dripping wet blonde bitch found with crabs in her mouth. Danny dreamed of her standing on the quayside, gesturing for Danny to come towards her, bloated, her blonde hair now wet with black seaweed as she lifted her dress. An endless stream of crabs emerged from her vagina, crabs the size of a fist, black in colour with massive right claws and evil red eyes. The crabs now covered her entire body, snapping away at him.

He had soaked the pillow and the duvet with sweat by the time he woke up. It was 9.20 am; he got up and headed straight for the kitchen; he had a stonking hangover and still felt drunk. The local news would be on at 9.30 am. Danny made himself a coffee. He pressed the remote and the TV built into the wall burst into life. There was news of an Egypt Air Airbus flight which had crashed. He watched it with disinterest. Then the exterior of

Claire's townhouse burst onto the screen. There was a white tent around the railings where Katie died. Red's photo came up next, on the top right-hand corner of the video footage of an armed policeman outside a room at a hospital. According to the reporter, Red was still alive, having been shot twice, once in the face! They were bringing in an army surgeon who had operated on soldiers with similar injuries. Another photo appeared; it was her reporter boyfriend who was also alive. It looked like Katie was the only one to have died last night; this was disappointing.

The reporter said that they were both expected to make a full recovery and that her boyfriend was a hero. Danny heard the grey-haired detective's voice. His face appeared and a reporter holding a microphone spoke to him. 'Can you tell us anything else, detective?'

'All I can say is that we are following a definite line of enquiry.'

'Can you tell us who the gunman was?'

'No comment, sorry, excuse me,' the grey-haired one said as he walked away from the reporter and up the steps and inside the flat. Great news that the ginger one was shot in the face; well done Katie for that one – she would not be back to work any time soon, maybe not at all. The grey one was supposed to be retired; would he stay the distance – would he want to continue after what happened? Katie was the one who attacked Red; would that take the heat from him? Did Katie manage to say the words 'This is for Danny'? He washed up his dishes before heading for the shower and looked in the mirror. He looked like shit. Danny took a long shower, fuck it, they were skin and bone just like him. Masturbating, he thought about Red, and decided that he did not have to run! He did not have to hide! NO! HE HAD TO KILL AND KILL THEM ALL! EVERY FUCKING LAST ONE OF THEM! All he had to do was take care of the detectives once and for all. He came on his hand and laughed out loud, his voice booming in the tiled bathroom. A small open window carried his voice outside and startled a crow who flew away.

Deer looked up from their grazing as his evil laughter carried out across the lochside.

Chapter 50

Red

John, the Chief and just about everyone on the force was at Gartnavel hospital. There were firearms officers inside and outside the hospital, and lots of them. Everyone who was off duty were also at the hospital. Claire was a popular detective, and police were protective when it came to their own. John was worried, first poor old Jed and now Claire. Claire had her suspicions about a male who worked on the park close to where the body was found. John suspected that she was working on him and felt guilty about not being there for her. He could not say he was happy to be back in his job; his trip to St Kilda was a million miles in the past. The killing of Jed kept him awake at night.

Claire was unable to have visitors although John and the Chief had managed to pop their heads round the door, but that was it. Claire did not look in good shape. A surgeon from the army was at her bedside, along with a nurse and a doctor. Her parents and friends occupied a room next door. John and the Chief went in and passed on their support. 'At least she is going to recover,' said John as Claire's mum gave him a hug. 'Yes,' she said, drying her eyes. 'Have you spoken with Colin yet?'

'No not yet,' replied John, 'we are both going there now.' They hugged and shook hands in turn before going to see Colin who was on the next floor down. John and the chief walked down in silence. He was keen to talk to Colin as they had to know what went on in that flat last night. Colin was on morphine when they went to speak to him directly after the incident. He had four broken ribs, a broken ankle, and multiple cuts and bruises but he, too, would make a full recovery.

John was pleased to see Colin sitting up well enough to have some soup, his face, neck, and arms criss-crossed with stiches from his window exit. He was pleased to see them both. 'Any more news on Claire?' were the first words from his mouth.

'She is doing fine,' replied John. 'Do you feel up to talking?' asked the Chief.

'Yes sure. I will start at the beginning; we had gone to bed about 10.30 pm. Claire was tired and, to be honest, so was I. Claire had a few glasses of wine and I had a few beers after dinner. We were both asleep pretty much as soon as we went to bed. I woke up later as I was needing to pee – too many beers. The cat was sleeping on my legs, and I pushed her off. The bedroom was light enough to see where you were going as it was illuminated by the red light coming from the digital alarm. The hall was also pretty much lit by the blue glow from the BT router on the table in the hall, so I did not turn any lights on. I spent a little longer in the toilet than I intended as I went for a number 1 and 2.'

Colin looked at them both, embarrassed, as if it was a crime to have a crap in your own house. 'I came out of the toilet and turned into the bedroom; that's when the first shot went off; there was a figure standing in front of me. You could clearly see the gun. I was scared as the second shot went off and just gave that person my best rugby tackle. It was a girl, and she was light, and we both sailed through the air. I could see Claire out of the corner of my eye, I think she was propelled by the force of the bullet and disappeared down the other side of the bed. There was a lot of noise; it got sore and cold at the same time and then massive pain and darkness. The next thing I knew I woke up here.'

'Anything else?' asked John.

'Oh yes, one other thing; the girl spoke. When I made contact with her, she was saying something to Claire. It sounded like 'this is for Da…!' She never finished what she was going to say.'

'Are you sure?'

'Yes, John, I am a journalist, listening is part of my job.' They all smiled. John had written everything down in his little black book. At 16 stone, Colin must have knocked the wind right out of the petite little killer's sails. They both said their farewells to Colin and now stood facing each other in the lift.

'I need you to give this case 100%, John.'

'Yes Chief, I know, I'm as keen to solve this case as you are.'

'I will handle the press conference; you get on your way and get me some results!'

They shook hands as the lift doors slid open, the Chief turning right towards the waiting press and John turning left towards the rear doors. John never got angry, and the Chief never swore. He had been called out at 12.30 am; it was now 11 am, he was tired, and the day was going to be long. He wished he were home with Heather.

He returned back to Pitt Street. The mood was quiet; the young cop who had earlier been working with Claire was waiting on John's return. Fingerprints had identified the killer as 24-year-old Katie Drummond from Dumfries. She was a long way from home and had been fingerprinted previously to eliminate her prints after her boss at a supermarket was murdered. Apparently, she knew his wife and had been to the victim's house on previous occasions.

John was no Columbo, but a previous murder connected to the same suspect as their shooter, now that was a coincidence and John did not believe in coincidences – what were the chances of that? John felt upset and responsible for Claire; he knew she was hooked on this Danny guy being her shooter and for the killing of the air stewardess, but without evidence, like a body for instance, there was still very little to go on. A search warrant would also be out of the question as neither himself nor Claire had much to go on and he believed that you should never bring a case to the prosecutor until you are one hundred percent sure, or thereabouts, of getting a conviction.

Door-to-door enquiries in and around Park Circus had revealed three witnesses who either saw or heard a motorbike. The shooter had not walked there and there was no sign of a car;

taxi companies were being eliminated but it was very unlikely that the female shooter went to Claire's flat by taxi.

CCTV, however, had shown a motorbike on Great Western Road not long after the shooting of Claire. Did Mr Fleming have a motorbike licence? Was he the shooter's accomplice? It was very plausible and needed looking into. John knew one thing – this bastard was evil beyond a doubt and could also be the one who had been responsible for killing Jed. In John's mind that was also a murder, the thought making him sick to his stomach. He decided to head home, he could work remotely from home, and he had not seen much of Heather the last few days. John had told her that Jed had died of natural causes – he did not have the heart or stomach to tell her what really happened. His two-hour drive would take him to Crianlarich, Tyndrum, Connel and then home. Music by Italian pianist Ludovico Einaudi played quietly through the speakers as he tried to get to grips with this case. He had instructed two detectives to travel south to Dumfries to investigate the dead Katie's background and the demise of her old boss and his missing wife; she could have been murdered by the same killer; it could well be that these people were all connected to the killer or killers. It was not unknown for besotted female partners to be involved in horrific murders and rapes committed by their evil partners. If old Jed's killing was by the same hand, then they were truly evil and a major threat to all people they came in contact with.

John did not believe this had started with Carolyn's horrific murder and thought it more likely that it was simply because her body had been discovered. The murder at the morgue was also a direct result of her murder. John had never heard of a murder victim's body ever having been stolen. That made two victims who were linked and two who were not, so far, but who could be. Throw Jed into the killings and the number would now be five in total that the police knew about. Serial killers were usually loners and Mr Fleming was a suspect, but he certainly was not a loner; he was in fact the opposite – a womaniser and probably on the verge of being a narcissist, which makes him part way there, but John, unlike Claire, was not convinced.

John felt sad within himself; he had thought this life was behind him and knew that if he had not answered that bloody call that day, Jed would still be alive, and they would still be on the JIP having a great time. This whole chapter of his life was ripping his heart out and he hated every second of it.

The only way this was going to end was when he caught whoever did this and he could then return to his retirement and get the hell out of Dodge for good; he would throw his phone in the sea and never get another one – ever!

Chapter 51

Heather

Danny was now determined to kill the grey-haired detective; he would soon be joining his stupid dog; he might even get a chance to kill Red also, but that would have to wait till the guys with guns were no longer protecting her. He intended to head for Connel, later that day, strike while the iron is hot and all that pish. He would indeed strike down anyone who stood in the way of his life, his existence. He deserved to live his life as he pleased, and God help those that stood in his way. A women book critic called Lyn some thing or another once called him a narcissist; she died a slow painful death for her comments. He went out to the 4 x 4 which was parked at the back of the house. He had packed a Smith and Wesson 45 and two clips, along with his usual date-rape bag contents of duct tape, rope, chloroform, a two-way radio, a knife, a compass, a balaclava and some dried food and water – his little goodie bag which he would transfer to the Audi when he was leaving.

He was beginning to recover from his booze binge the previous night, having drunk two litres of water which had certainly helped. He wondered what old Grey had done with his now dead dog and laughed his evil laugh. The sound echoed around the hills outside the barn. He wanted the old detective dead quickly and would enjoy killing him. Getting back to a normal life on the park had just come one step closer. He also felt horny for the first time in 24 hours.

Danny wore black jeans with a black sweatshirt and his favourite Doc Martens, black of course with a knife down the inside of his right boot. The drive round to Oban was spoiled by the low cloud and light rain. He would also have liked to have had lunch somewhere, but he was on a DO NOT BE SEEN DAY; he laughed at his own joke. He had a boner in his pants; where the fuck did that come from? He laughed to himself – some girl is going to be lucky tonight.

He reached the detective's house by 4 pm, hoping the old dude would be home for his dinner before six. There were no cops around which surprised him, after all it was only two weeks before that he had hanged Grey's stupid mutt. The lane beside the detective's house was quiet; there was a green Volvo X40 in beside the tree where he had hanged the dog.

Further along the road there was an old man in his seaside cottage tending the hundreds of pretty roses that not only grew on the walls of the house but all over the garden too. He was dressed as if from the forties with an old-style tan jungle safari hat on his head. He had an old Wolesley car in his driveway; it was cream coloured with lots of chrome; there was no one else around. Danny made his way along the single-track road and parked in the car park that overlooked the sea; the crap weather was keeping day trippers away, which suited him. He got out and removed his binoculars from his bag, scanning every inch around the house. There was definitely no-one watching it but him.

There was a woman in the kitchen, probably Grey's wife, at the kettle, probably making tea or coffee. She was a pretty looking 50 plus with grey-blonde hair and a good figure. Danny decided there and then that he would fuck the detective's wife in front of him before he killed them both. He could feel his erect cock pressing against the restraint of his trousers. 6 pm came and went and still no sign of the detective. By 6.30 pm Danny was getting pissed off.

Just then the wife came out of the house and reversed the Volvo out of the driveway. He decided to follow. His legs and arse were numb from sitting in the car for so long. The wife stopped 20 minutes later outside the swimming pool in Oban. She walked inside carrying a sports bag. Danny watched her from his car; she was heading for the pool. It looked like the little wife was going for a swim. Danny walked round the side of the building; it was of brick construction with a half round shaped roof. The grass surrounding its west side had benches where you could sit, and Danny did exactly that.

The benches faced away from the building, and he had to sit at an angle to see inside. Well, well, there she was and a fine body she had too. She was wearing a plain black one-piece bathing suit showing a very ample bosom and nice legs. There were about twenty other people there. And guess what she was doing. The pretty detective's wife was learning to swim!

He decided to head back and wait for them both at the bungalow; surely the detective would be back by now. But when he drove past, there was no detective to be seen. There was, however, a police car outside complete with two cops inside. Danny kept the car moving without missing a beat. Once back at the swimming pool, he was pleased to see the X40 still parked where she had left it. More to the point was the space right next to it. Exactly twelve minutes later the pretty lady walked out of the front door and headed straight for him. He got out of his car, went to the rear, and opened the boot.

He turned to face her. 'Excuse me,' he said as she placed her bag on the rear seat. She turned round in time to accept the chloroform rag that Danny put over her mouth. He looked around as he placed her inside, quickly taping her legs, arms, and mouth with duct tape. He whistled to himself as he reversed out of the parking space. Life was good; life was very good.

To be continued....................................

Printed in Great Britain
by Amazon

77969008R00253